CALICO HILL

CALICO HILL

by

CHRIS ALEXANDER

ASPEN LEAF PUBLISHING

This is a work of fiction. Names, characters, places, and incidents are either the product of the author's imagination or used fictitiously. Any reference to actual persons, living or dead, events, or locales is entirely coincidental.

Copyright © 2024 by Chris Alexander
All rights reserved.

No part of this book may be reproduced, distributed, or transmitted in any form or by any means, including photocopying, recording, or other electronic or mechanical methods, without the prior written permission of the publisher.

Published by Aspen Leaf Publishing, New York, NY

ISBN: 9798991012201
Library of Congress Control Number: 2024915312

For Ralph

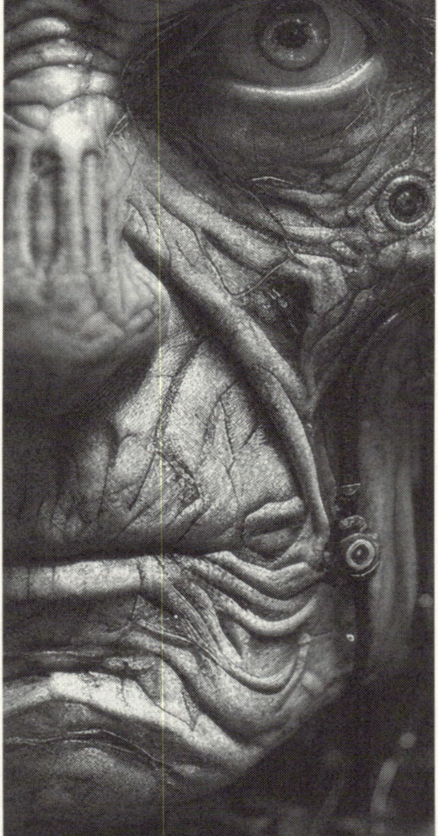

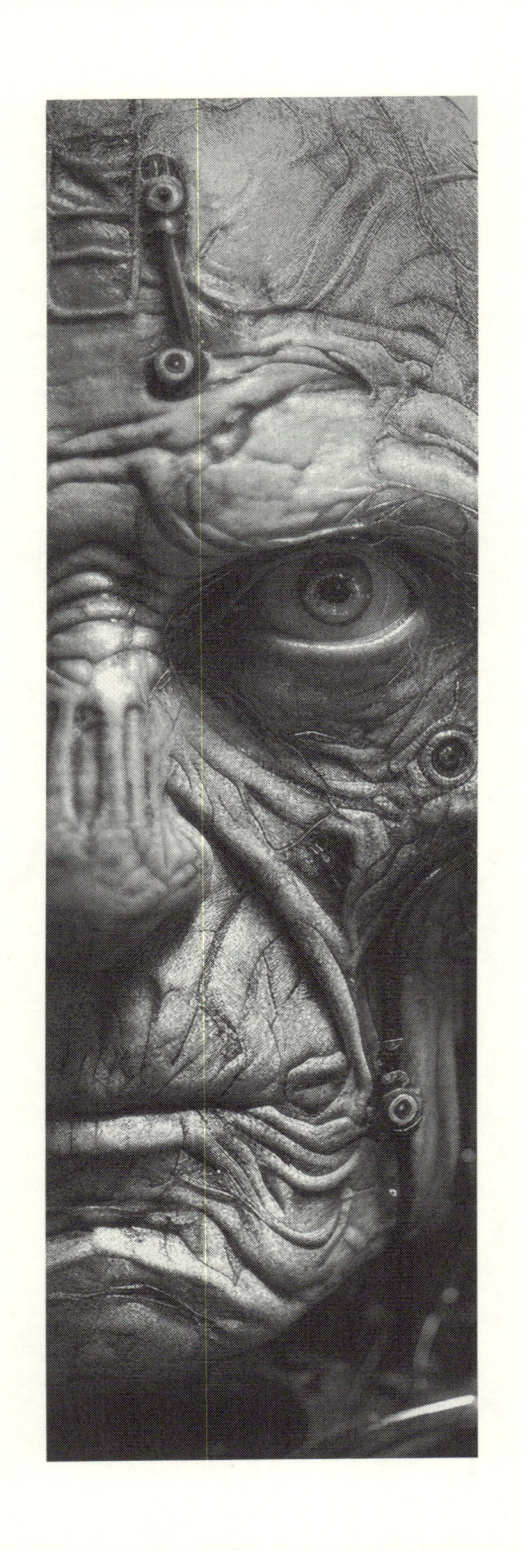

The sun sets.
The moon sets.
But they are not gone.
-Rumi

CHAPTER 1
CHARLES AND SALIM

YEAR: 2029

1,600 MILES SOUTH OF EASTER ISLAND

"Come say hi, Damien!"

"...No," said a faint voice from another room.

The woman's face on the monitor turned. Her eyes locked on her son, a game console in his tiny hands, his face obscured behind a mop of brown hair. Her smile faded. Her brow softened, and a defeated look flashed across her face.

She returned to the camera, eyes pierced through the glass, and smiled again.

"He's just playing with his game machine. He lost his first tooth today. He's been good–I mean..." She sighed and shook her head, "What am I even saying? The new doctor I took him to said his walking isn't getting any worse, which is good, I guess, but it isn't getting any better either."

She looked away.

"Damien was well-behaved with the doctor. He likes her. She's a nice woman down at the genetics lab on campus. They had this cardboard treasure chest full of candy by the door when we walked out. They let him take anything he wanted. Then, we walked down to the waterfront. Damien liked watching the sailboats."

She let out a heavy sigh that seemed to fill the thousands of miles of the space between them.

"That was nice. But he falls a lot, you know. He's weak. His legs, they're just not strong enough–"

She paused and turned to the camera.

"I wish we could talk like normal people, not through this one-way machine, with these recorded messages. But I know, I know, we can't do that. I know it's not safe. We miss you, Salim. I...I miss you."

The screen went black.

Yellow pixelated letters scrawled onto the screen:

END MESSAGE

Salim took a breath. Rivet-lined metal walls and a desk cluttered with keyboards, cables, crumpled clothes, and empty coffee mugs glowed in the soft light. The room grew noticeably darker as the single source of light, the communications console screen, faded to black.

He pressed a button to queue up the next recording.

Yellow text on the screen:

4... 3... 2... 1... RECORDING STARTED

"I miss you, Amy. I can't wait to be home." Salim looked directly into the tiny black dot at the top of the screen. He smiled and steadied his voice to control his trembling excitement. "We had a breakthrough last night. Our first viable subjects. A 99.97% match to a human lung. We've had full cellular oxygenation for over sixteen hours and a strong HLA match when adjusted for..." He paused, laughing softly to himself, "...it means it could work. I mean, it will work. I need to wrap up some loose ends here, but I'll be home before you know it. Another few months, maybe. We're so close!"

He paused, forgetting that the machine was still recording.

He saw his tired eyes in the reflection on the glass monitor.
"I love you, Amy."
He pressed the red button.
RECORDING ENDED
PROCESSING
ENCRYPTION BEGINNING
96 LEVELS
ENCRYPTION COMPLETE
MESSAGE SENT
The screen went blank. Salim looked at the two framed photographs on his desk beside the terminal. One of him and Amy, before Damien was born. Big smiles on their faces, with the exploding colors of Massachusetts fall foliage behind them. Amy took the other photograph. It sat in a large silver frame. Salim himself in an ill-fitting blue suit, standing to the left of Charles Sloan, grinning ear to ear, with a leucite podium at their side. Memories of that evening rushed into his mind. The 2026 Global Nations Bioethics Alliance Conference was hosted at MIT that year, and Charles and Salim were the center of attention with their work on human organ production using a revolutionary method that could replicate muscle and tissue such that it was indistinguishable from the target patient even at the cellular level. He looked back at their faces, beaming with hope and ambition. They were three champagnes deep and talking about changing the world.

Salim leaned back onto his metal cot. The digital clock beside the bed read 3:37 A.M.

Yellow block letters glowed on the screen even in its idle state:
PERSONAL TERMINAL OF DR. SALIM NARAM

The cot creaked when he stood up. He reached for the wooden cane that leaned beside the door frame and tightened the drawstring on his loose sweatpants. Wearing a faded Boston Bruins t-shirt, gray pants, and thick wool socks, he walked down the hall toward the lab.

The floor swayed gently with each step. He imagined the turbulent waves crashing against the hull, but the ship's careful engineering reduced that force to a subtle sway inside the ship.

Man conquered nature once again, he thought.

He bumped his shoulder against the wall. It had been thirty-seven long months, and he still hadn't gotten his sea legs.

But nothing ever went according to plan.

Salim descended a long metal staircase onto the lab's lower floor, his cane tapping softly on each step with a muted clang. When his eyes adjusted to the light, he could see the entire length of the ship.

It was a three-hundred-meter cargo ship Charles had purchased from an entrepreneur in Brazil who had specialized in the business of logistics. The old man was slowing down and wanted to spend more time with his grandchildren. He was looking to retire from a life of running freshly manufactured Volkswagens up the coast from their factories in São Paulo to the storage garages in San Diego, California. Charles bought five ships from the old man for a price that should have been illegal and, within a year, had them retrofitted to become a fleet of the world's most advanced seafaring scientific laboratories on the open seas. Operate freely, invisible to radar. It was the perfect site for cutting-edge research that pushed the boundaries beyond anything the GNBA could stomach. Wild experiments designed to peel back the mysteries of death, consciousness, pain, and identity while tossing ethical boundaries out the window. Experiments on primates, prisoners with terminal illnesses, and "re-acquired" human trafficked victims. Those five ships floated beyond any country's oceanic jurisdiction. It was the ideal plan, with the only vulnerabilities keeping Charles up at night being the unforgiving limitations of time and sea pirates.

Within the first three years of operations, four ships were

captured by pirates, their entire crew of scientists vanished, and ships sunk to the bottom of the ocean.

And then there was one ship left.

Salim looked down into a sprawling area in the belly of the vessel, lined bow to stern with three hundred illuminated glass cubes as tall as his chest and a meter deep. Each cube was filled with a liquid solution of saline and glucose to closely approximate the environment within the human body. Some cubes held artificial human hearts, others lungs, livers, eyes, and partial sections of brains. Vibration-dampening devices at the base of each cube held the tank level as the boat swayed.

Columns of bright green vines cascaded from the ceiling. They wrapped around pipes that snaked down the walls and fed into a grand reservoir slightly smaller than an Olympic-sized pool at the center of the room. The pool was full of flowers and patterned leaves of brilliant colors. A layer of viscous oil floated on the pool's surface.

Salim reached the bottom of the staircase and breathed in the humid air. It smelled like ocean water and decomposing leaves. To the uninitiated, the sight in front of him looked like a half-square-mile rainforest was plucked out of the Amazon jungle and set afloat on a ship in the Pacific Ocean.

He stopped to examine a round, flat leaf suspended from the wall and heard his mother's voice ringing clear in his head. A distant memory clawed its way to the forefront of his mind in a haze of sleeplessness. When he was just a boy, his mother would stroll with him along the rows of plants in their backyard garden in Cairo and say good morning to each plant. She would take his small hand in hers and guide his fingers along the ridges of the leaves, tracing each stem.

"My Salim," she would say, "Plants are our brothers and sisters. They are born, they grow, and they die, just like us. They accept the love of our earth and sun, just like we do."

He breathed in the fecund air. Could almost taste the soil on his tongue. He brushed his fingertips along that round, flat leaf and thought of those days long ago.

He sidled up to a glass cube. The steel plate mounted on the side read SPECIMEN 004. An immaculate human spinal column hung suspended in a clear liquid. He pressed his eyes inches away from the glass, letting his focus follow along the millions of striations of muscle tissue that make up a tapestry of cells. Accelerant lamps glowed bright azure as their light washed over the spinal column's extruded tissues, helping speed up cellular production.

The specimen levitated in a ghostly glow as if cradled by God's own hands.

"My gift," Salim whispered to himself, "to our world. And my Damien." He stared with reverence at the specimen.

A faint sound broke his concentration.

Beyond a shelf stacked with trays of sprouting seedlings, one of the IT server rooms was open, the door slightly ajar. A sliver of cold white light glowed from within the room.

He turned his head and heard a mix of voices coming from beyond the door. They exchanged words back and forth in real-time. Salim knew that only a direct channel unencrypted video call could do that. That type of transmission would breach ship security protocol and open up the entire operation to the prying ears of pirates.

"...The GNBA will convene next month," said a young woman, her voice compressed and tinny from the audio compression, "We have reason to believe they will move on article 530."

"An unprecedented overreach!" said another voice, a loud man trembling with anger.

"You're not immune, Charles," repeated the woman, "even at Point Nemo. If article 530 passes, you know we can't protect you. They'll throw everything they got at you. Life in prison.

They'll seize your ship and everything will–"

"I know!" Charles snapped, then paused to take a breath.

The room went silent. Then Charles replied in a hushed tone, his voice an unmistakable rumble, dry as rocks, "I'm aware of the risks," he said.

"And your partner," the woman asked, "Is he aware?"

"I'll talk to him, I'll–"

"Charles," the woman interrupted, "you have an asset of immeasurable value on your ship. We're prepared to provide you with unlimited resources. Labs, personnel, the best scientists from around the world, and an army of lawyers to keep the GNBA at bay. Our syndicate is prepared to commit a starter fund of $65 Billion for the first two years and a guaranteed $80 Billion after that."

The sound of rapid keyboard taps echoed from behind the door. Salim turned to head back toward the staircase and up to his room. He took one step, his foot brushing against the floor with an audible scrape. Then his cane tapped heavily on the stair step. A metallic ring cut through the ship's silence like a bell in the darkness.

Salim froze mid-step.

From behind the cracked door, the typing on the keyboard stopped.

A moment passed. The silence was expansive and deafening.

Salim slowly stepped forward and returned to his room to chase sleep again.

***

The next morning, the ocean was gentle and the floor of the ship was steady. Salim stood on the suspended metal walkway, his oversized white lab coat weighed down by tools in his pockets. He leaned on the railing, walking cane balanced against his hip. He unfastened a segment of the hose system that moved green fluids from the biological vats down to the organ-growing chambers below. He turned a wrench while holding a digital meter, watching as a glowing line danced across the screen. It was erratic at first, but after a moment, it slowed and hovered at the center of the screen.

Heavy footsteps approached from behind. The suspended walkway swayed.

"Recalibrating the flow valves again, I see?"

The smell of freshly brewed single-origin coffee filled the air.

"It's got to be the key, Charles," said Salim, not looking up from the hose, "I know it has to be."

Salim unlatched the wrench and turned around.

Charles stood at the end of the platform in his usual lab coat with an inquisitive smirk. He handed Salim a silver mug.

"You haven't been sleeping, my friend. I'm worried about you," said Charles.

Salim could feel Charles's eyes snaking across his face. His eyes must have looked tired, his hair barely kept, and day-old bandages grew crusty on his arms from harvesting multiple blood samples.

"We're on the doorstep of greatness, and we... I need you at your best."

"I know, you're right. I've been sleeping... fine."

Salim sipped the coffee. The sweet aroma cut through the musty air. He tasted the toasted flavors as the coffee hit his tongue, and the caffeine b-lined towards his bloodstream.

"It has to be the flow speed. It's the key. It must be," said Salim. He shook his head, mind sorting through formulas, searching desperately for the solution. "A perfectly regulated flow will increase the efficiency of the extruder wands and reduce lost-sector completions and nano-stitching errors. I know the field tensors are highly sensitive, but this will–"

"You think too small," Charles snapped, a whisper of anger rising behind his words. His brow pinched into a frown. He took a step back. "You look for greatness in minuscule things, but we both know this..." he waved his hands, motioning at the steel trellis above and the growing chambers in the ship floor below, "This will never be enough."

Salim sipped his coffee. Felt the surge of liquid energy. It was more potent than usual today.

"The Agency says we have less than ninety days before the GNBA comes after us," said Charles.

"The Agency?" said Salim, "So you've been talking to them again? Charles, we agreed years ago not to engage with them. That's the entire reason why we took the risk of coming out to Point Nemo. You know what they'll do with this technology if we achieve—"

"When we achieve 100% match," said Charles, "see for all your genius and empathy, that's your blind spot. You cannot dream big enough for what this technology will become."

"But that's how mankind has always built great things: by mastering the details. Perfection in each stone at Giza," Salim glanced over the railing at the grid of glowing glass cubes in the distance, and below them rows upon rows of metal vats filled with liquefied plant matter, bubbling under a haze of steam, "and soon, very soon, this will change everything. We will change everything, Charles! The end to senseless suffering. We will take the power from God's hands, and every child will know a new future of compassion and equity. Because of you and I! Because of us!"

Salim took a sip of his coffee and smiled.

"Every child... like Damien," said Charles.

Salim felt a tightness bloom in his chest. The massive room that overflowed with electronics and plastic tubing suddenly felt small.

"Yes," said Salim, turning to face Charles, "like my son."

"Then can't you see we are running out of time?" said Charles, his neck tense and words sharp, "That's why we need the Agency. The whole world, the future of our species, is within our grasp, Salim. We can solve this. And if the GNBA shuts us down before we finish our work..." Charles pauses to take a breath, a futile attempt to hide his frustration, "then we're not fulfilling our responsibility to the species."

"Not with the Agency, Charles. I will not stand by and let them pervert our technology for, for–"

Salim paused. The air in the room thickened, and Salim turned to look at Charles, a tall man with a trimmed white beard in a long gray lab coat. Salim watched Charles as his jaw twisted and the skin on his cheeks began to sag. His white lab coat stretched like taffy, and his arms, ears, and nose blurred at the edges until he became a cloud of colors and movements and was no longer Charles.

"I'm sorry, my friend," said Charles, "it's our duty to the species to become stronger and smarter and to achieve things we cannot even imagine today. That's going to take discipline and difficult decisions."

Salim felt his throat tighten.

"And the uncomfortable truth is: not everyone can be a part of that future."

A stinging sensation flooded his sinus cavity, and a splattering of blood erupted from his nose, painting his white lab coat red.

"This is the only way," said Charles, "and I couldn't have made it this far without you, and I promise to honor your work and contribution by seeing this through."

Salim's pulse grew heavy and pounded in his chest.

"You have my word that Amy and Damien will be taken care of."

Salim groped in the pocket of his lab coat and wrapped his

fingers around a sharp metal pen. He gripped it with a crushing force. His hands shook violently. He turned to Charles and reached out with a desperate thrust to the jugular, but his vision faded, and he lost his balance.

"I'm sorry, Salim," said Charles.

The coffee cup slipped from Salim's fingers. It bounced on the metal walkway, spilling steaming liquid through the grating onto the laboratory floor below. Nearly blind, Salim reached in the dark for anything to hold him up.

He grabbed the railing and tensed with all his remaining strength to hold himself up before the chemicals in his coffee suffocated his nerves and his knees buckled.

"This was necessary," said Charles, more a whisper to himself, "it needed to be done for the good of the species."

Salim felt a hand impact his chest, pushing him over the side of the metal railing. As his senses faded and his lungs collapsed, he felt the last rush of air sweep across his face as he plummeted toward the vat of steaming green liquid below. His body splashed, and steam swallowed him. Blood vessels ruptured, and organs were released from the tension of their cellular walls. Human and plant matter fused in a slurry of organic compounds that would soon begin their journey through a labyrinth of tubes into extruder wands of the specimen cases deep within the ship.

300 YEARS LATER

CHAPTER 2

THE KAIPHER

PRESENT DAY: JULY, 2330
SOMEWHERE OVER THE ATLANTIC OCEAN

Theo's blood was everywhere.

The faucet and mirror were painted red. The floor lurched, dropping only mere inches, but enough to kick him off balance. He slammed his palms into the sink to steady himself, the cracked plastic bending under his weight.

The aircraft moaned. Its engine strained like an overworked lawnmower, ripping through the ocean air currents. It sounded nothing like the finely tuned AGCO-X engines his father would rev up in the barn each morning as the sky blossomed from midnight blue to orange. Those engines hummed with a sweet vibration.

Under the flickering light in the rear lavatory of flight 805, Theoren Rousseau hunched over the sink and gathered fistfuls of paper towels to soak up the blood. He was on a mission to smuggle a silicon chip out of the Coastal territories and back to the Midlands. Shocking jolts of pain shot up his left shoulder from the silicon chip that sat lodged deep within his arm.

But the stitches weren't holding.

The bandage was slipping loose.

"Be invisible. No delays. Get to the Ranch," he whispered to himself, nearly inaudible, mouthing the words like an incantation.

He recalled the mission briefing, burned into his memory. Trent Blake, Commander of the Midland Guard, said it would be smooth. "Get in. Retrieve the chip. Slip out," Trent would say. But that was fourteen long months ago when Theo embedded himself in the Coastal city that sat upon what was left of Tallahassee, three miles beyond the massive concrete walls that plowed through the Blackwater River forest. His mission contact, Lena Galin, gave her life to extract the intel, plant the silicon chip, and get him on that plane.

It wasn't supposed to go like this.

But now it was up to him to finish the job.

They also told him of the high probability that there would be a Kaipher—or a grayskin, as some called them—aboard that flight to hunt him down before he could deliver the chip. Kaiphers were adept at blending in. It could be any of the passengers. But the Kaipher would not know who on board might have the chip.

Unless Theo made himself known. Then, it could all end badly.

Theo took a deep breath. He held it. The circulated air in the airplane bathroom was stale in his lungs. He closed his eyes and exhaled to focus on the moment, the mission.

Turbulence shook the cabin, but it didn't break his focus.

He opened his eyes to see a new face, full of resolve.

Is this how it happens? Is this how it all comes to an end, he thought?

His eyes narrowed. Jaw tightened.

"Be invisible. No delays. Get to the Ranch. Be invisible. No delays. Get to–."

A booming knock on the door shook him out of a trance. He recognized the harshness of his surroundings and the musty dampness weighing heavy in the air.

"Sir... sir? You have to take your seat," a voice called out from the other side of the door.

His hands shook as he dabbed red droplets and smeared blood on the paper towels. He quickly hid the towels in the refuse bin.

"One minute!" he said, hiding the panic in his voice. His jaw was shaking.

He'd come too far for this mission to unravel now.

He stacked a thick layer of toilet paper over the incision, pulled a roll of electrical tape from his back pocket, and looped the tape around his arm to form a rough tourniquet. It was too tight, but there was no time to redo it.

Theo wore a loose-fitting shirt the color of old oatmeal. It was nothing special to look at, and that was the point. Besides the lowered gaze and the slouched shoulders, Trent said it was the best way to blend in. Invisible. A nondescript, nameless, faceless Midlander like everyone else on that plane.

He rolled down his sleeve to cover the wound. The blood would eventually soak through, he thought, but it was secure for now.

"She'll see that blood there," the ghost of Sam's voice sidled up to Theo like a cold draft in the night. He spoke in faint, breathless sentences with the soft pitch of an innocent child of eight or nine, or about when Sam fell from the solar towers back home and died on the hard dirt while Theo watched, paralyzed with guilt. Sam's blood pooled red that day and turned the earth brown.

"They will all see your blood, Theo. She'll scream. She'll scream and make a scene and the Kaipher will see you and slice you open and gut you from head to toe right here on this pl–"

"Shut the–" Theo snapped back through clenched teeth at the invisible voice behind him. He checked the mirror again and saw him standing alone in the bathroom, only his exhausted eyes reflected in the dim light.

"Sir! Until the pilot turns on the lavatory light on—"

The bolt clicked, and Theo opened the door. It slammed louder than he expected. Cold air from the cabin rushed into the lavatory and chilled against his wet sleeve. Heads turned toward the sound.

Theo stood face-to-face with the flight attendant. Her silver name tag read "Mariette."

She was petite, with a navy blue top and maroon skirt that was commanding yet courteous.

Theo was sweating. His linen shirt was wrinkled, his pants an inch too long, and his sleeve was soaked. He looked like he was wearing hand-me-down clothes and lost a fight with a bottle of Jack.

Mariette recoiled at the sight of him.

"Sorry, it's the altitude," said Theo, "the turbulence, I mean, on planes. It gets to me."

Mariette looked him up and down.

"Happens all the time! I should know better than to expect it," he said, "but I'm feeling better, thanks."

"Very well then," said Mariette, assessing whether he would be a nuisance on her flight, "Good, now please take your seat."

He ambled toward his seat in row 57, eyes tracking along the floor, making quick glances up the aisle to analyze the passengers' movements. The carpet swished under his feet.

The plane jolted suddenly to the left, sending Theo off balance. He bumped against the headrest of a passenger who was deep asleep. He quickly regained his composure and calmly walked forward. The water on Theo's light-colored shirt formed a dark stain. He tried to cup his hand over the wet spot to hide it, but he knew from the right angle they would see it.

Passengers made eye contact with him but quickly looked away.

He felt their judging eyes on his back.

"The rear of the aircraft provides the best vantage point to notice suspicious behavior from other passengers," they had told him during the mission training, "it's the best place to become invisible."

Theo settled into his seat by the window, careful not to put pressure on his left arm. He leaned his head against the window and stared at the glossy sheen of the Atlantic Ocean twenty-nine thousand feet below. The setting sun reflected on an enormous cloud, engulfing it in neon pink light. He hadn't seen a fiery sun like that back home in many years. A deep chasm ran through that cloud, sculpting it into the gaping maw of a monster waiting to consume the world. A patient monster that outlasted its prey. He peered into its dark center and felt its gravity reaching across space, pulling him closer to its mouth. The pressure behind his eyes grew stronger. He closed his eyes and pinched his temples to find relief.

Memories from his training at the Ranch rushed through his mind. It was in a classroom back home in Oklahoma, bathed in dust and darkness, where Trent gave Theo his final briefing fourteen long months ago.

Months that felt like years.

As he stared out that window, Trent's voice from long ago rushed back.

"Have a seat," Trent had said then, standing at the front of that decaying classroom back at the Ranch, a sprawling three-hundred-acre compound in northern Oklahoma that was the home of the Midland Guard. A smile widened across Trent's face. He raised a hand, gesturing toward the rows of many chairs, "Anywhere you like, Theo."

Five rows of desks with attached metal chairs filled the abandoned space. Children once sat there, Theo had thought, back when there were more of them around. Before the country was ripped into pieces and the walls went up. Those wooden desktops were stained ink-black from years of use, and deep ravines scrawled into the wood, probably from pens and the occasional pocket knife.

Trent observed Theo pacing along the rows.

Theo selected a seat. A spot to the right of the center, in the second row. He looked around and examined the desks and the darkened windows. The lines carved into the desktop.

"Theo? Still with me?" Trent asked, tilting his head with the question.

He snapped out of a trance and looked up from the desk, fingers still resting within the eerily comfortable grooves.

"Yes."

Trent's outline was fuzzy in the dim light. Theo's eyes adjusted slowly. The desktop read like braille beneath his fingertips. Such a feeling of dark history embedded in that wood.

Theo thought of his father and remembered the reason for this journey he may never return from. But everything could change if Theo returned alive and with the chip.

He'd save his father, and he'd save the dying people of the Midlands.

He looked up, pointedly towards Trent, and hesitated before speaking.

"And our deal?" asked Theo.

Trent nodded.

"Still stands," he said, circling the room with slow, shuffling footsteps. "My boy, I can tell you care deeply about your father. And your sister, Lydia. I know you still carry the grief of losing your brother, Sam."

Sam. Hearing his brother's name sent a twisted pain shooting through his gut.

Theo's face flushed. The room grew suddenly warm.

"Once we build the Aeonite machine," Trent continued,

"your father will be the first Midlander to be healed. Son, you have my word. Given his years of invaluable service to our communities, Arthur more than deserves it. Without him, well, we'd probably have starved to death long ago at the rate the agricultural equipment had been failing."

Trent pulled a plastic cover off an object in the front of the room. It was a rectangular machine with a glass top.

"And you, my boy, well, you'll be the hero of the Midlands."

He placed a clear sheet of plastic on top of the machine, flipped a switch, and the room filled with a warm yellow glow. A diagram projected high onto the chalkboard walls. It was blurry around the edges, but Trent twisted a knob, and the center of the black-and-white photo snapped into focus.

"Theo," he said, "if everything goes according to plan, you should slip through undetected. We have a contact who has been living among the Coasters for over a year now. Her name's Lena. She has gained their trust. She will keep you hidden. And with a little luck, we will never have to worry about the Kaiphers."

Trent lit a hand-rolled cigarette and inhaled, letting smoke spill through his nostrils and tumble down like a cloud in front of the projector beam.

"But, well, you know what your father would say about luck."

Theo cleared his throat.

"Favors the prepared," said Theo.

Trent took a drag and exhaled. The room was filled with the medicinal stench of wolfberry and sweet ginseng.

"Exactly," said Trent, "and I need–we need you to be prepared."

Theo squinted to make out a tall figure in the grainy photograph. Half in shadow, half of the figure's torso was illuminated by an unseen light source out of frame. The light caught the outline of a face as the figure twisted to look back toward the camera.

Theo looked closer.

An apparatus in the figure's left hand. Short and elongated like a glowing rod with a waving rope sprouting from one end. It pulsed an electric blue—the color that a lightning storm glowed before bursting through midnight clouds.

An ominous halo surrounded the object.

Trent pointed toward the projected image.

"This is a photograph of a Kaipher we spotted roughly twenty years ago, hundreds of miles past the Coastal walls."

Trent was silent for a moment. He stared, captivated by the image on the wall.

"Hundreds of miles?" Theo asked.

"Yes," said Trent, "it's been puzzling us for a decade. Those walls are thirty feet thick of concrete, and the Sloan Coastal Republic hasn't been seen on the Midland side of the walls in over two hundred eighty years. Since they were built in 2049."

"So why now?" Theo asked

"That's exactly the question," said Trent.

"Why are they attacking us?" asked Theo.

"The attacks have seemed erratic at first. Many thought they were random, but then a pattern emerged."

"A pattern?"

"They seemed to appear whenever there was an instance of significant knowledge transfer. Schools, weapons factories, and the development of new medical treatments. We think they have one objective: to eliminate any innovation or advancement in the Midlands that might one day pose a threat to the future of the Sloan Coastal Republic. We don't know much about the Kaiphers but we know they are ruthless. They're strong and kill for sport. No, not sport. For exhilaration. They've been known to prolong the death of those they hunt, never going for a swift kill."

"But they must have a weakness of some kind," said Theo.

"During our observations we have never seen the Kaiphers

use ranged projectile weapons of any kind. It seems that they don't consider a kill honorable unless they are close enough to see the whites of their victim's eyes."

Trent looked up at the image on the screen.

"They're patient and smart, and they never stop."

"Never?" asked Theo.

Trent was silent. He wrinkled his nose and traced his fingers over the edge of the projector glass. Maybe he didn't want to answer the question. Or maybe he didn't want to confront the answer.

"So how do we... kill them?" Theo asked.

Trent drew a lungful of smoke. He puffed it through the lamp light. He looked away into a dark corner of the classroom and grew quiet for a moment. Then he spoke.

"We're not sure," said Trent.

"Not sure? Of what? What part?"

"We're not sure they can be killed."

Theo frowned and shook his head.

"But, they're human?"

"We think they were at one point, yes."

"Then they can die. All humans die."

Trent pointed his cigarette at the projected image, gesturing in a circle.

"We stopped this Kaipher at the Red Hills," he said, "It came all alone, in the night, and raided a village full of our best scientists and doctors who were developing new medicines. Their work was very promising. They were close to a breakthrough on a new remedy for the Dust Cough. We think the Kaipher was looking for a child, but that's beside the point."

"A child?"

"That doesn't matter. The point is seven of my men pumped its chest full of .45-70 slugs. Nearly a hundred rounds into center mass. Hand loads. Hot rounds. Its chest blew open like a flower.

I saw the body fall into a river with my own eyes and watched it disappear into the deep."

Trent gripped the cigarette between two fingers and leaned against a desk on the side of the room.

"A few weeks passed. Then we spotted another Kaipher in a town a few miles away, and I swear it was the same one. It cut down a school full of teachers in Clear Blossom."

Trent took a last drag, flicked the tip, and pressed the cigarette into the desk. White clouds shot out of his nostrils, and he rubbed his hands together.

"Based on observations in the field," said Trent, "the data we've captured seem to suggest corporeal annihilation as the only means to actually destroy them."

"Corporeal anni-hill-" said Theo. He spoke slowly, attempting to enunciate each syllable.

"Separation of the core body parts into minute pieces and moving them great enough distances from the central body mass. That's the only way to prevent the SCR from using the Aeonite machines to reanimate them and send them back into the field."

As Trent's words took hold, Theo stared at the projected image. The dark face looked in the other direction, but it felt like it would turn and look straight at Theo at any moment. The inevitability of the moment made the air in the room feel heavy. Palpable, like a domino teetering on edge.

Theo lost himself in the image. The Commander of the Midland Guard stood at the front of the classroom, cigarette in hand. His lips moved, and his hands swirled and prodded in the air, but Theo couldn't hear the words coming out of his mouth. The photograph tugged at Theo's chest as if bending space and time to pull him into the gray, smoke-filled scene. Beads of sweat formed on Theo's forehead. His fingers gripped the desk, and a warm vibration fluttered in his throat. For a moment, he couldn't breathe. All he could do was stare straight ahead into that projected image, captivated by the grainy, dark face of a Kaipher turning to meet his eyes.

That meeting was many months ago.

Now, the grinding vibration of the aircraft's engines ripped Theo back to reality, his gaze away among the clouds.

It's a miracle that these two-hundred-year-old junkers still fly, he thought, looking out the window at two worlds separated by a few inches of glass, plastic, and steel. And a gut feeling that even though he's so close to the end of this mission, mere hours away from becoming the hero of the Midlands. There was still plenty of time for something to go horribly wrong.

He buried the feeling.

He looked down to find his hands gripping hard on the airplane seat armrest, his fingers tensed like claws.

He scanned the back of passengers' heads for suspicious movements. Regular citizens of the Midlands: an elderly man in a gray jacket up front, some young families by the wing, teenagers who wore ragged scraps of twice-dyed linens. After wildfires raged across Arizona and New Mexico and wiped out thousands of acres of flax and cotton fields, simple goods like clothing were in short supply within the Midlands for the past decade.

Theo jolted to attention as the Captain's voice crackled over the ancient overhead speakers.

Soon, they would reach cruising altitude, and within the hour, they would pass through the freezing air of a hydronimbus ice storm, the Captain explained with a strained sound from decaying speakers. The aircraft's aging infrastructure couldn't project mid and low frequencies, leaving the announcements sounding like a vintage walkie-talkie.

Theo knew that cruising altitude meant the aircraft would pass out of range of Sloan Coastal Republic jamming towers positioned on mountaintops surrounding the coastal walls. Encrypted communications devices would soon come online. It also meant the SCR could pick up everything transmitted through their network of drones that, according to legend, roamed the skies just below the Kármán line.

Risky to transmit a message.

Risky to receive one.

"He's close, Theo," Sam's ghostly voice whispered.

Theo's eyes darted to the empty passenger seat beside him. Looking through the narrow opening between the headrests, he caught Mariette's direct gaze from afar. Up in the galley with a half-rusted coffee carafe in hand, she chatted with another flight attendant. Every few seconds, they both glanced in Theo's direction as they spoke.

"They live in their own prison of mediocrity," said Sam, "Watching the days tick away, accepting the inevitable end with a half smile and a shrug. And here you are, their big, strong savior, bringing home the machine to end all their suffering."

Theo could feel Sam's clenched, curled smile in his words.

A voice inside his head, but he felt real nonetheless.

"You must wonder, from time to time, how Trent knew so much about the SCR and what was beyond the walls. Hmm?" Sam continued, "The leader of the Midland Guard, who you risked your life for on this mission, and you don't even know the truth about his past."

Suddenly, Theo felt a faint vibration inside the pocket of his jacket.

"Don't listen to it," said the voice of Sam.

Theo shifted in his seat, extending his left arm to relieve pressure on his elbow.

"You're wondering if it's Trent. You're wondering if it's important. Trent said he wouldn't transmit under any circumstances, but you're wondering if circumstances have changed?"

Theo shut his eyes, took a deep breath, and held it. He tried to clear his head from the swirling doubts and willed Sam's voice to go away, at least until the mission was over.

Frost formed on Theo's window. Crystalline fingers crept across the glass. Massive weather events called Hydronimbus storms had become common over the last decade, decimating crops thousands of hectares at a time. Entire communities in the Midlands plunged into starvation overnight. Potatoes, soybeans and corn husks snap-frozen in the night. Every plant cell for miles ruptured, and nutrients died within seconds.

And for that relic of an aircraft, Theo knew this kind of storm meant turbulence.

He heard a faint hiss as the frost expanded on the glass. The hissing grew louder. Or at least he thought that's what he heard. He glanced quickly around to the other passengers. No one seemed to hear the noise or pay any attention.

The throbbing pain expanded up his shoulder, through his neck and pounded inside his head. He clenched his eyes against the pain.

He felt a second sharp vibration from within his jacket.

"Don't you do it," said Sam, "don't you do it."

Theo snapped open his eyes and stared at the empty seat beside him. Nothing but a ragged seat with frayed gray-blue fabric and a half-broken armrest with no padding. The metal bar of the armrest was exposed.

Sam is not here, he thought. He's dead. He's gone. He needs to get the hell out of my head.

In a flurry of small movements, Theo reached into his jacket, pulled out a small chrome device the size of an almond, and shoved it into his ear canal. He saw his reflection in the window, and a small red light illuminated as the transponder device woke from sleep.

A melodic tone rang, followed by three short beeps. Then, a woman's voice played back on the transponder. It was difficult to hear through terrible static, but Theo looked out the window and listened.

"Theo, son... Doctor Anderson here... Clinic over in Elkhart... they found your father's Bronco at the bottom of a ravine... trunk full of refilled oxygen tanks, we presume intended for your father... heavy rain and flooding, the worst it's been in years in these parts... landslides in the north wiped out a dozen homes and... sister Lydia believed to be the driver... no other occupants in the Bronco... very sorry... representative to identify the body before we–"

The static disappeared. The recording went silent. It was an abrupt ending, as if the signal was lost.

"Or someone shut it down," said the voice of Sam in a playful whisper.

Theo pulled the transponder from his ear. The red light had turned off. The device was unresponsive.

He observed the passenger movements, looking for anyone suspicious with an out-of-place device or someone who might have moved to a different seat. Everything and everyone was in the right place. Heads forward. Eyes down.

The frost grew thick on the window until Theo couldn't see anything but a wall of flat white.

"The storm," said Sam, "we're in the middle of–"

The plane lurched forward. It sent Theo's head forward, and he crashed back into the seat cushion.

Passengers let out a collective gasp, shocked by the unexpected movement.

When the jolt ended, Theo looked out the window again, tilting his head to see anything beyond the blanket of ice.

Trapped.

Then he looked down at the transponder in his hand, but his hand was empty.

The transponder was gone.

CALICO HILL

He quickly searched under the seat beside him.

He unbuckled and leaned out to look down the aisle.

Then he looked forward.

The transponder sat on the floor a few seats ahead.

The plane shook again. It jostled left, then right. A chorus of screams rang throughout the cabin. Then, as quickly as the turbulence arrived, it disappeared, and the plane steadied itself.

Theo watched in slow motion as the chrome-colored transponder rolled toward the front of the aircraft. It tumbled under a seat and spun around the undercarriage of one of the rows. It clinked against a seat up ahead near row twenty and rolled to a stop in the middle of the aisle—a shiny gem against the drab carpet.

A tiny voice pierced through the chaos.

"Daddy, what's that?" said a small boy seated nearby, pointing to the device.

Heads turned at the child's voice that sliced through the noise with its shrill pitch.

None of the passengers moved at first, until an elderly man in a dark gray jacket turned around and looked at Theo.

It had all the markings of a Kaipher. Theo should have seen it earlier. The wrinkles on its face were not from age but from repeated reconstruction. The unnatural eyes—one soulless black and the other steel blue. As the old figure stood up and entered the aisle, the top button of its shirt flapped open and exposed heavy studded scar lines up and down the gray skin of its neck and face, like a doll that's been stitched up one too many times. An unnaturally long life of being destroyed and rebuilt.

The Kaipher stood, a towering figure in the aisle, and picked up the chrome transponder off the floor to examine it closely. Its demeanor was machine-like, with eyes that scanned the transponder, following from one curve around to the dot that used to be illuminated red. In one seamless motion, it released its grip, dropped the transponder to the floor, and crushed it with a heavy stomp of a black boot.

With smooth movements, the Kaipher reached into the overhead compartment and grabbed a small backpack with two orange cords. It fastened the cords around its torso, clicked three metal buckles and pulled the harness tight around its waist.

Theo's hands were shaking. Sweat dripped from his brow. His left arm was splattered with blood, and his stitches were starting to give out. The silicon chip jostled within his muscle tissue. Blood pooled at his elbow. The pain was unbearable.

Theo slid back into his seat and pulled his seat belt tight. He looked up at the figure standing in the aisle and again met the Kaipher's eyes.

"They won't even do anything," said the ghost of Sam's voice, referring to the passengers, "they won't even stand and fight. Look at them. Cattle in a pen."

A wide grin extended across the Kaipher's face, stretching its scars unnaturally. Its skin like silk over rotting muscle. Amusement gleamed in its eyes.

Theo recognized that look. He knew that feeling well from the cold dewey mornings spent bowhunting whitetails in the Oklahoma woods when father was too weak to tend to the farm drones and food ran low. He remembered that point of no return when an arrow took flight from his stick bow and sailed like a whisper through a deer's flesh, the steel broadhead piercing skin and fat and muscle and punching through bone and erupting blood from the deer's lungs onto the forest floor. An individual life approached its terminal point. No turning back once the arrow was in motion.

But now Theo was the one being hunted.

Without breaking his gaze, the Kaipher drew a device from the backpack. From across the cabin, it looked like a small metal rod. Its gloved fingers curled around the handle as it clamped on the grip. Theo could almost hear the crinkle of leather as the Kaipher bent its knuckles. The top of the rod illuminated, and a small cap dislodged, spilling a thick, snaking coil of wire onto the drab carpeted floor.

Then, the wire glowed blue. It was bright, almost blinding, like it carried a powerful electrical charge.

The Kaipher raised a hand high into the air, holding the coil of glowing wire above its head. In a flash of motion, it flicked a wrist down and whipped the wire around in a single circular motion. The coil unspooled like a whip made of light and extended through the air.

Theo looked up. A circular line appeared across the fuselage's interior as if by sorcery.

It scrawled up the side of the aircraft windows, along the curve of the overhead storage compartments, and snaked across passenger seats.

The blue line intersected with a man in the aisle seat. The right half of his face slid to the floor in silence, spilling the contents of his head onto the rug like melted butter.

A woman's arm, sliced clean at the elbow, tumbled down the aisle. She shrieked and raised her bleeding stump into the air. Everyone watched in horror as it sprayed red up the side of the cabin walls.

A geometrically perfect line appeared along the walls. Beautiful, even, in its precision. It glowed blue. It pulsed and grew brighter until the cabin was flooded with a piercing light.

Theo heard a wall of sound blast through the cabin as the steel beams holding the aircraft together split. Freezing air burst into the cabin—louder than anything he had ever heard. The deep roaring of the engines filled his head as the fuselage began to bend. A sharp pain drilled into his ear from the deafening sound. Passengers' cries became inaudible. Mothers reached for their children as the wind whipped by. Oxygen masks fell.

Overhead bins shattered.

A tattered teddy bear floated through the cabin. Books, dresses, hats and earth-toned satchels fluttered into the sky. Mariette's body flew into the clouds as aluminum cans shot through the cabin, exploding like fireworks, coating the walls with sticky liquid.

Theo gripped his armrest tightly. He looked at the empty seat beside him and wished for Sam's voice to return, to keep him company in these final moments, but there was nothing but silence and emptiness in his head. The seats rattled. First rapidly, then slowly like a tugging earthquake. His vision started to fade as the G-forces ramped up. Chaos erupted around him.

Two hundred eighty-six souls plunged toward a violent death over the middle of the Atlantic Ocean.

With the air screaming into his ear, Theo tried to make peace with the end. But there was no peace. Only rage and the instinct to fight for any last chance at staying alive. He felt the weight of letting down his family—his brother, gone long ago; his sister, lost to a freak landslide; and his father, sitting alone back home with a dwindling oxygen supply. The thought crushed him. His town, all the Midlanders. They could have been saved. His mission was slipping away. Regret wrapped him like a blanket, and suddenly, he was a little boy, back home in his father's arms, tucking him under warm covers and drifting off into wondrous dreams.

The cabin shook and spun. Blaring sunlight darkened, and soon, everything was black.

He began to lose consciousness—a tumbling, brainless silence.

The roaring engine stopped, and everything went quiet.

Freefall.

As the aircraft fuselage split into two along the glowing blue line, the onrushing air currents drove the front half of the aircraft downward. Amidst the rumbling chaos, the seats behind the Kaipher fell smoothly out of sight. The Kaipher took a calculated step forward, unphased by the exploding air and shrapnel bursting around him. It planted a foot firmly onto the tail half of the plane.

The Kaipher looked at Theo one last time before it leaned out toward the clouds and dove towards the earth to pull his parachute.

CHAPTER 3
THE ISLAND

First, Theo felt the shock of cold metal digging into his abdomen.

He woke with nostrils full of dirt and smoke. He spit up a cocktail of blood that stained the green leaves below.

He groped for the buckle, fingers blindly crawling. It unfastened, and he tumbled forward out of the airplane seat, falling twelve feet onto the jungle floor. His head throbbed. Spikes of pain shot up from his arm down his spine. Smoke, mud, and trees surrounded him, and the sky was getting darker by the minute.

The air was moist. It smelled familiar, like the long, quiet days in the forest stalking Oklahoma whitetails, mixing with the welding fumes from back home. Then it all hit him. He pressed his hands to his head to brace against the shock of memories flooding in.

The Kaipher sliced the plane in half.

All this destruction in an attempt to hunt him down.

Guilt stirred in his gut. He tried to reconcile the immense loss of hundreds of Midlander souls, ripped out into the clouds. He reminded himself he was doing this to save his father and millions of other lives. At least one day, when the Aeonite machine gets built, that is.

Trent had told him the Kaiphers would go to any length to eradicate anyone who threatened the SCR and what they symbolized. There was no limit to the violence of action they would take to ensure the schematics never got beyond the walls. But Theo never imagined his actions would cause this.

He pushed himself up off the ground and wiped the mud off from the side of his face.

He thought back to his training at the Ranch: protect your world before protecting others.

Theo probed for injuries and found a bloodstain on the left side of his shirt. He began to panic. He looked at his arm, the stitches torn wide open. It was a miracle the electrical tape held as long as it did.

He leaned onto the metal frame of the aircraft seat and pushed himself up. At least his legs still worked. Standing wasn't too painful.

"Hello?" he screamed into the trees, hoping to contact any survivors.

The air was still. It was strange. There was no echo, no breeze.

The air tasted dead on his tongue.

Curiously, none of the leaves around him fluttered.

Everything was motionless.

This all felt wrong, he thought.

"Maybe you're dead," said the sudden voice of Sam, surrounding him in the empty forest, "Maybe this is limbo. Maybe you're stuck in a nightmare, tumbling through the sky?"

Theo shook his head to shoo away the voice and surveyed his surroundings. He landed at the base of a towering banyan tree. Its vines tangled so tight they formed a natural net. It was enough to slow his landing as his seat ripped through the upper canopy and tumbled to the forest floor like a human meteor. Enough to prevent him from becoming a puddle of blood and organs.

A few hundred meters in the distance, a long stretch of beach came into focus. Even with the sunset in total decline and the trees darkening, the bright pinwheel of the aircraft engine and a chunk of the torn fuselage glowed brilliantly beside pockets of towering flames.

Theo looked down at a long metal bar lying on the ground beside his aircraft seat. It must have been a joint supporting the reclining joint that snapped off during impact.

He grabbed it and shuffled it around in his hand to judge its weight and balance. A long curved bar that increased in thickness and weight toward the top.

It became a highly functional poor man's machete in the middle of this impossible jungle.

With his left arm a bloody mess and the steel bar in his right, Theo stepped forward over a tangle of vines toward the lights up ahead.

CHAPTER 4

THE BEACH

"The darkness... it sneaks up on you."

Since he was a teenager, in moments of overwhelming uncertainty, his father's voice would conjure in Theo's head as clearly as if he were standing right beside him. "You think it's hours away. You think you have all the time in the world. Then, all of a sudden, you're in it. And there's nothing you can do to get the daylight back." It was something his father had said during evenings on the Ranch as he would stare out beyond the tree line.

Theo trudged through the mud, following a narrow path between rows of spindly trees. Animals would follow a natural path like this, he thought. Efficient. Low resistance. An ideal location for a trap or a clear shooting land where whitetail deer would wander by.

But there were no animal tracks on the ground.

He looked up and compared the brightness of the tangerine sky peeking through the trees to the shadows growing under the canopy. Light was dwindling. He estimated he had less than an hour before total darkness.

Tall flames glowed in the distance.

Jet fuel burned at 1500 degrees Fahrenheit, turning the airplane's two-hundred-year-old industrial plastic composites into syrup. Toxic smoke billowed into the clouds. It stained the sky a nauseating green-gray.

Theo heaved his makeshift machete and chopped a path through vines as thick as his wrists. He swung violently at alternating angles, hacking repeatedly to sever thread-thin fibers, struggling to break through. Sticky sap flicked through the air. It splattered onto his cheeks and hair.

Theo swung again. One more chop.

Finally, the vine snapped.

A tangle of vines swung loose and thud against the tree trunk.

He was out of breath and hunched over to take a moment to recover. When he looked up, something caught his eye, even in the dying light. He paused and stepped closer to inspect the vine. He wiped perspiration from his eyes.

The vines unraveled like a rope of tiny fibers. Theo looked at the bark and surrounding leaves and watched, waiting for fluttering movements across the hundreds of crevices and folds in the bark. No ants, no beetles, no worms, no web residue from spiders or critters that exposed themselves in panic when leaves rustled, scurrying away to find new shelter.

No bugs. Leaves were smooth and bare.

And then he noticed: no birds either.

Theo pushed again, hacking tangles of waist-high bushes to make his way toward the light on the beach. He alternated between swinging his makeshift machete and cradling his wounded arm and used his right shoulder as a blunt tool to charge forward through the hanging leaves. Branches with pointy barbs scratched him, slicing tiny lines of blood across his exposed skin as he marched on.

He heard a rustling in the bushes off to his right. He froze in his tracks and held silent momentarily, listening for more.

A soft whimpering ahead, thirty or forty meters into the trees.

"Uh, hello?" Theo called out. He was half delirious from exhaustion and blood loss and suddenly heard the sound of his own voice—cautious and weak.

Silence.

"Is... is someone there?" he called out again.

He encountered a collapsed tree ahead. He braced the full weight of his body onto his right arm and hopped over the trunk. With his left arm bloodied and useless, his right arm was quickly becoming worn out. He pushed past the tree and squinted to let his eyes adjust to the fading light.

He saw a small clearing in the canopy ahead. Light poured from above and illuminated a flat, circular area like the single spotlight closing act of a stage play. A burnt orange backpack lay in the middle of the clearing, its contents strewn across the grass. Close by, one of the emergency exit doors from the plane sat wedged into the dirt with a trail of wires dangling in the dirt.

A small blinking light illuminated the exposed side panel.

Theo questioned if it was a beacon or could be transmitting their location.

There was a woman's body lying still, her leg trapped beneath the door.

As Theo stepped closer, he saw the carnage. The edge of the door wedged into her right leg, a few inches above her ankle. Her flesh was shattered, the white glint of exposed bone wet with blood.

He leaned closer, watching for movement from her chest, but she was gone.

His eyes shifted to the backpack.

Tools. Materials. Anything that could become a weapon.

He flipped the sack over and spilled out the remainder of its contents. Frayed pants. A hat. A chapter book with a partial cover missing. Gear salvaged from Midland junk shops.

He reached into the inner side pocket, hoping to find something that could be fashioned into a tool, and his fingers brushed against the bump of a long, cold handle. He pulled a medium-length leather sheath with a rusted knife inside it. Hand forged from a railroad tie, its blackened handle twisted like a tree trunk, and its blade shined silver along the sharpened edge.

Jackpot!

His mind rushed to something his father once said.

"A woodsman is nearly unstoppable with a good knife at his side," his father would say.

Now Theo had a good knife. But he didn't feel unstoppable.

He attached the sheath to his belt and anchored the knife to his side.

When he set the backpack down, something inside rattled. It sounded tinny and jumbled, like a pile of sticks. Around the side, another zipper on the pack came into view. It was easy to overlook, running the long way down along the shoulder strap.

He unzipped the pocket. Inside was a bundle of long, thin rods and a folded metal tool. Theo instantly recognized the straight lines, sharp points and pivoting joints that held it all together.

A folding recurve bow. Crafted of metal, with rust building up along the shoddy welds. Hand hammered limbs, a dozen arrows with broadheads sharpened to a razor edge, and dark brown burlap satchel to wrap it all up.

Midlanders always found a way to survive, he thought.

He slung the bow over his shoulder and marched ahead toward the glowing fires in the distance. Every step was lethargic. He wondered which wounds the adrenaline was shielding from his mind. His veins shot a rhythm of pain and exhaustion like a heavy, pounding clock.

After several hundred meters, he breached the tree line at the beach. Soft sand replaced the moist dirt that crushed underfoot.

The beach looked like a war zone.

Theo paused at the base of a tall, narrow tree that curved toward the ocean and surveyed the aftermath of the crash—what scattered shards remained of flight 805. The rear half of the fuselage came into view, illuminated by flames at its peaks and corners.

Yellow and orange outlines revealed the whole picture.

It was towering up close, with gaping holes that exposed entrails of wires and fluid tubes and sections where reinforced steel crumpled like paper. The line where the Kaipher sliced through the fuselage still glowed a faint blue. Its mathematical precision—straight and circular—felt alien among the curved metal panels that the tumbling g-forces had twisted into knots. Luminescent blue particles from the fuselage's edge scattered across the seats, along the inner cabin walls, and spilled outside into the surrounding sand.

Rows of burnt corpses sat intact, buckled tightly as the safety guidelines had instructed. Faces of entire families with flecks of blackened skin hanging from exposed bones. Hot air rose above the flames, sending clumps of hair and clothing fluttering gracefully away like summer dandelions. Next to the flickering firelight, white jawbones shined in the light—rows of skeletal smiles from a captive audience who enjoyed their last show as the pressure ripped the air from their lungs at thirty thousand feet.

They never had a chance.

Theo paused, taking in the silence of the beach against the background of soft, crackling flames.

Pockets of jet fuel burned near the wreckage. Smaller fires peppered the landscape in the distance.

Up ahead, a woman sat resting against a tree trunk. A man in a torn olive sweater tended to her wounds—a deep scrape on the side of her face—and lifted a metal water bottle to her mouth.

Behind a flaming stack of luggage, a young man emerged. He

crawled slowly up the beach, trying to escape the fire.

Theo saw him struggling and limped toward the wreckage toward the young man. He reached for the man's hand, latched on, and pulled him up the beach near the other survivors.

The young man collapsed beside the tree. When he turned, Theo could see the wound on his leg. It was crusted over with sand and dried blood.

The man in the olive sweater helped the woman take one last drink of water before turning to the young man lying flat on the sand.

"Are you a doctor?" said Theo, collapsing to his knees beside the other survivors.

The man looked over slowly as if dazed. His sweater was covered in soot from the flames and granules of dirt.

"Not exactly." the man said with a distant stare, "I just do what I can do to help." He seemed in shock, slowly becoming more detached from what was happening around him.

"I'm Bill," said the man in the olive sweater, "Bill Asher."

"I'm Theo."

Bill nodded, a faint smile appearing then quickly vanishing. He lifted up the young man's leg to inspect his wound, the left side of his thigh a mess of blood, muscle, and sand. The young man passed out. Alive but out cold from shock.

"The guy next to me got sucked out," said Bill, "I saw him disappear into the clouds. Terry, I think he said his name was. A guy from the north Midlands. Soybean farmer, he said. One minute he was there. Then he was... gone."

Bill tugged at the young man's pants to tear the fabric away from the wound. He cracked another metal canister and poured water to flush sand out of the cut.

"I just remember I couldn't breathe," said Bill, "for the longest time, I thought I was dead. Then I woke up on this beach. I don't remember how I got out of the plane. I've never seen so many dead people. They were all on fire and screaming. It was all so loud, and then just... silent."

Bill reached to check the young man's pulse and rolled a bundle of fallen leaves into a pillow-like lump to place under the young man's head.

"I just popped the buckle and started walking," he continued, "and I found her by this tree, and I didn't know what else to do, so I started making sure she was alright."

He paused and looked up at Theo.

"Looks like you took a good tumble yourself," said Bill, beginning to reach out toward Theo's arm, eyeing the ripped fabric and dark, dried stains, "want me to take a look?"

"No! No, uh, thank you," Theo said, jolting back and instinctively turning his body to put his left arm behind him, out of full view, "it's a bit of a gash, but nothing serious. I'll live."

Bill pulled his arm back. He tilted his head, eyes narrowed, looking Theo over with a suspicious frown.

"Well alright, buddy," said Bill, "suit yourself. Never can be too sure, though. Wounds have a way of getting themselves dirty, and before you know it, what started as a scratch blows up into a whole lot of something else. I've seen my share of wounds go bad quickly."

"We almost shouldn't be alive with a crash like that," Bill continued, "who even knows where the other half is."

"Other half?" asked Theo.

"Of the plane," said Bill, "we came down in the back half, but when it separated... when the Graysk–" Bill stammered, choking back tears, almost couldn't say the words. "What I'm saying is, the other half is either swept miles away into the ocean, or it's somewhere on this island."

Bill's face was overcome with confusion and grief. He set his water canister down, relaxed his arms at his sides, and looked out toward the horizon, a delicate orange line in the near dark.

Theo followed Bill's eyes and looked out toward the ocean. It was eerily familiar, with one important difference—the ocean has no waves. It was flat and still like a pane of glass. A reflective sheet extended out to where the ocean met the sky.

"We're dead," the woman sitting by the tree murmured to herself, as she looked out over the horizon, "This is death. This place isn't real. This, this—" she crumbled into a heavy sob.

"She has a point, Theeeeeeo," the sudden voice of Sam sidled up like a snake out of the jungle, a dagger-like hiss in his whispering tone, "Maybe you are dead. Maybe you've let everyone down. Maybe you've left Father all alone to suffocate in the dark back home at the Ranch."

Theo clenched his jaw and shook his head, beckoning the voice to go away.

"I don't understand," said Bill. He sighed with a defeated look, "None of this makes any sense."

"It was one of those grayskins. A Kaipher," Theo explained. Verbalizing it out in the open was disorienting. Surreal. Like the ground beneath him shifted. Saying its name pulled his attention back to his bleeding arm and the schematics saved on the silicon chip lodged deep in his muscle.

"As least I think it was," Theo backtracked, tucked his bloodied arm slowly behind his back, "I saw a strange man stand up just before—"

"Yeah, I saw him too," said Bill, "Old man. Real out of place. As soon as he showed his mangled face, I knew he was one of those SCR bastards."

Bill paused. He strained to hold back the confusion on his face, but deep wrinkles on his forehead and cheeks let it show. Not only the shock of the attack but something deeper. More insidious. He had the pale look of someone who had seen a ghost and was trying desperately to explain it all away.

"I'm a retired shipmaster," Bill said, "thirty-eight years and three months. Sailed military reconnaissance for the Midland Guard when I was young. Then cargo ships the rest of my career until I retired. Most of my life on the sea. But this doesn't make any sense."

Bill turned. Locked eyes with Theo.

"I've sailed all over these ocean routes in my youth. And here, out over the Atlantic," Bill swept a hand in front of him, gesturing toward the beach and the forest behind the tree line. "This–this is nowhere. It's not even a place–I mean, what I'm trying to say is there's nothing here. No land for a hundred miles. Not here. I've sailed it a thousand times over."

The woman beside the tree was quiet. She looked down and twirled her bracelet in between her fingers. She began hyperventilating while trying to hide it.

"Where are the waves, huh?" Looking at the flat reflective surface, Bill asked, "Why are there no insects flying around? Why is there no wind?"

Bill's questions hung in the air, unanswered. He became agitated. His hands shook. The water in his canister sloshed, and a little spilled out onto the sand.

"Something about this place is all wrong. I know it!" Bill said again, "I swear it.

The three of them sat, sharing a fleeting moment of silence. But it was quickly shattered by a deep, low hum in the distance. They turned their attention to the sky and listened together.

Theo felt his ribcage vibrate as a low tone grew louder, blanketing the beach in a wave of ominous sound.

A shape moved in the distance. The light in the sky shifted. Darkness arrived in full force.

The shape emerged from the gun-gray clouds. It came closer. It seemed like some sort of aircraft, but nothing like Theo had seen before. The parts were familiar but in all the wrong places. Like a machine cut up and riveted back together in a different combination. A wide, central fuselage shaped like an arrowhead. It had two circular discs on its underbelly that seemed to be the likely source of that monstrous vibration in the air.

The space around it seemed to distort as the craft approached.

"It's a miracle," the woman beside the tree said under her breath. Theo glanced back at her to see her smile.

"What is–," Bill started to speak, shaking his head, "how'd they get here so fast? We don't even know where here is!"

Bill looked at Theo.

"This doesn't feel right," Bill said, a worried frown on his face. He looked out over the water, searching in the dark. At the water's edge, a small burning seat cushion from the wreckage leaned against a pile of luggage and ignited a duffel bag into a bright inferno. From one bag to the next, they caught fire. A hardshell suitcase melted, and something burst inside, emitting a loud pop and sending white sparks in every direction.

The dark vibration was getting stronger.

It seeped into Theo's skull, shaking his ribcage. It was almost unbearable.

More survivors gathered up ahead to stare in the direction of the thrumming, dark sound. Limping figures made their way out from behind sand dunes and fallen trees and moved down the beach. Survivors climbed over bent sections of the cabin, avoiding pockets of flame. A tree engulfed in fire fell and crashed on the sand. Theo heard a mother shout at her children to keep up. An older man behind them cried out to his group that he was moving as quickly as possible.

Within minutes, the triangular craft flew overhead, and a second craft followed directly behind it. Two gray arrowhead shapes floated, loud and unusually low to the ground. Their engines whipped up a violent swirl of air. Burning embers flew from the wreckage up into the leaves and ignited the treetops.

Soon, large swaths of the forest began to burn.

The two crafts landed at the far end of the beach. Even in the darkness, Theo could see the faint outline of survivors shuffling down the beach toward the landing zone. Some ran. Others limped along as best they could.

"C'mon, we should get moving," Theo shouted to Bill and the woman by the tree. He waved his hands frantically, signaling them to start walking to the rescue craft.

The woman leaned against the tree and started to stand.

But Bill didn't move. He sat there with a look of dread on his face, staring off into the darkness shrouding the far side of the beach.

The crafts cut their engines, and the sound began to dissipate. Theo could see the rescue crew deplaning their crafts through the faint moonlight.

There were eleven or twelve of them in total. Black uniforms, barely muddied shapes in the darkness, wearing helmets with reflective face shields. Shoulder and chest-mounted electronics–maybe radios–glowed sharp blue dots in the distance.

Many survivors were grouped around.

The engines were dead silent.

The rescue crew formed a line in front of the aircraft, their dark suits becoming a row of blue dots piercing the shadows. Moonlight glanced off their helmets.

Suddenly they stood still. Not a single movement.

An uneasy silence fell upon the beach as a minute passed without movement.

Bill watched this unfold from across the beach. He slowly got to his feet.

"Something's not right about th–"

Then a loud crack of gunfire echoed down the beach.

CHAPTER 5

THE BANYAN TREE

The line of men shouldered automatic weapons and unleashed hell upon the survivors.

Theo watched from across the beach as flashes of blue light erupted from the barrels of their bullpup railguns. A volley of tungsten slugs, flying at hypersonic speeds, blanketed the beach and shredded the survivors into pieces. Limbs burst, and hemorrhaged blood flash-boiled, evaporating into the air. Within fifteen seconds, the gunfire ended. The beach was blanketed in silence, and not a soul was left alive. Only carnage. Corpses with monstrous, steaming holes blown through them. Exploded arms and torsos were strewn about the sand.

"Wh–why are they firing at–," Bill screamed as he ran toward the tree line.

"Run! We all need to move," Theo shouted back.

The woman beside him turned to look at Theo. By the time Theo looked back, half of her chest was a gaping red hole.

Theo ducked quietly under the nearest tree. He moved silently, falling back on his experience stalking whitetails in the woods. He rolled his feet to minimize the pop and snap of plants underfoot.

Bill turned to follow, his movements lumbering, his feet heavy and sluggish. He spun around and planted his foot in the soft sand. It sank and threw him off balance. He extended his arm out to steady himself, but his foot looped into the strap of a child's backpack, and he tripped on his next step. Bill tumbled to the ground, and his face impacted the sand.

A wisp of blue streaked through the air, and with a loud crack, a tree trunk exploded behind him. The trunk split in two, and feather-like fragments of superheated bark kicked into the air and fluttered around him like heavy dust.

There was a pause in the gunfire as soldiers ran down the beach toward them. Theo picked up the pace and bolted deeper into the trees.

Embers set fire to the canopy above. Glowing orange dots hovered in the distance like a thousand suns burning overhead. After several minutes, the flames began to illuminate their surroundings. Fallen trees and thick patches of green came into view.

Bill jolted up. Granules of sand speckled his cheek. He started to run after Theo. By then, he was a dozen paces away and quickly falling behind.

The soldiers reached the beach's edge, where the sand mixed into hardened clay. Their boots struck the dirt, and they ran faster with every footfall. In the dark, save for the faint glow from burning trees surrounding them, the soldiers were running and gunning blind.

Theo and Bill ran faster, dodging bundles of vines like webbed traps sprawled across the landscape. One trip and tumble would have meant certain death.

The soldiers were a hundred meters behind them and gaining.

Theo saw a tangle of vines hanging limp along the trunk of

two trees. It looked out of place and familiar. Then he recognized the path he hacked through the woods just an hour ago.

"This way," Theo shouted to Bill. He mustered every ounce of energy to maximize his fight or flight instinct.

A report of gunfire popped behind him. The soldiers were firing blindly in the dark, spraying bullets across the landscape.

Crack-k-k-k!

Heavy rounds ripped through leaves and shredded bark around them. Chunks of wood exploded and sprayed into their faces as they sprinted ahead, dodging rocks and fallen tree trunks. Theo found the path he had carved earlier with his makeshift machete and pushed harder to follow it, calling out to Bill behind him.

"Here!" shouted Theo.

He bent around waist-high roots and hopped over piles of branches. He pushed through razor-sharp barbs of wild, dry bushes.

Crack-k-k-k!

Blue streaks whipped through the air, this time so close that Theo could see it pointing straight ahead, leading down the path in front of him.

A round skipped off the ground and struck Bill. His left leg exploded into a cloud of fabric and muscle. Droplets of blood splashed onto the leaves as Bill tumbled to the ground, face-first into a web of crisscrossing vines.

Theo skidded to a halt and turned to look over his shoulder.

Bill reached to grab a vine to pull himself up. It stretched under his weight.

The soldiers' heavy boots pound the dirt in the distance.

"Leave him," Sam's voice appeared from behind, "There's no time."

Guilt flooded Theo's mind.

"If you help him, this mission is over. You'll be dead, and so will everyone back home. You have to move. NOW!" said Sam.

Theo spun around, and pushed into the darkness. He wanted to catch a last glimpse of Bill in the distance but didn't look back.

A heavy thud of boots grew louder. Theo knew that it wouldn't be long before the soldiers caught up to Bill and executed him on sight with a burst of high-velocity rounds. From the violence Theo witnessed on the beach, he could be sure it would be a quick death.

He was running on empty but summoned anything he could inside himself to keep pushing, keep running.

Another crack of gunfire. Blue streaks flew by, tungsten slugs speeding to the dark ahead. A vacuum of air pushed the leaves forward and then revered like a tide, pulling giant fan-shaped leaves backward.

The leaves shifted, and Theo saw an enormous banyan tree up ahead to the right. Roots as thick as telephone poles weaved in a labyrinth web. At the tree's base, there was a deep chasm in the dirt. It was filled with brackish water and shaped like a cave.

Probably deep enough for a person to crawl into, Theo thought.

It was the only way.

He couldn't run forever.

Theo jolted to the right. He was fifty meters away. He raced to the tree and dove under the root system. Dirt kicked up into the air. A flurry of splashes–louder than he intended–as he slipped into the crevice with muddy water rising to his chest. He stood, submerged and silent. He felt the cold soaking through his sleeve and seeping into the wound. The negative spaces filled with dark liquid.

Not a great place or time for an infection.

But there were other pressing dangers like the murderous soldiers hunting him.

The burning foliage surrounding him cast the massive banyan

tree in a soft amber light.

A crash of boots erupted nearby. Twigs snapped.

Theo watched from below ground level as two soldiers burst past the banyan tree in a full sprint. Their sounds disappeared into the distance. But within a few moments, their footsteps quickly slowed.

Silence.

Gunfire up ahead, erratic and scattered.

Their railguns spooled up and sent high-velocity slugs ripping through everything in sight. They swept left and right, up into the shadows of canopies, and punched glowing blue holes into thick tree trunks.

Frantic and unfocused.

Then the gunfire stopped.

Theo felt a soft rippling in the water with his slight movements. He sat in a moment of stillness and suddenly became aware of the absence of crickets chirping or flies buzzing.

Moments later, the soldiers' slow and cautious footsteps began to backtrack along their path. Soon, they entered the clearing directly across from the great banyan tree. Theo watched as the soldiers paused not far up ahead.

"... there's no way," said one soldier to the other with a voice distorted through a vocal amplifier in his helmet, "Blackburn said we need to shoot all of those dusties dead. That's the only way to be sure."

"No shit," said the second soldier, enraged. Theo could hear his clenched jaw from behind the voice amplifier. He bashed his rifle into a large, flat leaf beside him. It ripped from the stem and crashed to the ground. "But we won't find the chip now. Too dark. Come back in the morning. I'm sure you'll find it on one of the rotting corpses around here."

"Fucking dusties," said the first soldier, "we need to clear all this up before the first clients lands tomorrow. We can't have visitors seeing any of this. Blackburn will–"

"Nevermind Blackburn, this whole shitshow is his fault. He chose to take the whole plane down and couldn't even finish the job. This is the last time I'm cleaning up his damn mess."

"So what do we tell him?"

"Tell him we'll have it tomorrow."

"How're we going to find the chip in all this–"

"We get in early. We sweep up before the visitors arrive. Right now, I don't want to spend another minute in this hellhole. This island is fucking cursed, and I'm not going any further in there. Not now. Not in the dark. Can't see shit. I heard those.. things... whatever they are, they don't sleep. They're probably out now, just walking around and–"

"Calm the fuck down. Ok."

One of the soldiers turned to look around in a circle, scanning in the distance. Even with the trees on fire, it was futile in the darkness.

"You know how I feel about this place. This is bad juju, man. We shouldn't be here. No one should be here."

The radio beeped two sharp tones.

"Fine," the other soldier said, "Head back. I'll run a last sweep, and we'll call it. Tell the crew to be ready at 0500. Clients arrive at 0900. We find the chip, we clean this up and we get the hell out. You hear me?"

"Check," said the soldier. He nodded and turned to walk back toward the beach. Foliage crunched under his boots with every step. He faded into the darkness.

The remaining soldier looked around, lowered his rifle at his side, and raised a small backlit screen mounted on his wrist. He pulled it close to read it, the yellow-white glow of text reflected in his visor as he stared intently at the screen.

A tiny ember from a neighboring tree landed near Theo. A mound of dry foliage ignited, its flame coming to life in silence.

Theo watched as the flame expanded, its soft edge glowing brighter until it latched on the next branch and ignited anew.

He watched the fire take hold. Then he glanced back at the soldier, standing still with his attention on the wrist screen.

The flames, bending and expanding.

The soldier, distracted and unmoving.

A halo of smoke encircled the tree. It wafted across the surface of the mud.

Theo pressed a piece of cloth to his mouth.

The smoke became dense. It floated over the dark water under the tree and spread through the area.

Theo couldn't see exactly how thick it was and how it would, in daylight, visually obscure the entire forest floor in a thick haze.

But in the dark, he could smell it.

The soldier tapped a button on the wrist device, and the glow disappeared. He raised his rifle, resuming the search through the darkness with intent to destroy. He took one last slow, sweeping scan around him. Tension in his trigger finger. He nearly discharged his weapon simply for pleasure.

The smoke thickened. It penetrated the crevices beneath the tree roots.

After a moment, the soldier lowered his weapon. He took a slow step to turn back towards the beach.

Smoke seeped through the cloth, and Theo could feel it stinging his throat.

He coughed.

He startled himself and pulled the cloth tighter. It made it harder to breathe. His throat constricted, and the scratch of a heavier cough built in his chest.

The soldier stopped midstep and turned to his left, towards the direction of something he heard. A movement, or a sound. Or maybe it was nothing.

Theo froze.

The smoke burned his eyes. Filled his lungs.

The soldier walked slowly toward the tree, his rifle high and ready. His steps were cautious, but lacking direction. When he approached the banyan tree, he stopped and stood at the base of the trunk. Theo could hear the squeak of his leather boots and his vest, bulky and weighed down with radio gear, straps, and cords rustling against his nylon jacket.

"Shhhhhh," said Sam's voice, "Not the time to be making any noises."

Theo's eyes went wide. He knew Sam wasn't there. Only a voice in his head. But the intrusion startled him.

The soldier tried to locate the source of the noise he had heard. The muzzle of his bullpup rifle arced left, right, up towards the canopy, and back down toward the roots. He took a step forward. His boot pressed a thick rubber heel into the dirt, then rolled forward silently with pressure on the ball of his foot and toes.

"Too close for my liking," said Sam.

As he swept the rifle back and forth, Theo saw the blue glow inside its barrel where magnetic rails accumulated their charge and propelled each slug at unimaginable velocities.

Theo slowly moved his arm through the water so as not to stir up bubbles and reached toward the sheath on his belt. His fingers glided across the bump of the knife handle. He could hear the soldier's soft exhale above, so close he could hear it from behind the helmet.

Theo tightened his grip on the handle and slowly unsheathed the knife. His hand shook. Soft ripples expanded in the black water.

A rush of heat flooded his senses despite standing chin-deep in cold water. His body and mind recalled that primal feeling, that familiar burst of energy right before the leap–the moment at the cliff's edge before time tumbled into motion a series of irreversible events.

Theo cocked his arm back, prepared to strike out from underneath the roots. Took a deep, silent breath. Every muscle tensed.

The soldier took another step.

Paused.

Theo could smell the soldier's sweat through his shirt—cigarettes and engine grease. He froze, rifle pointed toward the tree.

Theo gripped hard on the knife, ready to unwind all of his remaining energy into a raging stab. Tremors built up in his muscles from the tension in his wrist.

The soldier squinted in the dark. The panel on his wrist illuminated a warm yellow light in his visor. He stood motionless for seconds that felt like agonizing hours. Then, like a weapon decocking, he lowered his rifle with a slow, reluctant motion. The coiled magnetic drive spun down and disengaged with an audible whine. The blue glow in the barrel faded to black.

With heavy footsteps—slow, then speeding—he marched back toward the direction of the beach and disappeared.

Theo took a breath and unclenched his grip on the knife. Even with muscles numb from the chilling water, he felt the blood rush back to his hand, and the divots in his palm where his fingernails dug deep began to decompress.

He exhaled, and his breath rippled over the water's surface.

Theo waited a moment and listened for footsteps. Then he slowly climbed out of the black water and wrangled every last ounce of energy to keep from collapsing onto the dirt. He stood and pulled at his sleeve, liquid releasing as he rumpled the fabric and saw the gaping wound on his arm. The open cavity was full of viscous fluid—a cloudy mix of blood and black mud. The surrounding muscle burned as he twisted his wrist to inspect his arm. It would get infected soon if it hadn't already begun. But that was a small price compared to getting your chest blown open by metal slugs.

He kept playing back the soldiers' words in his head. Something about their clients arriving in the morning and these mysterious things that never slept. And about the island being cursed.

"Tell me about it," Sam's voice sliced through the dark silence, "best not venture further into the forest, for that's where those... things they were talking about are."

"Well, I can't head back to the beach, now can I," replied Theo, speaking aloud in a harsh whisper.

"You could find a place to curl up and sleep, and hope those things don't pay you an unwanted visit in the dark," said Sam.

"Thanks for the advice," replied Theo.

As annoyed as Theo was with the voice in his head, a part of him was thankful for the company. Beneath the confident exterior and the risk-it-all attitude, there was a scared little boy who wanted nothing more than to be home with his father, sitting by the fire with a warm blanket while the fireflies speckled the landscape. Now, he was alone on a cursed island without a plan to get home. While the Midlands were dying and his father was alone with dwindling oxygen supplies.

Theo sighed.

"Wish you were here, Sam," said Theo, looking up past the trees at the dark blue sky, "I really do."

Nothing but silence in return.

Burning embers from a nearby tree rained down beside him. Theo strained his neck to see the pathway forward in the dark. A numbing pain jolted in his stomach, and he exhaled suddenly and violently, clutching his side and tensing his muscles against the fatigue settling in.

He made his way deeper into the forest. His breath grew heavy, coarse, and strained, the sound painfully loud amidst the stillness of the forest. It clawed at his eardrums against the background of unnerving silence. Besides the leaves that crunched under his feet, no crickets were chirping or flies buzzing. The flames surrounding him slowly subsided and reached a point where the orange embers faded, and the trees ahead were no longer burning.

"How the hell am I ever going to make it out of here?" Theo asked of the darkness.

Silence.

He wished he could curl up underneath a bush and sleep off this nightmare and wake to a different time and a different place. What a dream it would have been to walk off the plane and get into the truck headed back home. He didn't think about a future in which he never returns. There was no time to think about that.

He felt lost. He had never felt so far from home.

Then, an unsettling wind of deja vu hit him.

What if he'd been walking in circles all this time, and the trees played tricks in the dark? What if he took another step and collapsed to the dirt and surrendered and gave his body away in silent agony to nourish the forest's roots? Where was he even going?

Soon, the hard dirt disappeared, and the ground beneath him was soft moss covering the forest floor. It was spongy and moist. In the daylight, it must have been glorious. Emerald green with pockets of dew that shimmered when the sun shone through the canopy. But in the dark, one of the last burning branches cast a soft light on an object in the distance. Light reflected off its curves, and Theo realized it could only be one thing.

CHAPTER 6

NIGHT

The aircraft door was wedged into the dirt. Theo somehow circled around and found his way back. But how? Beside the door, the orange backpack contents were right where he left them. The woman's body was flat on the ground. Theo sidled up beside her and strained to find the right words, but all that was left in his head was rage and defeat. He bowed his head respectfully and found a soft patch of mossy ground to sit nearby.

Theo's eyelids grew heavy. He felt the tug of sleep getting stronger. The moss blanketing the earth beneath him felt cozy and familiar.

He looked up at the dark blue night sky. As a child, Theo, Sam, and Lydia would lie under the stars behind the house and play games, trying to name as many constellations as possible. Lydia would always win. Even though she was the youngest, she learned the fastest and memorized more constellations than Theo had ever heard of.

Lying here, on this impossible island in the middle of the Atlantic, Theo looked up beyond the canopy, looking for stars to connect like puzzle pieces, trying to locate Orion. He tried desperately to find any sense of the familiar, hoping that finding the same stars he looked at back home would make him feel a little less far away. But he squinted through the dark, and he searched and searched the sky until he stopped and gasped.

A jolt of terror shot through his heart.

This was all wrong.

Orion wasn't there.

The sky was... different.

There were no stars.

It was an empty black.

Lifeless and infinite.

Within minutes his eyelids shut and he fell towards sleep.

***

That night, Theo was plunged back into a recurring memory. A nightmare of the mistake that haunted him every day for the past four years.

Suddenly, he was in the kitchen back at the Ranch. His father had just arrived with a box of produce and grain from the Northwest Oklahoma Farmer's Enclave. During the decade earlier, farmers banded together, worked their fields, and offered crop yields to the community in exchange for anything else people needed to survive. Midlanders lined up once a month with goods to trade. Kerosine, hand tools, engine components, candle wax, bottled rainwater, soaps, livestock textiles, root vegetables, grain, and butter. Father always got a double serving, and the Midlanders were more than willing to offer it. Arthur Rousseau was the best engineer within a hundred miles, and no one would repair farm machinery like he could. No machines meant no crops, and no crops meant the end of the Midlands.

Theo remembered Sam bounding into the kitchen with a

box of carrots, onions, potatoes, chicken eggs, and a satchel overflowing with red tomatoes so vibrant one might think they were glowing.

Theo reached for the tomatoes and filled his cheeks with the sweet fruit.

"Theorennnnn!" his mother screamed, "Step away from those this minute. We eat as a family, and never before your father. You know this!"

As she wagged a pointed finger through the air, Theo scarfed down the remaining tomato in two cheek-swelling bites and grabbed another before running out of the house.

His mother put a cast iron pot on the stove and powered it on but found the reserves barely above fifty percent.

"Theo!" she yelled again, "did you clean off the panels as I asked you to? Theoooo?"

He bolted down the hill and found a shady spot under an oak tree beside a patch of wheat sprouting from the dirt. It was a perfect afternoon to waste the day and push his chores off until tomorrow.

Theo's pulse raced as he recalled the rest of the nightmare. In his sleep, he heaved and whimpered as the worst day of his life played out in front of him.

He remembered the smell of steel dust and diesel fuel from Father's workshop up the hill. A scrap yard lay in the distance with piles of faded green tractor hoods, chrome exhaust pipes, spools of copper wire, and a combine with bent corn headers. A partially disassembled pesticide-spraying drone sat splayed open like a patient on an operating table. Its propellers were removed, and resting beside its fuselage was a white chemical tank and brass nozzles patched with duct tape and epoxy.

Everything just had to keep going. Keep moving, no matter the cost.

Theo took a bite of his last tomato and looked up at the

monstrous clouds forming overhead. A storm was brewing, but it wouldn't strike the farm for at least a day.

Then he saw movement on the roof.

Sam was climbing the ladder towards the top of the tower where the solar panels were mounted. Gusts of winds swept up dust and crusted over the panels, so Theo's weekly chore was to climb to the top and clean the panels.

Theo knew every rung of that ladder like the creases on his hands. The rungs were once adorned with welded stippling to improve grip but now were worn smooth as glass from years of storms and intense sunlight.

Whatever man built, the earth tore down.

From a hundred meters away, he watched Sam ascend the ladder wearing Theo's gloves and boots. At least four sizes too big for Sam. Sam's legs would wiggle in the oversized boots, struggling to get a purchase on the rungs as he approached the halfway mark. Within minutes, Sam was five rungs away from the solar panel, and Theo could see him extending the brush pole in one hand while latching the other arm around the ladder.

Theo shot up and got to his feet. Tomato juice dribbled down his shirt.

Sam was reaching from too far down. The pole would never reach. He would lose his balance.

Theo burst into a sprint toward the house.

"Sam!" he screamed.

Sam swung the brush pole and made contact with the solar panel. He extended one arm as far as possible and gave it one solid swipe. A cloud of dust whipped away into the breeze.

Then Sam went for a second swipe to finish the job.

"Sammmmm, stop!" Theo screamed from across the field.

He reached out and made contact with the solar panel.

The wind shifted.

A puff of red dust shot into Sam's eyes.

Shocked and blinded, Sam loosened his grip and dropped the brush pole. It floated silently toward the house and smacked the roof with a loud metallic clang.

Sam tried to rub the dust out of his eyes, and with a flurry of motion, his foot slipped a rung.

Sam didn't scream.

When Sam hit the roof, it was with a thunderous boom that echoed through every room of the house. But when his limp body rolled toward the roof's edge and fell to the dirt, his landing was met with silence and an explosion of red dust erupting into the air.

Their mother burst through the door and rushed to her son. She cradled his head, wiping blood off of his temple.

When Theo arrived, coated in sweat from sprinting, he found his mother cradling Sam's mangled body as he writhed in her arms, hands contorting and legs kicking violently as if possessed. Tears streamed down his mother's face, and a circle of blood expanded on the dirt beneath Sam's body.

Theo woke from the nightmare, unable to breathe. He felt an immense weight on his chest, and all of a sudden, air rushed in with heaving breath. He wiped clumps of dried tears from his eyes.

His eyes were wide and alert. The sky above was crisp blue. The sunlight was sharp and assaulted his eyes. Morning had come upon the island. He tried to squint against the harsh light. He reached around to feel his surroundings—the soft, cool moss on the ground.

Then, his eyes adjusted.

To his right, the emergency door wedged into the dirt, wire innards shredded upon the ground, and the poor woman's body still beside the wreckage. Sunlight reflected off the door and bathed her corpse in a pool of hazy light. A solemn feeling was in the air as Theo sat there, looking upon the erected scene. One of mourning, of regret, and an unexplainable warmth.

He glanced at the gaping wound on his arm. Just hours ago, it was flushed with black mud and, on any other day, would have grown swollen red by now. But the wound was clean. The flesh, though still an open wound, looked healthy and robust.

Then, the nearby trees caught Theo's eye. Where they were once engulfed in flames and burnt to ash and embers, now the leaves were a radiant green under the clear daylight.

The soldier's words rang in his memory.

This island is fucking cursed.

At least he was still alive. At least he still had a chance. But morning had come, and the clock was ticking. The soldiers would return soon.

New smells of wildflowers, sagebrush, and mustard hit Theo as he sat up. The forest sat behind him, and in front of him was the beginning of a vast expanse of fields.

Then Theo heard a rustle in the grass up ahead. Someone was crying. It was soft and quiet with hurried, panicked breaths.

Theo got to his feet and walked into the field toward the direction of the sound. He raised his one good hand to shield his eyes from the sun, his wounded arm limp at his side.

He saw a figure crouched on the ground in the middle of the field. It's in silhouette, so he couldn't make out details. Only shadows.

Then, the light hit the side of his sister's face.

And she came into focus.

"Lydia?"

CHAPTER 7

THE HILLS

Theo looked at his sister with the clarity of the crisp morning air, standing together on this impossible island in the middle of the Atlantic Ocean. She was tall for her age. About fifteen.

She ran to him. Threw her arms around him in a hug that jolted him backward.

"Theo!" Lydia shouted. Her body was shaking. A parade of emotions fired all at once–happiness, relief... confusion. "Where are we, Theo? How did you get here? How did you...?"

The questions crashed into one another. An overwhelming cavern of emptiness with no answers to fill it. A cavern that felt lonelier each minute.

Up close, Theo saw the constellation of her freckles and that lighting bolt of energy in her eyes. Her hair was reddish brown, depending on how the light hit it. A color that had changed since she was a child. But standing there, in the middle of ankle-deep wild grass, he saw her hair glow like an unstable element, morphing from one shade of red to another like it was alive, almost iridescent at certain moments.

Theo squeezed the bridge of his nose and rubbed his eyes. Sweat and dried dirt rubbed off onto his fingers.

Maybe the fatigue is messing with my vision, he thought.

He looked over Lydia's shoulder and saw endless hills, curving and extending as far as the eye could see. A patchwork of hues—some vibrant as an emerald and others lush with grass the color of honey. Like a quilt of different colors rolled out to the horizon.

This wasn't just an island.

It was more than that.

The soldier's word: Cursed.

The entire landscape was draped in a dusty golden light. There was a thickness to the air, to the sunlight, like he could reach out and grab it.

Theo looked back at Lydia.

"You're so tall," said Theo, the words escaping his mouth almost involuntarily.

He'd been away from home for over a year, and the last time he saw her, she was a little girl. He couldn't help but smile, and for a few seconds, the terror of the previous twelve hours melted away like a morning frost. But the feeling didn't last.

"What are you... how did you get here?" Theo asked.

"I don't know, I... I... took Dad's Bronco to Mr. Jerreh's shop to get a new oxygen tank. He was closing up shop but told me he'd wait for me. It was late, I remember that, but it wasn't dark that night. I remember because the moon was so high. And then it started raining, and I–" she stopped mid-thought, silent for a moment, gaze fixed on Theo's eyes. Her shoulders lowered and posture deflated, "and I can't remember anything after that."

She frowned, lost in thought, then quickly looked away.

"Sam?" Lydia said, looking off to the edge of the grassy field.

Sam sat propped up on the ground with the grass brushing against his elbows.

Theo's heart pounded like a hammer. The air thickened in his throat, and his breathing became ragged and strained.

Sam wasn't a tall teenager like Lydia. He was a small boy with freckled cheeks and brushy hair. The same small boy that he was the day he fell off the solar tower and died in his mother's arms.

"But you were–" Lydia started to speak but lost the words.

Shock and sadness flushed across Theo's face.

"Oh, Sam," said Theo, "No... no... this is not real. This can't be real. Sam... you..."

Theo held back tears as they welled in his eyes.

"Died," said Theo.

That word.

It sucked the air out of the world.

He rested his eyes far into the distance and let everything in the foreground melt away. He tried to make sense of this impossible place, to put the puzzle pieces together and find the logical explanation. But there was none.

"Where's mom?" Sam's small voice cut through the confusion.

Lydia spun around and faced Theo, tears streaking down her face.

The Rousseau children united again on this impossible island.

"Theo," said Lydia, "what is going on? Where are we? How... Why are we... Please!"

Theo remembered the audio message on the transponder, which he listened to before the Kaipher destroyed the plane.

"Sam died years ago," said Lydia, "Theo... why is he here? Theo!? Why can't I remember how I got here?"

Her breathing quickened. Rapid and shallow.

"No. N-NO!" said Lydia. She held both arms out, palms open, and took a step backward in a defensive pose, "I don't know what's happening, and I don't know who or what you are," she pointed at Sam, then Theo, "but this is some kind of cruel joke. Whatever this game you're playing, this ends now!"

She stopped in her tracks, deflated. A child-like sadness on her face.

"I just want to go home," she said, looking at the ground, "I don't want to be HERE anymore."

Lydia shouted so loudly that it startled Sam, and he burst into tears before running into the distance. He disappeared into the tall grass.

Her brothers were at arm's length, but she was lost in this broken reality unraveling before her eyes. To Theo, she looked fifteen, but he could see in her eyes that she was a scared little girl who wanted nothing more than to be home under a soft wool blanket with her father and brothers sitting across the room and logs crackling in the hearth. Standing in this golden field so far from home, she looked so hopeless.

Theo detached from the moment and let his eyes rest on the curves of the landscape in the distance. He had used that technique in the forest to ease eye strain when his mind would play tricks on him during an early morning sit in a tree stand. Leaves, trees, squirrels, and branches would flutter, sway, and blend together. He looked to the hills ahead.

It was a bizarre sight, unlike any land he had seen back home. A patchwork of large mounds forming hills that curved and intersected. Each hill was a different shade of green, brown, or yellow. Some soft and dull, others exploding with so many brilliant colors it looked like an artist painted it.

Down the middle, a first pathway snaked its way through the hills. It curved and stretched. Wound up and down and disappeared behind the curve of the next hill. An undulating web of the most beautiful land Theo had ever seen. The paths extended far into the distance–probably nine or ten miles, Theo guessed, judging the way the line faded into shadow.

But something about this place was different.

The air felt all wrong. An uneasiness permeated the space. The sunlight and shadows looked different.

From where Theo was standing, the hills that dotted the landscape didn't follow the natural curve of the earth like the mountains back home that fade into a blue-gray fog as they reach close to the horizon.

A sound echoed across the landscape. A mechanical horn, like a conch but metallic and bright. It cut through the air and traveled a great distance with ease.

"There," Theo said, waving his hands, motioning for Lydia to crouch, "look beyond that bright yellow hill over the far crest. Something's moving."

A line of figures dressed in black with colorful embellishments upon their jackets walked down the path. A dozen walking figures at first, but then more joined the line. They moved with a slow and somber gait. Several hundred of them walking in line. Tiny figures on a slow, meandering journey from one hill to the next.

"We're not safe here, Theo," said Sam's voice like a ghost in the wind.

Theo spun around, but Sam was nowhere to be seen. He sighed and tried to understand what was happening in front of him. This place. These people. It didn't make sense. Theo knew the soldiers would be crashing through the forest any minute now. Whatever this place was, he needed a way out. Now.

As the line of figures loomed closer, Theo could hear shrieks of laughter and joy from small children.

"We need to get home," said Theo in a whisper.

Upon hearing the words, Lydia's face slowly rose, and the spark of life in her eyes flickered back. Sam, still a tiny boy, stayed sitting on the grass, his petrified eyes gazing upon Theo from afar.

Theo started walking along the edge of the field. He kept his posture low and stalked through the brush as silently as possible. He could hear Lydia following behind. The lines of figures marched closer. He listened to the children's voices echoing through the stale air. Theo continued following a great semicircular path that separated the hills from the forest—a threshold of some kind where one type of green grass met another type of yellow grass. Still, the stark color difference suggested it was manicured with an artificial precision seldom found in nature.

Theo picked up speed, carefully staying out of sight of the figures moving in the distance. By then, the line had disappeared, and the figures had fanned out, dispersed through the endless rows of hills.

The ankle-deep grass was soft, almost feather-like, and didn't rustle as loudly as Theo had expected. He pushed on with longer strides, moving close to a jogging pace.

Lydia was trailing not far behind until the air was sucked out of her lungs, and she cried a muffled, drowning scream.

CHAPTER 8
RELEASE

"Hehhhurrrggh," Lydia cried out, stopping in her tracks. Her body was seized by a jolt of paralysis. Her spine locked, her muscles contorted.

Theo spun around and lunged forward, resisting the instinct to run and help.

She's not the real Lydia, he thought.

Lydia raised her hands to her throat, scratching and clawing desperately for air. She choked. Her fingertips began to shimmer, their corporeal form blurring at its edges. Her hands transformed into a fine mist that ascended into the air like tendrils of smoke.

Her eyes widened, trying to process what was happening before her. She opened her mouth to scream, but nothing came out. Confusion ripped through her mind. Her wrists, forearms, elbows, and parts of her shoulders and chest began to blur. They transformed into a flesh-colored mist, expanding and swirling. It floated up into the glowing golden sky.

Overwhelmed and unable to breathe, Lydia took a step backward. She stumbled and fell. Her rear end impacted the soft ground. Within seconds, the mist contracted back toward her body. Her fingers, hands, and arms returned to their human form—the slender lines of a teenage girl.

She was hyperventilating.

She raised her hands to inspect her fingers and wrists, flipping palms in and palms out, rotating her arm and flexing her elbow to get a better look.

Her eyes went to Theo. She looked pained, silently calling for him to save her from that place.

She caught her breath and planted her fists into the soil, terrified that they might disappear into vapor once more. But she felt them, solid and stable, and leaned her weight forward to stand up.

She stepped forward and stretched her arm out, fingertips extended.

Another step.

Then another.

Her hands trembled and tears welled in her eyes, dread upon her face as she took another step forward. Her feet touched the edge of the field—the threshold where the green grass ended and a pristine sea of yellow grass began.

Only paces from Theo, Lydia's fingertips lost form again. They transformed into vapor and began to rise toward the sky in a spiral ascent.

She pulled her hand back.

"What's happening to me, Theo?" she asked in a fragile voice.

Theo and Lydia shared a moment of quiet at the threshold of the field, sitting with questions that didn't have answers. But they began to understand the truth that was revealing itself before their eyes.

"This place..." said Theo.

"It won't let me go," said Lydia.

Theo looked back at the figures marching in their direction.

A few hundred meters away, small clusters of figures walked up the path and split, two walking up the left hill and three walking up the right.

"I have to go alone," said Theo. He reached out to touch Lydia's hand. A wonderful relief to feel her warm skin and see the freckles on her face, but he knew deep in his bones that whatever was happening in this place, this wasn't the real Lydia.

"Find a safe place to hide," said Theo in his best brotherly voice.

Lydia began to cry, staring down at the threshold of the field. She nodded, "I know."

Theo stepped away and walked into the brush. He pushed forward with long, careful strides, following the curved edge of the field. He saw another field over the next hill. It was green and lush and flat. From a distance, he could almost recognize the silhouette of a small boy on a bright orange tricycle pedaling happily beside a tilting oak tree. He could hear the boy's bubbly and bright laughter and the squeak of the tricycle wheels as he pedaled furiously with his tiny legs.

Behind the boy was a burst of yellow blossoms on the next hill. An older man sat on a swaying bench, surrounded by a sea of sunflowers. He looked down the path and waved a brittle hand at a woman in a dark suit with neon lines. She was coming up the path, holding back trembling tears behind a beaming smile.

Farther in the distance, on another patch of bright green earth, a lone young woman stood in the grass flying a kite. It was blue with a green tail and hung impossibly in the sky, floating like a magic trick on an island with no wind. A man approached behind her with a surprise bouquet of flowers and a grieving look on his face.

The infinite expanse of hills to Theo's left.

The entrance to the forest to his right.

He wanted to look back, to see the outline of Lydia's tiny

body shrink into the distance, but he didn't. He stared straight ahead, sensing the weight of her stare from afar. Felt her fear like it was his own. Her dread and confusion like his own. It burned deep in his chest.

Was that a hallucination, he thought? Was he still sitting in the plane, plummeting to his death, his mind swirling through disconnected visions and oxygen-deprived madness?

Everything about Lydia was wrong.

Everything about this island was wrong.

He cut deeper into the forest, the golden grass disappearing behind chest-high vines and monstrous tree trunks. The light darkened as the canopy closed in from above.

Theo stopped and gave in to the urge to look back, but by then Lydia was far gone.

Then, through a narrow clearing between the trees, Theo looked out toward the golden patches of land and saw another figure standing alone in the middle of a field. Head bowed low, the figure stood motionless in the knee-high grass. It was unaware of Theo's presence. But something peculiar caught Theo's eye.

Short dark hair. A height and build similar to Theo. Shoulders curved like they were carrying the weight of the world, and eyes locked into a downward gaze.

Curious, Theo took a step toward the mysterious figure in the field. He stepped quietly in between the brittle stems of vines underfoot.

Theo crouched low but couldn't quite see its face. It was too far, and the figure stood with its body angled slightly away.

Then, the figure's head rose up. Sunlight caught the side of the man's nose, and he turned his head, revealing a terrifyingly familiar and brightly lit profile.

Theo froze.

Impossible, he thought.

His mind tried to process that moment. His body tensed as

he gasped and filled his lungs to the brim. He squinted, trying to get a better view of the man's face because what he encountered could not have been true.

Then Theo looked further, beyond the man standing in front of him. A second man and a third walked silently in a patch of grass a few hills away. Their slouch was too familiar, like the husk of a spent person, ground to dust by an unforgiving world.

Their faces were all the same.

When the sunlight hit just right, Theo saw what could only be the truth.

Their faces looked like his own.

In a flick of panic, he retreated from the edge of the field, retracing his steps and moving back into the depths of the forest. He took a deep breath to center himself, clearing his mind of the horror he saw across the field.

"Curioussssss," said Sam's voice. It came from the grasses behind him and surrounded Theo. He jumped at the sound.

"They'll be here soon, Theo," the voice continued, "to hunt you down like an animal. They're coming now. Can't you feeeeeel them getting closer? They're on their way."

Theo snapped back to attention.

He needed to find a way off the island. Fast.

He turned to look into the distance, away from the golden fields and back toward the island's exterior. He pushed farther into the forest, and after what felt like a hundred meters, he saw it—a tall white cylinder, half-covered in the soil, with the forest clinging like a cancerous growth.

The front half of the airplane fuselage was largely intact, save for the partially shattered cockpit section driven violently into the dirt. The ground was littered with metal panels ripped from their rivets during the crash. Fragments of the glass windshield remained in the frame, splitting the sunlight like a prism. The wreckage was an unexpected beacon of reflective light in the middle of the forest's dark canopy.

Luggage was strewn about the dirt like confetti. Backpacks, purses, loose satchels.

Theo looked down and saw a brown leather briefcase lodged under leaves beside his feet. He rustled through its contents. Binders, papers, metal pens, gold-rimmed glasses, and a snow globe. He picked it up and looked at it closely, watching white flakes swirl around a miniature hand-painted cottage surrounded by trees. A beam of sunlight pierced through the canopy and fell directly into the globe. He watched the light bend on the glass.

It was mesmerizing.

A moment of peace inside a tiny, fake world.

Up ahead, Theo stepped on a dark tangle of vines and almost tripped on a nylon backpack. New-growth vines wrapped tightly through its straps, snaking in and out of its zippers.

He ripped the pack from the vines and looked closer.

If he only crashed yesterday, how could these vines have grown so fast, he thought?

Or how much time had really passed?

Inside the pack was a jumble of wrenches, ratchets, screwdrivers, duct tape, a spray can of oil lubricant, and a small yellow repair manual with a pen and frayed papers that resembled a journal.

It must have been from the crew's engineer, he thought.

He strapped the pack onto his back and rummaged through the other pieces of exploded luggage like a rabid animal searching for food in a harsh winter.

He grabbed a box of cookie tins.

Then, a familiar feeling rumbled in Theo's chest. A deep vibration from a powerful engine.

"Ah, better late than never..." Sam's voice floated through the trees.

His heart lurched from its dark energy. A prickle of adrenaline.

The white face of the fuselage flickered in shadow. Theo looked up to see gray streaks in the impossible starless sky screaming through the air, the soldiers' crafts making their way back to the beach on the far side of the island.

"They'll be heeeeere... any minute nowww," said Sam.

Theo shook his head and slapped his temples to clear the noise from his mind.

He snapped back to reality.

Must get off this island, he thought.

Theo scanned the remaining luggage on the ground, his eyes jumping rapidly from one item to the next. He looked for anything useful.

Then the fuselage—a shining white carcass. The window was tinted deep maroon with dried blood. Bodies intact in their seats, burnt to blackened bone, and, in some cases, piles of ash.

Theo was sweating.

The forest smelled of jet fuel and vaporized soil, but still, like before, there was no movement in the air.

"What's the plan, Theooooo?" Sam's voice seemed to circle around him, faster and faster, "what's the next move?"

Theo looked around, breath huffing and speaking aloud to himself, "There's got to be... there must... something we can use to—"

His eyes locked onto the side of the fuselage. A small panel reinforced with three rows of metal rivets, a beacon light, and a stenciled text that read, "IN CASE OF WATER LANDING, PULL FOR INFLATABLE RAFT."

He rushed to the fuselage.

The vibration overhead grew stronger. It was crushing to stand, much less walk or lift anything at all.

Theo grabbed the panel with both hands and pulled with what little strength he had left. A jolt of pain ripped through his left arm, reminding him that his wound was still fragile.

He grabbed again with his right arm and wrenched his weight backward to pull with his body.

The latch popped. Hinges released. Theo tumbled back into the dirt.

In the distance, the vibration subsided.

"They've landed, Theeeeeooo," said Sam.

"Shut up!" Theo snapped, shouting into the empty forest.

He flicked open the backpack and stuffed anything he could find into it—a rain jacket, a cord from a lacrosse stick, an aluminum water canister, a flashlight, a jar of baby food, and a compass.

The soldiers would soon start their slow and methodical sweep of the island.

Theo shut the backpack and pushed forward into the forest.

He knew there was no time to stop, assess and plan. There was barely time to think. The only thing keeping him from a chest full of tungsten slugs was moving and hiding.

He ran toward the exterior of the island. The light from the beach leaked through the vines as he got closer. But as fast as he could run, we could never outrun the persistent, unnerving silence of the forest. Leaves slid and crunched under his feet. His ragged breath heaved loudly into the air as he surged forward.

Theo felt a vague force behind him—a tingling up his spine, like the monstrous cloud that floated outside the airplane window that tugged at his chest—and he turned to look over his shoulder.

Nothing but stillness and shadows.

"The soldiers couldn't have made it this far, this quickly," whispered the voice of Sam, "or could they?"

Soon, the ground beneath Theo softened. The dark soil turned to pillowy sand. The beach was close. Light burst through the trees, flooding the canopy's shadows in a sea of gold and white.

Theo stopped at the beach and looked out over the water. He exhaled loud, heaving breaths and inhaled what should have been the pungent, oceanic smell of salt and wind and kelp and sand. But he winced as the air filled his lungs, realizing it was stale and lifeless.

He looked toward the horizon and shook his head.

"Impossible," he whispered.

He wiped the sweat from his brow and rubbed his eyes as the scene in front of him came into focus.

The ocean was completely still. A single, glass-like plane just as he had seen on the other end of the island.

A mathematically perfect line.

A thick fog formed a band around the island at the farthest point upon the horizon, where the sky would meet the sea. A great ethereal barrier, like the outer defenses of a fortress, that floated over the sea.

Diffused rays of amber light bounced off the water. The whole scene defied explanation, but still, there was an undeniable grace and beauty in that water, like those nights staring into the fire that cracked in the hearth back home. Flames all at once glowing with light and receding into darkness.

Destruction and beauty in harmony.

He stared at the water, waiting for the breeze to arrive and produce the faintest wave. But the breeze never came, and nothing moved.

A perfect plane of water. Undisturbed and silent.

Not of this world, he thought.

Theo dropped the backpack at his side and reached down to touch the water, trepidation slowing his hand as his fingers inched toward the surface. The water enveloped his finger. It twisted and bent around his skin. It was a soft liquid with no temperature, like a figment of imagination from a dream.

"Everything about this place is wrong," Theo whispered to himself. He lifted his hand and watched the drop of water tumble down his finger and join the sea.

CHAPTER 9
FOG

Theo tightened his grip on the metal box, swung his hips back, unwound, and flung the box into the ocean. When it hit the water, it landed without a splash or sound. The water reformed itself around the box to accommodate its mass. Then the liquid touched the sensor, the trigger fired, and the box exploded. A bright yellow coil of rubber unfolded. After it had fully inflated, a second trigger fired, and the box disconnected itself from the raft.

The metal box slid deeper into the water.

Theo tossed his backpack into the raft and trudged into the unmoving water. It absorbed silently into the fabric of his pants. Sunlight was harsh as it bounced off the mirror-like water. It was like standing in the middle of a lightbulb.

It disoriented Theo, and he shielded his eyes from the harsh light.

He stretched one leg into the raft and collapsed onto the rubber platform.

Like the strike of a whip, a familiar high-pitched crack blasted through the distance. The soldiers were going through the forest just as Theo had predicted—slow and methodical, searching for the chip.

He ripped a sleeve from the rain jacket and wrapped it around the lacrosse stick, fastening it with the twine. He gave the knots a good pull to tighten and another for good measure. Within a few minutes, he plunged the makeshift paddle into the alien water and began to row.

He pulled the paddle on the left side, then the right, repeating until the raft floated away, heavy and sluggish.

Another crack in the distance.

Theo imagined them sweeping under every bundle of vines, fanning out in a grid formation, ripping through every piece of luggage scattered through the forest.

Hunting him.

Boots pounding the earth with orders to not return to the SCR base until the chip—lodged in Theo's arm—is retrieved.

"What's your plan, Theo?" Sam's voice floated on beside the raft.

Theo shook his head and focused on paddling, trying to gain momentum in the direction of the fog ring in the distance.

"A bright yellow raft. Smart," Sam continued, "There's no way they'll step through the tree line and see you all alone on the water, with nowhere to run. A slow-moving, bright target. The best kind of target."

He plunged the paddle into the water again.

He played through the scenarios in his head.

Make a move for the opposite side of the island?

Stay here and hide in the thick fog?

Die on the island or die on the water?

Combinations of actions and reactions and consequences that don't result in a gaping hole blown through his chest.

He imagined the tungsten slugs ripping through the raft, exploding its rubber walls and propelling him into the ocean.

As he floated silently toward the wall of fog, the shore receded into the distance until it became a delicate line separating the glowing ocean plane and the silhouette of trees.

Now that the raft gained momentum, Theo slowed to conserve his strength. He slouched to the bottom of the raft, his bloody arm extended over the water. The backpack was tucked close like a security blanket. It wasn't much, that bag of random things, but while floating into the unknown of the flat, alien ocean, it felt good to have anything at all.

The fog encircled the raft like giant arms. It closed off the view behind him. It was built of thick clouds and impenetrable to much of the sunlight.

The island faded.

The shore disappeared.

Theo floated on, surrounded by an impossible world of white.

He couldn't get the soldier's voice out of his head: This island is fucking cursed.

First seeing Sam. Then Lydia. Her hair shimmered like a dying star, and her fingers faded into vapor.

The vines grew back.

The birds and bugs and the breeze that wasn't there.

And the water.

He laid flat on the raft and let the day's exhaustion take over, spinning the questions through his head.

Not enough answers.

Then exhaustion became sleep. The danger looming beyond the fog was visceral, and the uncertainty of how he'd ever get out–or get home–lay heavy on Theo's mind.

***

Frost crystals formed on Theo's arm. He woke, arms tight against his body. Confused at first, but quickly snapped back to awareness by a sudden chill in the air.

He'd never felt so cold.

The chill penetrated deep, sending shivers down his legs. Laying on his back in this yellow raft in the middle of this incomprehensible ocean, Theo looked up into the fog.

His mouth was parched, and he couldn't remember the last time he ate or drank anything of substance. How long had he been asleep? He couldn't see the sky through the solid wall of white. He felt his energy level plummeting – the oncoming effects of dehydration.

The silence was a terrible force pressing against his skull. It reminded Theo of the forest that lingered just beyond, void of birds, spiders, fluttering leaves, and even the faintest touch of breeze. Floating on that water that looked like glass, wasting away in the freezing air.

As the hours ticked by, the way home–to return the chip and save the Midlands–looked increasingly uncertain.

The fog wrapped tighter around the raft.

The air grew colder still, crystals forming on his cheeks like crawling white spiders. The ice felt like it was seeping into his cells. It was difficult to take a full breath, his lungs scratchy and tight. Crystals bloomed inside his sinus cavity.

Theo curled himself into a ball as the cold overwhelmed him. His legs went numb. Then, his hands and fingers. He wished he could see the sky, a desperate plea to hold onto something in this world, but the sky was long gone.

Only white.

Cold.

An ocean of glass.

He closed his eyes and surrendered to the ice.

***

Theo awoke lying on a cot in a room he didn't recognize. The space was small. Metal panel walls closed in around him, and a small doorway led out to a hall filled with nothing but darkness. Straight lines of rivets scrawled up the wall and across the ceiling.

His head pounded. Sickness raged behind his eyes. The walls twisted and bent with each breath. He fell in and out of a delirious state, eyes crusted over with the dried tears he'd been weeping in his sleep.

Along the far wall strands of lightbulbs hung secured with metal pipes and scraps of rope. Long web-like lines of electrical wires swooped across the room. There was a jungle-like quality to the space, but built of steel, copper and polymers instead of earth, bark and leaves.

Is this some kind of prison, he thought? Did the Kaiphers pull his limp and mangled body from the raft?

He looked to his feet. Body covered with pelts from some kind of animal. From the familiar scent of decay that wafted over him, he knew they weren't dried properly. He was sweating under the animal skins, the cot beneath him damp and heat radiating from his head.

The fever persisted but was beginning to fade.

He tried wiping the sweat from his forehead but couldn't move his arm.

Ropes dug into his wrists. His hands were tied to the end of the cot, splinters cutting into his flesh with every movement.

Fragments of glass from broken light bulbs were scattered on the floor.

A translucent brown sludge speckled the floor.

From an adjacent room, a mechanical ticking sound echoed. The glow of warm light washed across the far wall. Theo heard the movement of gears and a ratchet tightening and loosening.

He flexed his arm, testing the rope. Clenched his jaw against the oncoming pain. The rope stretched a small distance. His sweat must have permeated its fibers and soaked into the rope. It was becoming pliable and soft.

Theo pulled again. It snagged on his wrist bone.

He twisted his body for one final pull, leaning in the opposite direction until two legs of the cot rose off the floor. He teetered off balance, until the cot came slamming down.

A metallic thump rang throughout the room, bouncing along the walls.

Something stirred in the other room.

The ratcheting sound went silent.

A lightbulb clinked against the cot, then rolled away. Theo felt his stomach lurch and his center of gravity shift. Then the lightbulb rolled back and forth and clinked against the cot once again.

I must be in some sort of transport vehicle, he thought. A truck? Or a ship?

At the end of the cavernous hallway, the glowing light flickered. Heavy footsteps echoed—a slow, pounding vibration on the floor—and a shadow slid across the wall.

Theo heard the click of a lightswitch. The room flooded in light from the bulbs hanging along the wall. It was harsh on his eyes. He winced, but as his eyes adjusted, details came to life—the makeshift wire and ill-fitting pipes fastened bulbs to the wall. Thick welds, knotted and ugly, secured shelves on the wall made of metal scraps. Machine components from unrecognizable contraptions piled on shelves and stacked in rows along the floor. Rusted gears, cloudy glass jars filled with bolts and washers and springs. Canisters of lubricant, bundles of cables and wires and ropes.

A figure appeared in the doorway. A large, looming man with a dirty leather apron and black welding mask on his face.

He walked toward Theo. Heavy steps rattled throughout the room when his black boots struck the ground like a hammer falling onto a hollow metal floor.

Theo pulled on his wrist trying desperately to break free as the figure inched closer. The rope stretched but the knot held.

Only paces away, there were sharp divots and blackened stains on the man's leather apron. Round metal studs lined the perimeter, and small loops of mismatched wire stitched up the gaps where studs were missing.

One last tug on the rope.

Theo's right hand broke free.

In a flash of movement, he grabbed the rolling lightbulb and smashed it on the floor. Glass fragments bouncing under the cot. He raised a defiant arm into the air, pointing the sharp tangle of metal and glass toward the approaching figure.

The pelts fell to the floor, exposing Theo's bare chest and left arm. And then he saw the fresh white bandages wrapped around his arm.

The skin around the wound had been cleaned.

No dirt. No blood.

The large man took a final step, the last thud echoing in the room.

Theo pointed the shattered bulb at the man's face, not backing down.

The man raised one thick arm and slowly lifted the black reflective visor. It swiveled and locked into place with a click, revealing soft eyes and a haggard beard.

CHAPTER 10

SCRAPER SHIP

"Oh, take it easy there, son," the man said, "calm yourself down."

"Cut me loose, now!" said Theo. He thrust his arm out, gripping tight onto the razor-sharp bulb.

"I'll be willing to cut you loose, but you're gonna have to tell who you are."

"You first!" said Theo. His jaw clenched. He broke his gaze from the large man's eyes long enough to see all manner of trinkets and tools on his apron–a ball-peen hammer, thick pliers, and a sheath that hid a fixed blade knife. A key ring with hex wrenches of various sizes was attached to a leather loop. And the tattered remains of welding gloves that had seen better days.

The man stepped forward. He towered over Theo. The cot leaned under his weight.

"You don't seem to be in much of a place to make demands, now are ya?" he said, "You see, I got my family here with me on this vessel, and they're the last thing that matters a damn to me in this broken world. So if I'm going to be allowing some stowaway boy with a bleeding' arm to be running loose in the bowels of my ship, I'm gonna have to know a few things: For one, who in the mighty hell are ya? And second, what were you doing in a raft in the middle of this ocean here?"

The man scratched two fingers through his beard, and keys jingled on his apron.

"I'm certainly not the brightest fellow, I'll admit to that, but I'm gonna need a little help understanding. You see, there ain't no land here, for a thousand miles north to south and laterally too. We found you in a raft with no food and no water. Now the explaining had better be starting if you want out of that rope anytime soon."

The man pulled a thick metal screw as long as his finger out of a pouch and proceeded to pick food scraps from between his teeth. His round beard bulged with each movement.

Theo unclenched his grip from the blub and let it tumble to the floor, partially out of surrender and partially from reaching the limits of exhaustion. He leaned back into the cot and let out a deep sigh.

"Theoren. Rousseau. Go by Theo."

"Now there's a start!" the man's bulging face stretched into a smile.

"I have a job to do... to finish," said Theo.

"A job, you say? Well, don't we all! And explain to me that raft. Why were you all the way out here?"

"There was an island. You see, my plane crashed, and these soldiers, they..."

Theo's gaze drifted as the shock of the memories flooded in.

Don't mention Lydia, he thought. Don't mention Sam.

Or any of the other unexplainable figures in that field of golden grass. He remembered their faces–their faces were his own.

"So I found this raft in the wreckage and tried to get off the island. But I floated off course, somewhere. I'm not sure where."

Theo looked up at the large man, unsure if he was stuttering his words. "and now I'm... here."

The large man studied Theo's eyes and the way he frowned. He glanced at Theo's arm, wrapped tight with a crisp, dry bandage, and the purple bruising already beginning to fade. He paused and let out a resigned breath.

"Name's Kristof," he said, standing tall with a firm posture and nodding slowly, "and this vessel here is my ship. Scraper #0347 of the mid-Atlantic fleet. Automated route F19."

Kristof unsheathed the knife from his apron and took a booming step forward.

And when the light hit it, Theo recognized that type of metal—a knife forged from a carbon steel railroad spike. Heated, twisted, hammered, flattened, then hardened. Its blade was chipped, black soot smeared across its twisted handle, and it was the same type of knife Theo found in the passenger's backpack.

Kristof raised the blade to Theo's face, the jagged edge hovering inches from his nose.

"My vessel. My rules. Understand? Any deviation, and you'd best believe I'll put this blade right through your chest," Kristof said, looking into Theo's eyes, "And I won't hesitate."

After a moment, Kristof cut the rope, and Theo raised his left arm. The bandage was straight and tight. Someone with medical training did this, he thought.

A small drop of blood leaked from the bandage as Theo stretched his arm. Kristof watched a dot form on the metal floor.

"Mae!" said Kristof, calling out behind him.

Another figure came through the doorway. A petite woman with graying hair, olive-colored overalls, and a frilly white scarf around her neck.

"Would you mind assisting our guest here," said Kristof, "with a new bandage?"

For a moment, Mae didn't move. Then, she took a hesitant

step and entered the room. She carried a small lantern in one hand and a small metal box in the other, with a slouching bag full of other supplies—ointment, gauze, twine, and a glass bottle labeled Isopropyl Alcohol.

"This here is Theo," said Kristof to Mae as she approached the cot, "and he's a good boy. He'll behave. Now, would you please, dear?"

Mae looked to Kristof, then back at Theo. He tried to sit up but nearly toppled over. Mae placed a hand on Theo's shoulder to stabilize him.

"Easy, son," said Mae, "Don't go moving around so much. You might still have some fever left in you, and you don't want to aggravate it now. You were nearly frozen through when we pulled you in from that raft. Cold through from head to damn toe. Never seen anything like that."

Mae set the lantern down on a table beside the cot. She cradled Theo's arm and swung open the lid of the small metal box. Stamped on the lid in mechanical lettering was PROPERTY OF SLOAN COASTAL REPUBLIC.

Suddenly, his pulse raced.

Forehead bloomed with heat.

Heart pounded at his temples.

Mae unwrapped the bandage. Theo winced at the sting of alcohol swabbing across his skin. Mae gripped his arm tightly and pressed into his skin at different spots.

"How'd you get this cut, son?" asked Mae.

Theo took a breath but did not answer.

"I've been tending to cuts and broken bones my entire life. Thought I'd seen everything. But nothing like this," said Mae, looking inquisitively at Theo, "Now don't go lying to me, son. That's not a good foot to start the journey on."

She inserted two fingers into a small jar and scooped out a dollop of green goo. Sticky like engine lube but with a smooth and elegant sheen. Before Theo could say anything, she pressed it deep into his wound cavity.

"I got bit," said Theo with short and quick words, "by something in the water. I must have passed out. Hadn't eaten for, I don't know how long. I came to with my arm hanging in the water, and the bite mark just appeared."

Theo kept his gaze low, trying to pull his eyes from the letters stamped into that metal box, but it tugged at him. His heart raced, the fever cascading back.

Mae paused.

She held half the bandage in the air and silently looked at Theo.

"Quite a clean cut there for an animal, son," said Mae.

Kristof tilted his head, his interest piqued.

Mae's eyes narrowed.

"And that rash on your neck. Something to keep an eye on, too. Nothing like anything I've seen before," said Mae.

He ran a gentle finger along his neck below the jawline and discovered a patch of dried skin extended down to his collarbone. The patches were hard, with bumps in a sharp pattern. Theo's memory returned to the ice on the airplane window before it tumbled out of the sky. Crystalline fingers envelop the plane. For a moment, he felt those same crystalline fingers, cold like night, wrapping around his throat and getting tighter.

He pressed his nail into the hardened skin and gave the slightest tug.

It felt good.

Mae watched him. Studied him.

She smiled a tense smile.

"But never you mind, I'm glad we found you in time. Praise be to Father Charles The Eternal," said Mae, turning to Kristof.

"Praise be, ah yes," said Kristof quickly, as if caught off guard, "to Father Charles."

Mae turned back to Theo.

"Praise be, "said Mae, "you should be patched up in no time. But you need to take it slow."

The finished bandage was taut and crisp—the work of someone who had applied many bandages in her day.

"Thank you," said Theo, nodding at the bandage, "for this, and for taking me in."

"Oh, son, don't you mention it," said Mae. "Don't be in a hurry to get up either. For now, I suggest resting as much as possible before we auto-dock in a couple of days."

"Auto-dock?" said Theo.

"Yes, son, of course," said Mae, "at the coast."

Theo looked at Kristof, his thick hand poised on the sheathed knife and a finger tapping the leather strap.

"Supper will be soon. At 18:00, son," said Kristof, "late, you don't eat. Meantime, behave yourself. We've only got another sixty or so hours, so you best use them well and get some good rest."

Theo nodded as Mae and Kristof disappeared down the hall. The walls flooded once again in warm orange light spilling out from a room he couldn't see.

His arm began to tingle as he sank his weight back into the cot. It was cold under the bandage, unlike any sensation he'd felt before. Almost like the salve his father used to make with boiled eucalyptus leaves, tree sap, distilled shine, and a mess of forest berries so purple they would stain the kitchen counter. The house would smell of after-rain and fresh earth when that pot would rise to a boil.

After what felt like several hours, the tingling in his arm grew stronger, like a million tiny bubbles dancing and popping under his skin. He raised his left arm toward the ceiling in disbelief. He braced against the expected jolt of pain, but when he softly clenched his fist he felt... nothing.

Theo slowly pushed himself up and tried to stand. Thick pelts formed a heap beside the cot. He stepped forward, hesitant, and put a small amount of weight on his foot. Then, another step. He squeezed and tensed his forearm muscles. They contracted under his skin. He turned his palm up and down, staring at this hand at every angle, marveling at what was happening in front of him.

A few days ago, his arm was a bloody mess.

Now, it felt barely more than a bruise.

"Impossssible," said Sam, his voice floating in a shadow in the corner of the room, "that's what you're thinking, isn't it? What kind of science could do that? Is it science? Or witchcraft?"

Theo spun around as if startled and stared at the empty room.

"How did it come to this, Theo? You should have been home by now, sitting beside the hearth at the Ranch. The road home was so close. Now you're where? The other side of the ocean? You could have been building the machine, Theo. You could have been saving lives."

Theo scowled into the empty air, annoyed at the voice that returned in his head.

He walked to the end of the room and looked down the hallway that snaked out of view.

Directly across the doorway, another room appeared. It was open. The inside was dark.

Theo entered the room and searched along the wall for a switch. With a click, lightbulbs illuminated, and a cavernous room revealed itself.

Monstrous barrels the size of small cars were stacked all around him. Hundreds, at least. Maybe thousands. They nearly reached the ceiling, their massive round curves forming what looked like row after row of impenetrable metal walls. Theo brushed his hand over the curves of one of the barrels. He felt the indent of sharp letters along the side: PROPERTY OF SLOAN COASTAL REPUBLIC.

They were barrels designed to store or transport some kind of liquid. Thick clamps secured the top of each barrel, and a column of small portholes ran along the side. The small portholes gave a glimpse of the amount of liquid stored within. Most were full. Green liquid appeared through the top portholes.

Some barrels were only partially full—not quite to the top—with a small visible pocket of empty air inside.

Theo caught his reflection in the porthole when the light hit the right angle. A young man with cinnamon-brown eyes, his face looked so small and fragile in that circular piece of glass. He looked down at his bandaged arm and felt so very far from home.

In the reflection, he saw the patches of whitened skin on his neck, like scales on a reptile. He ran a finger between the bumps, pressing at it, his bodily instinct proclaiming it as a foreign body that should be ripped off, scrubbed off, filed off, cut off. But as he moved his hand down his jawline, Theo realized this new deformation was very much a part of him.

Theo's thoughts were interrupted by a stampede of tiny feet thundering down the hallway. He quickly shut the lights and returned to his room with the cot.

The sound of pounding feet suddenly stopped just beyond view of the doorway, only to be replaced by the huffing of tiny, out-of-breath lungs.

Moments later, two short figures appeared in the corner of the doorway.

Then, the towering round shadow of another figure beside them.

"Evening there, Mister Theo," said Kristof, "these right here are our children. Our son, Puck, and our daughter, Penny."

Puck waved from behind Kristof's leg, a shy little movement half in light and half in shadow. He was a stout boy, hardly a day past six years old.

Penny nodded and stepped forward. She was older, maybe

twelve. Petite like her mother.

She stepped into the soft light of the table lamp. The orange flickering flames revealed her round cheeks and slender neck. Theo saw the face of a young girl appear—greenish eyes and a constellation of freckles on her nose, and her hair was reddish and brownish and seemed to twinkle, almost iridescent when the light would hit it in the just the right way and—

Lydia?

Theo's pulse skipped a beat and kicked into overdrive, pounding furiously in his chest.

The room was bending.

Her face was so clear, but he left her on that island. Now she's here, and they can be together again and—

Theo felt the fever rising. Beads of sweat bloomed on his forehead. The heat was unbearable.

It can't be Lydia, he thought. Impossible.

How was this happening?

Why was he hallucinating?

Theo jerked back in fright. A quick reaction: his left foot kicked against the metal wall and banged loudly, cutting the silence in the room.

Penny paused, frozen mid-step.

Kristof's posture straightened. His neck muscles tensed.

Lydia's face faded away, the sharpness of her features turning rounded, amorphous, and dissipating into a blob of shapes and colors.

The hallucination vanished.

Then Theo saw with a chilling clarity—Penny's face right in front of him. Her eyes were cloudy white, and her brow was hardened with a confidence not often found on the face of a child so young. She seemed to pierce through him with her intense gaze, her head tilting side to side with a nearly imperceptible movement to follow the sounds that bounced throughout the room.

Theo realized: Penny was blind.

She had a mottled red scar across the right side of her face. It was fading in spots but visible enough to make one wonder how she might have gotten it and how painful it might have been. From the looks of it, she would undoubtedly carry that scar for the rest of her life.

Kristof cleared his throat.

"Mae said you need to eat," he said, "but knew you might not be up for venturing around much. You ought to be getting as much rest as possible before we dock in about fifty-five hours. So she had the little ones here fix you up a supper plate."

Penny held a wooden tray with a large oval bowl filled with what looked like potatoes stewed with chopped fish parts floating in a thick reddish-brown gravy. Tiny drops of oil floated in the gravy, and the webbed tendrils of a fin poked out from under a potato near the bowl's rim. She placed it gently onto the table beside the cot, and the most heartwarming aroma filled the room.

"Mama says the fish heads are good for strength," said Penny, with a voice as small as her stature, "so make sure you eat up. Mama says you need it."

Theo smiled as he watched Penny retreat behind her father.

He sat in silence, and for a fleeting moment, home didn't feel so terribly far away.

"Thank you," said Theo, nearly at a loss for words, "This is so kind. I cannot wait to have it. It smells delightful."

Kristof nodded, and Theo caught the flash of an uneasy frown on his face as he looked Theo up and down before leading the children back down the hallway.

CHAPTER 11
ARROW

The room had gotten colder overnight. Was it night? Or day? How much time had really passed? Sitting in a damp gray metal room in the middle of the ship, Theo couldn't be sure. He pulled the animal pelts up to his neck and grabbed a second one to layer on top. Tucked it around his chin. His fingers brushed against the hard scales on his neck and paused momentarily, the sense of uneasiness mixing back in with the cold. He built a cocoon around himself, and slowly, the urge to shiver from the cold was subsiding.

A long metallic scratching sound echoed from down the hall. It was coming from the room with the orange light.

Some kind of file, he thought?

The sound scraped again. And again.

Metal or maybe wood?

Theo pulled the animal pelts tighter and settled deeper into the cot. He felt the ship's sway and became keenly aware that he was trapped in a vessel in the middle of the ocean, untold hundreds or thousands of miles away from home, with no plan to remedy the situation—how to get the chip home. In less than a few days, the ship will auto-dock on the coast in the middle of the hive, behind enemy lines in the heart of the SCR.

He slid his arm out from under the layer of pelts and checked the bandage. It was still taut and clean, but one corner of the bandage flapped loose. He reached over to lift the gauze, but to his surprise, all that was left of the gaping wound was a jagged red line. He tilted his head to get a closer look, turning it toward the dim light of the table lantern beside him.

"That's good stuff," said Kristof. He sidled quietly into the doorway, which was shocking considering how he lumbered around the ship with heavy footsteps.

"It keeps you going," he continued, "even in the worst of wounds. Straight from the bosom of good ol' Mother Earth. Where we all come from and where we all shall one day return."

Kristof cleared his throat, an uneasy seriousness coming into his voice.

"Say, uh, we found some interesting items with you on that raft."

Theo's mind fell into a panic. He tried recalling a mental inventory of the raft. His memory was jumbled from those last chaotic moments on the island.

Kristof tossed the pack onto the floor. It flapped open, revealing the top of the takedown recurve bow pulled from the woman's pack. It was rolled up with a dozen metal arrows and wrapped in a burlap cloth. The ragged, handmade fletching stuck out from under the cloth.

"My boy, can you shoot good?"

Theo considered the question.

"Well, I–"

"Can you shoot good? Can ya or can't ya?"

Theo sat up on the cot. His posture stiffened.

"I can, sir. Shoot. Very good."

"Good!" said Kristof, with a slap to his leather apron, "Tomorrow, at first light, I've got an important task I could use your helpin' on. It'll be a good way for you to pitch in and earn your keep around here."

"Feeding, yes," said Theo, "housing, well, I don't know about–"

"Or I could turn you loose to explore the freedoms of the great Atlantic Ocean?" said Kristof, spreading his arms in the air as if motioning toward the sweeping landscape, "unbound, nothing but the wind at your back. Free to pursue whatever course your heart desires on that little inflatable craft of yours."

Theo sighed.

"Yes sir, first light it is.

***

Kristof climbed a ladder at the crack of dawn. The rungs creaked as his boots slammed down on the metal bars. Theo followed close behind, his bow slung across his shoulder and a jumble of arrows in his hand. At the top of the ladder, Kristof leaned his weight into a metal handle and cranked it to unlock an external door. Large gears rotated, and four metal bolts slid inward, creating a clear path to push the door wide open.

A wall of daylight exploded into the cavern.

It took Theo a minute for his eyes to adjust.

They climbed to the deck. It was a wide, flat vessel that was mostly empty save for the captain's window at the front and rows of various jars and containers, metal lockboxes, cables, and tools are strewn about the floor. Toward one side of the deck, wooden cages burst with blooming plants reaching up toward the sky. Dark berries on twisted vines and leafy herbs Theo had never seen before.

At the far end of the deck, the tall white arms of the scraper mechanism hung off the back of the vessel. They were giant up close. Three crane arms extended out over the ocean, their sides patterned with hundreds of reinforcing bolts as big as Theo's fists. A wide base covered in weather-worn white paint sat underneath each arm. It was flaking off at the mechanical joints. It left such a towering impression on Theo that he wondered how the ship hadn't already toppled into the sea.

"There," said Kristof, his voice booming against the violent sound of the sea. He pointed a thick finger out over the water, aiming at the middle of the scraper mechanism. Theo could see a wild tangle of rope attached to the arm and something dragging behind the ship.

A disturbance in the waves suggested a large and heavy object.

"What is it?" said Theo.

"Whatever it is, it's slowing us down. We're losing twelve knots per day with that trash dragging behind us. It's enough that when we dock at the coast, we'll be low on our algae harvest. We've run sixty-three routes, and we've never come up short. Never. The SCR are strict bastards. Measure everything to the milligram. And the Grayskins are ruthless. I don't know how they'd react if we come up short, and I don't intend to find out!"

Grayskins.

Kaiphers.

The name shot a spike of panic into Theo's mind.

"I've been racking my brain," Kristof continued, "I can't think of how to get rid of that thing weighing us down. The only way, I thought, was to take a small boat out there and cut it down by hand. That wouldn't be easy."

"And you'd need to stop the ship," said Theo.

"Precisely," said Kristof, "But I'm afraid that's impossible. Even if I wanted to stop or change course, I can't. It's an auto-sailing vessel controlled by the SCR Capital Fleet Command

Center. The machine runs the routes. We just babysit it and empty the harvester into the barrels."

Theo looked out over the side of the vessel, the sunlight bouncing off the hull, making it refract like a crystal. He glanced back at the massive ropes coiled behind them, the pile of nets and scrap metal and cracked anchors, trying to think of another way to cut the object free.

"I was out of ideas until you washed up onto our little world here."

Kristof looked at Theo with a wide smile on his face.

"Almost like you and your little raft were delivered here for a reason."

His smile faded, and his brow turned tense with fear and desperation.

"Can you hit that, son?" Kristof asked, "That rope. With your bow. Can you cut it?"

Theo paused momentarily to take in the task in front of him. To understand what he was being asked to do. The wind rushed past his ears, and the vessel swayed as it sped across the ocean. He looked out over the side at the tangle of rope flailing in a swirl of foam and mist.

"I don't know," said Theo, "with the wind gusting like this, that's a nearly impossible shot."

"Focus, son. How far out do you think that is?"

Theo took a breath and covered his eyes from the sun as he stared intensely at the rope. He estimated the overall width of the vessel to be about forty meters and compared it to the length of the scraper arm towering over him. Then, he calculated the downward angle from the deck to the ropes below.

"I... don't know. I can't know for sure," said Theo.

"What's your best guess?" said Kristof, "What does your gut tell you? Deep down. Inside."

Theo sighed. Focus, he thought. Just like the woods back

home. High up in the tree. Whitetail bounding through the crunching autumn leaves, stopping with a jolt in the middle of a narrow opening between the trees. For a moment, the salty ocean was replaced by memories of the Oklahoma trees. The smell of redbuds and soapberries. He remembered the color of those leaves. The faintest hint of animal scent in the crisp air.

"Maybe fifty," said Theo, "fifty-five meters."

Kristof's face was intense and pleading.

"Can. You. Hit it, son?"

Theo felt the curve of the metal bow on his back. The nylon string was cool against his neck.

"Please, Theo. You have to try."

Theo looked at Kristof and nodded.

He held the bow out at arm's length, inspecting it. A tool that had changed very little since his ancestors hunted mammoths and bison hundreds of thousands of years ago. A young man, like himself, would have held a similar bow, calculating a shot that meant the difference between survival and starvation for his family. When he gripped the bow in his hand and fledged the taut string, he felt the whisper of a primal spirit in his veins.

He nocked an arrow on the bow. Pointed his shoulder toward his target. Focused on the ropes whipping and bending near the water below.

The breeze washed across his body from the back of his right shoulder to his left. A leftward rear crosswind. He compensated by aiming to the right of the rope and letting the breeze carry the arrow to his target.

Kristof watched intently in silence, looking at Theo, then back at the rope, then at Theo.

Theo tensed his back muscles and pulled the arrow back. Anchored at his jaw. Right pointer finger touched the corner of his mouth. The string, a hair away from touching the tip of his nose.

For a moment, the world dissolved. There was nothing except tension in his muscles, warm and raw, arrow poised on the rest, and the rope at fifty-five meters out.

He envisioned the arrow flying in a perfect arc, slicing the rope in half.

He took a breath.

Tensed his bow arm.

Drew the arrow back with controlled pressure.

Breathe. Pull. Pull. Pull. Breathe.

Release.

Theo and Kristoff watched as the arrow careened through the ocean air and struck the scraper's arm. It dug a black streak into the paint, and a spark flew inches to the left of the rope.

Kristof inhaled with a feeling of shock and surprise.

The leftward breeze, Theo thought.

He nocked another arrow.

Visualized the effortless arc through the air. The arrow's tip slicing through the fibers of the rope.

He drew back.

Tension in his back muscles.

Breathe. Pull. Pull. Pull. Breathe.

Shoot.

The second arrow flew true and silent like a whisper against the roaring sounds of the ocean. It floated through the salty air with ease.

Kristof watched, mouth open and jaw tense, unaware that he was holding his breath the entire time. His full focus was on the rope and the arrow racing toward it.

With a loud snap, the arrow sliced through the rope and plummeted into the water. The rope untangled with an audible rip, flailing in the wind until the last strand fell away and the shadow of the dragging object disappeared into the water.

"Ah! Ha! Son, you did it!" Kristof said with a booming voice and a teary smile. He clapped loudly with his thick hands. "That was an amazing feat there, son! Right down the middle! Almost cannot believe it!"

He took a few stumbling steps backward, clapping again.

Theo smiled, wide and beaming. His shoulders relaxed, and a sense of relief he hadn't felt in a long time washed over him.

"I didn't know you could do that. I mean, I sure as hell hoped you could but to be free of that, that–"

Kristof placed his hands on his head and looked out over the railing, a stunned look on his face.

He placed a heavy hand on Theo's shoulder.

"This saved us, son," said Kristof, "You saved us! Say, where in the world did you learn to shoot like that?"

"On a farm," said Theo, "In the Midlands."

The words spilled out. He considered if he'd already shared too much.

'Midlands, you say?" said Kristof. He was silent for a long moment. Too long. "And what the hell are you doing way out here?"

"Just trying to get home, sir. That's all."

Kristof nodded, slow and exaggerated, as if he had more to say but was holding his thoughts for another conversation, another time. He looked out over, lost in silent thought until something on the deck caught his eye.

"Come with me, son," said Kristof, "I've got something to show you."

Kristof lifted a white tarp to reveal a group of large containers made of clear plastic, each as big as a car engine. They were secured to the deck on all sides with a web of sun-bleached rope, fraying at the edges. Two dozen containers total, lined up in rows of six. Kristof knelt beside the container filled with the darkest liquid. It looked green-brown with murky shadows of items floating within it.

Theo watched over Kristof's shoulder as he unscrewed the cap of one of the containers and began sifting out a layer of brown foam from the surface of the liquid. He thrust a mesh scoop into the liquid, lifted it into the sunlight, and flung its contents back over his shoulder. It splattered on the deck behind him.

Theo looked over the deck at the waves tumbling over each other, and his thoughts trailed off. A sharp breeze gusted over the railing, chilling and salty. What a different world, he thought. A clear contrast from the island where the air was stale and tasteless. The water was flat as glass.

He felt an overwhelming urge to rub his calloused fingers across the ridges on his neck. They hadn't spread since yesterday, but the scales seemed hardened. He touched the sharp, crystalline pattern with his fingernail.

The scales. The island. The impossible cold fog. They must be connected, he thought.

"Look here, son," said Kristof, "are you paying attention? This here is the algae." He tipped the container to show Theo, then pointed to the giant scraper arms at the rear of the vessel that sat like steel praying mantises. "Almost every drop we harvest from those scrapers goes into the barrels below for the SCR. That's the job, and that's what we do. But once the quota is filled, I keep a little extra here for myself."

Kristof smiled as he scooped more foam. It made a wet slapping sound as it hit the deck.

"We mix it with fixings we grow here on the deck and brew up that salve you got stewing in your arm there."

He plunged tongs into the liquid and pulled out a mesh bag filled with a sticky blob of twigs, leaves, rocks, berries, and what looked like worm-like roots. Beside the bag, an electrical wire connected to a small solar panel behind the container.

"Mix in just the right amount of low current, strengthening the fibers and activating the low-level regenerative properties.

Enzymes and such. Three weeks baking in the sun, and then we're in business. The SCR bastards need not know about this, and they don't care. They get their harvest, and they leave us alone."

He stirred the tongs in the liquid.

"This does wonders for cuts and scrapes. Even do some magic on a broken bone if you give it time and patience. But it's only for surface wounds, you see. This ain't no miracle cure. It's nothing like the machines they have on the coast."

Kristof secured the tarp over the containers and picked up a box of small glass jars full of green liquid. He walked back toward the door.

Theo stayed back by the containers.

"Why–" Theo started to speak but searched for the right words, "why do you trust me?"

Kristof stopped and turned around the box, held in his thick hands, an uneasy look on his face.

"Trust? Who says I do?" said Kristof, "Should I have a reason not to?"

Theo shook his head and looked out over the horizon. He wondered how many nautical miles separate him from the Ranch.

Kristof looked at Theo, then followed his eyes toward the horizon.

The sun was a burning orange dot. Violent and pure and graceful all at once. Chaos and creation in a single life-giving star.

Kristof took a long breath.

"Every day, I think about what this world will be like without me. What will the sunrise look like on the day I'm not here to see it? What kind of world will be there for Mae? For Puck and Penny?"

He placed the box on the deck and raised a hand toward the sky.

"Every time I see that sun rising over those waters there, I know I'm another step closer to that day. To return to wherever life comes from. I don't have days to waste on thinking the worst of people. So sometimes, I take a tiny leap of faith, and try to believe people are good."

He turned back to Theo.

"So, don't you prove me wrong, son." said Kristof with a sly smile, "besides, I have zero worries about my ability to drop you like a dog if you give me a reason to." He chuckled and patted his knife sheath with pride.

"Grab that other box there, will ya?" said Kristof. He picked up the box at his feet and turned back toward the door.

"I lied to you," said Theo.

Kristof stopped. He let out a heavy sigh.

"The cut on my arm. It wasn't a seal."

"Well, that much I gathered, son," said Kristof, turning around, "because there ain't any animals out here on these waters that would bite like that. This is my sixty-sixth voyage along this route. I would know."

"I'm here to steal the machine," said Theo, "to build it back home in the Midlands. My people are dying. My father is dying."

Kristof looked at Theo in silence.

"The Aeonite schematics... I'm carrying them home."

"But, where are they?" said Kristof, "you didn't lose them at sea, did you?"

"No, they're here," said Theo, "with me."

Kristof tilted his head, a confused look on his face.

Theo looked down and pointed to the crisp white bandage on his arm.

CHAPTER 12

JUNK

His fever was breaking.

Theo dreamt about riding in the back of a giant car. As a child, he remembered his feet dangling off the edge of the seat, his rubber boots a few sizes too big. The world out the window was a blur of gray and black. Two men sat up front. The driver was silent. The other man smelled sharply of medicine. Whiffs of wolfberry and sweet ginseng on his jacket. Trent was his name. He was nice to Theo, spoke to him slowly, and was patient when Theo would get overwhelmed and cry.

Rain streaked down the side of the window. The glass was cold against Theo's tiny fingers. Much of that night was a jumble of faint memories, but even after many years, he'd never forgotten how dark it was.

They drove miles and miles in silence without passing a single house light. Until the car slowed and turned onto a gravel driveway, and he remembered the tires rumbled differently, somehow, but at such a young age, he couldn't quite understand why.

He remembered the faint glow of a dark rectangle up the long driveway ahead.

Fragments of memories: Trent exiting the car. The blast of cold rainy air coming into the vehicle. The clunk of the door slamming shut.

"It's ok to be scared, boy." said the driver, "they'll take good care of you. You'll be safe with them." His voice was kind. Theo couldn't see his face from the back seat, but it sounded like the driver was smiling.

"Arthur is a special man," he continued, "you'll learn so much from him. And Melody, oh she's going to love you so, so much. And she'll keep you well fed, oh my! What do you like to eat, boy? What's your favorite food?"

Theo couldn't remember if he responded or not. Maybe he just sat there in silence.

The driver chuckled to himself, looking out the rain-blurred window.

The memories were blending now.

Gravel crunching under his boots when the driver opened the door and Theo jumped down.

Rain pattering on his hood.

The cold air on his tiny cheeks.

The driver was walking him to the front of the house when slowly a door swung open. It was such a wide door that Theo remembered thinking the whole house was turning inside out. Trent stood there in the doorway, waving slowly at Theo, with a smile half obscured in shadow. Two other figures were standing beside him—a man and a woman.

Warm light spilled out from the home.

Theo shuffled over the threshold with tiny steps, and a puddle of rainwater formed at his feet.

A fireplace roared in the back corner. The room was warm and smelled of valerian root tea and earthy spices and wild forest and smoky firewood.

"Oh, you poor child. He must be so scared," said the woman, turning to Trent, "and you found him outside Imperial? What a tragedy. I can't even imagine what you've been through, child."

Theo remembered unframed canvases hung high all around the room. Taxidermied heads of beasts like monsters roaring and bursting out of the cream-colored walls. The chairs and couches were piled with lush animal furs.

"It's alright, boy," said Trent in a soft voice, "you're safe now. This is your home now. Everything's going to be alright."

Trent smiled and placed a gentle hand on Theo's shoulder.

"Melody. Arthur. Meet Theo."

Everything blurred into gray and black.

The cold air from the ship shook him from the dream.

Theo opened his eyes and found himself back in that rivet-lined room on a cot that swayed gently with the ship.

The room was no longer twisting, and he thought perhaps his fever had broken in the night. Moisture on his clothes suggested a cold sweat that had come and gone. But his mouth was dry as stone. He desperately needed something to drink.

Theo took the cup from the dinner tray and walked slowly down the dimly lit hallway. The hallway, which used to be pitch black, was indeed lit, but his eyes needed a moment to adjust. Slowly, the details emerged.

He was careful not to bump into any exposed pipes along the wall. Some pipes were as wide as his head. Others were slender, running overhead in five or six columns, transporting chemicals and gases throughout the ship.

A yellow warning light was blinking above a low-hanging valve. He ducked to avoid it.

When Theo turned a corner, he saw what looked like the galley ahead.

The sharp smell of fish, fry oil, and industrial degreaser hit him like a wall. The entrance was open, the metal door swung to the side, and its crank wheel protruded into the walkway. Rubber tubing ran along the door's outline, probably installed to create a seal. Fire suppression sprinklers hung above.

When he was steps away from the doorway, Theo heard a faint voice echo from the galley. It was Mae. She was whispering and emphasizing every other word with such emotion that it projected well beyond the confines of the galley.

"Think of your family's safety!" said Mae, "think of us! Think of me! What will the SCR do if they find out what we're doing... if they find out who he is!"

Theo froze mid-step and flattened himself against the wall, out of view. He watched their elongated shadows dancing along the far wall, reflecting off silver cabinets. Their heads and hands moved like an animated puppet show.

"I am!" said Kristof. He attempted to whisper, but his voice came out with a hushed boom. "I am thinking of us. All I ever do is think about this family!" That's what–"

"Well, I don't think you are," said Mae.

"Mae, don't you see? If that boy gets his plans to the Midlands–"

"If? IF? You're willing to put our lives on the line for an if? You're willing to wake up to the reality of the SCR boarding our ship and doing god knows what to me... Penny and Puck... and they'll kill you. That's a risk worth taking?"

"Imagine what it could mean for the rest of... all the people in..." Kristof paused, looked away with a far-off stare, entranced with the idea of changing the world.

"What about the people here? Your family?" said Mae.

They shared a tense moment of silence.

"It's too risky, Kristof."

"We need to do this. We need to do this for the future and for Penny. Mae, can't you see it's for Penny's future!"

"We need to get rid of him, Kristof. For our family."

"Imagine what it could mean for Penny if we could get her to a machine. If that boy gets the plans home and they build the machine, we could escape to the Midlands. If we stay here, Penny will never get–"

"Dear, I know you carry that burden, and it weighs on you every day." Mae looked up at Kristof, her movements growing somber.

"But it's not your fault," she said.

Theo watched their shadows standing face to face in silence.

"And it never was," she said, "Our Lord, Father Charles The Eternal, has a plan, and he walks with us through the good and the bad."

"Oh, don't you dare lecture me about our Lord," said Kristof, "what kind of a plan of his lets children grow up on the verge of starvation, imprisoned on this floating metal box, working as slaves for Aria Sloan–that dictator we've never even seen with our own eyes? What part of his plan puts someone like me out here, stuck for the rest of my life, running the same route over and over until the day I die and have to toss my body off the deck."

Mae was silent. Theo thought he heard the whimper of tears, but he couldn't be sure.

"But... you have your family." she said, "you have us."

Kristof's shadow paced back and forth in the room.

"I know," said Kristof, "I didn't mean... yes, I do. I'm sorry."

Their shadows came together and embraced.

"But this is bigger than us. There's too much at stake," said Kristof, "this is about the future."

Theo leaned forward, pressing his ear closer toward the door, trying to hear more clearly.

"We have to help him, Mae. Nothing will ever change if we don't take this chance right now. Puck will grow up running a scraper ship for the rest of his life. And Penny will... hell, I don't know. You know what they do to people who are unfit–"

"No!" said Mae firmly, "no, we don't speak of it."

A metallic clang echoed down the hallway. Theo looked down to find a pipe he had leaned against dislodged from the wall and the metal bracket coming loose.

He froze.

He took a deep breath, then shuffled his feet to pretend he was walking in the hallway. He dragged his feet louder near the door and took a hesitant step over the metal threshold into the galley.

"Oh," said Theo, "hello, I was getting some... water." He raised the cup awkwardly.

Kristof and Mae looked at him and didn't speak.

After a moment, Kristof nodded.

"Right, well then," said Kristof, "the sink, over there. A quarter turn for hot if you want it."

Mae sighed audibly and scowled at Theo. She turned to walk out of the room without saying a word.

Kristof reached one thick arm after Mae but lowered it when she disappeared.

Theo went to the sink and turned the knob. A sputtering sound erupted from a pipe deep in the wall. It was loud and rhythmic, like an old mechanical beast waking from slumber. Then, a few seconds later, a slow trickle of water emerged from the faucet.

It splashed into the bottom of the cup. Theo stared into the cup, wondering how anyone could cook with such low water pressure.

It filled. Theo waited. The silence in the room was unbearable.

"Son," said Kristof, speaking slowly, choosing his words carefully, "what's your plan?"

Theo looked up and considered the question.

It hung in the air between them.

"You said if you can get the chip home, your people in the Midlands can build the machine. A machine like they have. In the SCR. You can do that?"

Theo nodded. "Yes, I have engineers back home ready to start working on it now. I should have been... I was supposed to be back at the Ranch by now. We would've been far along in construction."

"So I'll ask again. What. Is. Your. Plan?"

Kristof tapped the counter with each word.

"Because we dock in just under thirty-two hours, and once we do, the SCR will be all over the vessel. It's their vessel, after all. I just look after it. So, how are you going to get from here, all the way back home to–"

"Oklahoma," said Theo.

"Oklahoma, alright."

"I've been thinking," said Theo, "thinking a lot. And all I need to do is find a train or something that heads back west. If I can get on board, or..."

Kristof snorted.

"Sneak on board a train?"

"Yeah."

"In SCR territory. You, a Midlander. This is your plan?"

"Well... yeah."

Kristof took a seat on a stool beside the walk-in refrigerator. His boots began to tap nervously. Eyes flicked back and forth around the room. His thoughts wound through ideas, problems, and solutions.

"Son, they'll put a bullet in you the minute your foot touches that dock. We'll dock near the Capital, and the coast will be crawling with soldiers. And for every fifty soldiers, there's bound to be a Grayskin nearby."

Kristof shook his head. He was breathing heavily and loudly. His anger bubbled up from a source Theo had yet to see.

He pounded a fist on the counter.

Theo flinched. Water spilled from his cup.

The loud bang filled the room.

"How dare you come in here, spinning fantasies of saving all those people with that damn chip in your arm, putting my family—*MY FAMILY*—at risk, at the center of all this. And all you got for a goddamn plan is to maybe find a train and maybe sneak onto it? You're going to have to do better than that, son!"

"I don't know how else to get this chip home," said Theo, "the only other way I'd know is to find a machine to read the files and transmit the data home. But that's going to be impossible on the coast. This chip is ancient tech. At least a hundred years old, maybe more. That's all we have in the Midlands, but no one will have a chip reader like that on the coast. They're too far ahead, moving too fast. Not a full year goes by before those Coasters throw out the old and get on with the new."

Kristof looked directly at Theo, an intense expression on his face.

"Old tech?"

"Yeah. Old." said Theo, his interest piqued, "what—why do you ask?"

"I don't know, it's probably nothing, but there was this one place..."

"Where? What is it?"

"Son, back when I was young, about your age, before this vessel and before I met Mae, I had nothing. No family. Never knew who my real parents were. No useful skills. I lived in this orphanage down on the southern coast. They called us Sents. We were the lowest group in a caste system running back hundreds of years. The SCR offered jobs to the poorest, most desperate of us. They needed a workforce to support the Republic. Nameless, faceless bodies to do jobs no one wanted. Life in dark mines, ripping rare metals from the earth. Being sent offshore to classified projects. Experiments, or worse. No one ever came back and no one knew what really happened to them. Every year, they needed a certain number of volunteers, but we didn't have a choice. Those who resisted were hanged in the streets. Unfit, they called us. So, when it was my turn, I enlisted."

Theo turned off the faucet and took a seat at the counter.

"The SCR," Kristof continued, "took me in. Trained me. And before shipping out, that took a truckload of us Sents in a transport up the southern coast all the way up to the docks. All kinds of people in that truck for days that seemed to never end. And I remember this one peculiar man. He was an older fellow from a group I'd never known about. Used to be a part of a strange religion a long time ago. This old man always wore drab clothes, ugly even. He had so much wisdom to share, so many stories about the world to tell, and all he'd talk about was this archive that existed two hundred years ago. I'd asked him where this archive was, but he'd never seen it with his own eyes. Said it was a legend passed down among his people. When times were different, many years ago, the archive was the center of their community. Like a church, almost. Before the SCR took full control of the information. They worshiped the idea of the archive even though none of them had ever seen it."

"Faith," said Theo, "that's what faith is, after all. Believing in something you've never actually seen and never had any proof of."

Kristof nodded.

"The Kingdom, they called it. The man I met said the coasters were blinded by their obsession for the future. The men of the Kingdom felt it their duty to secretly preserve the records of the past. But when I asked him, he said he didn't know the location. Didn't need to. He said he had his faith, and that's all he needed."

Kristof sighed and looked into the air, lost in a memory.

"I'll never forget that old fellow. Once we got to the dock, I didn't know what happened to him. Sometimes, I like to think he's somewhere out here, still holding on. Still keeping going in this cruel world.

"This Kingdom," said Theo, "you never found its location?"

Kristof turned to Theo.

"I don't know, son. Legend says it's within the Capital. Someplace in the city walls. And if you're seeking something from the past—like your chip reader—that's got to be your best chance of finding it."

Kristof raised a thick finger into the air.

"Son, I intend to help you, but I need you to promise me something in return."

"Promise?" asked Theo.

"Yes. I want you to promise me, and swear on your life, that when you get back home and build that machine, you make sure my Penny has a place in line to use it."

"Penny?"

"Yes," said Kristof.

Theo remembered Penny's cloudy white eyes.

"I see," said Theo, nodding, "Of course. Yes."

"Swear on your life, son. Promise me."

"Yes, I swear. You have my word."

Kristof nodded.

"Good man you are there. Now, we'll need to figure out a way to get you off this ship and into that city. Follow me. I have something I want to show you!"

***

Kristof reached into the dark.

Click.

Amber light flooded into the room. It was a warm color

reminiscent of the space between burning logs in a roaring fireplace. Shelves lined every wall in the long rectangular room, from floor to ceiling. Two wide tables with mechanical parts strewn in every direction. Tubes, wires, gears, excavated LED's. A wrench with half of its grip missing. Circular saw blades–some shiny and some rusted and bent. Sandpaper belts. Display panels with visible water damage and crushed screens.

And in the center of the room, a deconstructed engine lay flayed open on the table like a cadaver with its innards exposed. Beside the table, a large stool, like a throne, fit for a king.

"The scrapers, they pull up all kinds of junk from the ocean."

Kristof circled around the room, fingers tapping on various objects.

"This blade, you see here, from a drone," said Kristof, "It's hollow titanium with an internal lattice structure. Very strong. Very light. And this jar, full of spent fusion crystals. When they're fully charged, they can hold a ton of energy. They're depleted now. I never figured out how to recharge them."

Theo followed, looking with amazement at this treasure trove Kristof stashed in his ship–a graveyard of trash to the unimaginative observer, a shrine to innovation to others.

"An NPI-37 connector," Kristof said, pointing to a rusted spike with flecks of brilliant chrome shining through, "a neural probe interface, or what's left of it and not rusted away. For shootin' those fantasy programs into your brain!"

His hands floated up and down the shelves, juggling metal bins full of parts.

Magnets. Capacitors. An entire pouch full of thick rubber o-rings.

Theo noticed the remains of a small engine in the corner. He reached to touch one of its gears, ran his fingers across the greased metal, and pressed gently to see if it would turn. One of the gears turned, rotating a connected arm, which caused the second gear

CALICO HILL

to turn sequentially. On the side of the engine, four small canisters were mounted with tubes running the object's length.

"What's thi–"

Kristof turned around.

"No! DO NOT touch that!" he screamed, charging across the room to pull the engine away from Theo. Kristof was shaking, blowing big, angry breaths from his nostrils.

Theo flinched and stepped back, a shocked look on his face.

"This is... this... this..." Kristof looked down at the engine, at a loss for words, and tears welled in his eyes. He frowned, shook off the tears, and took a deep breath.

"Years ago," Kristof said with a shaking voice, "Penny began showing an interest in my tinkering. She'd come in and watch me take things apart. Asked me questions about this or that. 'Make the gear turn, daddy' she'd say. 'Turn it again,' she'd say. Eventually, she started helping me sort through the junk that came in from the scrapers. Small things at first."

Kristof's arms turned stiff, his face holding back rage and sadness.

"So one day, she picked this out of the junk pile. She was so excited. She wanted to try to take it apart, and I didn't want to discourage that spark in her eye, so I let her. And I should've been watching her. We never knew there was fluid still pressurized in these lines here. She cut one, and it sprayed all over her face. Burned her face. Got in her eyes."

Kristof placed the engine back on the shelf. He was quiet for a moment, staring at the engine.

"So today," said Kristof with a sigh, sadness in his voice, "that's a machine we don't touch."

He turned back to Theo, tears still drying on his cheeks and quickly walked over to a far shelf.

"About your plan... I've had some thoughts. The priority is to get you onto land, out of view of the SCR. And far away from the docks, which will be crawling with soldiers."

His eyes scanned the shelves while he talked. He reached into a bin on the top shelf and pulled out a strange apparatus.

"Here ya go," said Kristoff, handing Theo a spindly device with a round metal center the size of a baseball and rubber tubes extending out in multiple directions.

"That there goes in your nose, and that one in your mouth, and it turns algae into oxygen when you breathe in. But it's a delicate conversion process, so you've got to keep to slow, even breathing. Breathe too fast and you could clog the whole thing up, and before you know it, no more oxygen. Should last a couple of hours. That's my best guess, but I never got to test it."

Theo examined the device. He turned it over in his palm and immediately felt the subtle taste of bile in his throat. He felt his breathing speed up, fully aware that panicked breathing was exactly what Kristof said not to do.

Kristof slid two bins out from another shelf. He pulled out two pieces of a device that seemed to click together to form a handle with a hammer-like tip.

"This gadget here fires a magnetic pulse. Highly concentrated. Strong enough to blast through steel. But it's only got a few charges left, so be careful with that one."

Theo cradled the device in his hands, carefully pointing the tip in a clear direction. A mix of fear and curiosity on his face. When he looked up, Kristof was already on the other side of the room, bending to reach inside a low, squeaky drawer in the corner.

"This here. This is what I wanted to show you."

Kristof pulled out a brass monocular spyglass wrapped in a flap of soft cloth. As he unfurled it, the air filled with the ammoniac smell of metal cleaner. He cradled it like a delicate jewel in one massive hand, his other hand hovering nearby to catch it if it fell. On the table, he swept away pieces of crumpled wires and plastic shavings and he placed the spyglass gingerly onto the wooden surface.

Theo stepped up to the table.

"The Kingdom," said Kristof, "I don't remember much of what that old man said. It was so long ago. But what I do remember is the emblem drawn on his sash that he wore over his long shirt. A symbol of a lion."

He pointed to the small imprint on the end of the spyglass. It was a silhouetted outline of a lion perched atop a stone pedestal, with what looked like a column engraved on its left and a wreath of foliage flanking to its right.

"This same lion," said Kristof.

Theo placed a hand carefully over the engraving, running his fingertips over the bumps with a slow, delicate touch. He felt the ridges and curves of the metal.

"Find that lion, and you'll find the Kingdom. Find the Kingdom, and you'll find your chip reader."

CHAPTER 13

SCREAM

The morning of the docking sequence had arrived. An unsettling chill hung in the air, unfitting for the sunny blue skies overhead.

Theo lowered a hesitant foot into the liquid. The algae was unexpectedly warm. First, the front of his boot disappeared, then his heel and ankle slid into the brown-green syrup. It was thick, like wet sand. The liquid rose to surround his other ankle, then his leg, then expanding to envelop him entirely as he slid down into the barrel. He'd only seen them stacked like a wall of metal blocks, but the barrels were much larger up close than he remembered.

He took one last look at the family in front of him—Kristof and Mae standing beside the barrel, poised to help him climb inside. Puck and Penny stood at the far side of the room. Puck watched intently. Penny tilted her head to follow the sound of the metal latch opening and the green liquid sloshing.

Theo's feet touched the bottom.

He held the magnetic pulser above his shoulder, trying to

keep it dry and high above the liquid line. The rebreather was strapped around his neck, with a muzzle cupped over his mouth and tubes running up his nose.

Deep breaths. Slow, even breaths.

Kristof looked into Theo's eyes as if saying a silent prayer as he lifted the container lid and swung it over the top of the barrel.

In an instant, everything was black.

There were less than four inches of breathing room between the top of the algae and the barrel's inner rim.

"The darkness... it's freeing," said Sam's voice, suddenly rushing into Theo's mind. "Anything is possible in the dark, Theeeeo."

The only light that accompanied him was the small beam that shone through a circular porthole along the side of the barrel. A vertical row of eight portholes. Seven below the surface of the algae and one above. A faint glow came through the one at the top.

Theo waded over to the porthole, one hand pressing against the side of the barrel, and the other holding the magnetic pulser up high. Movement was sluggish in the thick algae. He angled his back to thrust forward with all his strength and pressed an eye up against the edge of the barrel.

Through the porthole, he saw the interior of a room bathed in light.

A small bird fluttered in from an open doorway. It traced low to the ground at first, then zipped up into the air at eye level and hovered in front of Kristof and his family. But when Theo looked closer, he realized it wasn't a bird but a tiny mechanical drone. It moved like a hummingbird, darting straight lines across the room. The drone produced a high-frequency noise for a split-second and projected a bright light from its body. The beam of light, tight like a laser, glowed and split into eight lines. Each beam of light locked onto each of their pupils and pulsed brighter and brighter.

Theo realized what was happening.

The beams from the drone were temporarily blinding them.

It was all about compliance and power.

Kristof, Mae, Puck, and Penny stood frozen, hands at their sides, panic across their faces. Kristof's hands twitched anxiously. He tugged at his apron and turned his face side to side, pupils shifting and searching. Mae did the same, taking a hesitant half-step backway to catch her balance, hands extending at her sides to steady herself. Her eyes darted around the room, the concern on her face slowly evolving into a silent terror.

The light on the wall flickered. Shadows stretched across the room and quickly disappeared.

"They're coming, Theo," said Sam, "in fact, they're already here."

Theo searched for a better angle through the tiny porthole.

Boots stomped into the room. Three soldiers don the same helmets and rifles as those on the island. They marched to opposite corners of the room, taking flanking positions beside the family.

The light on the wall flickered.

Another shadow.

A Kaipher appeared.

That slate jacket. Black boots. Short-cropped hair and mottled, sickly skin the color of dried-out animal flesh. It carried a distinct reddish hue to its skin like it had been weather-beaten from exposure to the elements. With controlled, deliberate movements, it entered the room.

It walked with a posture like a slow parade march—straight back, chin up.

"Misssster Kristof, good day," said the Kaipher with a raspy voice like air leaking from a pipe.

Theo could barely make out what he was saying. The sound through the barrel was deadened. His rebreather was locked tight against his mouth as he tried to take full, steady breaths, pacing his oxygen intake to make the filters last as long as possible.

Kristof, blinded and frozen in place, tried to look toward the direction of the Kaipher's voice.

"Yes, uh, sir."

"I assume our shipments are complete as instructed, Mr. Kristof?"

"Yes, sir. Complete, sir."

"Excellent. You have always been one of our most reliable producers, Mr. Kristof. You make Miss Sloan quite happy. She finds your work very satisfactory. And our Republic remains strong because of your contributions."

"Thank you, sir. My family and I are always in the service of the SCR."

A strong vibration rattled throughout the ship. Theo felt the barrel shake.

"As a direct result of your continued loyalty and reliability, Miss Sloan is prepared to add a twenty percent bonus to your contracted fee and an extra fifty food rations for your next run on route F19."

The Kaipher paced around the room. It stopped in front of Penny, bent down, and placed its face in front of hers. It then approached Puck, studying him like one would appraise valuable wares for sale. It inspected Mae up close, inches away from her face, its breath no doubt wafting over her as she struggled to see but the drone's light that shined into her eyes kept her in a state of blindness.

Another flicker of light across the wall.

Someone had entered the room, but it was out of view from Theo's porthole.

The vibration became stronger. A grinding sound came from outside the barrel, directly behind Theo. A mechanical whir spun up.

It was getting louder.

The barrel jolted.

Theo was moving. He felt gravity shift, and a rumbling machine lifted the barrel into the air.

As he moved, Theo caught a glimpse of the figure entering the room. It was a second Kaipher.

"Careful, Theo, careful. Slow, easy breaths," said Sam, "you wouldn't want to die drowning with algae burning through your lungs, would you? Burn so bad you'd want to scream, but no one would hear you."

The two Kaiphers approached each other and huddled into a corner to discuss a silent matter. After a moment, they nodded their heads in agreement.

The vibration stopped. Theo hung suspended high in the room, carried by a crane-like machine.

The first Kaipher with the red-hued face approached Kristof.

"Mr. Kristof, are we of the mutual understanding that your loyalty to the SCR is immutable and unyielding?"

Kristof's mouth opened. His eyes, blinded by the pulsing light, flicked left and right. He had a confused look on his face.

"Yes, sir. Unyielding," said Kristof with a stutter, "Im- immutable. I have always delivered what the SCR requests, sir."

"Magnificent!" said the Kaipher, "Miss Sloan will be overjoyed."

Its voice was dry as sand, with the twist of each word like a snake.

The Kaipher looked away and paused.

"But there is one more issue of importance we need to address, Mr. Kristof. A small, shall we call it... inconsistency. My associate has briefed me that we have discovered peculiar equipment on board your vessel. This is unexpected, given that we outfit your vessel with all supplies required to complete the job on the assigned scraping route. Nothing more. Nothing less."

The Kaipher paused. Silence filled the room.

"And yet here we are with an... inconsistency."

Mae took an audible, sharp breath. Her foot shuffled against the metal floor.

A soldier entered the room carrying Theo's deflated raft, its bright yellow rubber carcass limp and torn.

"Ahh, Theo,' said Sam, his voice overwhelming within the silence of the algae, "that looks familiar, doesn't it?"

The soldier tossed the raft to the floor. It folded over into a small heap.

The Kaipher cleared its throat, "Unfortunately, you don't have the ability of sight at the moment, so you must take my word for it, Mr. Kristof. But since we share such a high level of trust and understanding, I expect that shouldn't be a problem." It ran a gloved finger across the yellow rubber surface, producing a faint squeak.

"You see, the SCR equips every scraper vessel with four gray life rafts to save your precious lives in the event of a catastrophic event at sea."

It grabbed the edge of the folded raft and squeezed.

"We do not, however, equip vessels with yellow rafts. So, would you explain why one is aboard your ship, Mr. Kristof?"

Kristof took a breath to speak but paused to choose his next words carefully.

"Oh right... that-that got pulled up with the scraper. Many discarded items come up from the waters. It's nothing to pay any mind to. I will dispose of it immediately."

"Ah, please see that you do. Now, I must ask about a recent occurrence. We have information regarding a person, a very dangerous Midlander, that the SCR is very interested in speaking to. We believe this person was last seen near route F19 but has been missing for days. It is critical that we find this person. Would you know anything about that?"

"No sir," said Kristof, "it's been nothing but clear sailing along this route and no sign of a boy. Just good scrapes and quality product for the SCR, sir."

The Kaipher stood silent.

"Mr. Kristof, what an unfortunate place we have arrived at. Your service to the SCR has been impeccable over the years. Truly an outstanding provider for our great Republic. But Miss Sloan places loyalty at the highest level of importance. Without loyalty to the Republic, we would go back to living in that arcane existence those Midlander scum call a life. That would be a tragic sight."

Kristof shuffled his feet.

"But today, you have made me quite disappointed because you have broken that promise of loyalty."

Mae's breathing quickened. She panicked.

"This is not good, Theo," Sam's voice clawed back into his mind, "look at what you have done. They would have never been in this situation if you hadn't–"

"Papa?" cried Puck, looking around in the dark before him, arms restless at his side.

Penny's empty eyes looked toward the ceiling. She wept silently.

"Oh, I assure you, sir, we've done everything to code," said Kristof, "and any junk pulled up from the ocean will be discarded immediately; I will see to it my–"

His sentence was cut short as the Kaipher whipped a blade from its hip and plunged it deep into Kristof's neck.

Theo tried to scream, but the rebreather stifled the sound. He pressed his fists against the inside of the barrel, one hand bringing a crushing grip down on the magnetic pulser, nearly shattering it with his rage.

"K-Kristof? Kristof, dear? Wha-what is happening?" screamed Mae. She raised her hands, feeling the emptiness around her, struggling to find him.

She was flailing in a blind abyss.

Penny's face flooded with tears, and she fell to her knees. She cradled her head in her hands, shaking.

Kristof tried to speak. Only spurts of spit and gurgling sounds escaped his mouth. A silent curtain of blood spilled down his chest, staining his leather apron, and he began to wobble.

He stepped forward, quivering hands grabbing at his neck.

He took a second step and crashed to the floor.

The Kaipher moved away and watched Kristof fall, a pool of blood expanding around his large body.

"Search the vessel!" screamed the Kaipher.

The soldiers rushed from their flanking positions and disappeared through separate doorways.

"Secure the cargo! And do what you want with these pitiful souls; just get them out of my sight!"

Boots pounded the floor.

The barrel vibrated, and the machine whirred to life once more.

Theo stared out of the porthole at the scene in front of him. Kristof's body was a lifeless shape on the floor. His once imposing figure reduced to an unmoving object with the swipe of a blade. The Kaipher stepped over his body and disappeared from the room.

The barrel moved, and the porthole went black.

Mae and the children slid out of sight.

Theo's breathing quickened.

Panic and rage exploded in his veins.

"Why didn't you save them, Theo," whispered Sam, "you just watched from afar and let them die."

Theo shut his eyes and struggled to slow his breathing to preserve the air filter.

The surface of the algae sloshed as the barrel was carried

up and out of the vessel. After a moment, a blinding white light flooded the three-inch porthole. Sunlight! A welcome respite from the enclosed darkness of the container.

The barrel continued moving. It was smooth at first, but then everything stopped. A small engine spooled up with a series of metallic sounds, and something hit the side of the barrel with a thud.

Movement again!

Jerky and uneven.

I must have been handed off to a different transport mechanism, he thought. Theo imagined a tangle of robotic arms and spinning gears moving him along a conveyor belt.

Algae splashed into his face.

Theo wiped the porthole clean enough to look out at the world through the green-tinted glass.

He was moving in a transport vehicle. A long truck of some kind. He passes supply caches stacked on the docks. Large ships and smaller vehicles with sharp angles filled the scene. Dozens of soldiers in black helmets and green glowing rifles. Machinery with wires and antennae that glowed with a familiar blue.

And Kaiphers with their gray coats and black boots and dead eyes.

After nearly an hour on the transport, Theo felt the vehicle slow to a stop. Muffled voices from outside surrounded the barrel.

With a loud scraping sound, another machine took hold of the barrel. Something slammed against the side with a bang. Theo felt it jolt from side to side, and suddenly, he was rising into the air.

He twisted his neck to see out the porthole.

Rows of stacked barrels, ten or fifteen high, lined a cavernous warehouse.

Several barrels sit off to the side. It looked like their placement was yet to be assigned.

The algae sloshed once more.

He started moving.

The barrel rotated.

Then a thud.

It slowed to a crawl.

Theo looked through the porthole, trying to get a handle on his location, but he could barely see anything. Too much shadow. Two barrels beside him blocked half of his view. There was only the faint glow of outside light coming through the porthole.

He floated in an unnerving silence, exhaling controlled breaths into the rebreather. He listened intently to the noises from his surroundings, trying to pick up when the transport machine might return. He dreaded hearing the sound of that whirring engine once again.

"Look around, Theeeo," said Sam, "barrels stacked up high. Are they going to stack a barrel on top of you? Well, that wouldn't be good, now would it? How would you open the latch? How would you ever escape? Oh, that's right... you wouldn't. You would die here, floating in this tomb of algae."

Theo shook the voice away.

He waited for the engine sound to return, but only silence remained.

He thought an hour passed. Maybe two.

The outside light was fading.

It would be better to escape later in the day, he thought. Less chances of being spotted in the dark. But, on the other hand, he had no way of knowing how much oxygen was left.

Time seemed to slow as he continued to wait. He felt his head become heavy and wished he was far away from this terrible place. Back home with the season's first snow tumbling down from a light gray sky. Touching down with a soft landing on the fields outside and–

He felt so tired.

So much fatigue was lifting from his conscience.

The world felt a little lighter. The pain a little softer.

Peace washed over him.

What a wonderful feeling it would be to sleep, he thought. Just a short while to gather his strength. Close his eyes for a moment. Or two. And rest for a little while.

Then his heart raced with panic, and he realized: low oxygen!

He had depleted the rebreather and was suffocating slowly with each minute.

He needed to get out!

Theo raised the magnetic pulser, trying to scrape any residual algae off of its charging pads.

This better work, he thought.

He held the activation switch, pressing for several seconds like Kristof had shown him, waiting for the power light to illuminate.

His eyelids grew heavy. The urge to close his eyes was overwhelming.

The power light on the handle clicked on and put out a soft yellow glow in the darkness.

He felt a sudden calm fall upon him.

He dragged his fingers across the inside of the barrel, trying to feel for a bump in the metal—the ridge that marked the location of the first magnetic lock.

Everything was slippery under his fingers, the thick sludge heavy and dense.

Then he felt the metal ridge.

He jammed the magnetic pulser against the wall, carefully keeping it level and creating a solid contact.

Please be right, he thought.

He pressed the charge button to spool up the device. It illuminated bright green. He felt around for the trigger, fingers slipping.

He was fading fast.

Heart hammered at a rapid pace.

He jammed the trigger.

A high-pitched sound exploded from the device, and the first latch uncoupled with a loud mechanical click.

One more latch.

One hundred and eighty degrees opposite the first.

Kristof said it didn't have a ridge, but it was supposed to be there!

Theo reached across.

Everything was slipping.

It needed to line up to undo the latch. One inch off to the left or right, and it wouldn't work. He'd be trapped and drift off to a forever sleep.

He tried to line up the pulse gun but could only see a dark cavern with no reference points ahead.

He pressed the device to the wall.

Flushed and centered.

Pressed the charge button.

Greenlight.

Thumb on the button.

Please work, he thought.

He jammed the trigger.

CHAPTER 14

POWER STATION

The latch exploded with a heavy clunk.

Theo dug his heels into the floor and slammed his shoulder against the inside of the lid. It detached and swung upward along its hydraulic hinge.

Sweet, cold air flooded into the barrel.

He ripped the rebreather off his face and took a magnificent breath before doubling over the side of the barrel. Specks of algae and tendrils of spit hung from his mouth.

He tumbled to the ground and collapsed.

"This is all your fault, Theeeeeeo," said Sam's voice.

Ropes of bile erupted as he spilled the contents of his stomach, wheezing from airless lungs. Labored breaths turned into tears as he cried like a child on that frigid concrete floor.

"You left them all to die, Theeeo."

He cried for Kristof and the crushing feeling that there was nothing he could have done.

Green liquid turned to brown stains on the concrete floor.

I should never have come here, he thought. This was my

mission. My responsibility.

Theo's breaths echo through the rows of stacked barrels. He froze and splayed out on the floor, suddenly aware of how loud he was breathing. It was a cavernous warehouse with a high ceiling and two large metal doors on both sides. One was open, its rippled sheet metal fully retracted into the pulley mechanism above.

With lungs burning and eyes bloodshot red, he pulled himself up off the ground and listened around him for footsteps.

Alert for any hint of pounding boots and rifles, hot and ready to kill.

He heard nothing but silence.

The sun was setting. Bands of fire-red light streaked in from the open doorway. He thought he heard waves crashing just around the corner out of sight.

Brown puddles stained the floor. Soon, the dull stain of footprints would lead them right to him.

I need to get clean of this algae, he thought.

Theo stumbled forward, moving slowly on the slippery concrete toward the open door at the side of the warehouse. He paused at the door, listening again for any movements.

Silence.

Outside, endless rows of concrete platforms jutted up against the water's edge. Piles of crates and equipment were scattered everywhere. Vehicles and heavy machinery Theo had never seen before. Some of them secured behind chain link fences topped with razor wire.

Up ahead, there was an opening in the concrete. A narrow ramp angled down toward the water.

Theo hurried down the ramp. He heard the sound of waves splashing. The concrete was cracked, and exposed rebar shot up like weeds.

First, he threw the rebreather and the magnetic pulser into the ocean.

I can't have evidence lying around, he thought.

Without a second thought, Theo plunged headfirst into the water to clear the brown, caked-on sludge from his body.

Then the shock hit him.

The water was freezing.

It mainlined up his spine and jolted him awake.

When he realized what he'd done, his clothes were soaked.

He leaped backward, sucking in violent breaths of surprise, and crawled back up the ramp on elbows and knees. He hunched over into a fetal position, trying to compress his arms around himself to retain any heat.

N-n-need to find warmth, he thought, before it was too late.

Theo jumped to his feet and glanced back toward the warehouse. There was movement just beyond the door. The pounding of boots across the expanse of the warehouse. Some kind of patrol, or they're moving equipment, he thought.

He looked down, quickly reminded of his footprints stamped with water into the ground. It led directly from the warehouse door to the water's edge.

I cannot stay here, he thought. It's just a matter of time before they catch on.

A gust of wind swept across the water and sent chills down Theo's back.

He hopped forward and jogged down the edge of the water. His wet footfalls squeaked loudly against the soft sounds of ocean waves from his left. On his right, metal corpses of machinery were placed in crooked piles.

He searched for a place to get warm. Peered into tight spaces between equipment. Deep recesses under utility trucks and low-slung cables. But with a temperature that cold, it wouldn't be enough.

Behind him, rows of drones sat dormant on the concrete. One drone was covered in ice, and rust accumulated on its rotator arms. The other drones were wrapped tightly in thick black tarps. Theo untied a tarp and ripped it free. Specks of ice and water droplets scattered in every direction. He stepped back and took in the drone's massive size—helicopter-like blades folded flat sat level with his chest, its row of optical sensors bulbous like the eyes of a mechanical bumblebee. They were menacing in the dark under the glowing red light. He ran his fingers over the optical sensors. Even though all evidence suggested it was dead, he can't help but feel that at any moment it could spring to life.

He wrapped his entire body in the black tarp, the stiff nylon edge digging into his neck as he hobbled forward.

Theo's jaw tensed, and he began shivering uncontrollably. He gripped his torso tighter while he tried desperately to stay warm.

A few hundred meters ahead, Theo saw a faint, pulsing red light. It was beyond several rows of what looked like drones the size of a man's body. When a thick fog rolled in from the ocean and the light dispersed into the sky, a bright crimson glow rose toward the clouds.

Theo tried to jog faster. Behind him, his wet footsteps were slowly evaporating. But a stinging sensation built up in his boots. His socks, once soaked by the ocean water, are now almost frozen solid. Each step became more laborious, and his pace slowed.

About twenty meters ahead, he noticed razor wire perched atop a fence. As he moved closer, its sheer height came into view.

That fence must be fifteen feet high at least, he thought.

He peered through the wire. Twelve rectangular blocks the size of small houses were arranged in a grid formation, equidistant from each other. Each block was smooth and featureless from bottom to top, save for a small control panel at the base, which blinked with green and yellow lights. At the top of each block, towering at least ten meters high, white plumes of steam rose like storm clouds into the freezing fog above.

Theo felt the air around him grow a little warmer. A faint hum lingered in the thick air emanating from the blocks.

A power station of some kind, he thought?

The steam clouds swirled violently above.

Theo paced around the perimeter of the fence. He traced his hand up and down the chainlinks, searching for a latch, door, or any possible way in. It looked impenetrable from the outside.

Then, in the corner, he saw a curious line of small red dots. He stepped closer to investigate.

Sharp metal points shone in the darkness.

Someone cut an opening in the fence, he thought!

He ran his fingers over the chainlinks and pushed.

It bent.

He pulled back the fence and crawled through. When he let go, it sprang back and cut his hand. Narrow lines of blood formed on his fingertips.

Standing beside one of the power blocks, he felt a faint sensation seeping into his body, like he was stepping across the threshold of an invisible wall. A wave flowed in and out of him as he inched closer to the black monolith.

A deep vibration that dug into his chest. It was familiar, like the vibrations from the aircraft on the island.

To his left and to his right, more towering blocks point to the sky. Their red glowing shapes were menacing in the thick white fog. Far in the distance, beyond the last power block, there was nothing but a wall of darkness.

A welcome wave of warmth came upon him. It brought relief to his arms first, then his chest. He breathed in a lungful of warming air. It permeated his boots last, thawing his frozen socks and injecting feeling back into his toes.

He searched for any movement beyond the farthest power block but saw nothing. Nothing, except for the vibration in the air and the waves lapping nearby in the darkness.

What he wouldn't give for some company to make him feel like he wasn't thousands of miles from home, lost and abandoned forever. A kind, listening ear of another human.

Sam, he thought, how I wish you were here.

He braced for the whispering sound of Sam's voice to peer out from the recesses of his mind.

But there was nothing but silence.

He sat cold in the dark.

At the foot of the towering power block, Theo unfurled the tarp and lay on the ground, pressing his back hesitantly against the black metallic panel. It was warm against his body.

He couldn't shake the feeling that these blocks felt dangerous yet strangely protective.

He wrapped the tarp around his body to form a tight cocoon camouflaged in the shadows.

The electrical hum had returned. It cycled in and out every few minutes. To Theo, it felt like a lullaby that beckoned him toward sleep. His eyelids grew heavy. His mind drifted. The image of Mae and Puck and Penny burned into his mind. Their faces contorted in fear. The crushing feeling of being so helpless and leaving them to die on that vessel.

Then, a darker feeling clawed back into his mind.

The Kaipher's blade–a small length of forged metal that robbed a large man of his life. Memories of Kristof–the blood splashing over his apron. How empty he looked on the ground, face down in his own blood.

Theo curled tighter into the tarp. He surrendered to the warmth and let the black nylon material shield him from the horrors of the outside world.

He drifted to sleep in the red-glowing fog, preparing to meet the nightmares building inside his mind.

***

Theo woke to find an icy blade pressed to his throat and rancid breath blowing at his face. He opened his eyes and saw a slender, pock-marked face with a scraggly beard staring back.

"Don't bother reaching for it," said the man.

Theo ran his fingers over the sheath at his hip.

His knife was gone.

CHAPTER 15

OUT CITY

"Lovely blade you got here. I'll be sure to keep it in tippy-top shape," said a bearded man. A wide grin scrawled across his face, revealing a semi-toothless smile.

Behind the bearded man, two figures huddled close to the power block. They were hunched over the illuminated control panel, fiddling with wires and cables beside a large rectangular canister on the ground.

"The transfer won't work if you put kinks in the line! Hold it still!" shouted a spectacled man with a slender figure. His overcoat was much too long for his modest stature. The coat dragged lines on the sand behind him.

Standing beside the bespeckled man, a broad-shouldered brute with a head too small for his body hoisted a cable up to the control panel. He carried two giant bags on his back and a waist-pack bulging with tools and wires.

"I'm trying to! I'm holding it! I'm holding it!" said the large man. He fumbled his grip and wrapped the thick cable over his forearm for support. He strained to hold it straight.

"Well, try harder, you stupid oaf!" said the short man with the long coat.

The bearded man glanced back to this commotion, the knife still holding firmly at Theo's throat.

The blade was cold.

"Hey, go easy on him, Jay!" said the bearded man.

Theo felt the blade shaking under his jaw, tremors from the cold building in the bearded man's wrist.

"If he can't hold the goddamn cable in place, why the hell did we bring him, Deak?"

"I'm holding it! I'm holding it!"

"You're holding it all wrong! Look at the meter. Look! The cable needs to be straight, or the transfer will fail. You can't even do that right!"

"I'm helping!"

Jay frowned and pushed his glasses up the ridge of his nose. He scoffed loudly, then muttered two words to himself.

"Useless imbecile," said Jay under his breath.

The large man erupted into a tantrum.

"Bor isn't useless! Bor is helping! Bor can do this job! Bor is good!" he shouted. He ripped the cable from the power block, raised it high over his head, and slammed it onto the ground. The cable cracked open, flinging spirals of black tape and braided wire into the air.

"Goddamnit, Bor! Settled down!" yelled Deak, air shooting through the gap between his missing teeth.

Bor's tantrum subsided. Loud breaths shot out of his nostrils. He rested his arms by his side.

"We've only got two bricks left, so make good use of them," said Deak over his shoulder, "And youuuuu," he said, turning his attention back to Theo, "you'd better get gone real far real quick. This power block is ours, you hear? Don't get any clever ideas about siphoning our supply. It's our supply. We claimed it. Ours!"

Theo blinked and nodded slowly.

"*TELL ME YOU UNDERSTAND!*" screamed Deak. Spit flew into Theo's face, and rancid breath washed over him once again. Deak's eyes twitched, and the blade pressed deeper against Theo's skin.

He clenched his jaw.

"Understood," said Theo.

Deak squinted and looked Theo up and down.

"Now get out of my sight," he said, the toothless grin returning, "and thank you again for the thoughtful donation." He held up the knife, inspecting it into the light, "So generous of you to support our fledgling organization."

Theo slowly backed away.

Deak waved the knife around, stabbing the air in Theo's direction.

He turned away from the power station and slipped out through the opening in the chain-link fence.

Stripped of his possessions except for a tarp and a piece of rope, Theo trudged up the beach. For a moment, he looked back at the twelve black shapes jutting into the clouds. He pivoted around the side of the power station and peeked in between the blocks, hiding front sight while carefully observing thieves' movements. The bearded one, Deak, stood with his stolen blade in one hand, the other hand wagging an accusatory finger at the two other men.

He considered his options, maybe waiting until he had the element of surprise and finding a makeshift weapon to take them on, but he was outnumbered and running out of time. He tightened the tarp around his waist and continued down the coast.

As he got further from the power station, the fog began to dissipate. Behind the clouds, a clear black sky emerged, with a full moon shining as a beacon against a sea of stars. Only his footsteps scraping on the concrete and the ocean waves lapping nearby could be heard. Everything else was an unnerving silence. Before he knew it, he had covered several miles of coastline. The concrete beneath his feet had crumbled and faded away, and only sand was up ahead as far as the eye could see. Tendrils of seaweed sprouted along the beach like long fingers reaching out from the sea.

Theo got his first look at the Capital far off in the distance, but it was only a glimpse. He couldn't make out many details, but he could see a flat gray wall stretched for miles and sharp vertical lights beaming up into the sky under the dim moonlight. The region surrounding the Capital had an eerie glow; the lights would pulse and shift every few moments.

It sat upon the horizon like a mirage against the dark sky.

He was so transfixed by the Capital lights that he nearly tripped over a long metallic object at his feet. A long, thin tube with a broken rotating handle. He kicked it away. There was another object a few steps ahead. A bent plastic frame, possibly of a shattered display screen.

Further ahead, there were wires and plastic connectors and cables and gears and batteries and triangles of broken glass. As the moonlight illuminated the path ahead, Theo could see all of this trash leading up to the base of a mountain hundreds of meters wide. It was piled with tall, angled objects, with a sharp peak like a pyramid high above. Its jagged edge came into view against the starry sky.

There was no way around it. The mountain extended to the water's edge, spilling trash into the ocean. It smelled of decomposing plant life and entire worlds of flourishing bacterial colonies. Fish carcasses and barnacles lay beached, poisoned from the trash seeping into the water and rotting in the open air on the sand.

Theo smashed his boots firmly into the base of the mountain. He felt the sharp objects shifting beneath his feet, compacting under his weight. Muffled sounds of snapping plastic and metal crunched under his boots. As he climbed, more details emerged. Helmets and visors, cracked and bent, with entrails of wires. Display tablets—thousands of them—with shattered screens, bent, ripped into two with razor-thin chipsets exposed from within their body cavity. Metal boxes and bowls with thick inner linings. Kitchen appliances and small engines, with their exterior shells missing and inner compartments on display. In the cold silence of the night, the sharp cracking of discarded objects was deafening.

Then, the sound of children's laughter cut through the silence.

The crest of the trash mountain was a dozen meters away. Dark shapes darted across the mountain ridge. Two, maybe three small children with bags hoisted on their backs skipped across the sharp objects. Their movements were so effortless one might think they were floating. Laughter pierced the silence again as the children skipped down the far side of the mountain and disappeared into the dark, searching for parts to fill their bags and take back to the city below.

Theo placed his hand on the thick edge of a microwave for support. As he pushed up to take another step, he noticed its white bowl-like interior filled with clumps of soil. Two small green stems were sprouting, barely an inch or two in height. The sight of the plant made Theo pause.

Such a fragile life in the middle of so much destruction. In a world teetering on the edge, the courage for life to persevere and find a way.

Of all the places, you had to pick right here, he thought, looking down on the tiny budding plant.

When he reached the top of the ridge, he could see for miles. Behind him, the power station glowed red through the distant fog. To his left, the beams of the Capital skyward lights were getting brighter. To his right, rows of small buildings extended toward the horizon. Black fires burned in the distance. Shanties cobbled together of rusted metal and wooden boards. Tents made of tarp, some rounded like huts and others built of two poles flapping in the breeze. Hundreds of them. Maybe thousands. String lanterns lined the alleyways between buildings. Their bluish-white light cast a cold, dim aura over the town.

Theo heard a sound behind him. A melodic tone, like a whistle in the sky. It was growing louder. Closer. Faster. Like a single piano key hammering repeatedly. The whistling was overwhelming. It drilled into his ear.

Over the crest of a nearby mountain, Theo saw a fleet of drones ripping through the air toward him. They were flying fast and low. He had nowhere to hide, perched atop that dark mountain. The drones would soon be upon him, their engines raging at a high speed, getting louder.

Theo panicked and searched in the dark. He grabbed a loose piece of sheet metal, brushed it off, and flipped it onto his back to camouflage himself.

He tried to flatten his body against the mountain without impaling himself on the angular corners of metal and plastic beneath him. A wind gust swept over him.

"It was only a matter of time, Theo. But you led them here, didn't you?" said Sam.

The mountain started to shake. He could feel the objects under his body vibrate.

"The raft, then the footprints in the warehouse... you've been sloppy, Theo. A small, weak little boy."

Small granules of plastic scattered around him. Shredded strips of rubber and fabric swirled into the air.

The fleet was almost directly overhead. The ground shook violently. Light flickered with their shadows. Then, as quickly as they appeared, so did they vanish, rushing at full speed past Theo, making a direct line toward the glow of the Capital lights far in the distance.

Theo let out a harsh breath of relief, his heart hammering in his chest.

The sky was getting lighter.

The sun would soon rise.

He picked himself up.

Far in the distance, concrete pillars rose toward the sky. They loomed over the city full of huts and tents below. Stretches of old, winding highways, covered in green foliage with long vines that reached toward the ground.

The skeletal remains of a world from a long time ago.

Theo descended to the base of the mountain. A stinging aroma of chemicals filled the air. He resisted the urge to hurl right there onto the dirt, the toxic smells making him dizzy. He gulped in and held his breath, trying not to inhale any more of the fumes he already had. Wide metal barrels lined the alleys between the shanties and were all burning trash from the mountain: computer motherboards, compact battery packs, semiconductors, cables, and shattered flatscreens splayed open like a book. Occasionally, he heard a loud snap in one of the barrels, and white sparks shot into the sky. It pierced the quiet morning air.

Up ahead, a tall man slid open two metal doors to reveal an expansive room inside inside a dark, wide building. Rows of seats all faced a heavy table and a white chair at the front of the room. At the entrance, the sign read CHURCH OF FATHER CHARLES THE ETERNAL.

One by one, people shuffled down the alley from all directions, paused at the threshold of the tent, and recited the same line with a stumbling whispery breath: "Praise be to Father Charles, may his heart beat with my heart, blood be my blood, eternal and loving." They ducked their heads under the low entryway and stepped through the open doors.

After a few minutes, the doors shut and the morning air was

silent and still again.

Theo followed the direction of the drones, passing by brown wooden doors and brightly painted sheet metal walls of pink and blue and orange.

He walked down the coast, past a blur of narrow alleyways filled with crumbling structures, and ripped tents with wild dogs and chickens roaming the area, pecking and sniffing and digging at the barren ground, until he reached the edge of the settlement and was met by a flat, barren road ahead that led toward the Capital.

It was a straight shot to the steel-wire suspension bridge—that magnificent artifact of ancient brick, stone, and metal. Two massive towers stood hundreds of meters above the water. The sunlight, intense at that morning hour, bathed the bridge in a yellow glow. The weather-worn support cables were polished to a reflective finish. They shimmered like stars. In the sunlight, the side of the bridge became a single golden beam stretching across the water. Its underbelly of gray bricks and stone fell into shadow below.

From that vantage point, Theo got his first close-up view of the Capital.

It spanned the entire horizon—an island of metal, glass, and neon glowing colors. Shining silver towers shot up into the sky. He stepped back to marvel at the city's silhouette, shaped like sharpened swords as if they were preparing for war against the heavens above.

All Midlanders were taught to fear the Capital, but nothing could have prepared Theo for the rush of seeing the skyline. Standing in the wake of the city's extravagance, tears welled in Theo's eyes. His heart pounded with a swirl of emotions. Equal parts curiosity and fear.

Ashen white sea walls surrounded the perimeter of the island. Waves rose from the water and slapped the concrete walls.

Crumbling sheets of ice bumped against one another in the frozen river.

The road hit an incline on its way toward the bridge. Theo pushed ahead and approached an opening under a metal beam, its shadow painting sharp lines into the dirt road.

There was a barrier up ahead. He stepped to the edge. It was a crack in the concrete about two meters wide. The freezing waters churned below. Entire slabs of the road were missing; only the mangled mesh of rebar that once held them in place remained.

Two paths appeared on the other side of the gaping crevice. One path angled up the paved road toward a weather-beaten sign that read: UPPER LEVEL.

The other path extended down toward a barricade boarded up with wooden planks. Moss sprouted within the space between the planks, wet and glistening from the moisture in the air. Theo saw an opening in the darkness.

Above that opening, a metal sign read: LOWER LEVEL.

He paused, took a breath, and looked down at the faint red line scrawled across his arm where the incision had healed. He felt the weight of the chip buried within his arm–barely an ounce of silicon and copper, but heavy with the fate of millions of lives of Midlanders. The feeling crushed and energized him as he watched his muscles bulge beneath his skin, now healed and stronger than ever, thanks to Mae's healing salve.

This path was his burden.

His responsibility.

His oath to Trent and his silent promise to his father to build the machine that would save his life.

Theo exhaled. Focused on the task in front of him. The fortress-like bridge of steel and brick ahead. The sprawling expanse of sharp reflective shapes made up the Capital city and beyond.

Hang on, Father, I'm on my way home, he thought.

The answers were in there.

There was no turning back now.

Theo took five long steps back, and with a running start, he leaped over the concrete crevice. His boots slammed on the far side, and unable to control his momentum, he crashed into the wooden barricade with arms outstretched to slow his body.

A rusted bolt cracked overhead, sending the LOWER LEVEL metal sign swinging down in an arc.

He entered the hollow opening of metal, brick, and wood that made up the lower level of the bridge. The ceiling was boarded up in places, but bright sunlight burst through the open slits. All around him, stockpiles of construction supplies and heavy equipment lined the walkway. Pallets of bricks, cables as thick as his leg, spools of electrical wires with a rainbow of colored cables spilling out from their orange insulating lining.

Theo looked through the openings in the boards above and saw the massive brick towers looming closer with each step. Thicker than a dozen tree trunks and judging from the shadows stretching down the sides of the archway, Theo estimated they must have been at least fifty meters tall or more. He felt eclipsed by its mass, dwarfed by its immense weight pressing into the earth below.

Like the leg of a stone god that walked the earth.

Its gray brick arches were beaten by centuries of decay, unyielding to history.

There was a section of brick up ahead, where the base of the arch passed through the bridge and plunged toward the frozen waters beneath. It was obscured in shadow and crusted over with years of dirt.

Theo placed a hand over the brick and gently brushed away the dirt. It revealed a bronze plaque beneath. Thick numbers were cast into the metal.

18–

He swiped again.

−83

"1883," he spoke aloud to himself.

Suddenly, the bridge began to vibrate. The dirt melted off the plaque like a morning frost. The air around him filled with the suffocating smell of rusted metal, engine grease, and decomposing organic matter.

Footsteps pounded overhead.

Boots. Lots of them.

A heavy vehicle rolled across the upper level. Theo retreated behind a palate of thick wires, spools stacked as high as his shoulders.

The rattling intensified. Under the weight of many men, he heard the wooden beams overhead creak–an old structure from an old world still going strong.

Dirt trickled down from the slats above.

Soldiers, he thought. And that could only mean one thing: Kaiphers would be nearby.

Heavy knotted tires rolled overhead, following the soldiers' footsteps.

A wooden plank snapped, and a thin crack appeared above his head. But it held, and the soldiers didn't appear to notice.

The footsteps and the rumbling subsided, and Theo was left waiting in silence. He looked back at the bronze plaque to find it cleared of dirt, and a golden sheen began to shine through the soft brown coating.

He stepped closer to read: BROOKLYN BRIDGE 1883.

Suddenly, the faint squawk of a radio cut through the silence. That familiar sound of an electronically compressed voice from a sound amplifier embedded into a soldier's helmet.

"Look. There. A footprint. And there, too," said a soldier, "someone's in there."

"Yeah, you go check it out. Let me know what you find,"

another soldier said.

"The fuck man. You go!"

"What the hell, Gomez! Fine. Then, you do not move from this cover. I'm sure it's just a bundle of rats or some shit."

Theo heard boots shuffling. Rapid steps, soft at first but growing louder. Then, a hard stomp and crash. It sounded like one of them jumped across the crevice.

Theo hid behind the brick pillar and flattened himself into a shadow in the corner. He picked up two pieces of heavy rebar from the ground and noticed their rough ribbed pattern stamped into their sides.

Boots approached.

Then, the movement stopped.

Theo waited in silence, with only the churning of the waves below and the sound of his breath surrounding him.

He peered slowly around the pillar.

The soldier hunched low, staring intently at a spot on the ground that glowed in the sunlight. Theo's footprints in the dirt kicked up when the vehicles rolled by.

Theo hid back behind the pillar.

He heard the soldier's rifle spooling up. That familiar whine of magnetic rails charging.

The soldier approached slowly, his hips low and stance stabilized. Rifle high and ready, sweeping left and right in the patches of light and shadow.

"I know you're here," said the soldier. The softness of his voice was haunting through the electronic amplifier.

The soldier took a silent step, pressing his heel into the wood and rolling his foot forward.

"I can sss-smell you," said the soldier, his words trailing off under his breath, "like the cockroach you are."

He was getting closer. Mere steps from the pillar.

Theo tensed his grip on the rebar.

"Why won't you people ever learn," said the soldier in a soothing voice like one would speak to an injured child, "you're not suited for the future. You're not worthy of this new world. You had your run, but you're part of the past."

The soldier took another step closer. His movement was nearly silent, save for the softest crinkle of his leather boots. He searched the pockets of shadow with his rifle.

Frustration grew in the soldier's voice.

"Why can't you see the truth? You're nothing but a leech on this planet."

A swift breeze whipped across the bridge, and only silence remained.

Back toward the entrance, there was a crash of sound. The second soldier must have jumped the crevice. He would be there soon.

Theo saw the barrel of the rifle emerging from the side of the pillar.

"H-6. Got company. Weapons hot," the soldier whispered into his helmet microphone, "cover the rear."

Theo heard a radio confirmation squawk back toward the bridge entrance. The soldier's kinetic stabilizers locked into place from his boots to his legs, sounding like gears in a wind-up clock. The stabilizers clamped down on his hips and encased his chest. It was an elegantly designed exoskeleton, like a metallic spider web as it wrapped around his body, built to absorb the railgun's thunderous recoil.

Hiding behind the pillar, Theo watched as the rifle glided forward.

The soldier's movements were slow and smooth. Finger rested tense against the trigger of the railgun. He stepped forward into a sliver of bright sunlight and was exposed in plain view.

Theo's hands were tense. His grip trembled against his body. With one explosive motion, he raised the rebar in both hands and swung with an ax chop at the soldier's helmet. The knotted steel bars slammed against the soldier, shattering the side of his helmet.

His visor cracked, half of it fell to the ground—a curved piece of translucent composite material with a heads-up display flashing a dizzying array of colorful lines and numerical codes. The soldier whipped his head back and looked directly at Theo with one visible eye. His face was scarred and wrinkled like old leather. Stitch marks ran up and down his forehead and across his cheeks.

He raised the railgun to Theo's chest.

It charged up with a high-pitched whine.

Theo stared straight into the glowing green barrel.

He swung the rebar again, knocking the rifle out of the soldier's hands.

It crashed to the ground.

Theo thrust the second piece of rebar like a spear, plunging it through the center of the soldier's helmet, impaling him through his exposed cheek. The rebar blew through the back of the soldier's head, and his arms dropped limply by his side.

Theo yanked the rebar back. It was painted with a gloss of dark red blood.

The soldier collapsed.

The sound of heavy boots sprinted toward Theo. He turned to look in the direction of the pounding footsteps and saw the second soldier who came up the rear running with his rifle held high, glowing a radiant green.

And pointed right at Theo.

"Got you, you duster scum!" the soldier yelled as he planted his feet and let his suit's recoil-dampening mechanism lock into place before firing his weapon.

Theo flinched.

He anticipated the impact of the tungsten slug gliding through his chest. He shut his eyes, held his breath, and waited for the soft numbness of death.

Would it be a quick death to have your chest excavated and turned into a melting crater, he thought?

Then silence.

He heard the sound of metal and plastic composite clanging to the ground as the soldier dropped the railgun.

Theo opened his eyes and heard the soldier's muffled scream from under his helmet. Gloves clawed in panic, trying to remove his visor. Swirls of smoke erupted from the soldier's face. His skin melted under his helmet. The stinging scent of burning flesh filled the air.

It smelled like burning algae, Theo thought.

The soldier's helmet liquified as it melted into his head. As he ripped his helmet off at the last moment, his left eye burst from the intense heat, and greenish-red blood bubbled from his nose and mouth, his head melting into one amorphous blob of flesh and plastic.

The soldier's knees slammed onto the concrete.

His limp body fell to the floor.

Theo unclenched his eyes, stunned that his chest was intact and confused about how there was a mangled soldier's body in front of him.

"You're freakin' welcome," a shrill voice said from the shadows.

CHAPTER 16

THE GATE

A slender figure stepped into the light. It was a girl a few years older than Theo. He was startled and stepped back, shifting his weight to prepare for a fight or to run.

"How–how'd you... do that?" he asked, after a moment, nodding in the direction of the soldier's body, which had become a melted heap of blood and smoldering flesh.

"That? Easy," she said with a dismissive look. She gestured to an electronic device implanted beneath her skin above her wrist. "Just bypass their suit's central network unit, disable the power regulation system, and crank the circuit throughput sky high. Anything above three thousand pretty much turns them into toast. Easy remote hack. Any idiot can do it."

She squinted at Theo, "You're not from around here, are you?"

Theo opened his mouth to answer but was quickly cut off.

"Well, whoever you are," she said, "if you're looking to get inside the gates today, you'll have to wait until the shift change at sundown just like the rest of us peasants."

The girl shrugged, turned, and walked down the bridge into the shadows.

"Wait," said Theo. He stepped past the metal pillar to follow her, heading toward the bridge's center, "wait! Uh, what's your name?"

She didn't respond.

A swift ocean breeze slammed into his side, almost pushing him off balance.

Up ahead, he saw the girl sitting at the edge of the bridge, leaning against one of the pillars. Her scuffed black sneakers dangled freely off the edge of the bridge. Theo looked up and down both ends of the bridge, back toward the soldier's liquified corpse, but there was no one else around. She came here alone, her loosely cinched backpack flopped on the ground beside her.

Theo approached with hesitant footsteps, glancing up through the boards above to check for the movement of boots or tires or the glow of a soldier's rifle, but the coast was clear.

"I didn't catch your name," he whispered.

She turned and looked him up and down. Long since soaked through with ocean water, his clothes had dried with brown spotted stains from the algae.

"You don't have to whisper here. The wind drowns everything out." the girl pointed up to the wooden rafters above, "They can't hear us from the ninety-seventh pillar." She nodded toward the bridge's entrance, "to the hundred-and-seventh pillar right here." She slapped a hand against the metal pillar behind her. It made a flat thud and vibrated through the floor.

Theo nodded.

After a moment, he set the rebar down and sat at the base of a pillar across from her. In the warm glow of the afternoon light, he finally got a full view of her. Black jeans. Emerald green top, frayed in spots from wear. Long sleeves pinched at the elbow. Dark olive skin and short-cropped black hair with a streak of color singed into the side. An artificial reddish-violet that radiated in the sunlight. A faint glowing light from the computer device implanted above her wrist and a small knife sheath hooked to her belt.

Theo studied her as she stared out across the water. The air was quiet. Her expression, in one moment contemplative and searching, slowly shifted as if an uninvited memory slipped into her subconscious. Her eyebrows bent, and her lips curved downward. For a split second, a deep sadness washed over her face.

Her bag was a jumble of soft fabric. It slouched open, exposing stacks of slender orange bricks wrapped in tight plastic and small silver tubes with frayed red wires.

"Dee," she said.

Theo looked up from her bag. She was staring directly at him. Her eyes were light brown.

"It's short for Desiree," she said.

Theo's face went blank, his mind far away.

"It's my name," she said, nodding and sounding out each word.

"Right... yes, yes" he said, shaking his head, "I'm Theo Rousseau."

Then he heard it. The rumble grew in his chest. The deep vibration that he felt earlier in the day. The melodic whining, like a single musical note, blasting across the landscape. Theo spun around to see two black drones emerging from the haze in the distance. They were speeding directly toward him.

"The collectors will be here soon," said Dee. She spoke quietly as if narrating the events of the world around her to herself. "The sun will set. They rebuild. Then it all repeats."

She let out a long, defeated sigh as she stared at the horizon. Her eyes shifted to the stars in the sky–the first ones emerging as the daylight turned toward evening.

"You're either in the system, or you're out. Banished to the Out City or killed. There's no in-between."

She looked out over the settlement stretching across the landscape. Slums built of tarp tents and metal shacks, with the faint haze of toxic smoke blanketing the city.

"The soldiers, coasters, the entire SCR. Everyone with the blood of Father Charles flowing within them. Nothing changes." she added, "they never die... permanently, that is."

The whistling grew louder. The drones would soon be right on top of Theo and Dee. He could see their heads, round like a bumble bee, as the sunlight glinted off their hundreds of tiny optical lenses.

Two drones raced through the air.

They were a thousand meters away.

A bright spotlight appeared, sending a beam of light in Theo's direction. A wide section of the bridge was lit in a nauseating red glow.

Theo glanced down at his chest. It was solid red and glowing.

Five hundred meters away.

Thin lines began to form a geometric grid of thousands of hexagons that crawled over his entire body. It covered Dee's face, too. The lines expanded and spread across the steel beams above and the bricks and stone below.

He lifted his hand, watching the lines bend and slide across his palm. Dee watched Theo curiously as he played with the light splashing on his hands like liquid. She noticed his exposed neck as he turned to look at the drone flying across the sky. The crystalline pattern on his skin like a stain that refused to fade away.

A look of shock and surprise came across Dee's face.

Without thinking, she raised her hand to her neck and ran her fingers over the hardened grooves in her own skin.

The same mysterious pattern.

The mark of having visited a place not of this world.

"You've been there?" she said sharply, catching her breath as the words left her mouth. "You've been to Calico Hill!"

She spoke in a matter-of-fact tone. A question delivered as a confident statement.

"You know... the island!" she added.

Theo began to answer but was quickly startled by the drone appearing before him. Hundreds of pounds of metal and circuitry hovering in the cold air. A mechanical beast with the grace and agility of a hummingbird. He slid back from the edge of the bridge, making a poor attempt to hide his obvious panic. He kicked dirt up off the floorboards.

He stopped. He suddenly looked back at Dee, her fingers running along identical crystalline grooves on her neck.

Suddenly, the bridge slipped out of view, and Theo shuddered as cold air washed over him, his stomach lurched, and he tumbled into a disoriented memory of the island.

He stood in the middle of a golden field, surrounded by burning trees, looking at Lydia. Ashes floated in the breeze like first snow. Lydia's arms were stretched out toward him. Her fingers were tense. She was begging to be saved. Her eyes were swollen with tears and empty and terrified and lost.

The air smelled sour.

It reeked of death and ash.

Lydia wasn't real.

Lydia was a husk.

She took another step closer, and her hand tumbled into dust. Then, her arm. Then, her shoulder. She screamed as her body began to vibrate, a wretched shrill sound from a world away. Soon, her jaw lost form, and her peach-colored lips and shimmering auburn hair evaporated into the breeze. A cloud of ash sprinkled over Theo and faded away.

"Hellooo?" said Dee.

Theo blinked.

He was ripped out of a memory and found himself back on the bridge with Dee.

Cold metal beside him and wood planks beneath his feet.

The smell of ocean air, salt, and rust.

"What... was that place? That island?" asked Theo.

"You don't know?" said Dee, "you're the first person I've ever met outside of the SCR who has been there before."

She sighed and squinted to look at him, analyzing the details of his face, trying to unpack the puzzle of this stranger in front of her.

"Rumor was that the SCR stumbled upon it in the middle of the ocean while running their scraper ship routes. It doesn't have an actual name. It's just an island that appeared one day, a few hundred years ago. No one really knows where it came from. It's an impossible place. It shouldn't even exist."

"Who put it there?" asked Theo.

"Beats me. No one knows. It's like a myth that sounds like a lie, but it feels real enough that you want to believe it. When I was little, back when my parents were alive, they would drag me there every year on my little brother's birthday. We'd get on that plane, dressed in black, and go visit him. Brady was his name. Well, it couldn't have actually been him. That was impossible. But it looked like him, and his hair was soft like when he was alive. It felt real enough. He even smelled real, like grass and soil and peanut butter. And Brady's soft hands were warm, just like they really were."

She turned to look back out over the horizon.

"Some said it was an island of walking memories. Some said they were souls trapped in an in-between place before they went away... to wherever they went. Or maybe it's all just a fucked up hallucination meant to drive us mad."

She kicked a pebble off the side of the bridge and watched it ride the breeze down to the frozen waters below.

"You see, whenever my parents would take me out there, I would look out the airplane window and see that patchwork of different colored hills dotting the island. It looked like it stretched to the end of the earth, beyond the curve of the horizon. Impossible, I know. But nothing about that island was possible. It didn't make sense. And each tiny figure was standing out there, alone on a tiny hill, each hill with its own unique color, the landscape below looking like a calico cat. My heart would pound so hard I thought I'd be dead before we landed. I dreaded taking that flight, and my hands would shake every time I boarded that plane."

She looked down at her hands, half expecting them to shake from the memory. Long, slender fingers and soft palms bathed in the glowing red light from the approaching drones.

"I always looked for Brady's hill from my window," she smiled momentarily, and then it quickly disappeared, "It was the brightest green hill. And he'd always be riding his orange tricycle through the short grass when we'd show up."

"But why was the island crawling with soldiers?" Theo asked.

"All we know is that the island just appeared one day. Some people wondered if it had been there since the beginning of the world, hidden behind the wall of fog all along, and only now were we allowed to see it. Why now? No one knows. But once the SCR noticed it, they took it over and claimed it as their own. That's what they do best. Study it and inspect it. Determine how they can best exploit it as a resource. Lock it down to everyone except the highest bidders who could afford to pay to visit."

She tried to hold back tears as she spoke.

"Calico Hill. That's what I called it as a kid," said Dee, "all those years, my parents forced me to relive that hell while they lived in a world of delusion. They'd fly to visit him over and over, and he never aged. Always that little tyke with his orange tricycle.

All I know is I'm never returning to that godforsaken place."

The red light grew brighter. It was harsh, and Theo could barely keep his eyes open. The drone's engines were louder now—a sharp pulse that rattled inside his head. Metal tentacles unfolded from the drone's underbelly and extended out toward the soldier's body like long fingers. It wrapped around his legs and arms and scooped under his limp torso, lifting the body into the air. The tentacles formed a cage around the ragdolled body. Melted blood and flesh and gobs of liquified plastic slid down the drone's tentacles and dripped a hundred meters down onto the ice-covered river.

Red stains splattered onto the white ice below.

A second drone appeared behind the first one. It hovered closer and reached its tentacles deep into the bridge to remove the second soldier.

The bright projected lines began to fade. Lights began to flash, blinding pulses streaming across the bridge. Then the red light switched off.

The drones revved their engines to prepare for flight. They shifted their weight and swooped back under the bridge. Within seconds, they shot across the sky, speeding towards Out City's direction and ascending above the plumes of black smoke.

"It all repeats," said Dee, quietly like a whisper in the breeze.

An abrupt wind swept across the bridge. It shoved Theo forward, and he stepped toward the edge to steady himself and catch his balance. He took a breath and relaxed, taking in the full view of the world before him.

Theo stood perched on the edge of that monolith held up by stacks of brick and miles of steel cables. An engineering miracle erected centuries ago when the world was different. Built by the calloused and trembling hands of humans long since dead. Their muscles and bones fed to the earth. Their memories faded.

When the breeze hit him, it felt like he was flying. Floating above the world. Invincible. And suddenly, the enormity of his task—the chip, the Aeonite machine, the dying Midlanders, and his Father—it all came into focus like never before.

Theo turned toward the Capital. He stared at that fortress of glass and steel. Then looked back at Dee.

Until that moment, he hadn't noticed the soft hint of stitch lines running up her arms and alongside the nape of her neck.

"So you're one of them?" said Theo, pointing to her arm.

Dee considered Theo. Tilted her head in thought.

"You sure do have a lot of questions for a normal guy from Out City, Theo."

For the first time in a long time, Theo chuckled aloud.

"I assure you there's nothing normal about me."

"Well, questions are cool with me, but watch your back around here because sometimes walking around with lots of questions will get you into trouble... or worse."

Dee smiled.

"Used to be one of them," she said, "but that was a long time ago, way back in the before times. My family became a target of the SCR for charges of information treason. We were slated to be cast out of the system. You see, in the SCR, it was prohibited to possess written material that didn't come through the government. Everything you read, heard, watched, and saw was carefully curated and picked by Aria Sloan and her council of Kaiphers to ensure a strong alignment with the SCR's goals. But after Brady died, and then my parents soon after, I was the only one in my family left. An 'inconvenient liability' they called me."

"That's why you sneak around?" asked Theo.

"Have to. I was banished from all SCR metropolitan territories. The Out City took me in. Gave me a home. They're a quirky bunch—misfits and outcasts and others who don't fit the SCR's mold of a contributing citizen. The abused, the misshapen, the one in a trillion chance of being born weak or slow or... different. They carve out their place to survive, burn trash for fuel and warmth, and live their short, fragile lives with their children coughing under clouds of toxic fumes. You can't be rebuilt once you're out of the SCR system. Folks in Out City just slowly die a little each day. But they're good people. They'll show you their generosity if you give them a chance. Most of them, at least. And since I know my way around inside the Capital walls, I slip in and scavenge some things when people need them."

"That's what you need the explosives for? Scavenging?" said Theo, looking down toward her drawstring pack and orange bricks, explosives, and chrome detonators.

Dee replied with a smirk. Then, a sigh.

"Theo, have you ever experienced the feeling of waking up one morning knowing in your bones that you were going to change the world?"

Theo considered the question. He felt the muscles in his arms tingle for a fleeting moment.

"Well," Dee continued, "I have."

She reached over and cinched her pack shut, pulling it closer to her body.

Theo and Dee sat in a moment of silence. The sun inched closer to the horizon.

Theo frowned and started pacing back and forth.

"The soldiers won't even be back for another twelve hours, now that the collectors took them back to get rebuilt," Dee said, "and, as I said earlier, the guard shift change doesn't happen until just after sunset so you might as well take a seat and get cozy because you ain't going anywhere in that direction unless you want to head back where you came from."

"But the soldiers... what if they radioed for backup and–"

"I hacked their comms. They were fried to a crisp before you took the first swing with that rebar."

Theo stopped pacing.

"Ah, well, of course you did," said Theo with a smirk.

He sat near the edge and leaned against one of the steel beams.

"So if those were soldiers," said Theo, "what exactly are the Kaiphers?"

"Kaiphers?" asked Dee, "Oh, the Grayskins. The equalizers. They call themselves peacekeepers if you can call that peace. The greatest atrocities in human history have been committed under the excuse of peace. Grayskins made sure nothing threatened the power of the SCR. They hunt down any disturbances or the root of a future disturbance and eliminate them before they become a threat. Protests. Resistors. Dissenters. Saboteurs. Thieves. Grayskins patrol the SCR and hunt down and exterminate anyone and anything that goes against the SCR's view of the world."

"Their view?"

"That only the fit should survive," she said, "only the smartest, the richest, the strongest, the ones with the elite bloodlines... and anyone else is a burden of humanity's forward momentum into the future."

Dee looked toward the stars.

"Not fit," she said softly. Theo detected a hint of sadness in her voice as she spoke.

An hour passed. Maybe more.

Dee watched the sun's movement like a clock, biding time until the fuzzy orange circle positioned itself within a narrow slot between two angular towers in the Capital. Theo observed her silence. There was a calculated way about her underneath that enigmatic exterior.

The sky darkened. Slowly, then all at once. Clouds formed, and it started to rain. Dee got to her feet without a word and snapped her fingers in Theo's direction to get his attention, motioning that it was time to go.

Dee started to walk away, and Theo, not knowing what to

do next, leaped to his feet and followed. She led him across the beams to a gap in the bridge planks. She climbed up and bent her body to fit between two hulking pieces of ancient wood. Theo came up a few paces behind her, contorted his shoulders, and sucked in his stomach to fit, just barely, through the opening.

"There," she whispered, "the guards will change soon. Once they pass the threshold, there will be an eleven-minute, twenty-second window before the next guards arrive. All their defenses run on autopilot, and the systems reboot in a sequence."

Theo looked at the thick metal gate and slate gray towers at the end of the bridge, menacing and tall like the entrance to a fortress.

He turned to Dee with raised eyebrows.

"It's no biggie, chief," she said, "just avoid the scanners, and you're golden."

Dee moved ahead and dug her heels into a bent bolt protruding from one of the vertical beams. She climbed. Theo followed, trying to hide his fear and make his hesitant steps look confident while the rain began to pummel the bridge with heavy beads that blanketed every surface in a reflective sheen. At the top of the beam, they stepped out onto a large coiled cable. Theo looked down at its sharp ridges so tightly intertwined that he couldn't tell where one strand ended and the next began.

It was at least a meter wide, maybe more.

He couldn't wrap his arms around the cable if he tried.

How could any man have built this, he thought?

Raindrops curved down both sides of the cable, and the metal reflected with the bright twinkle of city lights. Dee walked ahead, moving with fast and sure steps. The metal was slippery under the worn threads of Theo's boots. Wind gusts tugged at his side. He took slow steps and tried to keep up with Dee's figure fading in an obscure gray haze up ahead.

Dee crouched on the cable and froze. She was perched on the

edge and looked down toward the end of the bridge a few meters away.

A pair of tall black towers below them overlooked the entrance gate like hawks. Two massive doors were only a short distance beyond the towers.

"We're almost there," Dee whispered, pointing to the edge of the bridge. Theo saw nothing but bricks and metal and bright reflections below. The lights were mesmerizing and caught his eye as he almost missed seeing Dee grab onto a cable, clamp her feet together, and slide down the side of the cable in one acrobatic feat. She landed deftly, out of sight from the sensor towers.

She shot Theo a look.

"C'mon," she whispered, then disappeared under the cover of shadows.

Theo followed. He kept his trembling steps centered on the cable, pressing each step into the metal to secure his footing.

But his foot started to slip, and he quickly spread his arms out to stabilize himself.

In a jolt of movement, he made the mistake of looking down at the fractal shapes of ice splashing hundreds of meters below where the bridge thrust into the river. The wind gusted once again, and at that moment, at the top of that bridge with the dark thunderous sky closing in from above. His insides felt a new level of cold.

"Almost there," he heard Dee's voice, a piercing whisper, from a spot in the shadows below, "let's get a move on!"

Theo reached the end of the walkway and grabbed the cable to slide down.

Clouds exploded above, and water came down in sheets, crashing against the wooden planks on the bridge below. Wind gusts swirled, and the temperature plummeted in a matter of seconds.

He reached out and curled his fingers around the line, forming a tight grip.

Felt a burst of air that was growing more powerful.

Bile rose from his stomach into his throat.

The wind whipped his hair in front of his face.

And then he realized: he was falling.

One foot slipped on the cold, slick metal, and Theo tumbled with outstretched arms and collided on the wooden road below with a wet thud.

Everything was black.

Lights and colors swirled in his head.

The world was empty, and he lay there in a cottony silence, rain slapping his face. Wet and cold in his eyes. Water fell into his nostrils. An electric jolt of pain flashed through his neck and back.

He heard Dee's voice.

She was screaming about time, or now, or being out of time or something.

He pushed himself up, straining to get a purchase on the slippery road, patches of skin on his palms and elbows ripped.

The fog cleared in his head. His vision snapped back to reality. Theo found himself staring up at two glowing optical lenses at the top of the tower looming down upon him like the eyes of a hulking cat inspecting cornered prey.

A blinding light burst overhead like an exploding star. The floodlights had turned on. Theo flinched at the sight of it. It blanketed the bridge in white light. Raindrops illuminated. Angled lines of water pelted the ground.

"Theo!"

He put his weight on his knee and stood up, shaky and unsteady.

He heard Dee screaming in the distance.

"We have to get out of here before–"

A tremor shook through the bridge.

A loud clang of metal was deafening. It startled Theo as he regained his balance.

The tremor grew to a persistent rumble as the wide metal doors began to slide, and the gate opened wide. Beams of violet and blue and orange lights burst through the cracks.

A voice boomed on the loudspeaker. It was the robotic voice of a woman. It was shrill and highly compressed.

"Welcome, Mr. Naram," the voice blasted from the top of the sensor towers.

Theo stared through the opening of the gate. Massive doors slid open to reveal illuminated neon roads, like crystal pathways snaking through the shimmering city of reflective surfaces and sharp angular lines. It was mesmerizing. Towering buildings were outlined in glowing, vibrant colors.

The raindrops subsided. Swirling winds began to die down. Clouds that once churned violently were abruptly frozen in time for an impossible moment. He felt the gravity of that place reaching across space, pulling him closer. An intense magnetism stretched throughout the cells within his muscles and bones.

A terrible feeling.

A freeing feeling.

Like a child staring into a lit match, understanding for the first time the beauty of a dancing flame and the allure of destruction.

The ringing in his ears began to clear.

A piercing voice cut through the confusion. It was piercing and growing louder.

"Theeeeo we neeeeeed to move now!" Dee screamed.

She was at the edge of the bridge, peeking out from the shadows with an outstretched arm and panic on her face.

Theo ran to her. Puddles splashed beneath his boots as they pounded the bridge. He caught her hand, slid under the bridge, and disappeared into a hidden pathway below.

Dee led him down crumbling concrete stairs. He tried to place his steps carefully, only able to see a few feet before him, praying that one misstep wouldn't send him tumbling into the darkness. Dee tugged on his arm as the steps gave way under their feet.

A sharp wind rushed past his face, and they slid down the steep interior of the cement sea wall. It was slick with a gelatinous substance, cold to the touch and absent of anything to grasp to slow his descent.

Theo was falling, accelerating faster and faster. He couldn't see what awaited him at the end of the slide. He was flailing, extending his feet out to brace for impact.

The air smelled strongly of salt, and then he heard a splash nearby as Dee plunged into a waist-high pool of water. Theo followed, crashing into the bone-chilling water a few seconds later. He tumbled forward and lay motionless for a moment to catch his breath before looking up to find Dee.

It was too dark to see anything, with only muted lights glowing like dim stars above. The air was eerily still. A strange but familiar feeling.

Dee emerged from the dark with a splash. Theo saw her shape walking closer. A blur at first, then the outline of her hair, face, and eyes.

He felt her fingers wrap around his wrist.

She twisted his arm behind his back, yanked him to his feet, and shoved him face-first into the cement wall.

The wall was frigid against his cheek. It was wet with a layer of slime.

Ocean waves growled on the other side of the sea wall, a loud rumbling like the churning stomach of a sleeping giant.

"That gate doesn't open for just anyone!" said Dee, anger rising in her voice.

Theo felt the prod of a cold gun barrel pressed into his neck.

"Now just who the hell are you, really?"

CHAPTER 17
THE FORGOTTEN CITY

The cold gun barrel was steady as it pressed into his flesh. Dee's hands didn't tremble. She was calculated. Experienced.

"I-I don't know what you're–"

"Your name! Your real name! Tell me what it is!"

Theo took a breath, unsure how to respond. A slug passed by his face, crawling along the sea wall and leaving a meandering trail of slime.

"Don't fuck with me. I'll coat this seawall with your brains! It'll be a feast for the slugs. They'll love it!"

Theo shifted his feet to find his balance.

"My name... is Theo Rousseau. I told you before. I swear it!"

"That's not what I heard on the scanner," said Dee, "it scanned you. It opened the gate for you. I've never seen that happen before for someone from Out City. Why? Who are you?"

"I'm not–"

"From around here?" said Dee, cutting him off, "Yeah, I hate to break it to you, but that's not going to fly anymore. The gate only opens for true Coasters who have the blood of Father

Charles in their veins. Those scanner towers can read your DNA. No one can fake that. Not even me. You lied to my fucking face."

Theo sighed.

"Alright, I lied. I'm sorry," said Theo, "but not about my name. I lied about what I'm doing here. My mission."

"We all got a mission, chief," said Dee, "we all got a fucking purpose. And I got my own things to take care of, and I don't have the luxury and time to deal with your bullshit."

Dee shoved him forward, pressing his face into the wall. She released his arm and stepped back, keeping the pistol raised at his center mass. Theo turned around slowly, half of his face glistening with sticky residue.

"You know what?" said Dee, after a sudden change of heart, "I don't care; I don't want to know."

Theo caught a glimpse of the revolver: a short barrel coated with rust and frayed duct tape around the grip. He looked at Dee and tilted his head in question.

"I bet you don't even have bullets in that thing, do you?" Theo said.

"I don't, do I? You want to find out?"

Dee took another step backward, the revolver aimed at Theo. Her heel caught the ridge of a cement curb, and she tumbled to the ground.

She flinched, firing the gun in Theo's direction.

A slug on the sea wall exploded in a puff of pebbles and slime. Theo quickly crouched to the side.

Dee clumsily got to her feet and wiped herself off. She took a breath and turned to Theo.

"I led you past the gates. Consider that my gift to you. Now, I want nothing to do with you, your lies, and whatever else you're involved in. I got my own thing going on, and it's bigger than you and bigger than me. You know what's the only thing I have left in this broken world? Justice! That's all I have. And I work alone."

Dee lowered the revolver.

"And don't you dare follow me," she added, "I swear if I catch you trailing the next time, I won't miss."

She turned, jogged down the block, rounded a building at the intersection, and disappeared into the shadows.

Theo got out of the water and collapsed onto the ground of cracked cement with patches of dark gray asphalt.

He rolled onto his back, soaked through to his core.

Up above, everything was darkness. It looked like he was in a cave of impossible size. The ceiling was hundreds of meters high. Tiny lights dotted the ceiling. Orange and white dots and sharp, thin lines that glowed at right angles. When his eyes acclimated to the light, he saw it in more detail: a patchwork of panels mounded high above. Illuminated gaps between the panels looked like artificial stars—a grid of giant columns surrounding him held up the Capital city above like stilts.

"They paved over the past," the snaking sound of Sam's voice revisited Theo in the moment of silence, "left it all behind to rot as they charged blindly into the future. I suppose it's the Coaster way, after all."

Theo got to his feet and looked around at the brick, metal, and glass buildings up and down the street. Sidewalks disappeared into a pitch-black infinity. The avenue straight ahead extended a mile or two before terminating at another seawall. The roads to his left and right ran far into the distance with no end in sight.

Strange bent shapes marked the path ahead. Traffic lights and ancient stop signs were tilted at odd angles. A flattened chain-link fence snaked across the street. A brick building with a red awning hung on to cracked bolts while the world decayed around it.

People used to live here, he thought.

Torn fabric drapes and triangles of broken glass where windows used to be.

In another time long ago, he thought.

Up ahead, there was a hole in the middle of the building as wide as a truck, as if a colossal machine plowed through, leaving a trail of destruction in its wake. Soft puffs of weeds pierced through the concrete.

Life discovered a way to keep going, he thought.

Swing sets. A jungle gym. Bent bicycle wheels emerged from the ground.

Rows and rows of houses led to an open plaza.

He looked up at the ceiling lights. Dots and lines of a soft glow leaked through the panels above. As he continued walking, the lights stayed fixed in space like the stars in the forest back home. It was an unnerving feeling to navigate that massive manmade cavern. Towering columns held up an entirely new city, street panel by street panel. They were the only things keeping it from collapsing onto the ancient ruins below.

"The new tide washes away the old in a cloud of brick and dust," said Sam's ghostly voice.

Theo sighed louder than he expected. His voice was swallowed by the darkness. Only silence remained.

He found a park bench to rest. It was missing two wooden slats, but those that remained had kept it standing for many years. Maybe decades. He lowered his weight onto the seat and an overwhelming wave of fatigue washed through his muscles and bones.

The plane. The island. The ship. The bridge. Now he sat on a decaying bench, lost in the forgotten wasteland of an old city.

This wasn't how it was supposed to go, he thought.

"If you were home," said Sam's voice emerging from the shadows, "Trent could have built the machine by now. And Father could have been–."

Theo shook away tears, and his body felt so heavy, tugging down toward the earth as his heart sank. The streets were lifeless. He was trapped in a metal and concrete cavern.

"A forgotten city," said Sam, "and a soon-to-be-forgotten son like you."

Theo scraped the back of his head on a bent piece of metal sticking through the wooden slats. It was a street sign connected to a pole jutting up from the sidewalk. He pushed it away from the bench, and a light layer of dust cascaded off the sign, revealing a rich green coat of paint. The letters underneath read: BOWERY.

Jolts of cramping pain shot through his back and neck as he lay down on the bench. He looked up at the soft glow of the manufactured constellations above and closed his eyes in the dusty light.

CHAPTER 18

NOODLES AND DUMPLINGS

He woke alone in the dark.

How long was I asleep, he thought?

With a parched throat and cramped neck, Theo sat up on the bench, which creaked as he moved. The sharp pinholes of light hadn't changed at all. They still shined through the panels high above.

In the distance was the base of the bridge, which connected to the seawall.

That must be south, he thought.

The road continued without end, fading into darkness in the other direction.

Theo started walking north with nothing but the shuffling of his feet to fill the silence.

The street widened. Skeletal remains of structures from a past world extended into the distance. Metal bars shaped like ladders hung up on the sides of buildings, their brick facades partially ripped to the ground. Some windows were utterly bare, and it was a miracle that others were still intact, with the occasional pane of broken glass. Fallen street lights crisscrossed the intersections. Holes ripped into the asphalt suggested the use of controlled demolition blasts.

There were explosive charges in Dee's pack, he remembered.

Theo peeked below the surface and saw the outline of tunnels, streets or even entire cities underground.

There was a faint light in the distance that flickered and then disappeared. Shapes blended together when everything was blurry, gray, and brown from fatigue.

Is this the direction Dee went, he thought?

The darkness never seemed to end. It was a lifeless world until Theo noticed one single door, far in the distance, several streets away.

As he approached the building, the door's outline became clear. A faint light shone through the hinges. He would never have caught it if the surroundings weren't so impossibly dark.

It was a nondescript building. Three stories tall, or at least that's what was still standing. Brick as dark as old timber. Stone sculptures adorned the window frames that had a distinct swooping curve like a bird's wings.

Theo stepped up to the illuminated door and slowly pulled the tall cylindrical handle. He peeked inside as the door swung open. Stairs led down toward an underground entrance; each step was immaculate. It was uncharacteristically clean, given the trash debris and black dust scattered throughout the streets. He stepped down the stairs and hesitated, glancing back as if expecting something hidden to stalk up from behind. But there was nothing but silence and empty streets.

Halfway down the stairs, he heard the muffled sound of music and laughter, glasses clinking, and chairs sliding across a hard floor. At the bottom of the stairs, he reached a large wooden door carved with intricate geometric patterns. Neon red, blue, and violet light bled through from behind the door.

Theo pushed it open.

He stumbled into a bustling scene and winced at bright lights and loud noises that assaulted his senses. Small tables lined the side walls. Patrons sat on mismatched stools and chairs, their body types and colorations as eclectic as their mismatched seating choices. Paper lanterns hung from the ceiling, bathing the room in a dream-like glow. There was a bar in the center with a dozen stools, half occupied by patrons slurping from bowls and drinking from frosted glasses.

After walking through a lifeless world for so long, Theo could hardly believe the scene unfolding before him, like a portal to another world entirely. Everyone in the room was so engrossed in conversation that no one paid Theo any attention until a familiar voice shouted from the back corner of the room.

"Well, well, well, if it ain't our lit-tle orphan!"

A wiry man with a disfigured face and scraggly beard approached Theo. Theo would have recognized those rat-like features and that pockmarked face anywhere.

"You've been following us, eh?" asked Deak, "Come to take back what was rightfully yours? Withdrawing your generous donation of resources to our organization?"

Deak sidled up to him and poked two bony fingers sharply against Theo's chest. Familiar memories came flooding back: being startled awake from a warm sleep with that rancid breath and that twitching left eye.

"Because I don't like to be followed," said Deak, "In fact, I don't like it when little daisies like you come gettin' the nerve to think you can just barge right in and disturb my eve-nin." Behind Deak, two familiar figures sat at a table. The short-statured one with glasses and the towering figure as wide as the door Theo had just come through, with a small head atop the man's shoulders.

In a flash of motion, Deak pressed a cold blade to Theo's neck.

Theo froze.

A pop of gunfire exploded.

The crowd fell silent like the air had been sucked out of the room.

Patrons stopped mid-conversation and stared at the altercation by the entrance. All eyes were on Deak's hand. Two fingers that were present a moment ago were missing, and red blood streamed down the newly exposed stump of a white knuckle.

"Gettheffffuck out, Deak!" yelled someone from the back of the room. She held a smoking snub-nosed revolver in her hand, and her speech was slurred. Theo recognized that revolver and that dark hair with a reddish-violet streak.

Deak howled in pain, and Theo reached up to liberate the knife from what was left of his bloody hand. Deak stumbled toward the door, one hand clenching his ruined fingers, and nearly crashed into a table before slipping out the door. His frantic footsteps smacked the wooden stairs on his way up. Big boy and spectacle man—Deak's two companions—looked at each other in shock and indecisiveness. After an awkward moment, they dropped their mugs and chopsticks and rushed out of the room.

Theo looked back at Dee. The revolver, still in hand, was pointed in his direction; her arm wobbled lightly as she leaned an elbow on the counter to stabilize herself. Then she turned around and nudged a stool open beside her.

Theo considered the invitation.

He wiped the knife across his pant leg, blood smearing across the collection of algae and slug-slime stains, and walked over to the open stool.

Red and purple lights shone brightly from lanterns above. The entire bar glowed in warm colors.

Theo sat, slid his stool forward, and set the knife on the counter.

Dee raised two fingers and waved at a tall man behind the

counter. He was rail-thin, with loose clothes that draped over his bony joints like a skeleton wrapped in fabric. The man stepped up to a rectangular machine behind the counter that was the size of a large semi-truck engine and typed a string of keystrokes onto an attached keyboard. Something in the machine spun and glowed molten red, and thirty seconds later, it let out a sharp sizzling sound similar to meat hitting a hot pan.

The machine dinged. The thin man reached into a side compartment and pulled out a bowl of steaming hot food. He slid it in front of Theo without saying a word.

"Thank you, Howie! Noodles and dumplings, dumplings and noodles," said Dee, hunched over and staring blankly into her bowl. "If you close your eyes while you chew, it's not terrible. The protein and fiber extruders here are pretty damn good. The flavor is seventy percent there, even if you don't have the implants."

Theo stared into his bowl at the long white tendrils and translucent blobs that resembled noodles and dumplings in a mysterious brown sauce.

The thin man refilled Dee's shot glass with a clear liquid. It smelled like a pipe degreaser.

"Implants?" said Theo.

"Yeah, up in here," said Dee, tapping a spot at the back of her head behind her left ear, "as long as those are calibrated correctly, you know, to the, uh," she snapped her fingers in the air, trying to recall the words, "the make and model of the protein extruder, it takes the slop from that machine and makes it taste like you're sitting at the counter at a noodle shop in Tokyo Station eating a late lunch during rush hour."

Theo grabbed a fork from a basket of utensils on the counter piled with chopsticks, soup spoons, and napkins. He poked at the contents of his bowl. When the first bite landed on his tongue, the chemicals in his brain kicked into overdrive, and he suddenly remembered that he hadn't eaten in at least a day. A ravaging hunger stormed from within, and he slurped down the noodles and dumplings so quickly that he placed the fork down with a breathless sigh.

He looked over and caught Dee staring at him, watching him eat. He couldn't tell if the look on her face was shock, disgust, or a mix of both.

"That was amazing," said Theo, his gaze pointing back at the extruder machine behind the counter.

"Do you... want..." said Dee.

"More?" said Theo with a snap response, "If, well, yeah... I mean, if–"

Dee waved at the thin man. He typed a string of numbers onto the keyboard. The machine whirred and spat out another steaming bowl.

"We got as much as we want until the protein blocks run out," said Dee, pointing to the stack of white boxes behind the extruder machine. "But the crowds have been slow lately since the SCR started raiding sections of Out City. Demolishing the shanties and ripping up the concrete and dirt. I don't know why. Nothing the SCR does makes sense anymore. And the Out City folks have been moving farther inland and are less willing to come down here to the Under City. So eat up, kid!"

Dee raised her glass and cheered the air.

"We only have the noodle bowl recipe in the system, for now at least. Thankfully it ain't half bad."

Theo pulled the bowl close and ate like a stray dog until the second bowl was empty. He belched as he wiped his chin.

"Someone's a fan of your work, Howie," said Dee to the thin man behind the counter. Howie chuckled. He pulled a dish towel from his apron, wiped down clean bowls, and stacked them into heavy plastic bins.

Theo looked around at the peculiar decor. Wood slab counter

and metal tabletops in the back. Paper lanterns stuck to the ceiling with string and tape. Mismatched stools and chairs. Everything, including tabletops and the extruder machine behind the counter, seemed to be resting on stacked plastic bins. The entire place was as temporary as a set from an elaborate stage play. Theo wondered if the whole joint could be packed into a few dozen boxes and moved if needed.

"How do the umm?" Theo pointed to the ceiling, motioning to the city above. "How do they not find you down here?"

"The SCR?" said Dee, "They couldn't care less. This place is dead to them. A non-threat, so they think." she chucked at her own words and slurped down a long gray-brown noodle. "Besides," she added, "we move around so often, they'd never be fast enough to notice. We move up and down the island whenever we want. We have thirteen whole miles of absolutely nothing but crumbling buildings and not a soul in sight, and that's just counting the surface streets. Don't even get me started on the mole people in the tunnels down below. So, we set this place up, have some fun, move, and we've never been in the same place twice."

Dee took a shot of a clear liquid in her cup. A stinging aroma hung in the air.

"Why'd you save me back there?" said Theo.

Dee considered him, for a moment, with a bend to her neck like she was struggling to stay vertical.

"I'mmmnotsure," she said, "Haven't made up my mind about you yet."

She wiped a hair out of her face.

"I've never seen that gate open for anyone from Out City before. Most of us die young. The misfits and the exiled. The SCR doesn't see us as much of a threat. In fact, it's too much work to hunt us all down. A waste of resources. Inefficient, they'd say. They just keep us out and turn a blind eye and wait for us to die out from pricking our foot on a rusted nail or getting a bad fit of pneumonia."

Dee scraped her chopsticks along the bottom of the bowl, soaking her last gelatinous blob, which was meant to taste like a dumpling, in a pool of thick sauce.

"That still doesn't explain..." she pointed her chopsticks at Theo, drawing circles in the air, "youuuu. Who are youuuu? And how did you open that gate?"

"I truly have no idea," said Theo, "It must be a glitch, or maybe the rain caused a short in their sensors."

"Nope, not a glitch," said Dee, "The SCR doesn't make mistakes like that. They can be slow and sometimes get in their own way. But if there's one thing I know, it's that they do not have glitches."

"I'm just a guy trying to get home. And I'm looking for a lion. I was told it's somewhere in the Capital, and it's my ticket out of here."

Dee turned silent. For a moment, she didn't breathe, just stared into her empty bowl. She painted thin lines of brown sauce along the inside of the bowl with her chopsticks. She frowned, wrestling with something inside her head, the alcoholic haze clearing and a singular dangerous thought emerging in her mind.

"Okay," she said into her bowl.

"Okay? To what? What does that mean?"

"The lion. I can take you."

Theo had a skeptical look on his face. He almost spoke, but didn't.

"I know where that is," she said, "it's here, but it's not in the Capital. It's underneath. I can show you, but I'll need something from you first."

And there is it, the barter, he thought.

"You run an errand for me, and I'll deliver you to the lion."

Theo sighed.

"What exactly do you have in mind?" he asked.

"Well, you seem to have a unique talent for getting into the Capital. That's a bit of a rare commodity around here. They pretty much rolled out the red carpet for you on the bridge. And as it turns out, there's something I need from up there," said Dee, pointing toward the ceiling.

"What kind of something?"

"Information. Signal frequencies, to be precise. The SCR keeps things locked down and has tight control over any information flowing in or out of the Capital—and the whole coast, for that matter—but not nearly to the same extent. They jam almost all of the wireless frequencies within the Capital except a few that are left open for Kaipher's operations. But I can't get close enough to scan for the open frequencies."

"And you need these frequencies for?"

"Remember, back on the bridge, when I said I knew in my bones that I would change the world? Well, I'm going to. But those details are above your pay grade, chief," said Dee with a smirk, poking her chopskins in his direction.

Theo rolled his eyes and sighed.

"You said you can't scan for them yourself. What exactly does 'close enough' mean?"

"Inside the upper walls. Inside the Capital."

"Let me guess... that's where you need me?"

Dee raised a half-full shot glass, clinked a cheer into the air, and drank. She reached into her bag and pulled out a small metal device barely larger than the palm of her hand. The device had a tiny screen on one side and a battery pack stuck to the back with thin beads of hardened epoxy.

"I need you to take this scanner and walk through the Capital streets until you find five open frequencies," Dee pointed to the screen on the device that was actively scanning the airwaves, "when you see this line jump up, you push this button here to record the frequency on the local onboard memory. Get me five, and the job's gone. Then I'll take you to your lion."

"Woah, woah, wait a second," said Theo, "You want me to–"

"Yes. Walk through the Capital and get five frequencies."

"I heard you, but..." Theo took the device into his hand, flipped it over, and examined it, feeling its weight and balance. "You said these are the same frequencies the Kaiphers use, right? So what's to stop them from shooting me on site?"

"Well, they scanned your eyes and opened the gates for you, so in theory that shouldn't happen."

"In theory?!"

***

Theo tensed his grip around a knotted steel cable and tried to hide the fact that his hands were shaking. He placed another hand on the cable and watched a curve ripple up the ladder. It was a hideous thing–this ladder Dee and her people built out of surplus metal cables stolen from the bridge. It was braided and clamped in spots. Misshapen joints reinforced each rung. But what it lacked in looks, it made up for in durability.

Theo gave it another tug.

Not an elegant design, but it'll probably last a decade, he thought.

"And remember," said Dee, "as soon as you reach the surface, put on the suit. It'll help you blend in with the populace. Luminescent filaments embedded into the suit will light up from your body's electromagnetism, so you don't need to do anything to activate it. Just make sure you wear it at all times, otherwise–"

Dee tilted her head and looked away instead of finishing her sentence.

Theo stood at the base of the concrete column. It rose at least a hundred meters into the air and disappeared into the hazy darkness.

Dee watched him look up and down the length of the column, sizing it up.

"And no matter what, don't ever, ever look down," said Dee.

Theo frowned and let out a glimpse of a smirk.

"Oh, and one more thing–"

"Another thing?"

"Yes," said Dee, walking up to fiddle with the straps on Theo's backpack. She yanked on each strap to check that it was tight. His body jerked back from the motion. "You know, just to be sure. You don't want this thing swinging loose when you're a hundred meters up with no backup safety line and climbing in the pitch dark–"

"Okay, okay," said Theo. He raised a hand and looked away, "I've heard enough. Let's get this thing done."

"And remember," said Dee, "Five codes. Find them, push the button, and then get the fuck out of there."

Theo nodded.

He inserted a radio transmitter into his right ear and patted his hands against his pockets one last time to make sure he had Dee's transponder device.

He looked up. A trail of silver cables snaked up into the dark.

High above, the constellation of lights twinkled from the Capital city.

He stepped onto the first rung of the ladder.

CHAPTER 19
THE CAPITAL

Theo kept climbing, unaware of how much time had passed. He still couldn't see the top of the ladder.

Was this how Sam felt in his last moments, he thought? The pull of gravity below him, his fingers tight with fear around the metal rung.

When Theo reached the halfway point of the ladder, the faint outline of the top rung emerged out of the darkness. His mind flooded with the sound of Sam falling, nothing but the calm passing of wind, and otherwise the deathly silence of his brother's tiny, flailing body speeding through the air.

An icy feeling shot through Theo's body. His chest tightened, and his breath became strained. When his focus returned, he found himself looking directly down the ladder into the darkness.

Exactly what Dee cautioned against.

He tensed his arms and pulled his body close to the ladder. The abrupt movement sent twists rippling up and down the ladder. It whipped him side to side, swinging in the air, and he slammed his elbows against the concrete column. He hugged the steel cables and took a deep breath.

Once the ladder steadied, he continued to climb. The outline of the world above appeared. Glowing dots like stars in the sky stretched across the grid of panels—dark patches in some areas and sharp angled lines of light in others where the panels intersected.

Ten more rungs.

He kept climbing.

Theo reached the top of the ladder. There was a gap in the street right above his head. Light bloomed through jagged opening. He could see the entire picture now: the new Capital city built upon panels held up by concrete columns high above the old abandoned city below.

He reached in and pushed up with all his strength until a small panel swiveled open like a miniature door.

The city was made of pink and orange light. It smelled of fresh rain. The light was blinding as he pulled himself through the doorway.

Theo stuck his head out and cautiously looked around. He was in a back alley of some kind, positioned in a dark corner between a glass-walled building to his left and a metal-paneled building to his right. The smooth artificial ground was covered in rain puddles, creating a kaleidoscope of reflected light.

Seeing no one around, Theo pushed through the opening. As his foot left the ladder, his backpack snagged on the sharp edge of the panel, and he heard the sound of a violent rip coming from behind him.

"Shit," he whispered, falling to the wet ground, instantly soaked through to his underwear. He swiveled the backpack around to inspect the damage. There was a tear down the left side, and the clothing inside looked torn.

Dee had told him over and over to put the suit on the moment he arrived.

He pulled the jumble of navy blue fabric from the backpack and unfolded the jacket. He put it on, pulled the collar taut. It was a sharp, crisp fit.

Theo crouched and checked that the alley was clear. He stood up slowly, listening carefully to the whisper of strange sounds floating by. The air was cool. A refreshing after-rain sweet.

Suddenly, the wall beside him was washed in a flood of pink light. Then, a garbage dumpster to his left turned bright red.

He looked down at the jacket. It was illuminating with thin colors of light circling his collar, gliding down his sharp shoulders and running the length of his arms. Dee had said the filaments would light up from his body's electromagnetism.

A warmth bloomed in his chest, feeding the light source and brightening the jacket's colors. For a moment, the jacket was more than an accessory, the light more than a decoration. It was a part of him—an extension of the light that burned within. He knew he had never been here before, worn these clothes in this alien place, but yet an oddly familiar feeling rushed over him, one that was comforting.

Like childhood. Like his own blood.

It was like coming home.

A sound at the end of the alleyway.

Footsteps and laughter. It was getting closer. He eyed a nearby doorway just beyond the dumpster. He tucked the ripped backpack under the dumpster. As he glanced down at the illuminated jacket, the left sleeve peeled off from the shoulder and hung halfway detached and dangling.

When he tore the backpack, the jacket inside tore as well.

Footsteps stopped. A spark of high-pitched laughter echoed down the alley. Then silence. Theo pulled the loose fabric back over his shoulder and peeked around the corner.

A young couple stood a dozen meters away, pinned against the wall. His sleeves glowed blue, and her dress was ruby red.

His lips were on hers. Their colors melded into the same shade of orange like a sunrise. The colors pulsed together in sequence when they touched. They were silent and distracted.

Theo bolted across the alley toward a doorway, trying not to slip on the rain puddles dotting the ground. He crashed through the door into a long gray hallway that reeked of stale tobacco. A broken light flickered overhead. Sounds of bells and musical instruments grew louder from the other end of the hall.

He followed the sound. He turned another corner and came to an interior door. The door muffled the loud noises and blasting music, but much of it still leaked through.

He opened the interior door and entered a cavernous room hazy with cigarette smoke and smelling like sweaty upholstery. The light was cold and harsh to his eyes. The carpet was angry yellow with dark orange stripes. All along the walls were narrow rows of Pachinko machines, hundreds of them, in long lines that curved in such a way to visually obscure the exits of the room. It seemed to stretch on forever like a maze of maddening colors and sounds. The noise was unbearable, like an alarm clock spinning out of control, hammering shrill musical tones deep into his ear.

People dressed in illuminated clothes lined the seats, their faces sunken and spines twisted and hunched from sitting for many hours.

"Ha-HAAAAAHHHH!" a man shook with jubilant laughter as his machine struck a winning play. Theo started to walk past the man when he suddenly burst out again into a loud, gut-wrenching sob. From afar, it must have sounded like a murder was taking place. Tears streamed from the man's eyes. His shoulders quivered uncontrollably like he was possessed by a manic spirit. He took a sharp puff of a mechanical inhaler that flooded his lungs with calming chemicals, and his mood shifted again. He stared at his winnings with swollen red eyes and a blank, dead stare, drool pooling on his lips as heavy tokens tumbled into the metal receptacle beside him.

Theo walked on, moving down the aisle of machines, and slipped past people with erratic emotional outbursts that came and went with each play.

He heard status crackle in his earpiece. As if by reflex, he reached into his pocket and gripped Dee's frequency recorder.

"You there?" said Dee.

"Copy."

"You need to get out in the open before you can run a scan."

Theo moved toward the front of the building, where glass doors with gold trim adorned the entrance. He walked past the last row of machines banging with jackpot bells and came across a floor-to-ceiling tower of holographic display panels. Light hit the grid of reflective nodes, and a larger-than-life three-dimensional image of a nude woman appeared. She was dancing and spinning, the projected light struggling to pierce the smoky air. The advertisement voiceover came over directional speakers, but Theo could hardly recognize a word from the cacophony of the sound.

He pushed through the glass doors and spilled into an open plaza teeming with neon people.

A tiny silver drone fluttered above Theo's head and swooped down to hover at eye level a few meters away.

Like the drone that blinded Kristof, he thought.

It scanned his eyes.

"Mr. Naram! Book your visit today to the great and magnificent island between two worlds!"

He watched as a three-dimensional model of his face floated above the drone. The person in the image—it was Theo, but it wasn't Theo—raised a pair of chrome sunglasses to his face. The man smiled a wide, beaming grin, and the sunglasses illuminated. Other figures join him to his left and right. An elderly man and woman stepped forward into the three-dimensional image, and a young boy with short-cropped hair appeared beside them. They smiled, embraced, and watched the sunset together in a golden field of grass.

"A magical place like no other, Mr. Naram! On the island between two worlds, goodbye mustn't be forever. Book your visit today on SCR daily charter flights!"

"Hey, chief!"

Dee's voice snapped him back to reality and the mission at hand.

"Pull up the scanner," she continued, "you might be in a good spot to pick up something."

"Copy," Theo whispered.

He found an inconspicuous area under the shadow of a street lantern, which was wrapped with a colorful, snaking vine from a nearby potted plant.

He pulled the scanner from his pocket.

A series of numerical digits spun up and down. The digital bar jumped halfway to the top of the meter. It was a medium-strength frequency, but not quite what he was looking for.

Theo walked through the plaza past a group of people in colorful suits and dresses. One man with an angular mustache cut into sharp lines, with thin metal glasses with no lenses. The man smiled, delivering the punchline of a joke and bathing in praise as the group laughed. Their clothing pulsed in unison with bright golden lights as they walked along as a group, synced in their movements and their social behaviors.

Theo watched the group walk by, and when he turned around, he almost collided with a tall, thin woman with a bright violet eye. Her figure seemed odd, verging on distorted, resembling the attributes of a limber animal as much as a human being. She stared directly at him as she sidled by. He was so distracted by her eyes that seemed to glow from within her skull that he almost missed a small but essential detail: studded bumps running up her neck as if her skin had recently been stitched back together.

After the woman walked past him, Theo stopped in his tracks, looked up towards the open sky, and saw them.

Three figures with bags over their heads hung by a dark wire that would have entirely disappeared against the dim blue sky if it weren't for the glow of the street lamp. They hung motionless, with the letters NOT FIT scrawled across their naked chests by a sharp blade. Dark lines of dried blood clung to their skin, faded by several days of intense sunlight.

Theo gasped.

"Wha-what is it," said Dee.

He looked around at all the people in vibrant dresses going about their business, unphased by the bodies hanging for all to see.

"No, it's just, um, bodies... there are bodies... hanging," said Theo.

Dee was silent.

"Two adults and a..." Theo struggled to finish his sentence, "... a kid."

"Yeah," she said, "that's what they do to those who don't fall in line. Those who are not fit for the future."

Theo could hear her hands forming air quotes around her words. He scoffed, half out of disgust and half out of surrender.

"And who decides who is fit or not?" said Theo.

"Simple," said Dee, "Aria Sloan. Always."

Her voice cut out to static for a moment.

"Just be thankful they're not executing people in the streets right now," she added, "or not today, at least."

Theo looked at the frequency scanner. A tall black bar jumped to the medium-high mark. He stepped to his left and turned, watching the bar drop lower. There was only one direction remaining to chase the frequency. He looked up toward the bodies and walked forward. The black bar leaped on the scanner.

Now, he stood in the middle of the open plaza. People swirled around him, paying him no attention. Directly above him, Theo saw the undersides of their feet, blackened with filth and decay.

The scanner vibrated.

Theo pushed the button.

"Great! The first one is done!" said Dee. Now, see if you can make your way north to the entertainment district. There's likely to be a ton of signals there."

Theo looked back at the room full of gambling machines behind the gold-rimmed doors.

"The casinos... that wasn't the entertainment?"

"Oh, fella, you don't even know," said Dee.

He turned a corner onto a side street where the ground became a mix of glass and slate gray panels. He tapped his foot against the material. It was some kind of polymer or metal he had never seen before.

Above, Theo saw towers extending into the sky until their tops disappeared into the dark clouds. They were thin and angular constructions, like blades thrusting toward the heavens, with reflective sides smooth as glass.

He rechecked the scanner.

Another medium-high blip.

Close.

The crowd became denser as he entered the entertainment district. The light was brighter there—more ambient and full, like it was bouncing off of every surface, surrounding him with brilliant blues, pinks, and reds. The air smelled faintly of chemical exhaust, booze, and tobacco.

For a moment, he could see the fascination: to live in a place so energized with stimuli, one street more wild than the next.

Another crowd passed by, erupting in shrill laughter like a pack of banshees. They seemed to pay him no attention except for one man walking to the side of the group. He seemed to be alone. Theo had the unnerving sense that the man was staring at him.

After the group walked by, Theo lost track of the lone man.

"Mr. Naram!"

An artificial voice startled Theo. He looked up at the facade of a building plastered with digital screens. A silver advertisement drone fluttered towards his face.

"Have you ever wanted to feel the thrill of true revenge?" the drone announced with a theatrical flair in its voice, "now you can experience the highly anticipated new feature at the SCR Colosseum: 'Murder Your Ex' is a full immersion experience. Choose from seventeen pre-scripted scenarios and ten different methods of murder. Book today! Virtual options are available for instant streaming, or you can upgrade to the forced-immersion package for a real-life flesh-and-blood thrill!"

A scream from across the street startled Theo.

A large audience gathered around a row of screens, and more people flooded forward for a better view. A man's face appeared, duplicated across nine monstrous screens. He was probably in his mid-thirties with sunken cheekbones and a concerning, almost ghost-white pallor to his skin. His breath was heavy and strained. Victory shined in his eyes under glaring stadium lights. According to the on-screen graphical overlay, he had just won a race. He waved to the crowd and walked off the field.

Then the camera zoomed out. Another man appeared on the field. It zoomed out further. Two women stood beside him. They all wore metal collars around their necks packed with explosive cord. Panicked, they tried to pry the collars off. Their faces contorted into terrible shapes as they tugged against the metal clasp. One woman crouched to the ground and tried to bash the collar against the hard clay dirt to break it. Tears erupted from her face as she pounded it again and again with no luck.

The crowd chanted, "Not fit! Not fit! Not fit!" in unison at the top of their lungs.

An angry man in the audience groaned in disappointment as he watched his money vanish on a lost bet. Back on the field, the metal collars detonated with a sharp pop, and the contestants' bodies separated into pieces, limbs tumbling onto the astroturf. The screen turned dark red for a split second, then cleared.

The audience shouted, laughed, and raged. Money exchanged hands, and a fresh batch of contestants queued up for the next race.

Theo's heart sank as he watched this horrific scene play out in front of him: gamblers betting on human races and exterminating the losers.

Drones rushed onto the field to remove the bodies and spray down the blood. The TV programming flipped to a commercial advertisement for a new hallucinogenic pill.

Theo's pocket vibrated.

Another signal.

He pulled out the device, saw a high-strength bar, and quickly pressed the record button.

Then he saw it.

Far across the crowd, behind a group of teenagers huddled against the exterior of a glowing arcade building.

That lone figure in a gray coat.

Those unmistakable eyes–steel blue and coal black.

The Kaipher from the plane.

CHAPTER 20
LION

"I see you got a second one!" said Dee.

Theo ignored the voice in his earpiece. He recognized the Kaipher's eyes.

"Good goin'! Now just get three more and... Theo, are you there?"

He ducked below the Kaiper's line of sight, positioning a crowd of people in the way. He moved quickly to the nearest entrance of the next building and slipped in through two majestic red doors. The interior was dim, stuffy with humid air, and illuminated by a grid of spotlights in the ceiling that mimicked a star-filled night sky.

"Ah. Mr. Naram!" a woman said, "I see this is–" she glanced down at a handheld tablet, "your third visit to WorldScape? Welcome back!"

Theo did not recognize the place. The mirrored walls, the drooping wall sconces, and a circle of plush reclining chairs. Half of them were occupied by people lying back, motionless.

He couldn't tell if they were sleeping or dead or someplace

in between.

"Mr. Naram?" said the woman.

Theo looked at her confused and quickly realized his sleeve was coming apart. He pulled it up.

"Mr. Naram, may I tell you about our newest WorldScape experience? 'Tau Ceti Heist' is quite exhilarating and very popular! It's a race against time to stop a transport shuttle full of kindergarteners rigged to explode if it drops below 500 kp/h! And if you haven't yet tried our newest NeuralSync technology, I assure you that the new beta 3.2 is indistinguishable from–"

"You still with me, chief?" Dee's voice chimed in his ear.

"Huh? Oh, yeah," said Theo.

"Oh, excellent," said the woman holding the tablet, "what version of the neural implant did you say you–"

"Oh, sorry, no, no, but thanks," said Theo.

"Thanks?" said Dee, "what are you–"

His pocket vibrated.

Theo pushed past the woman and ran behind the reception desk.

"Oh! Excuse me, Mr. Naram, you can't–"

He rounded a corner down a long hallway. An open door to his left was stacked with storage shelves full of silver needles the lengths of his hand. He jumped into the closet, shut the door, and pulled out the frequency scanner.

A high-strength signal!

He jammed the record button.

Then, the scanner vibrated again.

He pressed the button a second time.

"Sir? Sir! Mr. Naram, I must ask you to pay for a service or leave." The woman's muffled voice came from behind the door, coming closer. He heard handles turn and other doors clicking open.

She was searching for him.

"Theo?" said Dee, "you still there?"

"Huh, yeah, yeah," he said breathlessly.

The woman's footsteps came closer.

"Amazing. I don't know how you did that, but... two in the same spot!" said Dee, "the frequency density wherever you are must be off the freakin' charts. They must be operating some serious equipment, streaming data from a thousand server nodes into one—"

"Can't talk, gotta run!"

Theo slipped out of the closet and barreled down the back-office hallway deeper into the building. A stampede of footsteps burst into a run behind him. He followed the hallway down a set of stairs and came to a door set in the shadows at the far end of the building.

He ran at full speed.

He cranked the handle and slammed his shoulder into the door. It burst open with a thunderous bang, and he found himself in a new place—a different alley.

It was empty.

Behind him, the bright light of a Kaipher's whip flashed, and the door sliced in half. Theo heard the sharp crack and felt the shock of electricity sizzling in the moist air. Half of the door bounced to the ground, glowing blue slanted lines where it had been sliced into two.

Theo ran down the alley and took the first left.

"Th-Theo? What is happening? Talk to me!" said Dee, panic coming through her usually confident facade for the first time.

"A Kaipher!"

"What?!"

"They must have picked up my trail when I scanned their frequencies."

He was nearly out of breath. He slipped a right, flew down a short set of stairs, and ran toward a building with solid fuschia on all sides.

"I just need," he said between breaths, "the fifth... frequency."

"What? No, no, fuck the frequencies, just get out of there! Head to the exit hatch!"

He was three blocks away from an exit.

A crowd of jubilant people walked by, activating invisible energy fields above their heads like electric umbrellas to block out the rain. Light raindrops glowed white as they trickled down the energy shield and glowed wild colors like shooting stars in front of their faces.

He sprinted through them, almost knocking down a woman with glowing filaments stitched onto her lips.

Two blocks away.

Theo felt a dark and dreaded force behind him but didn't dare to look back.

One block away.

He needed to lose the Kaipher before going to the escape hatch; otherwise, he'd be followed and jeopardize Dee's entire system. He saw the alley straight ahead, where Dee said the hatch was located. He was so close, but he decided to pivot right and head up a side street to bait the Kaipher in a different direction.

Shops lined the streets. A bodega selling starch proteins, virtual reality sex shops, and facial reconstruction boutiques. A family of still-bleeding corpses were propped up on a street corner with letters carved into their naked chests: NOT FIT.

His pocket vibrated.

Theo darted around another corner, thumb fumbling for the button in his pocket. After another two left turns, he couldn't see any trace of the Kaipher behind him.

He jammed the button and captured the fifth frequency.

He raced down a narrow alleyway.

"Where the fuck is the–"

"The building exhaust pipe," said Dee, "fourth one. Just

below it. Look for the yellow mark on the valve handle."

Theo jerked to a stop in front of the fourth pipe jutting from the wall and saw a slight indentation in the corner where rainwater wasn't pooling. In fact, the water was silently draining, which indicated that there was an opening in the ground.

He looked back.

Nothing but silence.

Theo flipped the hatch, shut it behind him, and began his descent down a ladder into the dark, forgotten Under City below.

***

Theo leaped down from the ladder. His boots splashed in a shallow puddle of rainwater dripping down from the column.

"What the hell, Dee!" he said, breathless, "Who are... what are... what in the actual fucking hell is wrong with those people up there?"

"They're... it's just," said Dee.

"Bodies in the street. People being murdered, exploded for, for, for entertainment?"

"It's the SCR," said Dee, "They created this world, and when you're inside, you can't tell up from down. It's so easy to fall into it and never come back out. I mean, my family did."

Theo caught his breath, put his hands on his knees, and stood tall to face Dee. He reached into the bottom of his pocket, revealed the frequency scanner, and handed it to Dee. Tears welled in her eyes as she reached out slowly and took the device, emotions running deep at this moment she'd waited for for so long.

"What's your plan," Theo asked with a head tilt, "with all those frequencies? Why did you need them? And why were they so important that you sent me there to risk my life to get them?"

Dee looked down at the wet ground, trying to formulate her answer.

"You knew what I was walking into, didn't you?" said Theo, "you knew the dangers, and you sent me anyway!"

"This world," she said, "what it represents is everything I lost and that was taken away from me. Live forever, they said. Life without loss, grief, or loneliness. Unlimited pleasure and excitement. No more aging. No more suffering. No death. Just a couple hours in the machine to become good as new. It was almost salvation, you know. But now it's something else. Now, it's becoming a cancer on the people it was supposed to empower."

Theo took a breath.

"What are you saying?"

"I'm saying there's a reckoning around the corner. And all those frequencies you got me were the last piece of the puzzle to bring this godforsaken place to its knees."

Theo thought he saw the hint of a smile for a moment.

"You've fulfilled your end of the deal," she said matter-of-factly, "and I thank you for that. Truly, I do! I know the risks you put yourself in and appreciate what you've done for me."

"Risk... that's for sure," he said.

"Now, I'm happy to deliver what you've been searching for."

Dee nodded, calling Theo's attention to something behind him. She pressed a button and swiped across her wrist to activate an LED torch embedded under her skin. After a second, a wide beam of light shot out from her wrist. It pierced through the darkness and illuminated a giant stone statue of a lion.

Theo turned to see the sculpture of the majestic creature and struggled to breathe as if the wind was ripped from his lungs. Memories of Kristof's workshop back on the Scraper ship raced through his mind—the smell of gear grease, oiled leather, and burned solder. How he unwrapped the fabric from around the brass monocular spyglass with such care as if it might crumble in his hands like sand. How he would float from shelf to shelf, with curious fingertips pinching and twisting objects collected from the deep ocean.

Theo looked at the enormousness of the stone animal before him.

"How did you know it would be right here?" said Theo, gesturing toward the sculpture and pointing out that everything around them was a fading wasteland.

"We've got sixteen entrance ladders scattered throughout the Under City and rotate them every eleven days. Many ways in and many ways out, so it always keeps the SCR guessing. Today, when you said you wanted to find the lion statue, I remembered that one of my ladders from the current rotation would lead right here.

Theo nodded and cleared his throat.

"So?"

"So..." Dee replied.

"Will you at least walk me to the door?" he said.

Dee chuckled with a half-smile.

"I thought you'd never ask, chief."

***

They walked down a series of shallow steps from the street that led to the side entrance to a large building that used to be white but was tinged a gray-orange hue from many years of decay. The gate was partially barricaded from the outside with a pile of wooden beams and crumbled bricks stacked at jagged angles. But Theo saw an opening at one end, possibly large enough for a person to slip through. He entered first and came up against a metal door with glass panels. Dee followed. Most of the panels were shattered, but some still had triangles of glass wedged into the frame. Dee pointed her torch over Theo's shoulder and lit up the door. It was locked shut with a thick metal chain and rusted padlock.

Theo let out a faint chuckle.

"The rust," he said, "does wonders on the springs. Eats it up from the inside."

He searched through the scraps of metal, stone, wood, and brick littering the ground. Dee swept the light toward the ground to follow his movements. He grabbed a long piece of metal with a tip pointed like a screwdriver in one hand and a heavy round stone in the other. He inserted the metal spike between the shackle and the locking bar, raised the stone above his head, and slammed it down onto the back of the metal spike.

The padlock cracked into two and fell in silence to the ground.

"I bet you couldn't have hacked that one," said Theo with a smirk, "Sometimes, old-school problems need old-school solutions."

Even with the deep shadows on her face, he could see that Dee was not amused.

They pushed together on the door and opened into a long, expansive room. White pedestals lined the perimeter, some with cracked marble busts and others bare with nothing upon them.

As they traveled deeper into the building, Dee swept her wrist torch across to illuminate the walls. Paintings by Albert Bierstadt and Emanuel Leutze sat stacked with dozens of other canvases wrapped in fabric along the wall. Poems by Ralph Waldo Emerson were scrawled in elegant calligraphy across the decaying walls.

Ancient art from an ancient time. Theo ran his hands over one of the paintings, sweeping lines into the dust.

"Art really is immortality," he said, more as a whisper to himself as he looked closer at the names on the paintings.

Theo opened a door at the far end of the hall to reveal a room as tall as it was wide, with ceilings reaching at least forty meters. Remnants of chandeliers hung from the ceiling, and above their decorative glass beads was an intricate pattern of etched wooden panels. Bookshelves lined the wall all around him, filled with thousands of preserved texts of various sizes and shapes—novels, encyclopedias, bibles, atlases, and volumes of articles, essays, and poems.

Dee stepped through the doorway, clutching her chest in shock. She surveyed the room, mouth open with a twisted look of joy and fear, or maybe both at the same time.

"Oh. God," she said, each word rolling slowly out of her, "If the SCR knew this was here... I don't even know. They must have missed it completely."

"Missed it?"

"The SCR doesn't allow books from around the world, much less a freakin' library. Those were disposed of long ago when the walls first went up, and Aria Sloan was gaining power among the coastal leaders. All sources of knowledge–the digital books or neural upload training catalogs–come from the SCR information office. After all, the easiest way to control a population is to keep them blind to the past."

She stepped up to a nearby shelf and drew a book with the same care she would use to handle a newborn. It had a green cloth jacket, frayed strands unraveling at the edges, and gold leaf along the side of the pages. She opened the book to a page, breathed in the musty printed paper and ink and words written from another time, and was lost in silence for a moment that felt like hours. Theo sidled up to her and noticed the title of the book: Nineteen Eighty-Four.

"I was told what I'm looking for is in one of the lower levels," said Theo, sensing the pull of time and wanting to move on.

Dee nodded and tossed the slim green book into her drawstring bag. They exited through doors on the northern side of the grand book-lined room and came across a wide marble staircase that twisted down into lower levels engulfed in darkness. Dee let out an audible sigh that followed them down the steps, the sound bouncing off the muraled walls and eventually dissolving into a ghostly silence.

The stairs descended deep into the earth, five or six levels down. When they reached the bottom, the stairs ended and spilled out into a large room that seemed to span the entire width of the building. The marble tiles that once covered the floor of the rest of the building ended. In the darkness, they could hear the taps of their footsteps disappear, and the sounds of gritty shuffling from an unfinished concrete floor took their place. Dee raised her wrist torch and bounced a soft light off the ceiling. It was a massive square room with the ceiling much lower than the floors above. Columns spaced through the room kept the immense weight of the building from crashing down, and the piles of objects around the perimeter suggested it was used as a strange kind of dumping ground for machinery of all types. Computer monitors, server stacks, electronic consoles with glass tubes and missing knobs, and exposed wires running tight loops around fuses and circuits. Plastic cases that cracked from age.

Dee's face flushed with excitement. She ran to a pile of semiconductors and began fishing through the parts, tossing aside the cracked and bent chips and pulling out the good ones to slip into her backpack.

Light from her wrist torch bounced up and down as she rummaged through the bin. Angular shadows stretched across the ceiling. Theo looked around at the broken machines—nothing but trash. He plunged a hand into a pile of twisted cables and examined the assortment of colors, widths, and connector types. In the far corner of the room, in the blackest patch of shadow, something caught Theo's eye. It was hard to see in the dark, but with the quickest flash of light bouncing off the walls from Dee's torch, he thought he saw a light.

A single, delicate light.

It blinked and repeated at a constant interval.

It looked yellow and was a tiny, thin blip in the dark.

A cursor on the screen.

CHAPTER 21

HOLOGRAM MAN

The cursor's soft glow was hypnotic. Theo couldn't pull his eyes away from the screen. It pulsed from across the room, compelling him to look closer like a force of gravity pulling at him. To place a finger on a key and press.

Behind him, Dee was rummaging through components, looking intensely for something.

Theo began moving in the direction of the screen. He passed by a crumbling stack of server racks. The pile tilted and bent in on itself like a falling tower. Beyond the servers was a console from some kind of control room with a connected chair for an operator. Plastic was flaking off, and what used to be leather on the seat cushion was decaying into a fine powder. These objects had been lying dormant for decades.

A motor suddenly whirred to life. Theo jumped and looked to his left, startled by the noise. He instinctively raised his hands in a defense posture.

It was a slender machine with a long metal neck. The top, which extended high over Theo's head, must have been seven or eight feet tall. At its tip, a bulb started to glow reddish-yellow, then white.

He recognized that device. It was a projector, not unlike the type Trent used to display photographs at his initial briefing months ago. And it came to life with that familiar warm glow.

"Was this you?" Theo whispered to Dee, "Did you turn this on?"

"Me? No, what is that?" said Dee. She had both hands full, stripping wires from a pile of trash and stuffing them into her backpack.

Specks of light hovered over a small platform beneath the projector, like a stage getting ready for a performance. Slowly, the cloud of particles drifted closer together and began to approximate the shape and stature of an illuminated man.

"You sure you didn't push any buttons over there? Or..."

"What? No, no, I didn't touch a thi–"

"We-we-we-WELCOME to the library's newest summer exhibit: A 200-Year Retrospective to celebrate the SCR's magnificent past and usher in an even more prosperous future!" A small hologram about two feet high of a cartoon man in a striped three-piece suit, gray hat, and a beaming theatrical smile appeared. The electronic voice of a male announcer blasted from the device's side-mounted speakers. He spoke with an enthusiasm that would be well suited to introduce a high-flying circus act.

Theo shot Dee an awkward look.

"I swear I didn't touch anything," she said, raising both hands and stepping back from the bin.

The hologram man spun around in a flourish and continued.

"Come along as we learn about the history of the greatest republic to grace this fine earth."

The second lens mounted on the side of the machine tilted down and shot a beam of light into Theo's eye.

The machine buzzed and beeped.

"Greetings, Mr. Naram, welcome to the tour. We're so thrilled to see you again since your last visit sixteen months ago."

Theo winced and blinked repeatedly in disbelief until the light beam shut off.

"We're going to go on a journey, and every journey starts in the same place. The beginning."

The smiling man moved his hands with wild gestures carefully coordinated with the script.

"The year was 2029. Two enterprising scientists built an offshore laboratory in the bellows of an old Freightliner ship. Dr. Charles Sloan and Dr. Salim Naram were geniuses ahead of their time, dedicating their work to improve the future longevity of the human species. Through years of arduous tests, two scientists discovered a process to harvest nutrient-rich algae from the ocean floor and harness it as nature's fuel to regrow human organs. They used samples of their DNA to seed the first viable test subjects, and through their bravery and perseverance, the first Aeonite machine was invented."

The holographic man pulled a slender glass beaker from his coat pocket and laughed as it began bubbling and steaming for comedic effect.

"Shortly after the Aeonite machine's invention, Dr. Salim Naram disappeared under unexplained circumstances that have kept conspiracy theorists guessing to this day. Some called him a weak man, prone to extreme jealousy of his genius partner, Dr. Sloan. In fact, Dr. Naram's journal entries that surfaced long after his disappearance suggested evidence of psychotic episodes. Unfortunately the journals were never verified by a third party source, but Dr. Sloan had testified to its contents and had confirmed this to be true. Some said Dr. Naram secretly never believed in humanity's full potential and tried to sabotage the project. But others believed he went mad and abandoned Dr. Sloan without warning. Whatever Dr. Naram's cowardly reasoning, Dr. Sloan persevered despite the odds, and continued developing the miracle machine."

"Over the next two hundred years, the Aeonite machine was the catalyst for progress in the United States. Citizens in coastal states banded together and formed a perfect society dedicated to human success, education, wealth, and engineering knowledge. In a sweeping gesture of love, Dr. Sloan honored every Coastal citizen by infusing a fragment of his DNA into every tissue and organ reconstruction operation in the Aeonite machine. By doing this, he graced all Coastal citizens with a small yet everlasting connection to his eternal love. When the Secure Horizon Act was passed in 2071, and the walls along both coasts were erected shortly after in 2078, the coastal states secured their place in history as the premier territories most fit for the future. Today, under the leadership of the great Aria Sloan, the prodigal descendent of Dr. Charles Sloan, the Sloan Coastal Republic continues to be a shining example of humankind's peak potential. To learn more, press the keypad below to continue to the next chap chap chap chap chap chap CHAP CHAP CHAP–"

After a moment of looping, the system powered down and attempted to restart itself.

Dee turned to Theo, beginning to form a sentence but stopping to gather her thoughts.

"Theo," she said finally, "back on the bridge, it addressed you as Mr. Naram."

Theo nodded with a puzzled look.

"And now this machine called you Mr. Naram," she continued.

"I know," he said.

"But he's been dead for..."

"Yeah."

"Two hundred years."

"Yeah, I know. It doesn't make any sense. They must have

their records crossed or something—a glitch in the database."

Dee frowned as a look of dread and skepticism came over her face.

"Theo," she said, "when you climbed to the surface of the Capital, did you get scanned again? Did they recognize—"

The machine whirred back to life.

"La-La-Ladies and gentlemen, what a treat we have for the new winter exhibit... the animated man took the stage again, "a deep dive into the most important story ever told, and one that may sound familiar or even surprise you!"

Theo thumbed a button on the keypad below the hologram, but the machine didn't respond. The animated man pulled a pair of binoculars from an invisible pouch, raised them to his eyes, and looked directly at Theo. He tried a different button and pressed harder, trying to turn it off.

"It's the greatest story in the history of your life. This winter, the library presents Project: YOU!"

Theo kicked the side of the machine.

"Step right up and—"

The side-mounted lens glowed again and flashed a beam of light directly into Theo's pupils.

The machine made a loud scrambling sound. The animated man jerked unnaturally back and forth before settling into a welcoming, open-palmed pose.

"Male. Age: twenty-one years, seven months, and thirteen days. Bloodline lineage: Naram. Let us go on a journey, Mr. Naram. Theo Julis Naram, born May 17, 2308. Notable ancestors include..."

The projector beam flickered as the computer paused to search its database.

"Dr. Salim Naram, born August 8, 1987, died unknown, co-inventor of the Aeonite machine... data missing file corrupt-up-up-up-upted. That concludes your journey, Mr. Naram. We hope you have enjoyed Project: YOU, and thank you for visiting our exhibit today!"

The lens glowed once more and flashed quickly in Dee's direction.

"Female. Age: twenty-three years, two months, and eleven days. Bloodline lineage: Canterbury. Let us go on a journey, Ms. Canterbury. Desire Elizabeth Canterbury, born July 7, 2306–"

Dee stepped up and typed forcefully on the keypad.

"No, no, no! Stop it! Turn it OFF!"

She pounded her fist against the machine.

"Notable ancestors include Marvin Canterbury, politician, and Lily Anne Canterbury (West), nurse in the SCR Uprising. Father: Benedict James Canterbury. Mother: Maureen–"

"I don't want to hear her NAME!" she shouted, kicking against the machine and tapping rapidly on her wrist device to try to override the machine.

"Father: Benedict James Canterbury. Born: December 14, 2268. Died: April 28, 2316. Dissenter. Unfit for the future. Mother: Maureen Shavaughn. Born: August 3, 2270. Died: April 28, 2313. Dissenter. Unfit for the future."

Dee collapsed at the sound of her parents' names, her mouth open wide, quivering uncontrollably as she knew what name would be read aloud next.

"Sibling: Brady Canterbury. Born: February 21, 2309. Died: November 6, 2313. Dissenter. Unfit for the future."

She let out a wail of anguish after hearing Brady's name, folding her body low against the floor in tears, shaking with deep, pained breaths.

"That concludes your journey, Ms. Canterbury. We hope you have enjoyed Project: YOU, and thank you for visiting our exhibit today!"

The projector light dimmed until the room was black once more. Theo rushed to put an arm around her while she cried in the dark, the lone blinking cursor casting a haunting glow on a computer screen across the room.

"I haven't heard their names in years. I thought I could get through life just letting them all go," she said through the tears, "But I can't. It's too much. Everything is too much."

She was quiet for a moment. Theo could sense her looking off into the dark.

"My mother, she was far from perfect," said Dee in almost a whisper, "she was the head of this group that called themselves the Night Scribes. The Scribes would collect pieces of books found throughout the land and reconstruct them page by page in secret. This was illegal under SCR law. They were building a compendium book of written documents about history, science, and art outside of the SCR's surveillance, outside the bounds of SCR approved information. My mother was the keeper of the files, she organized and transcribed everything, and the entire Scribe network reported to her. She united them. She loved the work. And loved the people. Maybe loved them more than her own family. One night my mother went to meet one of the partner Scribes and collect the newly discovered pages, but the SCR tracked her down and captured her. They demanded the names of others in the network, but my mother wouldn't give them up. She risked everything to protect their names. Until the SCR came and took my brother Brady in broad daylight and used him to get my mother to talk. I was supposed to watch Brady that day, and protect him, but I couldn't. I tried to stop them but they took him. He was four years old. Brady was the sweetest, funniest, gentle boy."

"And the next morning," she continued, "to send a signal to my mother and the rest of the Scribes, we woke up to find Brady hanging from a streetlamp."

Dee caught her breath in between the tears.

"After all of that, my mother, she was broken. I knew her

mind was there, but her heart was long gone. One morning I woke up and she just stopped speaking. She stopped reading. She just couldn't handle life anymore. She became obsessed with visiting Calico Hill to see Brady."

"She insisted we go back again and again," she continued, "She started losing touch with reality, until she couldn't stand leaving Brady again. So on the flight, she stepped into the bathroom and swallowed an entire bottle of sleeping pills. She died on that island, hoping that she'd be reunited with Brady, but it didn't work. And she was gone forever."

She clenched her jaw in anger.

"One minute Brady was there and the next minute... gone," said Dee, "The SCR took him from me. Took my whole life away that day."

"Dee, I never would have gotten this far without you. Why are you helping me?"

At first, she didn't speak. Her silence was heavier than any words.

"I never did tell you who I was on the bridge that day, did I?" said Dee.

Theo thought for a moment.

"No," he said.

"My life," said Dee, "isn't much these days. Sure, I help out some friends in Out City occasionally, siphoning off some SCR supplies when I can. My family is gone, and I kept thinking I'd one day figure out something real in my life—some reason to belong, a purpose to keep going, a connection to anything. But the days are shorter and shorter, and the months pass in a blink, and there's nothing left for me."

Dee looked up, her tears drying in the soft light. Theo could barely see the outline of her hair in the dark.

"The truth is," she continued, "I go up to the bridge some days and look out over the water and feel the freezing open air below me and the blue sky above and wonder if that might be the best place to put an end to it all. To be so high above the water, feeling like I'm flying. I've thought about it a lot for years. But I guess I–I wasn't brave enough. I didn't have the guts. So I'd sit alone in the cold air until one day, you showed up and needed me to save your life. And it was intoxicating, you know, being needed again. For once in a very long time."

"Dee, you're the bravest person I've met this side of the wall," said Theo, "I hoped you'd never see my hands trembling all those times I followed behind you on the bridge."

They share a moment of silence in the darkness deep underground beneath a forgotten city.

"Come with me," said Theo, "help me finish my mission. I need to get the Aeonite schematics back home so the people in the Midlands can live. We can save millions of people. The SCR doesn't deserve to keep this for themselves when families, children, and elderly people are dying every day. You can stick it to the SCR once and for all and open the floodgates by getting this technology out from behind the walls. We can build a good world. A free world. It doesn't have to turn out like this place ever again."

***

Theo sat in a creaky padded chair, watching Dee tinker with wires on a machine across the room. She hunched over, reaching inside an open panel of another projector machine, stripping two multi-colored wires to expose their metallic insides. The single bulb at the top of the machine glowed and cast the room in a drowsy amber light. She pulled two wires and pressed the tips together. A spark flashed for a split second, then an arc of electricity, constant and blue. She plunged the blade of Theo's railroad knife into the middle of the arc and watched it heat up

CALICO HILL

until a faint orange glow appeared. Then she pulled it back, and a swirl of smoke appeared.

"It's clean," said Dee, holding the knife up and inspecting the scratched gray blade with its twisted handle, "Well, not clean, but sterile enough."

"That'll have to do," said Theo.

He fidgeted in the chair, his sleeve rolled up and his body leaning to put weight on his left arm. The marks on his skin from the first incision had almost entirely healed, save for a faint red line one could easily mistake for a scratch.

That salve from Mae was a miracle, he thought.

It was almost as if the chip was never tucked into his arm, and the cut was never there in the first place.

Dee reached over and gave Theo the knife.

He paused for a moment, examining the blade in his hand. The weight of it in his palm. The twists in the handle. He'd waited for this moment since his first briefing with Trent in that smoky classroom. And once he'd set foot on that plane, this moment haunted him, knowing it was around the corner but looming closer each day.

Theo yearned for the day he could exhale, knowing the schematics were coming home to the Midlands. He wanted more than anything to let that pain flow out of his body like a river held behind a dam.

"You okay, chief?" Dee asked.

"Yeah, I'm just... yeah, I'm good."

Theo took the knife in his hand and tightened his grip.

"So I guess this is it," he said, "everything good?"

Dee pulled the machine's light closer, trying to cast more light on his arm.

"You're good. You got this."

Theo folded two strips of rubber that Dee had found in the bundle of cables and stuffed them between his teeth.

His breathing quickened. He bit down softly on the rubber, which flexed under the strain of his jaw.

He tensed his fingers, trying to shake the tremors beginning to emerge. They were seeping up through his muscles, taking control of his hand. His hand shook. His fingers turned ice cold. He inhaled deep, sharp breaths and exhaled slowly and silently.

Dee sat a few paces away, leaning against a stack of old servers and watching Theo lift the knife. She shuffled her feet, a concerned look on her face.

The blade hovered over his arm.

The point pressed into his skin.

It bent the hairs on his arm.

His breathing was quick and sharp and getting louder. Spit pooled at his teeth as he clenched on the rubber strap.

He took a deep breath and pushed air through his teeth like the sound of a kettle close to boiling.

He tensed his grip. The knife hovered. He raised it an inch, lowered it, and raised it again. He tried to wrestle the strength to initiate his own torrent of pain.

Spit hung from his teeth.

Finally, he opened his mouth and let the strap fall.

"I-I can't... I can't do it. I–"

His eyes bulged and flushed with redness, tears a moment away.

He lowered the knife and let it tumble onto his lap.

"I need you to do it."

"Do... it?" said Dee, "You mean, cut the chip out of your arm?"

Theo sighed.

"Yes."

Dee took a deep breath and nodded to Theo.

He handed her the knife, stuffed the rubber strap into his mouth, and leaned into his chair.

Dee balanced the knife in her hand. She squeezed the twisted grip.

She placed a finger on Theo's arm.

Her touch was electric and cold.

"Sorry."

"No, it's fine."

"Right here?" she asked, pointing to a small spot on his skin.

He looked down.

"Yeah."

"Okay."

Dee took a breath.

"Y-you're sure about this?"

"Goddamnit, just do–"

She plunged the knife into his arm.

CHAPTER 22

UPLOAD

Blood pooled at the tip of the blade. Dee dragged the knife back to widen the opening.

Theo bore down on the rubber strap, his jaw muscles popping as he let out a strained scream.

When the opening was large enough, Dee jammed two fingers into the wound and probed through his muscle tissue, searching for the chip.

Theo's breathing grew faster.

He peeked down at the blood dribbling over the side of his arm. A feeling of lightness flooded his mind. He was floating. He struggled to tense his neck to keep his head up.

"I can't feel anything! It's not here—"

"Itttsssss thrrrrrr!" Theo mumbled through clenched teeth.

Beads of sweat accumulated on his forehead and dripped down his cheeks.

He was fading.

The pain was overwhelming.

A wave of hellfire shot up his arm, across his shoulder, and up his neck. It sat behind his eyes, sharp and paralyzing.

"Wait!" said Dee, "I think I feel something!" she wiggled her fingers deep within the opening. Blood bubbled to the surface. Every movement sent a jolt of agony up Theo's arm.

She pressed against the edge of a small piece of plastic. It was tiny, barely larger than a fingernail. But the blood made it slippery and nearly impossible to grasp.

She tried to get a purchase on the chip to wiggle it free. She twisted her hand again, wrapped one finger around the side of the chip, and pulled.

Theo's head fell back against the chair.

He tumbled into silence.

***

He woke up gasping, filling his lungs with the musty air of that dark basement. It smelled of decaying plastic and aerosolized glue. Ancient air that had been trapped underground for decades.

"I tried to stop the bleeding," said Dee, leaning over Theo's arm, "you're fine, but you need to keep pressure on that bandage."

His arm was wrapped in a shabby bandage of ripped cloth tightened with a plastic cord-management zip tie that Theo presumed Dee pulled from inside an old computer tower.

"Please tell me you got it!"

"I got it, I got it," said Dee. She held a tiny sliver of plastic up to the projector light. It was such a small thing, held softly between two fingers, its edges glowing as it caught the light from above. It was a simple square of protective clear material, inside of which a small black chip suspended in the middle as if weightless.

Tears welled in Theo's eyes as he squinted and looked closely at the chip. He remembered his stomach lurching when the plane tumbled through the air. The bodies were charred black with fire, nothing but bones that used to be people strapped to those airplane seats. Countless deaths and unimaginable pain. For that chip.

He grit his teeth and leaned onto his bleeding arm as he attempted to stand up.

"What are you doing? You need to sit!" said Dee, her voice more urgent than ever. "You just had your arm excavated, and you passed out cold. Now is not the time to be—"

"It's... fine," he said slowly, hobbling ahead with one arm clutching the other, the chip in its protective case held tightly in his hand.

"I can't waste any more time," he said. "I need to transmit the data home."

Blood dripped onto the unfinished concrete floor. It marked a trail behind him before quickly absorbing into the porous material.

Dee fired up her wrist torch and lit the corner of the room with the blinking computer console. Theo stumbled forward toward the machine. It was ancient technology; he could tell from the yellowed plastic panels that formed a frame around the screen. Keys were missing on the keyboard, but it was powered on, and there was a slim flip-up panel below with the screen and various input sockets.

His eyes were fixed on that panel as he moved with slow steps. Each footfall brought a wave of fatigue, and his arm screamed with pain like his bones were on fire.

He shut out the pain.

It's just my body sending signals to my brain, he thought. The pain was not within; it was external. For a moment, he closed his eyes and retreated within himself, envisioning his body as a vessel insulated from the outside world. He chose not to be hurt by that which was not a part of him.

He chose stillness.

He chose silence.

Theo opened his eyes and focused on the mission at hand. The blinking cursor on the screen beckoned him with a heavy force that rivaled gravity. It tugged at him, and in a moment of hallucination, he heard his heartbeat throbbing in his ears in rhythm with the blinking cursor. With each beat, the room seemed to grow darker, and the pain that screamed in his body was numbed.

He stumbled and almost collapsed, but Dee rushed to his side and held him by his shoulder. His left arm dangled like a dead leaf.

"This is everything," Theo mumbled under his breath, fatigue taking over him, "this is my whole world. Right here. This chip."

Dee set him down in front of the computer screen, its blinking cursor like a blinding strobe in the dim basement light, and Theo sank to his knees. He reached a finger to flip up the yellowed plastic panel below the screen. It had nine slots total, arranged in rows by size: small to large. Theo pulled out the chip recently excavated from his arm and stared at it closely. He popped open the protective clamshell case and revealed a small black square that held the complete schematics of the Aeonite machine. It was a beautiful thing. Matte black. Pristine. An elegant line of gold contact points as thin as a few strands of hair lined one side of the chip.

With careful fingers and steady breath, Theo inserted the chip into the reader slot that matched its size and width. It slid in with minimal tension and let out a reassuring click.

***

Theo tapped the keyboard to wake the computer. The dim cursor brightened and waited patiently for instructions.

"How'd you know this machine would have a compatible chip reader?" asked Dee.

Theo shook his head, "I don't. I didn't. Call it a hunch, I guess. But when I saw it across the room, and it was the only machine still connected to power—except for the tour guide machine, of course—I... I just had this feeling."

Dee flashed a concerned look on her face.

"But this is a graveyard of computers," she said, "and this is the only one working. That isn't even remotely suspicious to you. That only one here—"

"I know it's the one, Dee!" said Theo, fatigue showing on his face and desperation in his voice. "It feels like a dream like I've been here before or seen something like this. It's all too familiar. But it feels so right. This is the path. I know it. And I've come so far. This is the way."

Dee glanced around, letting her eyes follow the edge of the residual light spilling from the side of her wrist torch. To her left, the machine with bent plastic with a cracked glass monitor. It was in bad shape. A rectangular cabinet stood shoulder height to the right with rows of read-out dials. It looked to be well preserved but without a power supply.

Both machines were dead. This one, conveniently, was operational.

Theo called up a command prompt and instructed the computer to read the data on the chip.

71,058,824 FILES

FILE HEALTH: 97.3%

He ran a command to search for an active network connection. It returned 12 connections. 11 were blocked, but one was open and active.

"There we go!" said Theo, "all I need is one."

"One? What do you mean by one?" said Dee, distracted and flipping switches on a nearby computer console.

"An open connection to transfer files," said Theo.

FILE STATUS: COPIED TO LOCAL DRIVE

He queued up the files to prepare to send. A motor spun within the machine, a disc powering up. Fans whirred to life and pushed a small cloud of dust out of the ventilation grates at the back of the computer.

"Now, I just need to remember the node code for Trent's lab," he said.

The computer Dee was tinkering with powered up, and an array of multicolored dots illuminated along the side of the console. She was staring intently at the screen, paying less attention to whatever Theo was doing and becoming more engrossed in a library of images she had managed to find.

Dee leaned back from the monitor and gasped.

"There's no way," she said to herself in nearly a whisper, "this... this is the motherlode. It's everything. This is everything. I cannot believe it."

She tapped repeatedly on a key, then faster and faster, pounding harder onto the keyboard. Black-and-white images flashed on the screen: cross-section diagrams of buildings, housing foundations, tunnels, sewers, subway networks, electrical wiring plans, pipes extending and curving, and electronic transmission terminals denoted by small antennae symbols.

She stopped tapping.

She leaned toward the screen, her eyes inches from the glass.

The image frozen on the screen was a structural schematic of the concrete columns that held up the Capital. All 173 columns, with lines revealing how they were assembled, like puzzle pieces, bases connected to middles that sat beneath the crown that fanned out to support the black panels above. Information about the types of materials used in assembly, precise concrete formulas, and, most importantly, a map of the weight distribution shared among all the columns. The immense weight of the buildings above held in careful balance for maximum efficiency, the least waste, and a negligible risk of failure.

Dee's eyes were transfixed on one distinct graph.

"Thirteen," she whispered, her breathing growing rapid with excitement. She repeated the words as she stared at the screen, "Thirteen. Thirteen. Thirteen columns!"

A list on the screen showed which columns bore the Capital City's heaviest load and the corresponding weakest points within their concrete construction.

She pulled her wrist device close to the machine and plugged in a slender cable. A green light blinked as she initiated a data download.

Theo tended to his computer and paid Dee no attention.

"Seven, eight, two," said Theo, punching the computer keys with his one functional hand. The yellow numbers lit up on the screen.

He struggled to remember the next string.

"Two, two… one, I think."

Dee unplugged the cable from the computer. She sat back and exhaled, trying to hide a beaming smile. She glanced at the ceiling, mouthed silent words into the air, closed her eyes briefly and then turned her attention back to Theo.

The last three numbers, what were they, he thought?

He levitated his fingers over the keyboard as if willing the keys to identify themselves through telepathy.

I remember six, he thought.

He pressed 6.

Maybe four?

He hesitated a moment, then pressed the number 4 key.

The last one… the last one, he thought.

The pain came roaring back, a dull ache in his arm that rippled throughout his body.

Theo struggled to remember. Trent had shown it to him in that smoky classroom. He slid a white paper with numbers printed on it across the desk to Theo. But that memory was fading.

Theo stared at the row of numbers on the keyboard. A lightness came upon him. He felt like he was floating, consciousness hanging on by ragged threads as he noticed the blood dripping from his arm. The numbers pulled him like that all too familiar gravity—a dark and heavy feeling of tunnel vision that overtook his mind.

He tried hard to concentrate again. He remembered Trent in the room and it was hot and the metal chair was cold against his leg and there were back-lit microfiche and maps drawn out on plastic film and–.

"Eight! That has to be it!" said Theo, the words tumbling out of the memory.

He punched the number eight key, and the screen lit up.

DATA STAGING COMPLETE. TRANSMIT? Y/N

He took a breath, his mind and heart filling all at once with the ghosts of those who had been lost to get these schematics. All that suffering. The sacrifice.

He pressed **Y** and hit **ENTER**.

The cursor on the screen was responsive at first, blinking in silence as if the machine was thinking. Then, it refreshed and showed a pixelated progress bar illustrated by a row of periods and a counting percentage meter.

22%

37%

The counter slowed and paused.

71%

92%

It took its time to send the last packets of data.

Finally, the screen refreshed with a new message:

99%

TRANSMISSION COMPLETE

Theo exhaled sharply, never realizing that he was, in fact, holding his breath as he typed the last keystrokes and waited for something, anything, to happen.

He looked at the tiny yellow letters on the screen and felt a sudden rush of panic.

Is that it, he thought? Theo couldn't believe it. It didn't feel right. Was it over just like that?

His mind raced as he imagined tiny packages of information soaring through fibers in the ground, catapulting into the clouds to ping-pong across satellites, and showing up as a quiet beep on a computer in Trent's lab somewhere far away.

Would they even be waiting for the transmission, he thought? They could have easily assumed he was dead.

Theo pressed his palm against his eye and rubbed away the building tension.

Then, without warning, a string of new text flowed silently on the screen. The pixelated yellow letters were piercing in the darkness.

REROUTING

REROUTING

PACKET INTERCEPTED

"What the hell is—"

REROUTING

REROUTING

He stared at the screen, eyes unable to tear away, his breath frozen in his chest.

Please go through, he thought.

STATUS......

TRANSMISSION RECEIVED

Theo gasped, and Dee looked over.

"You did it?" she asked, leaning in close beside Theo, her eyes transfixed on the glowing screen, "you actually did the damn thing?"

"I...I"

"Woah!" she said, "so does this mean..."

"The Midlanders, my people, they'll have the plans. They can build the Aeonite machine!"

Theo smiled, half out of joy and half out of relief and release from carrying the agonizing burden with him every day. The questions that had floated in the unknown all this time: would he make it? Would he die trying? Would the Midlands waste away to nothing after all?

Maybe Theo smiled for all of those reasons.

He saw Dee smiling wide beside him, reading the numbers on the screen. It was the purest happiness he had seen on her face since meeting her that stormy day on the bridge.

"You... actually did it," she said, turning to look at Theo, "I mean, I never really doubted you, but it's one thing to have a plan and another to–"

Theo leaned forward and pressed his lips to hers in the middle of her sentence. She kissed him back for the briefest moment but quickly pulled away. She gasped a sharp breath, and her eyes looked to the floor.

"I'm sorry, I–"

"No, don't be."

Theo and Dee shared a moment of silence in the middle of that musty basement under a forgotten city, two people crawling back from a dark place but never letting the world break them.

"Thanks for, you know, sticking with me all this time," said Theo.

Dee nodded, collected herself, and looked at Theo.

"It's been my pleasure," she said with a smile and matter-of-fact tone, like a captain signing off after a long and eventful voyage.

"Now, let's find a way out of this grim place, shall we?" said Dee.

***

"Can you walk?"

"Yeah, I'll be fine," said Theo, feeling a strange sense of Deja Vu as he limped forward, one arm in wretched pain and the other gripping the bandage with light compressions.

Dee walked at his side, leading the way with her wrist torch blasting through the darkness. Half of her attention was fixed on the path ahead, the other half trained on Theo's wobbling steps, while she kept one hand tense and ready to grab him if he fell.

They passed a wooden door with a stenciled letter that said MAINTENANCE OFFICE SHIPPING AND LOADING.

Theo stopped.

"I don't remember this door," he said, "do you?"

"I think we came in through the other side of the room. But I don't know."

Theo considered the door.

"Why don't we go this way," he said, "if it's for loading, then it must have a faster way to the surface. A faster way out of here."

Dee flashed her light on the door. It bounced in the tight quarters of the hallway, and she winced at the sudden brightness.

Then she swung the light behind her to illuminate the original place from where they entered. That way would lead up the staircase, through the tall room with the chandelier, and up and out the side of the building past the stone lions.

It was a long way.

"We should leave the same way we came," she said, "leave minimal footprints. I mean, I'm sure we're in the clear here, but you never know what might catch up with you when you least expect it."

Theo made a groaning sound but quickly cut it short to mask his pain.

"The SCR might not be the smartest, but they can be tricky sometimes," she said.

"But this way might be faster, he said, "and hey, if it's not, we can always go the way we came. That'll be our plan B. Yeah?"

Dee sighed.

Theo grabbed the door handle to the Maintenance office and gave it a cautious turn. He moved slowly at first, then waited for each latch mechanism to clear and click into place. It moved smoothly, and the door popped loose. The hinges creaked with an almost sorrowful sound.

He looked back at Dee with a satisfied look on his face.

She shrugged and nodded.

As Theo opened the door, Dee pointed her wrist torch into the room, slicing the angles like a pie to ensure it was clear of surprises.

The long, narrow room expanded into a wide opening at the far end. Near the back of the room, a loading elevator sat idle with its sliding cage door half-open. The walls were peeling. Years of wallpaper and paint cascaded like tumbling water, colors of white and gray and textured patterns. Rows and rows of small drawers were lined along the wall. They stored a catalog of maintenance records, each note card marked by year and month. Theo picked one up to inspect it. February 2082. March 2082. April 2082. Then, the dates seemed to end.

Dee pointed her light toward the elevator.

"There!" she said.

Theo walked up to the threshold of the half-open elevator and pulled back the gate. It dragged along a groove in the floor, rusted by years of inactivity and neglect.

"If there's residual power coming into those computers," said Dee, "there's a chance there might be some flowing to the elevator."

"Let's hope," said Theo.

They stepped into the car. Theo slid the grate closed, giving it a tug with all his body weight to close the gap of the last few inches. It dragged with a terrible squeal.

Dee lit up a metal box at the rear of the elevator car. It was caked in rust and was missing a panel, but when she looked closer, she saw a single lever protruding outward.

It read: B3, B2, B1, GRD.

She cranked the lever to GRD.

Silence.

"Ummm," she said.

"Maybe there's a—"

Something rumbled beneath them and startled Theo. The car lurched down an inch, then stopped. Moments later, with a soft vibration, the car began to rise. Theo and Dee watched the maintenance office floor disappear below them, followed by two more industrial metal doors that slid into view and disappeared. Finally, the elevator car rolled to a crawl and jerked violently one last time as it stopped at the ground floor.

Dee reached to grab the wall and caught her balance as the car stopped.

Theo peeled back the gate.

A heavy metal door stood before them, a faint light leaking through its hinges and around the edge. Theo looked to Dee, who raised her brow and shrugged with approval.

He tried the handle and prepared himself to push through the door, which looked encrusted with rust and debris. He bent his knees and lowered his hips and started to press the door forward with all of his weight.

But after a light touch, the heavy door swung free.

It moved effortlessly and smoothly.

The door didn't even make a sound, he thought. Were the hinges greased recently?

"That was... weird," said Dee.

They stepped into the dim light of the forgotten city. A forest of concrete columns extended into the distance, and scrap-lined streets crisscrossed for miles in each direction.

Theo breathed in a lungful of the sweet air of accomplishment, even though it smelled of decaying bricks and spilled fuel. It filled his chest with an ease he hadn't felt in months.

"Do you smell that?" said Theo, sniffing into the darkness. "What is that, diesel?"

Theo turned to Dee, but she was gone.

Confused, he looked back toward the elevator corridor where they had come from.

It was empty.

His head was plunged into a black bag, which tightened around his throat. Thickly gloved hands held it tight behind him. The fabric scratched at his neck and was thick enough to block out all light.

He was trapped in the dark.

Entirely alone.

Someone swept his leg and wrestled him to the ground.

Theo tried to kick free, but his boots slipped on the soft gravel, and he couldn't get leverage on anything solid.

He didn't feel the needle prick his neck until it was too late. Liquid sleep flooded his veins until the world was silent.

CHAPTER 23

ARIA

"You're right on time. I had a feeling we would be seeing you again."

Theo heard a woman's voice through a speaker.

"Mr. Blake is certainly relentless, isn't he?" said the woman.

He opened his eyes and blinked repeatedly to shake away the mental cobwebs.

Trent, he thought? Why is she talking about Trent?

It took six seconds for the blurriness to subside.

"You've demonstrated tremendous fortitude in your journey here, Theo. Admirably more impressive than the last one."

He tried to turn his head, but movement was limited. He tugged at his arms, but he couldn't move. He searched the room, looking in all corners of his field of view. His arms were secured with metal cuffs that latched across his wrists and above his elbow.

It was a stark white room. Empty at first, then details emerged slowly as his eyes acclimated to the intense light. Smooth, glossy tiles lined the walls and floor. The ceiling was tall. He was strapped down to a flat metal slab that was rotated vertically, so he felt like he was standing up against a cold wall.

Ankles and legs were also locked. From the corner of his eye, a mechanical arm appeared and lowered from a bulky contraption mounted on the ceiling.

The mechanical arm lowered a screen in front of his face.

A woman's face appeared on the screen, shoulders and up. She was beautiful, with an intensely symmetrical face, short-cropped hair, and an immaculately tailored suit jacket with intricate embroidery that suggested an air of privilege and unquestioned authority.

"Theo," the voice said, "I am Aria Sloan. The Sloan Coastal Republic is the enterprise under my command."

She smiled. It was warm and welcoming. Her eyebrows tilted upwards, alluring and disarming.

"I know why you have come, Theo. I can only imagine the terrible things you must have heard about us. Many of your brothers have been here before, and I have no doubt Mr. Blake will continue to send more of you as long as he remains alive."

Her voice had a soothing tone.

"All I ask of you is that you grant me a moment of grace and give me a chance to show you that things may not be what they seem. I worry you may have the wrong impression of us. Will you allow me that, Theo?"

He didn't respond. He tugged at the cuffs. Tried to kick at the foot harness but could not begin to flex his legs.

Four soldiers entered the room and took sentry positions to Theo's left and right. Then, a familiar black boot emerged from behind the screen. That long slate coat flapped in the air as it moved. A Kaipher stepped out from behind the shadow.

Theo knew those deep stitch marks and the leathery skin that stretched over muscle in unnatural ways looked familiar. The scuffed handle of an energy whip protruded from the holster on its waist.

Blackburn! The Kaipher from the plane, he recalled. The commander of the soldiers on the island.

Aria tilted her face forward toward the camera. The articulating arm carried the screen closer to Theo's face. It enveloped his field of view. It was suffocating.

"We are the SCR. This is the reality of this place and the vital work we do," said Aria.

Theo's pulse raced. His blood boiled, and his face flushed crimson.

"For over 250 years," she continued, "the SCR has been dedicated to the prosperity and perpetual improvement of the human species. History has taught us that bold action sometimes requires difficult decisions, and let me tell you from experience that this has not been easy. Hard choices are often misunderstood by those who must be left behind if humanity is to thrive for another thousand years."

"Theo, there is no easy way to say this, but our planet is in peril. You have experienced the storms and seen the rising oceans, but I am afraid that's just the beginning. It is much worse than many are aware. Within the next five hundred years, we will face detrimental resource constraints. Food, fuel, and building supplies. Within another four hundred years, the earth will slowly slide toward the inevitable: a planet unfit to sustain life. Climate degradation is happening at a scale we could not previously have imagined. The evidence is damning. Melting polar regions have caused a redistribution of mass among the planet's surface, causing the earth's rotation to slow. This is irreversible, despite our best efforts to find a solution. And that's not the most terrifying fact. Several centuries ago, we were on a trajectory toward the goal of becoming a multi-planetary species, but wars between nations and strife over resources consumed us. We, as a species, failed. We were tragically behind in aerospace technology and ill-equipped to explore the stars. We missed our window to leave this planet, and now our fate has been sealed."

"Humanity is dying, Theo," she continued, "And we, the SCR, have taken on the burden of ensuring humanity has the best possible chance of survival. With dwindling resources, sacrifices must be made. Only those with the most potential to serve the future of humanity must be allowed to continue. We are the elites, Theo. The smartest, strongest, those with the most steadfast resolve and resilience under pressure. Our extended lifespan allows us to pursue research spanning multiple generations, compounding our knowledge and innovation. We are the future, Theo. And to ensure the prosperity of future generations, we must make sure our limited resources go to those who are fittest for that future. That means some, unfortunately, must be left behind."

"It is my responsibility to protect the SCR," she continued, "I don't know if those who oppose us will ever quite understand what we are striving for..."

Aria paused. For a moment, there was a flicker of unease in her eyes. It lingered but disappeared quickly and was replaced with a machine-like coldness.

"But now, far too much is at stake."

A second screen lowered from the mechanical arm and moved close to Theo's face, filling his field of view. One screen of Aria Sloan was on the left, and the other screen on the right was black. The background flickered to life as the display panel powered up.

It was a satellite video feed of a flat, brown landscape. Trees peppered the surroundings, and a flat wooden structure sat in the middle. It was a wide building with three partitions connected by interlocking corridors. Machine parts were scattered along one side of the building. Details emerged as the satellite feed optimized its display resolution, and Theo recognized the scene.

It was the Ranch.

"Theo, you've been in a medically induced coma for sixteen days. We woke you today because today is a very momentous occasion."

The image on the screen zoomed in on two figures climbing a ladder, tightening joints on a tall array of cylindrical objects housed within a metal cage.

"During the time you were out, your friends at the Ranch were busy. In fact, they've made an admirable amount of progress on building the Aeonite machine."

The figures on the screen descended the ladder and disappeared beneath the roof of the building. After a moment, they reappeared carrying a coil of thick cables. It snaked across the ground behind them. They connected the cables to the base of the machine, one figure holding the cable in place, the other tightening the connection point.

"We predicted that you would look for a means to transmit the stolen data. Given the circumstances in which you found yourself—alone and so far from home with no help and no resources—it was the only logical course of action. After all, Theo, the probability of you returning home alive to deliver the chip was virtually zero."

Theo turned his attention from the small figures on the screen to Aria's face. Her jaw and lips tightened, and her eyes grew narrower. She had the look of a predator marveling at its superiority as its trapped prey squirmed helplessly.

"We started to track you from the Scraper ship, Theo, but thought we had lost you until you scanned your eyes on that bridge. And I knew, at that moment, we had found you. By the time you initiated that data file transfer, we were ready to intercept the data."

"Our Aeonite machine is incredibly difficult to replicate," she continued, "given the complexity of the schematics, the most logical place someone may begin is with the assembly of the energy storage apparatus. So, we made a small change to the plan. A small change... but a significant one. You see, a functioning

Aeonite machine requires a carefully regulated current to ensure the extruder wands operate correctly. Otherwise, the integrity of the reconstructed cellular walls will suffer a catastrophic failure. However, with one minor change to the files, the machine would return the electrical current to the storage apparatus instead of sending it to the extruder wands."

Her smile widened, and her eyes grew larger as she observed Theo's gaze darting around the corners of the white room. He struggled to piece together the information, following the trail of clues to see where it would lead.

"In theory, upon initiating the first power-up sequence, what may seem like a normal power cycle will quickly result in a... spectacular event."

Theo looked at Aria on the screen. Their eyes connected momentarily before she quickly looked off-camera toward the second screen.

"There... ah yes! It looks like we are seeing movement on the ground! Yes, yes. Enhance the image! Get up close on that satellite feed. It looks like they may be attempting the first power-up sequence soon. Let's see how this little experiment plays out, shall we?"

The figures on the screen were nothing more than clumps of pixels. They climbed over one another to attach a cable. The lens on the satellite broadcast zoomed out to include the entirety of the building and surrounding trees. Theo remembered that road where trucks strained to climb up the steep incline beside the buildings.

At first, nothing happened. It was a tense and silent moment. Then, the screen flashed white for one-sixtieth of a second, and smoke and debris blanketed the countryside in a gray smudge.

Theo screamed at the monitor in front of him. He begged Aria to stop. Blood rushed to his head as he ran his vocal cords ragged. He couldn't hear the words coming out of his mouth, his mind racing into overdrive, trying to process the nightmare unfolding before him. His ears popped from the pressure and the volume of his own voice.

The smoke began to clear. Shattered boards and torn branches were thrown across the dirt. There was a blackened pit in the middle of the screen with specks of small fires, but everything else was flattened. Gone. Empty. No bodies in sight, or at least no identifiable shapes that suggested human-like bodies with limbs intact. Pixelated artifacts on the screen looked like they could have been remnants of legs or arms, or maybe they were just shards of tree trunks. Theo couldn't tell for certain.

It looked as if there was nothing there to begin with.

"No, NOOO!" he screamed again.

Amidst the screaming and silent explosion on the screen, Theo couldn't feel his saliva as it dripped from his lips and his face contorted into painful shapes.

"Noooooooo..." he said, quietly this time. Barely a whisper of air seeped from his lungs because he had nothing left.

"I am so sorry, Theo," said Aria, "I know how hard this must be for you to watch, but I am afraid it was a necessary precaution."

Theo couldn't comprehend what she was saying. The pressure in his ears drowned out her words, and he couldn't pull his eyes away from the image on the satellite feed.

"These people... they're not like you, Theo. They're not fit for the future that humanity desperately needs."

The small fires died out along the edge of the black spot where Trent's lab once lived.

"They're not like us, as much as you might think. They would have become a burden. A burden that our world is simply not capable of supporting. They would have held us back back back back BACK BACK BACK BACK–"

The image of Aria melted into a kaleidoscope of colorful pixels on the screen. Her face bent into unnatural angles, and her voice glitched. Words became a tangle of syllables like a computer rushing to reassemble data packets with missing information.

"BACK BACK BACK BA BA BA BA BA CK CK CK–"

Both screens shut off.

Then, the lights in the room went dark. Everything went black except for the dim glow of white LEDs atop the exit door.

There was a loud sizzling sound very close to Theo, and the smell of burnt hair and flesh filled the room. He recognized that sound and that smell.

Theo tugged at the cuffs around his elbow. They unlocked and swung loose. He pulled his hands free, kicked open the cuffs at his ankle and broke free. He slid forward and landed with his bare feet on the cold tiled floor.

In the darkness, he could barely see the outline of soldiers lying motionless on the ground. Their helmets melted into a steaming soup of flesh and brain matter. The Kaipher lay beside them, disoriented, searching the walls for a switch.

Theo looked toward the far end of the room.

The door was wide open.

He could see down the entire length of the connecting hallway. The next three doors were also open, and the hallway was clear. Faint lights on each door marked the way like stars in the night.

The floor shook. Theo felt the soft vibration of an explosion far in the distance. Pebbles of debris shuffled loose from the ceiling and pecked at his head, landing in his hair.

Emergency lights flipped on with a sharp mechanical click. The room was flooded in a dreary red light.

The Kaipher started to move. It raised its hand in front of its face to block out the flash glow of light directly above it.

Theo burst into a full sprint down the corridor. Lights streaked by in a blurry stream of cold air and adrenaline. His bare feet smacked the tile floor, heels pounding heavily as he rushed past open door after open door.

The loudspeaker boomed overhead.

It was Aria's voice.

"Theo, you disappoint me."

Her voice was different that time. Mixed with a lower octave of a man's voice.

Demonic and shifting unnatural.

"I had a hundred opportunities to kill you, but I welcomed you here thinking this time would be different from the others."

The voice twisted. It changed from Aria into someone else. Something else. It was cold and computational. Machine-like.

Theo reached the end of the hallway and turned a corner. He shot past more doors with connected observational windows, clean rooms, tubes and vials with glowing liquids, and gurneys with sheet-covered bodies.

"We are ushering in humanity's next phase of superiority, Theo. You could have been a part of that, but I see you have made your choice. You have chosen to fade into the past with the rest of those Midlander cockroaches."

The humanity in her voice was slowly siphoning away.

The hallway curved, and Theo stopped abruptly at a fork. It split to the left or the right. He looked down each hallway. They were full of identical featureless doorways and smooth white walls.

He was trapped in a maze.

"What a meaningless existence. Your actions prove that you reek of inferiority. You, Theoren Rousseau, are unfit for the future! So be it!"

Theo struggled to make up his mind: left or right, left or right. Confusion overwhelmed him, and the voice booming through the overhead speaker drilled into his mind.

"So. Be. It. So. Be. It."

It repeated like a haunting mantra echoing down the halls.

The sound vibrations were palpable. The air was thick with that insidious, electric voice. He could feel the sound waves seeping into his bones.

"SO SO SO SO BE BE BE IT IT IT IT IT–"

The voice spun out of control like a program stuck in a loop. It was getting louder. It was unbearable.

"IT IT IT IT IIIIIII–"

Then a cold hand grabbed his shoulder from behind.

CHAPTER 24

THE TRAIN

Theo jumped forward and spun around.

It was Dee.

"GO LEFT!" she screamed, her strained voice competing with the sound of the booming overhead speakers.

They raced down the left corridor towards a single elevator door. Dee jumped into the elevator and tapped furiously on her wrist device. She pressed her wrist against the elevator control panel, trying different combinations of codes, each resulting in a blinking red light and a harsh buzzing tone.

"GET IN!" she screamed at Theo.

She tried the panel buttons again.

It buzzed again and displayed a red glowing light.

"Dee, you're bleeding," said Theo, noticing dried streaks of blood down the side of Dee's face, "What, what is happening?" She didn't respond. She was focused on the elevator panel, gritting her teeth in frustration.

Theo looked back and forth at Dee, the red light on the elevator panel, and the long, empty corridor.

"Why aren't we moving?" he asked, the strain in his voice bleeding through his calm veneer.

She tapped again.

Red light.

"I'm TRYING!" said Dee.

Theo looked down the corridor. The shadow of a moving figure appeared in the distance. The sound of heavy boots in pursuit echoed from afar, getting closer with each second.

The blue glow of the Kaipher's energy whip filled the corridor with a ghostly light.

Dee tapped her device again, and the light turned green. The elevator doors started to slide closed, and she let out a breath of relief.

The Kaipher rounded the corner, spotted them, and barreled down the corridor. Its energy whip flailed gracefully like a kite tail in the breeze, and whenever it brushed against the sidewall, sparks popped like fireworks.

It was halfway down the corridor and racing directly for them.

The elevator doors shut, and the motorized lock mechanism engaged. The car began to descend with a soft vibration.

The Kaipher's boots pounded on the other side of the door, thunderous and close. Then, the footsteps suddenly stopped.

A flash of blue light exploded into the interior of the elevator car as the Kaipher's whip pierced through the metal walls, and a sharp, straight line appeared glowing on the ceiling. A triangular chunk of the ceiling ripped off and tumbled down the adjacent shaft. Freezing cold air flooded the car with an audible woosh. Through the opening, Dee watched tubes and wires and metal beams slide up and out of view as the elevator descended. Theo's stomach lurched as the car gained speed, causing the walls to vibrate. The floors kept rushing by, and for a moment, he thought the car might come crashing to a fiery wreck at the bottom of the shaft but it still kept going.

How tall is this building, he thought?

Theo looked at Dee, his eyes filling with terror as the descent continued.

Suddenly, the elevator jolted to a stop on the ground floor. The doors whipped open, and Dee led Theo out of the building through a nondescript, rusted door. It was the type of door no one bothered paying attention to unless they had a predetermined route and a calculated plan.

They spilled out into the bright daylight of a Capital street.

"Hurry, this way!" screamed Dee.

"I think... I think we lost it, for now at least."

"No, it's not the Kaipher we need to get away from." said Dee, "all the plans have changed. The balance of power is shifting," she spoke in bursts in between pained breaths, "They raided Out City. They leveled the shanties. They must have gotten some indicator, some hint at things to come. But there's no more time now! Our timeline has moved up!"

She bounded around a corner down an alleyway and rolled a pile of trash containers out of the way.

"Our timeli—what is going on, Dee?"

She reached under a pile of wet leaves and pulled a hand-crank lever to reveal an open hatch.

"Here!"

"But—"

"Go, Theo! NOW!"

He lowered himself into the hatch and stretched his ragged bare feet, feeling for the first rung of the cable ladder. He felt the cold contact of metal and slowly lowered his weight onto the rung. Dee dragged two large trash containers back into place to camouflage the hatch and shut it behind her as they climbed back into the Under City. The rumbling in the distance was getting louder as Theo reached the bottom of the ladder, his wet bare feet instantly blackened when he touched the dirt.

Dee pulled on the ladder to dislodge it from the panels above. It fell into an unruly heap.

"We need to get clear of the Capital, Theo,"

"What? Why, Dee?"

"You remember those charges I had in my pack? The orange ones?"

"Yeah."

"Well, that's why!" said Dee, "The Capital is going to be a crater in the earth soon. I set charges on the thirteen most load-bearing columns holding up the city. The first three went off successfully. It sent quakes all through the buildings, and the SCR is spooked. They're searching for the other charges as we speak. This is the end, Theo! Cutting down the snake at its head! But we're running out of time!"

Dee took off running toward a dip in the pavement up ahead.

Theo tried to catch his breath and make sense of all the information Dee had just given him, but when a panel high above him cracked with a pop that sounded like thunder, he quickly picked up his feet and rushed after her.

Dee was a blurry shadow running ahead in the dark. Theo followed and climbed down the steps of an old-world escalator overrun with wild plants. He took each step carefully, the metal grates pressing painfully into the skin of his bare feet. It looked as if it hadn't been powered up in years or centuries.

Rows of parallel escalators formed lines to his left and right. Then, all led downward toward a tunnel that opened into a wide, empty plaza with a concave roof of steel and patterned glass. It may have been stained glass once, in another life long ago, but all of its glamor was lost to the dust and shadows.

A disc-shaped chunk of concrete hung from the ceiling.

Light bled in from the forgotten city streets above.

"Hurry!" shouted Dee, rushing down more steps and

descending deeper into the darkness. "They'll be on us any second!"

Gone was the musty smell of brick and dirt. The air transformed like Theo had been transported into a new world. It became thick. Dank water, subterranean mold, and the earthy scent of moss filled the cavern.

"Where the hell are you going?" shouted Theo, "Where- what are we looking for?"

His feet pounded the partially tiled floor, skipping over splinters of rotting wood.

"A way out of all of this!" said Dee, words filling gaps between breaths, "I've made my decision!"

"Your what? What decision?"

"To come with you," said Dee. She came to a halt at the entrance to the final staircase, which plummeted into nothingness. It was the final level of the underground tunnels beneath the forgotten city.

"While they held you, the SCR, I was trying to devise a plan to get you out. And it gave me time to think. And I realized you're right. You've always been right. There's nothing for me here, now. Nothing for me anymore. But if I can be useful there and contribute something to your people... I'm in. I'm all in."

Theo nodded and smiled and, for the first time since being captive in that white room, began to feel the faint swell of hope return.

They descended the last staircase, zigzagging through the pitch dark, hands groping the railing to guide them.

Dee switched on her wrist torch, and white light flooded the scene. The stairs opened into an underground train yard with hundreds of tracks extending far beyond the throw of Dee's light. Rows upon rows of tracks, some barren, and several overgrown with snaking vines drawing nourishment from the moisture in the air. Segments of the train yard were indistinguishable from an Amazon jungle, given the explosion of greenery and years of uninterrupted growth.

Dee's eyes darted back and forth between the train cars.

"Find one with a plow!" she shouted.

"A plow?"

"For clearing snow. It's a big hunk of metal on the front of–"

"I know what a plow is!"

"Then why did you–"

"There!" said Theo, pointing to a silver stretch of train cars three rows over.

They hopped over the tracks.

Needles of pain shot up Theo's bare feet, but he kept moving.

He tried to step around the small, sharp pebbles by balancing atop the flat metal tracks, but the pebbles scattered everywhere by the thousands, and he couldn't avoid them.

Dee reached the train first and unlatched the door to the front cab. She hopped inside, and light from her torch glowed through the windows.

A short while later, slowed by his bruised feet, Theo approached the front cab. He quickly looked over his shoulder, feeling like someone was watching him, but the darkness was empty and silent. He stepped into the cab.

Dee was cranking furiously on the lever on the center panel. The waist-high dashboard was split into three panels, and the windshield, with its vast glass panel and metal frame, looked to be intact. The dashboard was a crowded patchwork of instruments and digital displays on the left and circular dials of various sizes on the right.

She cranked a lever again and pressed a wide, yellow button. She braced, expecting something to happen, but the train remained quiet.

"No power," she said, "this is not good. Not good!"

"These things are probably a hundred years old. What did

you expect?"

"This whole place is connected. I studied the blueprints and the power routing diagrams. Everything is connected," she flipped a switch that should have toggled an overhead light, "even though they wired the Capital above with a gazillion megawatts of power, they never separated it from the grid down here."

Dee spoke quickly, spreading her fingers across three buttons, and pressing and holding to initiate a reset but it didn't work.

"The Capital is siphoning all the power," she said, a concerned look on her face as she turned to look at the outline of Theo's face in the bouncing light.

"You look at me like I'm supposed to know what any of that—"

"It means we can't power the train until I blow the last charges and take out the central power station. Only then will the power route here, where we need it."

Theo shook his head, trying to follow along.

"And the central station is where exactly?"

Dee pointed upward toward the ceiling.

"Awesome."

"Directly above us," said Dee, "if we blow that, we need to get out of here right fuckin' quick."

The train vibrated.

A faraway explosion reverberated like a muffled gong through the underground station.

"And when you hit the switch and blow it, how long do we have before everything comes tumbling down?"

Dee shrugged. She shook her head, the beam of light sweeping up and down on the wall.

"A minute. Maybe more."

"And you actually think this will work?"

"In theory, yes."

"In theory..." said Theo, quietly, more to himself than to Dee. He took a deep breath and looked out at the long lines of tracks extending into the darkness. He thought of the people who used to ride these trains long ago, in another time, and they seemed like they were in another world entirely. Where were they going? To be with family? To escape heartbreak? A ghostly vision of thousands of people boarding and sitting and shuffling about flooded his mind.

"Dee, I trust you," he said, "if you say it will work, then it'll work. I wouldn't have gotten that far without you. So let's blow this and get the hell out."

She smiled across the left side of her face, the right side holding onto a hint of doubt.

Dee nodded.

"If we're going to do this, we need to clear the tracks. Once the power comes on, we'll only have seconds to get going, and we need to move. Or else."

"Okay," said Theo. He shifted weight on his feet, and when the light bounced across the cabin, Dee noticed the dark splotches of blood on the metal floor of the train car. It started at the doorway and scrawled its way to a mess of red smeared under Theo's feet.

"You're bleeding!"

Theo looked down at the blood with a sharp gasp, "It was so dark. I didn't know it was this bad."

Dee reached for a first aid kit mounted on the wall and ripped it down. The front panel unlatched and popped open in a cloud of dust. She coughed and swiped her hand through the air to clear the brown cloud lingering around her face.

"Here," she said, handing Theo an ancient roll of medical gauze wrapped in petrified plastic. It cracked like an autumn leaf.

"Wrap that up. I'll make a pass around the train to check the tracks. I'll be back in sixty seconds, and we'll blow this thing. Good?"

Theo nodded.

"Good."

Dee jumped past the steps and disappeared outside the car door. The interior plunged into darkness as light from Dee's wrist torch bounced and reflected across surfaces outside. Theo reached into the first aid kit and pulled what looked like a dried-up emergency flare from the piles of items.

"Let's see if you go one more light in you, shall we?"

He struck the tip, and the flare erupted into a fountain of sparks. It filled the cabin with white smoke, and he quickly tossed it away. The flare bounced down the steps and landed outside beside the tracks.

He rolled the gauze, coughing as the smoke cleared, and wrapped his bleeding foot. He planted it down, braced for pain, and wrapped the other foot.

As the cabin dimmed again, Theo's mind raced with doubts he had been ignoring. But in the moments of quiet, when distractions have faded out of sight, that's when the demons came out.

What if she's wrong, he thought? What if we die down here? Crushed in the darkness beneath a million tons of rubble. Entombed forever in dust. The Midlands would never know how hard he tried to get home. How close he had almost come.

He tied the gauze and rested his foot.

He wondered what difference he could still make. The Ranch was flattened and turned into a smoking crater. They were all dead. He wasn't even sure there was anything to return to, even if he could make it all the way home.

The sound of metal sliding against metal squeaked outside the train car.

"Dee?"

Silence.

The flare began to dim but still sent warm pulses of light through the doorway.

Another sound. Something plodding across the ground.

Theo felt the train car jolt and the wheels swayed freely.

The flare was almost out. It popped spectacularly as it neared the end of its fuel, sending sparks into the air and across to the nearby set of tracks.

Then the light died.

Darkness came creeping back.

"Dee? That you?"

Nothing but silence.

Only the soft and distant crunch of gravel under boots.

CHAPTER 25

ACCELERATION

Dee stepped into the car. She reflected her light off the metal ceiling.

Theo exhaled loudly and startled her, causing her to nearly trip on the steps. She pointed the light toward his gauze-wrapped feet.

"Not pretty, but it'll hold," he said.

"Excellent. I managed to clear some debris off the rear tracks, so we're clear on that side, and the plow should handle the rest upfront. I tried to decouple the rear cars to get to us on the move faster, but most of them were rusted shut. I could only disconnect the one nine cars back, so we'll be dragging a little weight, but that'll have to do."

They both jolted to attention as a loud crash echoed from the stairwell across the trainyard. Theo felt an electricity in the air that was not there a moment ago.

He knew the Kaipher was near.

"We're out of time," said Dee, "we need to go."

Theo nodded, "I'm with you. Let's light it up."

He looked out through the windshield. The railroad tracks disappeared into a darkness so black one could think they had discovered the end of the earth. Dee took a breath and looked ahead into the looming darkness.

She mouthed a silent prayer.

She tapped a command into her wrist terminal and held her hands over the train's control panel. One hand ready to punch the GO button, and the other poised over the lever, rocked fully to the rear position.

The ceiling vibrated. Dust fell, and pieces of concrete dislodged from the ceiling and bounced off the train's roof like hail.

Silence.

"Was that it?" said Theo, "That didn't feel like–"

A second explosion rocked the ceiling, and the rumbling became a deep, ear-shattering thunder.

Dee watched the control panel, her forehead tense and eyes unblinking. Beads of sweat gathered on her face. Her eyes flicked back and forth across the instrument panel and the tiny glass status light on the right side of the dash. She counted seconds that felt like hours, waiting for the perfect moment when the power would reroute from the capital above to the subterranean networks that powered the trains.

After a few seconds, the light glowed with a soft amber-like color of honey.

"Rockin'!"

She punched the yellow button and thrust the lever forward until it locked into the top-speed position.

The floor vibrated. The car hummed to life. A slow turn of the piston began, and torque built up in the engine. The rumbling grew louder, and it pounded into Theo's eardrum like a heavy punch to the temple.

The train began to move.

It rolled forward on the tracks.

For a quick moment, it lurched backward, straining to pick up the weight of the cars behind it. Then, it started to speed up.

Debris overhead came crashing down in basketball-sized pieces. Aerosolized concrete dusted the windshield in a thick layer of gray.

"Can't this thing go any faster?" Theo smacked the side of the wall with his palm.

"Hey, it just needs a minute to gain some speed."

"Do we even have a minute?"

"We have one," said Dee, "Only one. And it'll have to do!"

Twenty yards ahead, a metal beam fell from the ceiling and came to rest perpendicular to the tracks.

"Hold on!" said Dee.

The plow kicked the beam aside in a crash of metal-on-metal. The train jolted from the impact.

Finally, the speed increased.

Dee tapped her fingers across the bottom of the control panel and flipped a switch. A single headlight came to life, spreading a dim orange beam over the tracks.

The chassis vibrated even more as the engine built up power. Dust puffed off the train like a rainy mist in the night.

After another moment of darkness, they emerged out of the tunnel.

Daylight flooded through the windows.

The way forward was clear, metal tracks and small round stones paving the way. Overgrown foliage hung over the sides of the tunnel like green waterfalls. It was apparent that the tracks hadn't been used in many years. The rumbling intensified, and Theo looked out the window towards the tunnel where they escaped, just in time to see the city fall.

He remembered those tall, reflective towers, how they looked so small, sitting upon the horizon when he was traveling up the beach. Now, up close, they were monstrous marvels of engineering, glistening in the bright sunlight. In the center of the Capital, one of the tallest buildings began to shudder and then flex inwards. From a distance, they looked like swords made of diamonds piercing the veil of the blue sky above.

Then, a second tower, adjacent to the first but shorter and wider in shape, sank behind the others and disappeared from the skyline. A white cloud began to gather behind the silhouette of the capital.

One by one, the columns snapped like twigs. Streets collapsed. Glass shattered and rained down on the upper capital streets, shining like a cloud of glitter.

Explosions flattened the Under City beneath a cover of clouds and dust. Buildings imploding under their own weight expelled shockwaves of violent energy laterally, ripping glass from windows, pummeling bricks into powder, and peppering the concrete sea wall that had held for several centuries with thousands of tiny holes. Within seconds, holes spread to cracks across the sea wall, crawling dark trails up its cold surface until the concrete could handle no more and surrendered to the immense pressure.

The sea wall collapsed, and torrents of water rushed in.

Slowly, then all at once, the capital folded in on its own foundation.

Memories of the explosion at the Ranch flickered through Theo's mind. Like a flashbulb, vivid images burst in and out of his consciousness. He remembered the cold feeling of the metal table on his skin, the straps digging into his wrist. How that wave of white light took over the screen that hung down from the ceiling. And seeing the place where Trent's Aeonite machine had been constructed turned into a blackened crater. An entire story blinked out of existence as Aria Sloan's wretched smiling face and empathic eyes mouthed meaningless words on the adjacent screen.

He watched the Capital buildings fall and exhaled.

After such a cacophony of destruction, the silence that followed was unnerving. Theo collapsed onto the floor of the train car and leaned his head against a storage cabinet. He watched as leafless trees whipped by and clouds stretched across the horizon like a single white brush stroke.

The train hit a straight stretch of open track, and the ride became smooth.

Dee sat against the padded conductor's stool, head bowed, half in disbelief and half in terror at the thought of her deepest, darkest desire—to flatten the capital—coming true after all those years of pain. She struggled to breathe. Tears tried to claw their way out, but the sorrow was drowned out by so many confusing emotions. After a moment, her body and mind collapsed under the pressure. She spun around and retched a mess onto the metal floor.

Theo stared at the clouds as the train chugged forward, trying to avoid looking over at Dee falling apart for fear it would also give him permission to break. He, too, wrestled with the slow, encroaching feeling of doom that came with traveling the final leg of a journey without knowing if there was a destination to greet you at the end.

He kept replaying the images on the screen, unable to get them out of his mind. The building vanished in a white flash of fire.

That really happened, he thought. Or did it? He wrestled with the truth in his head. He saw it with his own eyes. Was it real? His mind resisted it. It wouldn't let him accept it. Back in the capital, he had seen how displays could be manipulated to create intricate holographic light shows. Anything could be adjusted, edited, or misrepresented on video or digitally created entirely anew out of absolutely nothing.

Theo closed his eyes and felt the light rumble of the train's wheels bumping over the tracks, its suspension smoothing the ride.

No, it was real, he thought. It happened. He had to accept it. He would know it when he saw it in person.

"See what?" asked Dee, returning to life from being a heap on the floor.

Theo realized he must have been muttering to himself. He wondered how much she heard and how much he might have said.

"So, that's it," said Theo, "We're home free now. We ride off into the sunset?"

Dee coughed up a storm of dry, putrid air.

"No," she said, shaking her head, "no... no... that's not it."

A pained look came across Theo's face, and he was suddenly more alert and present.

"There's one more problem," she said, wiping her mouth and taking a deep breath. She looked out the windshield at the tracks that curved gently in the distance.

"The Roanoke gate. At the outer wall."

Theo remembered hearing about the wall when he was growing up. It was built in 2078 when the coastal states broke away from the midlands. It took nearly a decade to build, and thousands of lives were lost during construction. But individual loss was simply fuel for thrusting humanity into the future. That was the SCR way.

"I tried to open the gate," she continued, "but they locked the network. I hoped that if the Capital was disrupted, I'd be cleared for one last hack on an open frequency before the city fell. They must have initiated the frequency reset as a last measure shortly before the buildings came down."

A rough vibration came up through the floor. The smooth rails hit an uneven patch of earth, and the train's suspension fought hard to absorb it.

Theo exhaled a sharp lung-full of air. Fatigue bore down on him as he looked at his bloodied feet.

"So we've managed to not die and make it this far despite impossible odds," said Theo, "only to now be barreling down the tracks heading for a solid concrete wall?"

Dee sighed, resigning to her own fatigue.

"Well, you're not wrong," she said.

"And how long do we have until, you know?"

"At this speed, maybe twenty minutes. Twenty-five tops."

"Uh-huh."

Theo imagined how nice it would be to float among those white clouds right about then, floating free, high above the earth and all of its problems. War, death, arrogance, hatred, division, disease, pain, grief.

To just fly away.

Then, a swift wind surged in through the open door. It was cold and gusted into his eyes. He was wide awake.

"Wait," said Theo, "how many blast charges do you have left?"

"Charges? I think I used them all. They're gone."

Theo reached for Dee's pack, slouched on the floor like a rumple of fabric under the train conductor's seat. He plunged a hand into the pack, fumbling along one edge and sweeping his fingers into the corner.

He stopped.

He looked at Dee. Their eyes met.

He pulled a small orange object from the pack. It was wrapped in plastic and had a mess of twine tied hurriedly around its middle.

Dee looked at the blast charge, then looked ahead at the tracks racing toward them. Theo could see her mind calculating a way forward. She tilted her head. She opened her mouth to speak but hesitated.

"We can blow it," said Theo, "right? Blow the gate?"

Dee shook her head.

"That's assuming we can stop this train long enough to get out and place the charge. No, nope, it won't work."

"Ok, ok. What about some way to shoot it in front us before the train reaches the—"

"It doesn't even matter," she said, "those walls are over a hundred years old. They're thirty feet of concrete. Maybe more. Probably more. One charge wouldn't make a dent."

"Well, then, there must be some kind of weak point or a place where the blast charge could, you know, exploit some point with a—"

"My original plan was to remove the electronic lock that engages to keep it shut. If I could have gotten that to disengage with a remote hack... ah, but it doesn't even make a difference because those fuckers scrambled everything, and now I have nothing to work with."

She jabbed a finger on her wrist device repeatedly until it stopped responding, then smacked it with a swipe of her hand.

"There's nothing. Nothing. It's game over."

"Wait. Stop. Tell me more about that gate."

"The gate? It's impossibly tall and thick with solid concrete and—"

"No, no, the locks."

"The electronic locks sit at the base of the gates and keep them closed. When they disengage, the gate swings freely, but it's too heavy for a mechanical apparatus to open, so soldiers at the wall operate it manually."

Theo listened intently, tilting his head as he felt the weight of the orange explosive charge shuffling around in his palm.

"So the lock disconnects," she continued, "the soldiers operate a gear that swings it open. Then they close it and re-engage the lock to hold it in place."

"And if, IF, we can get this charge on one of the locks, will the gate swing freely?"

"Well, yeah. Yes. What are you—"

"And if the gate swung free, we could use the plow on the front as a battering ram?"

Dee winced and shook her head.

"You want to take this hunk of metal and turn it into a battering ram at 135 miles per hour? With us still on it? Are you insane?"

"It could work, couldn't it?"

"I don't... well, even if it wasn't an insane idea, and even if we had a way to shoot the charge directly at the lock, and even if the gate opened at the right time, we still only have one charge. One shot. That's it."

Theo sighed.

"We've come so far," he said, "sometimes all you need is one shot."

Dee tried to hide her mounting worries behind a smile, but it was all too evident to Theo that this may not play out in their favor. She looked up at the ceiling of the train car, her eyes sweeping down the metal columns and across the control panel adorned with knobs and buttons and spinning dials as if letting the beauty of that moment sink in before it all became a smoldering wreck of fire and bent metal.

Theo watched her think.

The ride was smooth as they hit another straight stretch of even track through the wilderness. They sat in a moment of peace, interrupted by the loss of the past and unknowns of the future.

Suddenly, the train shook with a violent jolt.

Dee was thrown to the floor, and Theo crashed his head into the corner of a metal handrail. He was disoriented. He got up, slowly trying to put weight on his bloody feet once again. The train was still intact, and they were still alive.

He looked over to Dee.

"What the hell was–"

Another earth-shaking boom rumbled from the back of the train.

There was a tight curve in the tracks coming up ahead. Theo watched the landscape out the window shift, trees sinking further into the distance. They hit a flat stretch of track beside a barren field. Dark rocks peeked out of the dirt and peppered the landscape.

Across the field, the last car became visible as the train entered the middle of a long, sweeping curve.

Theo could see a figure appear in the last train car—the ninth car. It was a person. It walked forward, stepping into the eighth train car. It loomed with slow steps, and Theo squinted to follow its movements, like a phantom figure, disappearing and reappearing in the spaces between the seats, behind the open windows, and on the threshold of the door as it swung open.

The figure entered the seventh car.

"Dee!" said Theo, eyes locked on the figure, one arm reaching back to see if she was alright.

"Yeah? Uhh."

"Look! There!" he pointed at the far end of the train.

The figure slid into the sixth car.

Back at the end of the train electric blue lines glowed brightly across its metal walls.

CHAPTER 26

BLACKBURN

Blackburn, he thought!

"It's that Kaipher," said Theo, "I know it from the island. How the hell did it find us here?"

"Oh god," said Dee, face contorted in pain and body still reeling from being rag-dolled across the floor.

"How much longer till the wall?"

"Maybe ten," she said with strained breaths, "but if we slow down now, it'll get right on top of us. We'll be dead."

"Fuck. We're dead either way."

Theo watched the train doors slide open and shut at the entrance to the fifth car. The dark outline of the figure loomed closer.

The train exited the curved part of the track and resumed along a straight path. The surrounding terrain became noticeably rocky, and Theo swayed and bumped against the wall as the suspension navigated bumps in the tracks. He held an arm out to steady himself.

On the straight track, Theo could no longer see where the

CALICO HILL

Kaipher was.

This is not good, he thought.

He spun around and looked at Dee. She had a hand on her head.

"Dee, you said we can decouple the cars. Back there, in the station, remember?"

"Yeah, I tried a few in the back, but they were all rusted shut. I could only get the tenth car to budge and break free."

"What about the second car?"

Dee looked up.

"I never tried the second car," she said, "I thought we'd need the weight to hold us together to plow through the debris on the tracks."

"But we're clear of all that debris now."

"I... yeah, I guess you're—"

"Dee," said Theo, speaking slowly and deliberately, pounding his words into the air like his life depended on it, "Can you decouple the second car?"

"I-I don't know if—"

Dee heard him, but the words were heavy like syrup in her brain. The jolt had rattled her hard, and she was trying to keep up with what was unfolding around her: the countdown to the wall, the Kaipher in pursuit, and the cold air blasting loudly through the train car.

"Can. You. Decouple. The Car."

In the distance, Theo thought he heard the sharp sound of a train door sliding open, then rolling shut with a heavy thunk.

"I think I can," said Dee, looking more awake.

"Dee, I need you to do it! Now! RIGHT NOW! GET UP! Go to the end of that car and DECOUPLE THE SECOND CAR! You need to do it before the Kaipher gets any closer!"

Dee focused. She took in Theo's words. He saw her eyes light up, clarity rushing in with a shot of adrenaline.

She leaped to her feet, arms out to maintain her balance in the swaying car. She stumbled toward the door and tugged on the latch. It flew open, and frigid air burst through the car like a hurricane.

Theo watched her from across the car. She reached below the floor where the train cars connected. The train hit another soft bump, and she collided with the side wall but held herself steady.

The sound of the metal door was clear in the distance. It slid open, the latch engaged, the tumbler rotated, and it closed with a metallic clank.

The Kaipher was closing in.

"I almost got it!" she screamed over the thunderous wind, her voice straining. She swung her arm below, pulled and twisted at something Theo couldn't see.

From the corner of his eye, Theo saw the edge of a face obscured in shadow. It appeared in the second car as the windows swayed around the soft bend in the tracks.

Leathery skin, wrinkled and studded. Dark blotches of brown and red spots along its neck and cheeks. Those empty eyes, one steel gray and another as blue as a cold mist over the ocean.

"Ok, I think I've got it!" Dee yelled again, her hand out of view, cranking a mechanism in the undercarriage of the car, "ALMOST. GOT IT. HERE WE G–"

A blinding flash of blue light.

Theo winced.

His retinas tingled with the pain of a thousand soft pinpricks. Then, the sensation quickly faded.

The Kaipher's energy whip sliced an opening in the second train car, and a geometric shape appeared on the front of the cabin. It took the wind a moment to grab the freshly cut sheet metal. It rattled in the breeze, jostling in place, but soon the air whipped under the opening and levitated the dissected part of the train like a feather in the breeze.

Dee pulled her arm back and decoupled the second car.

A part of the hitch fell onto the track.

It dragged behind the speeding train, sending a shower of white sparks erupting into the air. The wind whipped into the second train car.

The gap between the cars slowly widened, and the second car began to recede into the distance.

Dee pushed back onto the floor, one leg dangling off the side. She rolled over and got to her feet, grabbing the wall to steady herself as the car wobbled from the sudden weight change.

Suddenly, the air was terribly cold.

Dee looked up in time to see the Kaipher's arm stretched high overhead, muscles tense and arced back.

Its electric whip unfurled through the exposed sky, marking a wide and wicked curve.

It sliced through metal and glass.

And flesh.

And muscle.

And bone.

Dee's blood sprayed like fireworks.

A blue line zipped across her right arm.

The moment lasted a mere quarter of a second, but time felt like it had stretched for minutes. The side of her body pulsed with a brilliant blue glimmer, and then the brightness quickly vanished.

Her arm slipped silently into the wind, not like an appendage previously connected to her body, but rather like a branch flowing in a river, disconnected, foreign, and free. It twisted in the breeze and disappeared behind the mountain of sparks shooting up behind the train car.

She opened her mouth to scream, veins protruding from her neck.

Theo couldn't hear her.

Everything was deafening.

Metal grinding on metal, the air ripping past his ears.

Dee collapsed to the floor.

Behind her, the train car rolled farther into the distance as it gradually decelerated, but Theo could still see the Kaipher's eyes locked on to him, staring without blinking, clear as day, his eyes penetrating through the veil of sparks cascading around him.

Theo reached for the last remaining demolition charge. The slick plastic wrapper was soft in his hand. It warmed within his sweaty palm.

A tiny object with the capability of such world-shattering destruction.

Dee writhed on the floor, blood streaking down her arm. Singed black at her elbow stump. Dark liquid escaping below the burnt patches of skin.

Theo stared into the forest of sparks, with the Kaipher's eyes looming behind it.

He crushed the explosive in his hand and focused on the Kaipher standing at the edge of the second train car. Theo knew the second train car was seconds away from being too far out of range. He channeled his fury and sadness and threw the charge. It streaked through the air, a tiny orange blur, spinning along its course, flying straight and true like an arrow seeking its prey.

It disappeared behind the shower of sparks erupting into the air.

A violent tremor shook the train as the Kaipher separated into wet pieces in a brilliant white light.

The blast propelled the second train car farther into the distance.

Every surface was crawling with fire.

Its body vaporized above the waist, the train's metal walls smeared with a liquid that looked similar to human blood but with a green tint and fibrous texture.

So it wasn't quite human after all.

Theo watched the weak remains of its body collapse as the train car disappeared around a curve in the tracks, receding into the shadows. The legs were nothing but stumps.

He rushed to Dee. She was splayed out on the floor, burns across her face and arm pulsing hot blood.

He bolted to the front of the car, pulled the ancient first aid box from the floor, and rushed back to Dee. She was slipping in and out of consciousness. He wrapped a tourniquet around her arm as best he could and ratcheted it tight. She writhed on the floor. Theo unrolled a spool of gauze and wrapped it around her arm stump to slow the bleeding.

"I'm so sorry," she said, "I–"

"Stop," he said, "You saved us. The Kaipher's gone, and we broke free from the other cars."

Dee slowly regained consciousness. She searched the car and saw her bag, a rumpled pile of fabric, flat and empty.

"No, no!" she moaned, her breath weak and words soft.

"What? What is it?"

"That was our last charge," she strained to get air through her lungs without wincing in pain, "now there's no chance of opening the gate."

The car swayed.

A wave of warm air rushed in.

Theo held Dee in his arms on the floor of the train car, the bleeding slowing and their few quiet minutes slipping away before the train reached the wall. He looked at the control panel in front of the car. Levers and dials displaying full speed, straight course, zero deviation from a set and unchanging destination.

Then, in the center, the shaft with the red knob.

The speed control!

He leaped forward to get a closer look. A full spread of switches with protective flaps and a flat display screen with numbers spinning wildly out of control.

He pulled the red knob back with soft pressure at first, but after it failed to budge, he wrapped another hand around the knob and leaned his body weight into it, trying to lower the train's speed.

It was locked.

It wouldn't budge at all.

Beside the shaft, a digital panel read:

OVERRIDE IN PROGRESS
ADMINISTRATIVE LOCKDOWN COMMENCING

His stomach twisted.

He stepped back and took in the view of the cab. All the hinges and knobs, and rivets connecting sheet metal together with fabric, plastic, and glass. He imagined it all consumed by fire, burning, curling under the severe heat, flames hopping from one melting surface to the next. The fumes would be stinging and sour and poisoning the air. Those same flames would leap from the dashboard onto his own body, softening his flesh and turning his arm into liquid, bones into ash.

What will people think when they come across our ripped and blackened bodies, he thought? That they almost made it out alive? Or their death, like their lives, were meaningless? Part of an inescapable past, like wind churning mountains into sand.

He imagined the cab crashing, gravity flinging him forward, his body breaking faster than his brain could register the pain of the impact.

A loud rattling sound from the wheels pounded into his ears.

He stepped away from the dashboard and went back to check on Dee. She was semi-conscious and hanging on. She lifted her head long enough to point a finger toward the windshield.

The Roanoke gate.

Theo watched it looming from a few miles away. A solid block of gray, lacking any texture or distinguishing features.

Nothing but an interruption of the otherwise smooth line of the wall connecting one end of the horizon to the other. As they raced closer, the dark mass of the concrete wall came into view. At least thirty meters tall, it swallowed the surrounding trees in shadow.

A new feeling of numbness flooded his body like a warm blanket. A paralysis that overtakes you when riding on an unstoppable train barreling toward inevitable death.

Dee reached for Theo's hand and interlocked her fingers with his. She squeezed, her hand still warm despite the blood loss.

He squeezed back.

They sat in silence, breathing softly and listening to the rhythm of the railroad tracks. The cabin started to vibrate. It was gentle at first but grew into a concerning rumble. A loose knob on a storage cabinet rattled.

The sky grew darker. Light bled from the clouds and cast the world in a blanket of gray. The color of sickness and decay.

Theo closed his eyes and turned his attention to the vibration forming up from the floor and seeping into his body. He imagined Dee was doing the same thing but didn't bother to look in her direction. In his last moments of life, even with a warm body leaning against his own, he felt so alone. Even more alone than the night on the beach huddled against the power blocks, wrapped in a tarp desperately trying to fend off the cold.

Another bump trickled up from the tracks below.

Then another.

A violent jolt.

In an instant, the cabin went dark.

Black as night and swallowed into a void.

Is this death, he thought? Darkness, but without the smell of burning metal that he had expected?

A shockwave of mountain air passed through the cabin with a percussive blast, like standing beside a cannon, with an ear-shaking sound that emptied Theo's lungs and just as quickly filled the void with air from a new world.

The cabin filled with blinding sunlight. Theo shielded his eyes and watched through the cabin's rear windows as the once fortress-like wall shrank to a line and fell off into the distance. He felt Dee shifting under his arm.

"What happened?" said Dee, head on a swivel and beginning to sit up.

Theo started out the window in silence. The gray clouds dissipated into white and resumed their place on the mantle of the blue sky. Wisps of white scrawled across the horizon.

"I don't understand," said Dee, "the gate... how, how did the gate open? I mean, if we couldn't do it then," she turned to look at Theo, "what, or who opened it?"

Theo shook his head, not knowing where to start with finding an answer or even how to process what just happened. He had no words. They watched as the trees sped by, green smears against the golden landscape beyond.

CHAPTER 27

ARRIVAL

A familiar smell of burning diesel and charred metal filled the air. That blend of different materials fused under intense temperatures from raging flames, like the scrap piles his father used to burn far off in the hills. Arthur had forbidden Theo from leaving the house and left him to watch the plume from afar, out of reach of the toxic fumes, as Arthur father stacked contaminated wood planks and chemically treated pipes and bent sheets of thin metal, ignited over a curved mound of twigs, branches, and pinecones cleared from the forest floor.

Theo knew he could never get that day back, but the memory felt all too close as those familiar smells floated throughout the train cabin and escaped out through the shattered windows.

He wondered how long he had been asleep.

Dee's voice was a soft exhale. She was curled up on the floor beside him, out cold, one arm clutching the stump of the other arm, cradling it as the train rocked from side to side.

Theo stood up, legs steady on the swaying floor, muscles fatigued, and his head spinning from the chaos of the last few hours. Or days? He shielded his eyes from the sunlight blasting through the windshield, and after a moment, the landscape around him came into focus.

Flat plains of golden grass to the south, floating among barren spots of dark red dirt. The roaring wind spun dust high into the air. It formed shapes, twisted up into the sky, and then disappeared. To the north, majestic rock formations bulged out of the red earth. Mountains were carved and flattened by the wind, with surfaces of such geometrical strangeness that Theo wondered how nature could have made such a thing out of the earth.

That stench of burning metal stung Theo's senses and plunged him back into the present moment. A thought crossed his mind to seek out the source of the burning smell, to confirm that what he feared wasn't actually true.

But part of him already knew.

It was real all along.

What he saw on the screen wasn't a digital manifestation.

Out toward the western sky, the clouds above were stained gray. A thin black plume of smoke still rose from beyond the hills. No one could have survived that. He rubbed the red marks on his wrist where the straps held him down in the room with the Kaiphers and Aria Sloan floating on the screen in front of him. Images flashed into his mind of his people being annihilated in a fiery shockwave from the bird's-eye vantage point of the drone.

The memory of watching the blast on the screen, with the circular force that rippled across the dirt for a mile, made him nauseous.

He looked away and noticed a change on the LED panel next to the speed lever. The words "**OVERRIDE IN PROGRESS. ADMINISTRATIVE LOCKDOWN COMMENCING**" were gone. He gripped the lever, and tried to pull it downward one notch. It slid freely, no longer locked in place. The hum of the train engine grew softer. The train slowed by five miles per hour.

Rocky formations whipped by at a slower pace. Shocked, he looked back at Dee, sitting up against the silver cabinet. Her freshly woken face began to recognize the change in the train's speed.

She smiled an exhausted smile.

Theo pulled down on the lever.

The engine quieted from a scream to a soft metal-on-metal grind, eventually stopping entirely after a few minutes.

Theo's eyes welled with tears. The familiar scents of Oklahoma, which he used to call home, were gone, swallowed by the blackened air of destruction. He had finally arrived at the place known as home, which he never thought he'd see again.

And because of him, because of what he had done, there may have been nothing left.

He held tight to the side rail and descended the train's steps. His bandaged feet dragged in the dirt, leaving heavy tracks. He hunched over and scooped up a handful of red granules from the ground, rolled them in his palm, and let them glide freely through his fingers back to the earth. Tears fell from his cheeks, hit the dirt, and dark spots formed.

Behind him, Dee stumbled to her feet and deboarded the train. She placed her hand on Theo's shoulder without a word, and no words were needed. They looked upon the scarred countryside in silence.

Theo cradled his head in his hands. His family was gone. Any chance of building the Aeonite machine was lost. Sorrow flooded his heart like a new, foreign blood pumping through his veins. It was heavy and thick. Paralyzing.

Dee knew the feeling of having your entire world ripped from your life. The worst part was never the anguish of death or the unimaginable weight of sorrow. The worst was the sensation of living inside your own skin the next morning when the sun inevitably rises, and the world awakens, and everything you worked for and every single person you knew and loved no longer existed.

She stared across the tree line in the distance, where the forest ended and the flat, red, rocky earth began. It looked relatively untouched, just far enough to be outside the blast radius.

A faint light flashed from behind one of the trees.

Dee tried to find the source of the light, but as quickly as the flash appeared, it was gone. After a moment, she thought nothing of it and tried to think of something to say to Theo, who was crumpled on his knees, slogging through the depths of loss she had once lived through.

The light flashed again.

This time, she paid attention and caught the source. It was just beyond the fourth tree.

Another flash.

"Theo, look," she said, "There. Did you see that?"

He looked up slowly, exhaled a lung full of heavy air, and wiped the streaming tears from his face. Red dirt smeared across his forehead.

Another flash of light. That time, it was two in a row and brighter.

"You see?" said Dee, pointing off toward the trees, "there!"

"Yeah," he said, shaking the cloudiness from his eyes. Theo looked across the terrain, searching for anything moving or making a sound. There was nothing but stillness, interrupted only by the pattering feet of a lizard that shuffled out of a bush and dashed across the dirt in front of them.

Another flash of light. One bright flash.

Theo and Dee looked at each other. Their eyes met, Dee nodded, and the decision to embark was made.

They rummaged quickly through the compartments in the train and scraped together any supplies they could find in the shocking clarity of daylight. Theo loaded what was left of the ancient first aid kit into a ragged duffel bag behind the front seat with the words "MAINTENANCE" printed on its side. Dee tossed in flares and two large screwdrivers she found in one of the side drawers behind the seats.

They stepped off the train together, and at that moment, Theo saw the full extent of the damage at the rear of the train car. Severed cables trailed behind the car like mechanical tendrils, their exterior wrapping frayed and the inner electrical fibers exposed. The edge of the car was flame-kissed black. Its plastic exterior panels sagged from the fierce heat of the explosion that shattered the Kaipher into wet pieces. Sitting atop the railroad tracks that snaked off toward the horizon, the train looked like a battle-worn warrior taking its last breath, fulfilling its purpose to the end.

Theo gave a silent nod of gratitude to the train and strode off toward the trees.

They walked through sparse brush and flat land riddled with snake holes. The air began to change when they arrived within a few hundred yards of the tree line. Smells of fungi and moss and wet bark floated through the breeze and began to drown out the stench of smoke.

Another flash of light ahead.

Theo stopped. He held out a hand to grab Dee's shoulder. They stood frozen in place, cautious and unaware of how they were shifting their weight to the balls of their feet, knees slightly bent. The instinct of fighters forced to run.

In the distance, a melodic whistle rang through the air like the middle notes of a flute.

Slowly, a face emerged from behind a tree. It was a young girl, possibly fourteen or fifteen. Then, from behind another tree, a boy popped up, and then another boy appeared beside the first. Their faces were all painted with smeared green pigment. The whites of their eyes popped like diamonds against their camouflaged skin.

Their unkempt hair and ragged clothing—a blend of leather scraps with mismatched military-style uniforms—looked weathered from the outdoors.

Theo's tight brow loosened, his frown softened at the sight of these young people—they looked like kids—as they emerged from the woods.

Fifty yards away, Theo and Dee slowed. He looked at Dee with uncertainty, trying to sense her reaction, but Dee never took her eyes off the tree line.

As the figures came forward, the young girl in the center with wild hair pulled a pump shotgun from behind her back and trained the bead on Theo's center mass.

"These your people?" Dee whispered, keeping an eye on the girl walking towards them.

"Don't think so," Theo replied.

The boys to the left and right revealed their weapons—a revolver and bowie knife on the left and an AK-style rifle with a rope sling and dented barrel on the right.

Theo tensed again. For being just kids, they had a decent amount of firepower among them.

"Stop!" yelled the girl with the wild hair in a high, squeaky tone. Her voice, in any other context, would sound innocent, but there was a strain in her words as she attempted to sound commanding.

Theo slowly raised his hands in a sign of non-aggression.

"Not another step!" the girl yelled.

She approached cautiously, the shotgun barrel holding aim at Theo. The boys came closer with weapons drawn, encircling Theo and Dee.

"You there," said the girl, gesturing the shotgun at Theo, "state your name!"

He took a breath.

"Theo," he said, "Rousseau."

"Check!" said the girl.

"Check!" echoed the two boys."

"And who exactly are you?" Theo asked.

"We're here to take you in. Been camped out here waiting for six days," said the girl, "we were supposed to be the welcome wagon, but then that happened," she pointed toward the smoking hills in the distance, then looked back at Theo, "And now Trent wants you back."

The wild-haired girl made a clicking sound with her mouth, spat on the dirt and said, "But he didn't exactly specify a preference of alive or dead."

"Trent?" said Theo, gasping a lung full of air. His chest tightened upon hearing that name. "He's... alive? How did, I mean, where... Does this mean—"

"Shut it!" snapped the girl, "Now... who the hell is she? We only had you on the list."

Theo looked at Dee, her one hand raised, the other stump of bloody bandages hanging by her side.

"She's... a good friend," said Theo, "a partner. She helped me escape the Capital."

The young girl with the wild hair didn't respond.

"I wouldn't be alive if it weren't for her," said Theo.

The two boys exchanged glances with the wild-haired girl, who was clearly in a position of authority. They were looking to follow her lead.

"Dee," said Theo, "her name is Dee."

"Fine," said the girl, "we'll let Trent sort you all out."

"But she's not on the list," said one of the young boys through clenched teeth, a sharp complaint of defiance fired back at the young girl.

"Cuffs! Now," said the wild-haired girl, "do it!"

The boys looked at each other and shrugged. In the distance, one of the boys flicked his wrist into the air. A split second later, two pairs of metal handcuffs hit the dirt beside Theo's feet, kicking up a cloud of red dust that slanted away into the breeze.

"C'mon!" yelled the girl, "that way." She tilted her head to gesture toward the trees.

Dee looked at Theo.

"Cuffs or buckshot, your choice, mister!"

"But," Theo started to gesture towards Dee and her bloody arm, "she doesn't have, um–"

"Fine," said the girl, "Cuff yourself and then she to you. Let's get on with it!"

Theo clicked the handcuffs onto his wrists and secured Dee's one hand to his own.

The kids shuffled forward through the red dirt and briefly lowered their weapons. They spread out, flanking Theo and Dee, and cleared a middle path toward the tree line.

"Let's go! Got to get moving!" said the wild-haired girl, "that way," she tilted her head, gesturing toward the trees.

Theo and Dee tugged at the handcuffs, looked at each other for a moment, and, out of options, reluctantly stepped forward.

"C'mon," shouted the boy to their left, his pre-pubescent voice squeaking.

Theo winced at the boy's tone and started to walk faster. The boy kicked a cloud of dust. It flew up into Theo's nostrils and he spasmed a violent cough.

"We ain't got all fuckin' day!" said the boy.

The wild-haired girl protested.

"Hey, chill, Darcy!" she shouted, "we got 'em. Job's finished. We'll be home soon enough, and then you can go off and torture bugs in the woods or whatever the hell else you run off and do."

The five of them hiked in silence, the rhythmic sound of their dragging feet reducing the tension in the air, if only for a few fleeting moments. The treeline loomed closer, and the details once hidden in the shadows started to emerge–the sharp ridges running up the bark, the tufts of moss blooming on the exposed roots, and clumps of fungi sprouting from dark crevices. The world was so full of life under that forest canopy. Quite the opposite of the naked, blackened dirt of the blast site a few hundred yards away.

Theo felt a poke at his back as the boy to his left nudged him forward.

"You do know who I am, don't you?" said Theo.

"Yeah, you're a fuckin' liability, that's what I know," said the wild-hair girl.

"I got in, I got the plans, I did what Trent asked—"

"And we got blown up," the boy on the left interrupted, "I could give two shits what happened on the coast. Those SCR scum are dead to me. But here, that smoking crater over there, that's what happened on this side of the wall. Some good you did."

Theo was fuming.

"I risked my life for—"

The wild-haired girl interrupted him again.

"And how do we know you ain't workin' for the SCR now? And you brought back your Coaster girlfriend. Why in the hell should we even trust anything you're sayin'?"

"The explosion was not my fault," Theo said with a sigh, "the SCR altered the data during the transmission. They sabotaged the plans and tricked the engineers into building a makeshift bomb!"

His plea was met with silence. The boy to his left kicked a fern bush until its leaves were ripped to pieces. The fern rustled loudly in the calm forest air.

"There was nothing I could do!" said Theo, "I couldn't warn them. I was chained to a table until she—SHE broke me out of there and saved my life."

Theo looked at Dee. She rolled a half-smile across her mouth.

"Then why did you even bother to come back, huh? You must have some kind of death wish showing your face around here," said the wild-haired girl.

"Because I can still help," said Theo, "I want to help. We want to help."

"Enough!" snapped the wild-haired girl, "we'll let Trent sort you out. And who knows what he'll have planned for her. The fuck if I care."

The five followed a snaking path through the trees, the leaves above becoming noticeably thicker and taller with each step. Eventually, the light dimmed, and they reached a downhill slope of dirt practically invisible in the darkness. The wild-haired girl stepped to the front of the group, her stringy hair bouncing with each step, scratching audibly against the fabric of her jacket. She smelled like she had spent significant time in the forest.

She reached into the shadows and strained to pull on a heavy lever. The loud sound of metal grinding against metal sliced through the still air.

A doorway appeared in the earth.

CHAPTER 28
BUNKER 55

The wild-haired girl swung the shotgun behind her back and opened the heavy door. It dragged open and revealed a rectangular tunnel, and when the light from the setting sun leaked through the canopy at just the right angle, the outlines of stairs appeared as they faded into the depths.

The two boys stepped to the side and gestured for Theo and Dee to enter first. Their sharp frowns and rigid body language made it seem less an invitation and more a command. Theo twisted to fit through the narrow opening and descended into the darkness, stepping sideways and stretching his cuffed hand behind him as Dee followed. She contorted her one usable arm. The cuffs began to slice at her wrists.

They marched in a slow, long descent without a single spoken word down what seemed like four or five floors beneath the earth. Theo focused on placing his feet carefully on each concrete step, checking that Dee wasn't far behind. He imagined how a tumble down that staircase would hurt like holy hell.

Soon, an illuminated doorway floated in the darkness like a

mirage in an ocean of black. It was a second metal door. The wild-haired girl manipulated the mechanism on the door and slid it open.

When Theo reached the bottom of the staircase, the subterranean air was cool and musty. Wet metal walls lent a sweet smell that reminded him of evenings that followed a rainstorm.

He stepped over the threshold and entered the narrow room. Piles of rope, braided metal cables, bins overflowing with hand tools, shovels, and pickaxes hung on the wall for quick access. Vertical ridges crimped into the metal walls ran from the floor to the ceiling. After a moment, Theo recognized the thick metal beams that extended the length of the room and joined the ceiling to the wall.

The bunker was built with a sprawling network of connected shipping containers—the same containers that traveled hundreds of miles from state to state carrying produce and farm equipment throughout the Midlands.

They followed the wild-haired girl, her shotgun slung low and close to her chest for rapid acquisition and passed through several long rooms before coming to a stop. Theo reached the opening and noticed jagged edges along the seams connecting one container to the next like someone traced a circle with a plasma torch without much concern for smoothing the edges. It was a haphazard job done by builders in a rush.

They entered a long corridor that looked to be the central throughway of the compound. It stretched far in one direction and joined some additional rooms laterally to create wide spaces.

The next room was larger. Desks, file cabinets, and a jungle of wires snaked along the walls, swooping over lamps and chairs like spiderwebs. Containers welded to the left and right created a double-wide barrack. Walls were stacked with bunk beds with stained linens. Cots covered the floors between the bed frames. Pillows, blankets, and duffel bags were strewn about.

Theo thought there must be a hundred shipping containers here. It must have taken years, maybe decades, to build them. But the location—under the protective cover of the forest canopy, away from the spying eye of the SCR drones—made perfect sense.

Theo and Dee followed the wild-haired girl to the largest room they'd encountered so far. The two boys armed with the A.K. and the revolver followed behind. It was a pentagonal room with an unusually low ceiling. It was the central hub of the compound, with long hallways branching off in different directions like the spokes of a wheel.

It was unmistakably a war room. Clusters of desks encircled a chalkboard in the center. Communications equipment around the perimeter. The scent of cigarette smoke and stale coffee and stress-amped sweat filled the room.

"Clear out for a sec!" the wild-haired girl shouted, sending a handful of people seated at desks shuffling away down the halls.

She turned to face Theo. A red mark formed on her neck where the shotgun strap was too big and heavy for her small stature. She whipped a key from her pocket with a jingle and stepped forward.

She unlocked Theo's cuffs.

"Thank you," he said with a long sigh, "that was beginning to leave a mark."

The boy with the revolver stepped behind Dee, pulled a black hood over her head, sinched it tight along her neck, and kicked her in the back with the heel of his boot.

"No!" screamed Theo.

Dee crashed into a desk and tumbled to the ground. Chairs fell to the side, and when the cacophony turned to silence, the only sound left in the room was Dee's strained breathing through heavy tears.

The wild-haired girl saw Theo beginning to step forward and raised her shotgun to his chest.

"Not one more step!" she said, "she's not one of us, Theo, and frankly, I don't know if you are anymore. No matter what she told you or promised you, she's SCR, and you need to get that INTO YOUR HEAD! The Kaiphers murdered hundreds, most of our families, our friends, our smartest doctors and engineers. The SCR has sentenced millions to die of starvation and disease. Do not forget that. You may not have seen it with your own eyes, but I have."

"Do not ATTEMPT to explain to me what's at stake," said Theo through clenched teeth, "I fucking know what's at stake."

She looked Theo in the eyes and, after a moment, let out a resigned sigh. The shotgun barrel hovered inches from his chest.

"She'll be moved to a more secure location until we can be confident she doesn't pose a threat."

Theo was breathing rapidly, his ribcage heaving with anger.

"As for you," she said, "I have my orders. He wants to see you. This way."

All emotion disappeared from her face. She waved the shotgun with a blank stare.

"That means now, Theo!"

He gave her a stern look with violence in his eyes and stepped forward down the hallway.

As he walked away, he heard the two boys scooping Dee's half-limp body off the floor and dragging her down the hallway in the opposite direction.

It was a long, empty corridor. String lights snaked down the hallways like fireflies in the night. After a certain point, when the second container connected to the third and the fourth, the walls began to change. When he stepped over the next threshold, he was shocked to see that the floor, ceiling, and walls were clean. Pristine, even. Likely scrubbed and washed meticulously by some poor kid.

They reached the end of the hallway. Theo approached a

doorway at the far side of the room, with the wild-haired girl following close behind.

He stopped and turned.

The wild-haired girl nodded.

"He's waiting for you," she said with a gentle tone he'd never heard before in previous interactions. Then she slung the shotgun over her shoulder, turned, and walked back toward the war room.

Theo stood there, motionless, watching her walk away. The walls were strangely clean, a sight so alien in such a decaying world.

An uneasy feeling ran up his spine like a cold draft.

There was a door at the end of the hall.

White light spilled through the door seams. It wasn't very bright but looked different from the other lights hanging around the compound. It was the first bluish light he had seen, and it was a cold, hard assault on his eyes.

He stared at the straight metal bar of the door handle. It taunted him like a gravitational pull, flooding his mind with a dark, sinking feeling as he stood in that empty hallway. His chest tightened. It grew heavy and warm. That same dark feeling he felt on the plane and again at the top of the bridge—a force beyond his world pulling him forward.

He took a deep breath, held it in his lungs, and steeled himself for whatever was behind that door.

Then, after a moment, he turned the handle.

The light was overwhelming, not in brightness, but in sharpness and shocking clarity.

It was an empty room, save for a row of three oxygen tanks and a hospital bed centered along the far wall.

He took a step forward.

There was a figure in the bed obscured by crumpled blankets. Oxygen mask. Plastic tubs and IV drips.

The outline of a small body. It sank into the old foam mattress.

A wrinkled hand rested limply beside the railing.//
Chest rose and fell with such fragile movements.//
Theo stopped.//
His breath froze.//
Heart was pounding like a hammer in his ears.//
One word sprung from his mind, down to his heart, and through his lips.

"...Father?"

CHAPTER 29
LEGACY

Theo could hardly breathe.

"I thought you… were dead," he said softly to the unmoving, silent shape on the bed, "I thought all of you were dead."

And the part he didn't speak out loud…

From the explosion, he thought. The one that wouldn't have happened if I didn't plug into that computer.

Theo's hands were shaking. His fingers curled over the bed rail and gripped so hard he barely noticed the fingernail marks that burned red into his palms.

"Dad," he said, voice low and barely a whisper, "I failed you. I should have never left. I should have stayed, and maybe if I had gone into town that night instead of Lydia, she'd still be alive."

Alive. The word made him lightheaded.

His heart wanted to burst like a crumbling dam, vent the pressure through the cracks, and explode thunderous waves into the open air. He struggled to catch his breath, reaching deep for the right syllables to form words to construct sentences to convey his truth: that he had brought nothing but death and destruction upon his family. And all that, to speak inadequate words aloud to a dying old man in an underground bunker.

There was a soft click of the door handle and the shuffling sound of someone entering the room.

"He can hear you, Theo. But he can't speak or move. It's been three days since he slipped into a coma."

Theo glanced back with a quick movement and faced Trent Blake.

He was a short man in ill-fitting military-style brown pants and a slate gray T-shirt. His hair was slicked back under a hairnet, and his nitrile-gloved hands were gripped tightly on a metal walking cane by his side. It had only been fourteen months since Theo had last seen him, but he looked like he had aged several years.

"Arthur's lungs are the least of our worries now," said Trent, "I'm afraid this time it has spread again. This time, the liver. I'm down nine people since the explosion, but the specialists I have left are monitoring him closely. I owe Arthur that much. We all owe your father."

Tears welled in Theo's eyes. He tried to speak but couldn't find the right words to make the situation any better. He just took a slow breath and let a sigh hang in the air.

"I'm sorry," said Theo, "you trusted me to bring it home, and I–"

A compassionate smile flashed across Trent's face but quickly disappeared. He nodded and looked down at his feet, staring in silence, his body bending as he leaned severely onto his cane.

"Son, every well-planned operation includes redundancy measures. When we started building the first Aeonite machine, we produced duplicate parts as spares. It was the only logical thing to do, as certain components needed custom machining, and while investing the time and material to produce one, it only made sense to make several more. They were stored in secondary and tertiary locations. One of which was this compound."

Trent raised a hand and gestured to the surrounding facilities.

"After the first machine was lost in the blast, we immediately pulled the parts out of storage and began building the second. I knew we couldn't finish it. Without the schematics, we only got so far. The output wouldn't be viable. Tissue build tests resulted in only a 93% success rate. That simply wasn't enough. Cells and fibers would bind but suffer catastrophic breakdown within mere hours, sometimes minutes. I had hoped that if we started construction, we'd be ready to complete it by the time you returned. But in the end, we find ourselves here, back at the beginning."

Trent looked away to the far side of the room, his gaze lost in a thousand-yard stare.

"I suppose I'll have to send another," he said under his breath, the words a mere thought floating in the air.

"Another?" asked Theo.

The door behind them cracked open a few inches with a light click. A man stood just out of view, but when the light reached his face, Theo could see the man's olive-toned skin and the side of his face with jet-black hair falling in waves down to his ears.

"Mr. Trent, sir," the man said from behind the door.

"Yes. Tell me."

"It's the girl, sir. The outsider."

Trent grunted.

"We got something out of her. I think you should come see–"

"Ah, right then, yes," said Trent.

"The girl? What did you do to Dee?" said Theo, his voice stressing into a higher octave, "where is she? Where are you keeping her?"

Without another word, Trent turned and exited. He slipped behind the door, his cane the last to disappear. The latch clicked loudly into place.

Theo stomped across the room and pulled on the handle.

It was locked.

He pulled again. He pressed his weight onto his palms and bore down onto the thin metal bar, but it didn't budge. In a fit of rage, he landed a firm kick in the center of the door, his heel smashing with a violent thud. The door rattled at its hinges, but the lock held.

Theo collapsed into a chair in the corner. He looked across at his father's small body on the bed, getting weaker by the minute as the illness burned from cell to cell like an unchecked wildfire.

Three days in a coma, he thought. I missed him by three days.

Several minutes passed. Then the latch clicked, and Trent's face peeked through the half-opened door.

"Son," he said in a calm tone, "Theo, come. Now."

Theo followed Trent down a labyrinth of corridors, passing rows of open doors with observation windows. Trent was silent the entire walk, save for the shuffle and tap of his cane on the metal floor.

"Where are we going?" asked Theo.

Trent didn't respond.

"Where is Dee? Where are you keeping her? What do you want with her?"

His questions went unanswered in the quiet echo of the hallways, gray metal walls reflecting the dim glow of light bulbs strung as far as he could see.

There was a flurry of activity behind one of the doors. Theo glanced through the observation window. The room burst with the sterile glow of daylight-spectrum lights. Men in protective white suits tinkered with machinery. One of them carried a circular piece of metal to the center of the room and attached it to a long cylindrical object. It was bright silver, shaped like a metal radius and ulna. The piece clicked into place, and the object articulated like a ball bearing joint as the workers jabbed slender tools into its insides.

They passed another room that glowed orange and green. Tubes and barrels were stacked along ceiling-high shelves.

The next room caught Theo's eye. Bunk beds lined the walls in rows of four. Some beds were occupied by the sleeping children, their small bodies wrapped in thick white blankets. They all had identical black hair.

"Here," said Trent.

He opened a door, and they entered a dark room that reeked of blood.

Three figures were standing in the room. A fourth figure was crouched on the ground against the far wall.

When Theo's eyes adjusted to the light he saw Dee crumpled on the floor, head barely holding up, blood and tears and spit running down the side of her mouth.

A quarter of her face was plastered in black and red bruises.

Theo's pulse ripped into overdrive.

"What the fuck did you–"

Then Theo looked into the eyes of the three men standing in the room.

Their eyes were identical to his own.

They had his hair.

His skin.

His nose.

His ears.

The way the corners of his mouth bent downward when he clenched his jaw out of rage or paralyzing fear.

Theirs did, too.

Trent turned to Theo and saw his face turn ghostly white.

"Theo," he said, "Meet Armand, Allen and Arnaut."

Theo didn't speak. His racing thoughts ground to a halt as he confronted three men who were clones of himself.

"Your... brothers, I suppose, in a way," said Trent, "you all share a special bond. A common bond. Well, you and the other ninety-seven of you. It's a great honor you should be proud of to be part of something so magnificent. To share a touch of DNA from our lost prodigal Father, my long-lost relative, Dr. Salim Naram."

"I don't... I can't," Theo mumbled incoherent sounds but couldn't find the words.

"I know this is a lot to take in," said Trent, "especially being one of the shielded. You see, some of your brothers grew up knowing of their family members, but others I had to isolate as a control. It was an experiment, if you want to call it that, to see which one of you would rise up to your full potential and make it home alive with the schematic. Many of them fumbled their mission, some in spectacular ways, dying before even stealing the files, or in some wretched alleyway in the Capital, ripped to shreds by a Kaipher. They took many of you. But you, Theo, my son, you were unique. The first, among many, to find your way home.

"Now, I applaud you for our triumphant effort," he continued, "but there is still one line of inquiry that needs to be resolved."

He pulled a silver 1911 pistol from a concealed holster and pointed the barrel at Dee's face. She tried to raise her head to meet his gaze, but all she could do was wince through her one blinking eye, the other swollen over from the beating.

"Was this your planning, son?" asked Trent, "why the data dump? What was your end game?"

"Wh-what data dump?" said Theo, confused and breath quickened as Trent's finger rested softly on the trigger of the gun. Like tension screws in his mind, twisted with each second, he looked at the clones to his left and right and Dee, bloodied on the floor. Trent, neck throbbed red with rage, mouthed words Theo could barely follow amidst the chaos.

"The computer embedded in her arm," said Trent, "contained

seventeen terabytes of schematics of the entire Capital city. Archives going back decades. I'd wager to guess that no living person on this side of the wall has ever seen these. Why, Theo? What's the play here?"

Theo shuffled his feet uncomfortably, unsure how to respond.

Trent pointed to a metal hard drive enclosure that one of the clones held tightly by his side.

"We pulled a copy and encrypted it onto that drive. It's isolated until we decide how to proceed. What did the SCR want us to do, Theo? Upload all of this to our network? Then what? Initiate a remote attack on our infrastructure? Or would they ping our servers to triangulate our secondary and tertiary locations? Or permanently cut our power and send Kaiphers knocking on our door in the night like they did all those years ago? Well, I won't have any of it. It's not worth risking everything we've built here. Keeping her alive is not worth the risk."

Trent cocked the hammer on the pistol.

"Trent, there is no plan!" Theo pleaded, "I promise you there's nothing–"

"I'm going to need more than that son."

"I don't, I just don't know–" said Theo.

Dee spat a mouthful of blood onto the floor.

"It wasn't him," she said, straining to get the words out, "It wasn't Theo. He had nothing to do with it. The files were mine. I found them underneath the Capital, in the basement of the Kingdom."

"I will not let my legacy go to ruin because of one worthless Coaster girl," said Trent, "if you are lying, girl, I promise you, you will be mine to kill."

"No!" pleaded Dee through oncoming tears, "Right before Theo transmitted his message, I copied the entire archive. I used it to identify the structural weak points in the columns. For the explosive charges. To bring down the Capital."

Dee retched a heavy cough. Spit and tears ran down her chin.

"Thirteen columns," she said softly, "thirteen... thirteen charges."

Trent blinked, his face softened as he put the pieces together.

"The Capital..." said Trent, his words almost a whisper, "that was... you."

"Sir," one of the clones said for the first time in a voice and tenor eerily similar to Theo's, "If the girl did indeed clone the entire archive, and that process was completed before the Aeonite plans were sabotaged... there is a chance the original, unaltered schematics for the machine could be intact on that drive."

Trent decocked the pistol and lowered it slowly.

Then, with a quick glance and a nod, the three clones straightened their postures and followed Trent out of the room.

The door clicked softly behind them. Their hurried footsteps echoed down the hallway.

Theo ran to Dee.

He pressed his palm to her cheek and raised her weak head. She looked at him through one eye and spoke in whispers.

"You're all the same," she said, words squeaking through her ragged lungs, "I thought your people would be different, but they're just like the SCR. You're all the same."

"Dee," he said, "I'm so sorry they treated you this way. When they finally see that you've brought the real schematics, they'll build the machine and we can build you a new arm!" He smiled, but it faded quickly when she didn't share his enthusiasm. Her face twisted with a venomous look in her eyes.

She burst out laughing and spit blood onto the floor.

"What makes you think they'll do anything other than execute me and move on?" she said, "another body paving the way for your machine. How many people had to die all these years, all those clones, to finally get a fighting chance to secure the schematics? What's one more worthless Coaster girl after all?"

"Dee, you're not just one more–"

"Fuck you! I'm sick of your compassion. When are you going to wake the fuck up and learn that the world doesn't work like that?"

Theo shook his head in silence, unsure of what to say.

"Please leave," said Dee, "just... leave."

"Dee, I–"

"Fucking go! I don't want you here anymore. Get out of my sight!"

CHAPTER 30

BROTHERS

Theo returned to the room and sat beside his father's bed. The blip on the monitor held steady. Arthur's chest rose and fell; he lay motionless like a sleeping child. He still hadn't woken up, and as the days went by, there was less and less reason to believe he would.

"There's so much I wish I could tell you," Theo whispered. He reached out and took his father's frail hand in his own. "Dad, please wake up." His throat choked as he said the words, but his plea was met by silence. Until the click of the door behind him jostled his attention.

Trent cleared his throat.

"I realize we may have gotten off on the wrong foot since your arrival... I mean, well, your return," he said, shuffling into the room, "I want to apologize. This is not the way I had envisioned your homecoming, but after the events of the last few days, I admit I was beginning to think you'd been lost just like the others. Any hope that you'd return at all was slipping away. But here you are. In the flesh. You've made it, and you've done a remarkable job, son."

Trent sat in a chair on the far side of the room.

"There is so much you don't know, and I imagine that must feel unfair. Perhaps even frightening. I know at your age—"

"My age? Quit speaking to me like I'm a child. You need to tell me what's going on, and you need to tell me now. Why are you holding Dee? And who are those... those..."

"The boys?" Trent sighed and leaned back. The chair creaked under his movement. "Yes, well, where do I even begin? They are my creation, as you are my creation. And you are our salvation. Born of my own genetic material, you share the DNA with a long and important lineage of warriors."

Memories flashed across Theo's mind of men on the island whose faces bared a striking resemblance to him. Their faces, their hair, and skin when the sunlight touched their silhouette.

Faces like his own.

"Noble crusaders in the three-hundred-year war for equity," explained Trent, "For the end of suffering. For a fighting chance to be a part of humanity's story. The SCR wanted to starve us into oblivion, let disease and suffering and time take its toll and do the dirty work they were too cowardly to do themselves. They fought us with time and patience. We fought for a chance for our people of the Midlands to live on."

Theo remembered the sensor tower from that rainy night on the bridge. Bright light beams shot into his eye and scanned him. The metal gears unlatched and the gate at the end of the bridge swung freely open. It welcomed him into the Capital like he was one of them.

"For the past thirty-two years," Trent continued, "I have raised your brothers, prepared you all to storm the Capital and take back what we have a right to own. We launched dozens of missions: coming in from the water, tunneling under the sea wall, and even running high-altitude air jumps onto tower roofs. Many died, and only one other brought back a passenger as you did. We were fighting for our rightful claim—a human right—to the Aeonite apparatus, invented by my ancestor, Dr. Salim Naram. For years, I was the only one who knew of his sacrifice—his cold-blooded murder and cover-up by his partner, Dr. Sloan. I have dedicated my life to avenging his memory and seeing that his work is returned to the people it was intended to benefit. All we needed was one fully intact schematic, and we could build our own machine for the Midlands!"

"And you call yourself a warrior?" said Theo, "sending us to fight your war for you? Why didn't you go to the coast? Why didn't you fight?"

Trent exhaled a tense breath. He looked down at his cane, dragged it, and tapped it twice on the floor.

"Because I was too late, Theo," he said, "I waited too long. Look, tell me this: have you ever felt a faint tingle in your leg after running or straining your back to lift something heavy? That pinch in your muscle and you wonder if it's a nerve, but you shrug it off and blame it on not having enough rest or soreness that you'll toughen up and forget? And you tell yourself to walk it off, you'll get over it?"

Theo thought back to a time in Oklahoma, climbing into his tree stand before the sun came up, feeling a jolt like an electric shock ride up his leg for a fleeting moment. It was gone almost before he noticed. He blamed it on the biting morning cold. But then it happened two more times a few years later.

"It's called hereditary spastic paraplegia," said Trent, "And you get over it because you're young. It hasn't had a chance to overtake your body yet. But by the time you hit forty, the deterioration is irreversible. Walking eventually becomes difficult. You learn to live with a cane at your side. And in your fifties, well, there's a significant chance of full loss of motor function."

Theo shook his head.

"No, no, that doesn't make any... what makes you so confident that it will happen?" he asked.

"Because it's my life too," said Trent, "It's the reality I know, and I live, but some days are hard. It's in my genes. Our genes. From my father, and his father, and his father... and it is in you too. All your brothers will suffer the same way eventually. I didn't have the technology at the time to sequence the gene and correct it. But maybe with the Aeonite machine, we have a chance. My specialists say that if we combine the phase scanner with another connected module—"

"Stop," said Theo, raising his palms into the air, "just... stop. You mean to tell me that you shipped us off on the mission before our legs would suddenly stop working?"

"Yes."

"But, how could you—"

"I know it's difficult, son, but there was only a particular window of time that you and your brothers could have a real chance at changing our future."

"But you said I was the first to bring back the schematics. Surely others must have made it back."

Trent looked away, his eyes escaping to a far-off memory.

"A few did," he said, "but you've seen what the world is like out there. Food is scarce. Medical supplies are dwindling. Antibiotics and blood are nearly gone, and our doctors and scientists are being hunted by the SCR. People dying at rates we haven't seen in two hundred years from a common cold or a mild cut on their hand. Flu striking down entire families. Theo, you need to understand that the state of the Midlands is fragile. We can barely keep our own people alive. Extra mouths to feed creates a strain on the already fragile infrastructure."

"What are you saying?" said Theo, "what happened to the others who didn't make it back?"

"If they managed to return but failed their missions..."

Trent took a breath.

"Those who no longer had a role here had to be removed. Some escaped to the mountains and—"

"Removed? What does that mean? You murdered them?"

"Theo, son, you have to understand—"

"What did you do, take them behind a shed and put a bullet in their head?"

"Ammo is scarce as well, but I assure you it was peaceful—"

"Peaceful? Like how you treated Dee? I see what happens to people who suddenly become extraneous to your cause."

"Resources all across the Midlands were nearly gone. We barely had food stocked for nine days at a time. Then what? What would you have done, Theo? No crops because we have no machines to tend the crops. We had to look forward, focus on the future, on securing the Aeonite machine no matter the cost. No matter the sacrifice."

"At the cost of innocent lives. I get it. My brothers and I are nothing but pawns in your game. Just like that. An expendable resource for the Midlands. You brought us into this world, so you feel you have the permission to remove us."

Trent's face went expressionless like a stone.

"Yes. Yes, I do. Because they—"

"Didn't have a role anymore? They weren't fit for the idea of the future you planned in your head? Dee was right; you're no different than the SCR."

The words hung heavy in the air.

The walls seemed to close in, and the temperature in the room grew warm.

Trent's anger boiled.

He whipped his cane into the air and jabbed it at Theo's throat. He leaned his weight into the cane, pressing hard on Theo's neck.

"You listen to me, you little self-righteous shit," Trent's voice was sharp, words escaping his clenched jaws in tight bursts of air, "you had better recognize your place in this world. In my world!"

Trent's breath was heavy. He paused, jaw loosened, blinking rapidly like someone waking from a dream. He quickly pulled his cane back from Theo's throat.

"I apologize, son," he said, "you have accomplished more than any of your brothers before you. You deserve better from me. I owe you better than that. I am in your debt."

The door behind them opened. A man stepped in wearing a plastic clean suit and protective eyewear. It was the same gear Theo had seen people wearing in the engineering lab he passed down the corridor.

"Mr. Trent," said the man partially obscured behind the door.

Trent grunted. "Tell me," he said.

"We got it, sir."

Trent turned toward the door, a look of intense clarity on his face.

"What are you saying? Speak clearly now."

"The plans, sir. Schematics. We ran the numbers. Projections show anticipated successful tissue fusion rate."

"How successful?"

"Fully, sir. Completely. Over 99.998%, sir."

Trent looked back and forth at Theo and then at the man in the doorway. The man in the plastic suit nodded.

"Are you telling me it's... it's..."

"The real thing, sir."

CHAPTER 31
ARTHUR ROUSSEAU

MAY, 2310
ELKHART, OKLAHOMA

Arthur curled his fingers around a loose steel bolt on the side of a claw-footed wood stove. The bolt spun freely in his hand. He reached to a side table and, without looking, his fingers crawled over a pile of loose tools, jostling a screwdriver aside. He drew a short wrench from the pile and reached down to twist the bolt. After it was tightened, he gave it a final twist for good measure.

Soft rain tapped on the roof and the wrap-around wooden porch outside. The air in the house was cold that evening. He saw his breath before it quickly faded.

Arthur loosened his grip on the wrench and pulled his right hand back to his chest. His fingers and wrist started to shake. A tremor was building.

He looked down at his dry, cracked skin, unable to shake the feeling that his hands, once his most important tool, no longer felt like a part of him. He felt betrayed by his own body.

"Dear?" Melody called from the other room, "Bergamot or Chamomile is all that's left unless you want that foul valerian root from the cellar." He heard the faint clink of mugs and spoons and drawers and cupboards opening and clasping shut, "I know it's good for health and all, but Lordy, does it make a room smell like an old farmer's wet boot." He heard the shuffle of her soft footsteps approaching. She entered the living room with a white wool shawl cascading down her shoulders and an oversized green sweater draping over her round, pregnant belly.

Arthur quickly concealed his hand with a grease-stained rag and pretended to rub a fleck of black soot from his knuckles. He loaded the wood stove with two oak logs placed atop a fluff of kindling and used the backside of a pocket knife to strike a flint rod and light the fire.

Melody set a tray down with two ceramic mugs and a clump of herb bread and took a seat on her cushioned wooden rocker.

A soft bell chimed three times from overhead in the kitchen. It was a signal that a vehicle had entered the premises and was beginning its long journey along the stretch of wooded driveway. A weight sensor buried ten inches below the gravel detected heavy movements, like vehicles. A small solar panel mounted in the crook of a nearby Sycamore tree powered the sensor. It was reliable and efficient, with few moving parts to get clogged up when the red dust blew heavily into town.

Arthur glanced at the wall clock. 10:53 pm. There was only one person who would show up unannounced at such an hour.

The bell chimed twice. The vehicle was four hundred meters away.

Melody settled into her chair, grabbed a mug, and breathed in a lung full of rising steam. She pulled a fur blanket over her lap, waiting for the burning logs to warm the air.

Arthur walked to the door with slow, resigned steps.

The bell chimed once. Headlights washed over the closed curtains, and they heard the crunch of gravel dragging under heavy tires.

Melody let her eyes float along the wall from one painting

to the next—the comfort of each memory washing over her. She became transfixed on a painting above the hearth, no bigger than the lid of a shoebox, of a lake and a fiery red sunset. She remembered the tug of her arm as she folded globs of crimson and ochre paint and pressed the brush into the canvas to paint the edge where the sunlight met the hills. Light flicks of her wrist created the delicate trees.

Arthur opened the door. The smell of cold rain and dogwood trees wafted in. A stout man stood at the threshold, his figure outlined by the vehicle's headlights.

"Trent," said Arthur, lowering his eyes. The man at the door nodded.

"Evening," said Trent in a quiet voice.

Arthur glanced over Trent's shoulder at the black vehicle with thick tires idling behind him. Bright beams of cold white light shimmered in the rain.

"I'm sorry to show up unannounced and so late," said Trent.

"No, no, please think nothing of it," said Arthur, "Come inside, out of that rain."

Trent tracked in a puddle of water with his leather boots. His long brown coat almost touched the floor. He paused and glanced toward the logs crackling in the hearth. Light gleamed off the metal brace running up the length of his right leg and the 1911 on his belt as he turned, coat swaying open, the pistol's silver handle with bleached bone inlay like a jewel in the dark. Melody sat up from her chair. She forced a polite smile.

"Ma'am", Trent nodded.

"Mr. Trent," replied Melody with a nod, glancing at the puddle of water on the wooden floor and then her eyes focusing on the 1911.

"You still feel the need to bring that into our home?" she asked.

Trent brushed a finger along his side, felt for the steel grip of the exposed pistol, and flicked his coat flap over to cover his sidearm.

"Melody!" Arthur snapped.

A half smile came across Trent's face, and he raised a hand, a soft gesture with a palm open.

"It's alright," Trent said to Arthur, "A force of habit, that's all. That's my old-world upbringing, I suppose." A quick chuckle shot out of the side of his mouth. "Well then... I won't keep you folks for very long," he continued, putting a reassuring hand on Arthur's shoulder, "Like I said, I do apologize for the intrusion, but I'm afraid I have an urgent situation, and it could not wait 'till morning."

Arthur frowned, straightened his posture, and nodded.

"Yesterday," Trent said, "we had our first report of a Kaipher spotted more than eight hundred miles past the coastal wall. That's deep in the Midland states."

"But the SCR has never pushed beyond the walls before, let alone eight hundred miles," said Arthur.

Trent sighed. "Yes," he continued, "but in the past seventy-two hours, they've wiped out three towns in east Texas. Three hundred and seven dead. One survivor."

"That doesn't make any sense," said Arthur, shaking his head. He started pacing around the room, foot tapping nervously on the knotted floorboards, raising his right hand to scratch his forehead but quickly plunging it into his pocket before it started to shake. He stopped and turned around.

"Why would they come that far? Why now? What could they be searching for?" asked Arthur.

"It's not what," said Trent, "it's who."

Melody paused mid-sip and set her steaming mug down. It landed with a clunk on the heavy wooden table.

"Trent," she started to speak, somewhat startled at the sound of her voice piercing the cabin air, "you mentioned that there was one survivor."

Arthur frowned, looked at Melody, then back at Trent.

"I'm afraid so," said Trent, "and that brings me to why I'm here. I need a favor—we need a favor. I need someone I can trust."

Trent looked at Melody, her belly bulging under the fur blanket.

"A stable home. A family I can trust".

Outside there was the faint click of the car door opening, and it shut softly with a thump a moment later.

"Our only survivor from the events of the past few days," said Trent, looking down as he selected his words, "is... a boy."

A crumbling log in the hearth snapped and broke the silence in the room.

"We think he's four years old, maybe five. His entire family was murdered when the Kaiphers rolled through the town at night. Cut them down in their sleep. Never had a chance."

Trent took a breath and let out a deep sigh.

"I need you to watch over him," he said, "protect him, teach him, guide him, and raise him as your own. Only four souls know about this arrangement. My driver and us three, standing here in this room."

Melody had a concerned look on her face. She turned to Arthur.

"Please, I am calling on you at a time of great need," said Trent, "This is important. I believe this boy could have a larger meaning than any of us can understand right now, but I need people I can trust fully and completely. Will you help?"

Arthur turned to Melody. Her worried look faded as she surrendered to the reality unfolding before her. She looked to Arthur, nodded slowly, then turned away to face the hearth and let her thoughts get lost in the fire.

"For the Midlands, you can count on us," said Arthur.

Trent nodded, "I am indebted to you. Both of you. Truly."

He turned to raise a hand and wave at a small rain-soaked figure standing in the shadows on the porch.

With soft steps, the boy shuffled through the door. Dark hair, olive skin, a small round face covered in shadow until he stepped into the light. He looked up, eyes exploring the unframed canvas paintings and animal mounts adorning the walls in the hallway, and the black stove raging with fire in the living room in front of wooden chairs covered in blankets and patchwork pillows. The room smelled of tea and spices and bear hides and firewood.

"It's okay, son," Trent said to the boy in a soft voice, "This home can be your home now, and everything's going to be alright."

The boy looked up in silence with cinnamon-brown eyes and a mop of wet hair, black as the midnight country sky.

"Melody and Arthur," said Trent, "meet Theo."

CHAPTER 32

AEONITE

PRESENT DAY

Theo woke in a dim room with a single warm glow pulsing from the machines beside his father's bed. But something felt off. He didn't remember falling asleep in a chair. In fact, he couldn't remember sitting on the left side of his father's bed, right next to the IV drip. Hunger lurched inside him, and he reached for a tray of bread, carrots, coffee, and water that Trent's people had left for him. There were no clocks on the wall. Were there clocks before? No access to natural light anywhere in that underground compound. He couldn't tell if it was day or night, but he felt as if he hadn't seen another soul for many hours.

There was a computer terminal on a desk in the back of the room.

Was the computer there the entire time, he thought? He tried to rewind his memories of the room, but he couldn't be sure.

It was covered in an opaque plastic sheet with a thick layer of dust, smooth as untouched snow, which seemed to suggest the machine hadn't been touched in months or years. Then, he inspected the underside of the desk. The drawers were empty, and there were faint drag marks on the floor as if it had been recently moved.

Under the plastic sheet, a faint yellow light glowed on the bottom left corner of the boxy monitor.

Theo ripped back the sheet. Dust flaked onto the floor and clouded the air. He tried powering up the computer terminal. It whirred to life, and a yellow cursor appeared on the screen.

Maybe there's something I can find out about Dad's diagnosis, he thought.

He tapped enter on the keyboard. A menu of four options appeared on the screen, along with lists of folders with a blinking cursor beside the first one.

INVENTORY DATABASE
SURFACE REPORTS
MISSION ARCHIVES
MAINTENANCE LOGS

He tapped to move the cursor. It hovered over **INVENTORY DATABASE**, and he pressed enter.

He browsed spreadsheets full of equipment lists, dates of shipments, and storage locations across the Midlands, from Texas to New Mexico to Kansas and beyond. Beakers, car engines, cables, batteries, capacitors, resistors, syringes, and tools all moved through an intricate supply chain. When the AI-driven machines stopped working, they cannibalized abandoned hospitals and medical clinics. Defunct car factories, full of useful parts, became resource treasure troves.

No useful information about his father.

He backed out of the folder and explored **MISSION ARCHIVES**. The screen flooded with text of mission descriptions, everything from personnel intake reports to training protocols to launch dates and multi-page risk analysis reports. He clicked through. Pages flashed across the screen.

Aman, age 17, diver and proficient in underwater demolition.

The insertion zone was the Atlantic Ocean, fifty miles offshore. His plan was to approach under cover of night, plant explosives on the southern sea wall, and create a breach large enough to flood the undercity. He would take advantage of the ensuing chaos to infiltrate the Capital, access the SCR production facilities, and obtain the Aeonite schematics. But the pressure relief valve on his oxygen tank froze, and he died before ever reaching the sea wall.

Albert, age 28, high altitude parachutist and expert survivalist. While training for his mission, he took only a knife and a length of rope and went to live in the Ouachita National Forest alone for 180 days. His plan was to parachute into the mountains near Lake Champlain, live off the land, conduct long-range reconnaissance, and find a way to slip into the Capital undetected. He buried his parachute upon landing, but a Kaipher patrol to the north discovered his parachute after heavy rains washed away the dirt. They tracked him two hundred miles to the south and killed him in his sleep in his camp just ten miles from the Capital.

Theo scrolled through more entries. Pilots, hackers, mechanics—all manner of tactics that those boys were sent in to deploy. All dead before the age of 30.

This mission, this war, was the only thing they'd ever known in their young lives. They were bred to perform, to serve, and to die. They never had a choice.

He shut down the computer terminal and stepped away, exhaustion hitting him after reading those briefings.

Theo moved to the door and pressed on the handle. To his surprise, the latch clicked, and the door opened. The hallway was dim and looked abandoned. Rooms at the end of the corridor were dark.

He stepped into the hallway and walked back toward the war room, following the spoke of the compound towards its central hub.

The cavernous room was swallowed in tense silence. He

peeked around the corner and down another corridor, stretching off in different directions, but all of the adjacent rooms were also dark. Desks, beds, and swivel chairs were all empty.

A ribbon of smoke trailed into the air like a ghost. It caught Theo's eye, and he noticed a single cigarette butt that was recently pressed into a mug on a desk.

Where the hell did everyone go, he thought?

He backtracked toward his father's room and moved in the direction of the room where Dee was held. He passed a door labeled Delta Lab. The engineering room—once buzzing with technicians building the metal arm—was empty. Not only were the people missing, but the machinery and supplies were gone as well. Tool racks and shelves were bare.

He looked into the next room, which housed the bunk beds. It was dark, with not a soul in sight.

Something was wrong.

Something was happening.

He could feel it.

A frantic walk turned into a slow jog. He moved faster down the hall. Lonely footsteps echoed off the corrugated metal walls.

The door to the right was left wide open. Gamma Lab, the placard read. The room that once stored silver canisters full of green, glowing liquid was now empty. The canisters were missing, and the room was dark like the rest.

Suddenly, all the lights in the compound pulsed brightly in unison. Then they flickered and dimmed. A few seconds later, it happened again. The light glowed bright, then dimmed, repeating in a looping sequence.

Something was using an immense amount of power, he thought.

Theo reached the room where Dee was being held. He pounded his shoulder into the middle of the door to force it open. It jostled free, and Theo rumbled into an empty room.

Dee was gone. The blood that used to stain the walls was gone. The floor was mopped clean and a strong stench of bleach and lemon-scented industrial cleaner hung in the air. From the look of the room, one would never know what had happened in there.

For a moment, Theo questioned everything. Was he living in a hallucination fueled by exhaustion and dehydration? Were Trent and the clones even real? Or was everyone already dead, and this was his mind's elegant way of shielding him from facing a torrent of grief? The puzzle pieces didn't add up, and Theo wished desperately to wake from this twisted dream.

The room vibrated. A powdering of soil shook loose from the sheet metal ceiling above. It peppered Theo's shoulders and dusted his hair with dirt.

He looked back down the hallway. The lights pulsed and dimmed, repeating the loop. This time, the intervals between each burst of light were getting shorter, and the pulses were speeding up.

He ran down the corridor past the labs and storage rooms and reached a bend in the hallway. Behind its doors, a room glowing with a bright light was at the end of the corridor.

The placard read: Alpha Lab.

Rapid voices bounced back and forth in discussion from behind the door. He heard Trent's voice, and then other voices joined. Some of them sounded younger.

Theo pressed on the handle and opened the door just as Trent was stepping into the Aeonite machine.

It was a large contraption constructed of metal and tubes and cables that snaked like vines across the room. The mechanical arm that Theo had seen the engineers building earlier was mounted onto the head of the machine, looming over a flat metal bed. The entire abomination looked like a robotic coffin.

Theo's stomach twisted at the sight of it.

Trent lowered his head and laid flat on a metal slab. He turned as Theo stepped into view, and an eerie smile came across his face.

"Ah, Theo!" said Trent, "Wonderful of you to join us in this truly magnificent moment. One that you made possible, of course."

He gestured up to the mechanical arm and pointed in circles around the room.

"Everything here, the miracle that will revolutionize the Midlands, would have never come to fruition if not for you, son."

"Fourteen months ago," said Theo, "you promised me my father would be the first one to be cured. That was the deal, Trent."

"Oh Theo, I love Arthur like a brother. We, all of us, our entire community, owe him so much. But we have to face the truth that his condition has progressed too quickly, and it's beyond our ability to help."

"What do you mean beyond? The Aeonite machine can heal anything."

"You need to understand that we only have a limited amount of serum, and until we can synthesize more at a much faster pace, we only have enough for one reconstruction operation for now."

"This is not what you promised. This was not the deal!"

"Theo, I cannot argue with science. It takes approximately 7.8 liters of serum for one operation. We've barely scraped together 10 liters. We can only replicate so much, so quickly."

"10.3 liters, actually," said a clone that was staring unblinkingly at a computer screen, "cellular replication from the SCR algae sample is a slow procedure, fraught with errors. Until we learn more and refine our technology. Which we will, but that will take time."

Theo's blood was boiling.

"Time," he said through clenched teeth, "that's exactly what my father doesn't have."

"Son, Arthur is beyond help," said Trent, "We needed to make the difficult decision to focus on those who have the greatest potential to contribute to the community."

The clone at the computer added, "We should be able to reproduce a viable replacement fluid for the serum from the moss that grows abundantly on the forest floor. That has shown promising results. We'll know more after further testing in about thirty-two days—"

"My father may not have thirty-two days!" Theo shouted. Clones to his left and right stiffened their posture.

"I'm sorry, Theo," said Trent, as he stretched his neck to relax on the metal table, "I'm afraid we must move forward. It's what Arthur would have wanted. For the good of the Midlands."

Theo took a step forward, his hands knotted into tight fists and rage burning through his veins. The clones beside him sensed his movement and rushed toward him. They grappled him to the ground. One clone locked Theo's arms behind his back. The other pressed a knee into his back and leaned his weight onto Theo.

"You fucking coward!" Theo screamed into the floor tile, "You promised!"

A clone technician stepped up to the machine and pulled straps over Trent's arms and legs. They clicked into place and tightened. Then he lowered the glass panel over the top of Trent's body. It floated smoothly with assistance from a hydraulic arm.

The machine latched shut. A motor at its base vibrated to life.

The other clone sitting beside a computer started a timer.

"Phase load beginning," he announced, "injection in 3... 2... 1..."

A circle of condensation appeared on the glass above Trent's head.

"Commence phase one," said the clone, eyes never turning

away from the computer screen, "preparing fusion site."

Metal arms within the coffin-like machine activated. They swung into the air and danced side to side with wicked-fast precision, making minute incisions at Trent's neck, chest, spine, hip, and legs.

"Phase two. Beginning build. Extruder wands functioning at..." the clone leaned forward to read the screen, "optimal levels. "Duration: seventy seconds."

The metal arm spun in place. It swapped out one tool attachment for another. Scalpels rotated and tucked back into the machine, and dozens of small spikes appeared in their place, a dense bundle of needles like a mechanical cactus. Along the side, clear plastic tubes coiled like springs flushed with a liquid from the connected canisters. They flushed a greenish-brown color. Large tubes funneled through plastic connectors to small tubes, squeezing the liquid into smaller and smaller channels. Flow speeds increased as electrical currents hummed and rocketed the liquid into injection ports on the end of each metal spike.

The arm turned, jabbing into Trent's neck, back, and leg with short, abrupt movements. His body jiggled as the machine made rapid work of the build process.

Then, the arms folded back, retracting into standby mode. Bright lights inside the machine blasted Trent's body with a flood of ultraviolet light.

"Curing phase commencing," said the clone, "Duration: one hundred and twenty seconds." He turned his head slightly to the side, eyes breaking away from the screen for the first time. "This is the most critical step," he explained, "One that has yielded... inconsistent results in the past."

Theo huffed air into the floor tiles and wiggled his body against the grip of the clones holding him down.

Then the light in the machine turned off. The enclosure went dark.

"The sequence is com–" said the clone at the computer, "wait, wait, it's…"

A piercing tone rang out from the machine.

The top panel began to lift slowly to the side along its hydraulic hinges.

"It's complete… yes, complete," said the clone with a sigh of relief.

Theo fidgeted and turned enough to look at the machine.

The other clones around the room turned, setting down pens and clipboards on tables.

For a moment, the whole room was silent.

No movement from the machine.

Then, a long, deep exhale.

Trent lifted an arm out of the machine, gripped the side wall, and slowly lifted himself up. He managed to sit up and winced from each movement of his muscles. His face was flush with pain. Recent incisions still raged red across his skin.

Then a grin appeared on his face, wide and thin, like a pencil line from ear to ear.

No one in the room made a sound.

The clones gathered closer, waiting with bated breath to see what would happen next.

Trent turned and lowered one leg onto the floor. Small droplets of blood dripped down his calf but quickly stopped as the coagulants finished curing. He pulled his other leg around. He moved slowly, cautiously, testing each movement, anticipating the shock of pain.

He slid forward to the edge of the bed, shifted his weight onto his heels, and began to stand. He straightened his posture, raised his hands at his side, and stretched his back muscles. He looked up at the ceiling for a long minute, mouthing a silent prayer to the corrugated metal panels above. Trent looked as though he might cry, but he simply shut his eyes and took a breath.

With all eyes on him, Trent took three steps into the center of the room, his nude body glistening with a sheen of condensation and splotches of still-moist blood. Stitch lines were throbbing up his legs, buttocks, back, and neck. It curved along the valleys of his muscles and terminated at the base of his skull.

He took six slow steps without his cane.

He moved with perfect balance, a posture of strength and confidence. His pale skin looked youthful, and his body was cured and restored.

The clone by the computer looked back at the screen.

The Aeonite machine began beeping incessantly.

"Oh no," said the clone, "No, no, this can't be... lost-sector completions are out of range. Much too high. No. In the hundreds? No, that can't... that means–" He spun his chair around and locked eyes on Trent.

Trent stopped mid-step. His smile slowly faded, and a look of torment flashed across his face. His eyes were wide, and his mouth loosened like he was going to hurl or pass out.

Or worse.

Then the muscles on his leg began to twitch. They sagged toward the floor, skin stretching like putty, red lines of hot blood creeping down his calf.

Stitch lines along his back began to loosen. Grayish-red liquid oozed from the incision lines on his back and neck.

He let out a deep, guttural moan of pain and rage. His fists clenched, and he pulled his arms close to his naked torso as an instinctual act of self-preservation.

The clones all around him circled, filling all corners of the room, eyes trained on Trent in utter shock and fascination.

Muscles detached from bone.

Organs tumbled out of his abdominal cavity.

His skin sagged, and half of his body began to melt to the floor like warm wax.

Trent died in a writhing, steaming pile of blood, muscles, and skin.

The clone technician panicked and pounded the keyboard. Numbers and line graphs flew across the computer screen.

"I... I... don't understand," said the clone, his composure breaking and tears pushing through, "how could it—"

He stared at numbers rising in columns. Punched a keystroke, and the screen was changed to a plot graph with dots of various sizes.

Another clone across the room dropped a metal canister and fled out the door. It landed with a thud and a highly viscous brown liquid leaked onto the floor and slowly expanded.

"The field tensors! They're all wrong!" said the clone at the computer, "it needs to be recalibrated. Then it will work. It should have worked, but the flow speed was too high. That's it. That will do it. We must correct it and prepare another build!"

The clone standing beside the Aeonite machine collapsed to the floor, weeping like a child. His body shivered uncontrollably.

Theo observed the room, watching this nightmare play out. The clones all around him—barely teenagers—with child-like faces cracking under pressure. They were losing their sense of reality, unable to tear their eyes from the puddle on the floor that used to be their father, their creator, and their leader. Their God.

He sensed his opportunity and lunged across the room toward the pile of clothing and boots beside the Aeonite machine. He plunged a hand into the folds of Trent's crumpled jacket, fingers groping blindly for the thick ridges of the leather strap and holster. His thumb brushed against the coiled stitching and his palm quickly found a purchase on the grip of the 1911 pistol.

Theo spun around and aimed at the two clones who, a moment ago, were grinding his face into the metal floor. He wanted so badly to pull the trigger and watch the heavy .45 caliber bullet rip open their artificially grown chests and hear their bodies drop to the floor. The blast would be deafening. The recoil would be a shock to his wrist.

He started backing slowly toward the doorway. He pointed the pistol at the clones, shifting his aim back and forth from one clone to the next.

They all stepped back.

Nobody moved.

The clones froze, watching him inch closer toward the door.

He punched through the door and ran down the corridor toward his father's room, thinking and praying that this would be the chance he had been waiting for.

One more operation. Maybe not a complete bodily reconstruction because the clones needed more time to develop the serum, but something, anything, to help his father, begin the healing process, and take away his pain.

Allow him to wake up and talk to Theo again.

As his feet struck the floor, Theo played the image in his head. His father getting rebuilt, waking up, breathing new air through lungs free of disease, smiling at the sight of Theo, hugging him, mouthing the words, "My son, you've done it, you've saved us all." But he couldn't hear the words because the vision faded into a blur of twisting hallways and the rhythmic pounding of his footfalls, so loud in the empty corridor.

He pushed open the door.

Against the pale light, his father's shrunken body lay still on the bed.

And a flat line scrolled across the monitor.

CHAPTER 33

REBUILDING

Theo woke to a hand nudging his shoulder. Radio equipment, coiled cords, microphones, headsets, and powered-off display screens surrounded him with the musty stench of aging rubber and old copper wiring.

He was sprawled across a desk in the cavernous communications room.

The hand nudged him again.

Theo groaned and slowly opened his eyes.

The walls were plastered with paper maps with bright marker outlines of encampments and cities and travel routes. A grid of LED bulbs twinkled with an array of colors on a panel mounted high above the desk.

His temple was heavy and pounding, his head a dead weight as he tried to move but could barely keep his eyes open. The smell of alcohol and body odor mixed with rifle cleaner and dirt from the ceiling filled the room with a unique scent reminiscent of an animal's den.

"You stink, chief."

Theo mumbled awake. He lifted his arm and knocked over two empty glass bottles. A few hours ago–or a few days, he couldn't quite be sure–they were filled with unidentifiable liquor stashed in the desk drawer. One of the clones had been running a small batch distillery as a side hustle to kill time underground, presumably in a lab down the hall utilizing fermented mushrooms from the surface. The empty bottles clanged to the floor with an ear-splitting rattle.

"That I do," said Theo, mostly to himself. He turned his head as the maps and papers tumbled into focus.

He recognized that voice.

"Dee? You're back?"

Her face was peppered with cuts, and the side of her jaw had a hint of fading purple. It was still swollen but healing quickly.

"Never really went anywhere," she said with a sigh, "after they pulled the files, they moved me to a bunk room at the other end of the compound. Then everyone just vanished. Emptied out and left me all by myself. Luckily they removed my restraints. Then the lights started going haywire, and I found the door unlocked and I started to wandering around but I haven't seen a single person since."

Theo tried to sit up. He winced as the cold edge of the desk dug into his side. He pulled himself up and fought the stirring urge to projectile vomit across the floor.

"I was too weak to go anywhere," she continued, "so I stayed in that room. I don't know how long I was in there. Time passes so strangely here. Day and night don't exist. It's one long blur. I'd fall asleep like a dog on the cold metal floor and wake up, and every day, a tray with food would appear by the door. It must've been a few days. Maybe three. I'm not really sure."

Theo fanned the fabric of his shirt and leaned forward to get a whiff of his own scent, pretending to shift to a more comfortable position on the desk. He winced at the odor but continued as if nothing happened. He let his eyes wander, getting lost in the curves of the ceiling. Metal panels bent under the crushing weight of the earth above. Granules of soil leaked through small tears in the hurriedly welded seams.

"Is this what it feels like... to want to jump?" he asked, staring at the ceiling.

Dee took a breath. Her demeanor softened. Her voice grew quieter.

"Like the world doesn't want you?" said Dee, "and everything you once called home doesn't exist anymore? So therefore, why should you exist? Yeah, that's exactly the feeling."

Tears welled in Theo's eyes.

"Like you're stranded on a raft," he said, "all alone, in waters that go on forever in every direction. Floating in an infinite ocean, and when you close your eyes, you feel like the last person on earth. You look out at the horizon, and it's flat and hard and sterile. Everything is cold. No one to call out to. No one is coming to help. Just you and your own fucking self."

Theo wiped his eyes.

"But if I had just–"

"Don't," said Dee, "You can't do that. You can't waste time in the past. It'll consume you if you let it."

"Then how do you live like this?" he asked.

"It never really goes away," said Dee, "you just keep living, keep breathing, keep waking up and choosing to see the sunrise and eventually you make space for it, you make space for all that emptiness. Like a compartment in your backpack, it lives there. You take it with you. It never goes away. It just becomes a part of you."

"I can't believe he's gone," said Theo, "I mean, even when he was lying there in that bed, he couldn't speak, couldn't even look at me, was barely breathing, but he was there.... There, with me."

Theo raised his arms, gesturing in the empty air with outstretched hands, pretending to touch an invisible force in front of him that was no longer there.

"Right now, you don't have the luxury of shutting down," said Dee, "right now, your people need you. You brought back the plans... well, technically, I brought back the plans–"

"And I brought you back, so–"

Dee nodded, a faint smile appearing on her bruised face.

"Don't shut us out, Theo. Don't shut me out. Not now. Not when the machine is working. They only need one more small test operation before it is complete. Ready for prime time. You'll be known as the one who saved the Midlands!"

Dee swiped her hand through the air, outlining an invisible newspaper headline, "Theo Rousseau Brings Aeonite Machine to Towns Across the Midlands, and the crowd goes wild! Ahhhh!"

Theo chuckled, "Why is there a crowd reading a newspaper and cheering?"

"Because anything can happen in the future," said Dee.

Theo's smile faded quickly.

"And my father won't be there to see it."

"He will. He is. He'll never truly go away. You'll carry him with you until it's your turn."

Theo's face was filled with tension, his eyes welled with tears, and his cheeks burned red.

"But now," said Dee, "Right now, the people who are still alive need you. They need a leader. The clones will follow you. You've proven yourself. They'll believe in you if you just give them a chance."

Theo looked at Dee, locking eyes with her for the first time during their conversation. Wet streaks ran down his face.

"Like I believe in you," she said.

She reached out and grabbed his hand.

"It's time to finish your mission, Theo."

***

Theo stepped into the Alpha Lab. Only a handful of clones were left. It looked as though they were working through the night to fix the Aeonite machine. The air was thick with the fresh scent of blood, bleach, and artificial lemon cleaner. Cables crisscrossed the room in haphazard lines. All the machinery had been rearranged. The desks and tables were pushed to new locations. Brown stains lingered on the floor where Trent's body had fallen to pieces.

One of the clones balanced on a ladder above the machine in a precarious position, holding a tube with outstretched arms over the top of a metal bar. Another clone lay on his back, tinkering with wires bursting out of an exposed panel on the underside of the machine.

The room became silent when all hands stopped, and eyes turned toward Theo. The one at the computer was still seated, typing furiously as usual.

Theo watched the boys' faces.

It's all they have lived for, he thought.

Then his heart skipped a beat as he realized the truth: it was all he had lived for, too.

Their soft eyes, and pale skin, seemed to be aging in surprising and unnatural places. One was going gray in streaks along his temple. Another had drooping, dark circles under his eyes. The clone sitting at the computer stopped typing.

"We fixed it," he said with a hint of desperation in his trembling voice, with a mechanical pencil twirling between his fingers, "the flow valves weren't calibrated correctly and the power throughput was all wrong. But we corrected it now. It will work!"

Another clone behind him stepped forward to read the computer screen.

"It will work," the other clone said, emerging with a trembling smile and fighting back tears.

A clone, possibly the youngest one, held a red spiral notebook by his side. He was crouched in the far corner, partially obscured behind a cabinet full of glass jars.

"We don't have a serum for a full reconstruction operation. That will take time. But we can do a partial. We're extracting what we can from the moss samples we found growing in a crack in the walls of the bunk room. It's not the biggest sample, but the health of the cellular walls indicates it's a pristine specimen. We think we can get a viable quantity out of it. It will work!"

One by one, they nod their heads and smile. On the brink of tears, hearts breaking at the thought of their precious machine failing. Only half-hearted smiles were saving them from breaking beyond reproach.

Theo sensed Dee's presence standing behind him. He paused in thought.

"You said you don't have enough for a full operation," said Theo, "but what if a partial was all we needed?"

The clone with the notebook turned to look at Dee. She stood with her left shoulder forward, unconsciously tucking her missing limb behind her body, out of view. The clone looked at her intensely, running back-of-the-napkin calculations in his mind.

He nodded at Theo. "It will work," he said with a compassionate smile.

"Then let's fire up the machine," said Theo, "I want so badly for this to work, and I know you all want this too," he turned to look at Dee, "so let's get started with one of our own."

The clone with the notebook smiled wider.

"Yes, sir!"

For a moment, Dee didn't move. She stood there with a look of fear and apprehension on her face.

"You're going to be fine," said Theo, "you deserve this. After all, you and your files did save us."

Dee smiled and nodded. She stepped forward, climbed into the Aeonite machine, and laid flat on the cold metal plank. A clone approached the side of the machine and reached in to gently remove the bandages on what remained of her right arm. The exposed skin was furiously red and irritated. He sprayed it with a disinfecting solution that sizzled, and a white foam bubbled across her skin but quickly disappeared. She winced at the sharp jolt of pain. When he was finished, the clone lowered the protective panel over her body and encased Dee in what looked like a glass and metal cocoon.

The clone sitting beside the computer flicked a rapid series of commands into the keyboard. Line graphs and columns of code flooded the screen.

"Initiating phase one," said the clone.

Theo watched from across the room. His face, stoic and calm, hands balled into tense fists, and remnants of his raging hangover clawing their way back into his head. Inside, he grew more and more nauseous by the minute.

"Sequencing sample."

The clone entered a sequence of numbers matching the column on the left side of the screen to the column on the right side of the screen.

"Serum staged."

Clear tubes extracted liquid from canisters stacked beside the machine. They flushed with a vibrant greenish-gray color.

"Serum activated. Construction beginning."

A warm sensation blossomed in Theo's chest as he watched the Aeonite machine go to work on Dee. The arm of the machine extended and contracted, spinning in place and switching tooltips and instruments like a dealer shuffling cards. In a flash of sadness, he imagined his father lying on that table, the machine's spindly arms opening his ribcage, removing his cancer-eaten lungs, and sculpting him a new pair. Extruding new years of life into an old man's frail body. What a gift it would have been to let his father breathe new air with new lungs.

Then, his father would never die.

And Theo would never be alone.

Time warped as he lost himself in imagination. He didn't hear the clone's last two announcements of the curing phase or the beginning of the sterilization procedure. Minutes waiting for the operation to finish whipped by in what felt like mere seconds. A clone in a white lab coat stepped up to the Aeonite machine, rotated a latch, and lifted the glass and steel panel.

Somewhere in another reality, another timeline or another world, Theo saw his father's fingers curl around the edge of the machine, arm emerge into the air while he sat up with a smile from ear to ear.

But it was Dee's hand that shot into the air and not his father's. Her skin still held a residual glow under the curing light. She looked at her hand in disbelief. She stretched her fingers to form a loose fist. Testing the boundaries of her newly constructed arm with each movement, wincing expectantly at the thought of pain.

The clones gathered around Dee, analyzing her every move, examining her body from all angles. But when she rotated her palm inside and out, the realization overwhelmed her: the machine worked, and she will be able to live as a whole person once again.

And the larger truth was on display to the entire room: that life across the Midlands was about to change forever.

CHAPTER 34

GODSPEED

The sky burned crimson with the setting sun as ten motorcycle engines rumbled to life. Bursts of piston fire rang through the darkening trees. The boys twisted their handles and revved the engines.

A clone named Adam pulled a strap on his backpack. The canvas bag wrapped tightly around a bundle of hard drives—eleven drives in total—loaded with the Aeonite schematics, parts lists, lab test audio diaries, prototype data exports, and detailed instructions on how to strip down an eighteen-wheeler truck into usable parts to build it.

Theo looked at the boys, their packs cinched tight, mounted on a row of motorcycles.

"My brothers," he projected with a deep and confident tone, "ride hard through the night!" His back was straight, stomach tight, belting the words of a leader.

"The rubber bladders full of fuel tied to the back of your bike should give you an extra six hundred miles of range. The caffeine chews in your pocket should keep you alert. You have your assigned destinations. You know what you must do, and you know what is at stake! They are waiting for you. They are relying on you. And I... I am counting on you."

The engines revved.

The boys roared and cheered.

"You were destined for this moment," he continued, pausing to reflect on the weight of his words, "You were put here for a reason. You were the ones who needed to take on this task. It has always been you. You were destined to bring the Aeonite machine to our Midlands. You will fight through the darkness of the night and ride until you cannot ride anymore."

Theo took a breath and felt the frigid forest air chill his lungs.

"Tonight, my brothers, you are the Midland's best hope."

He called their assigned designations.

"Oklahoma City!"

"Check!"

"Tulsa!"

"Check!"

"Wichita!"

"Check!"

The engines revved louder. Fireflies gathered around the boys, encircling them in a ring of twinkling lights.

"Dallas!"

"Check!"

"Kansas City!"

"Check!"

"Memphis!"

"Check!"

"Jackson!"

"Check!"

The ground rumbled.

"Santa Fe!"

"Check!"

"St. Louis!"

"Check!"

A swift and warm breeze ripped through the trees.

"And last, San Antonio!"

"That's a check, sir!"

"Ride hard," said Theo, words beaming directly from his gut, "and do not stop. Do not give the Kaiphers a chance to track you. If you keep moving, you stay alive. And everyone will live. When each of your Aeonite machines is operational, prioritize the sick, the weak, and the elderly. Never let anyone jump the line. Everyone deserves a chance to live on!"

Theo raised a hand into the air.

"Godspeed, my brothers!"

The motorcycles took off with a thunderous roar. Some headed north. Others to the east, and west, and two to the south. The ground shook and Theo's heart was full as they blazed on at full throttle.

Ten boys on bikes raced the setting sun to the horizon.

***

Several days had passed since the messengers rode off into the night. Theo and Dee climbed the bunker steps into the forest and emerged to find the black starry sky glowing a deep blue. The sun would rise soon. Faint rays of warm reds and oranges pierced the horizon.

"It's time to begin a new world," said Dee, "it's what your father would have wanted."

Theo looked at the pinpricks of light in the sky. Many stars faded with the morning, but a few burned brightly, violently raging in the vacuum of space, stubbornly hanging on.

"He died not knowing if we made it," said Theo, "I was too late. And he never had a chance to see this world being built. To see that in the end, we would be okay. The Midlands would be okay. The people he cherished and the communities he served all those years would all be okay."

Theo stared at a bright star and thought it might have been Alpha Centauri. He wondered how many years the light from that burning ball of gas had been traveling through the cosmos to meet him that day, at that moment, in the form of a white dot in the Oklahoma sky.

"I just wish there was a way to tell him. Wherever he is. No matter how far away he journeyed. Just one last time to let him know we're okay. And the future he made possible for the Midlands is a good future."

Dee turned to him.

"Theo... I can think of a way."

CHAPTER 35

A FLAME

"So, you've been flying since–"

"Since I could walk, just about," said the clone in the pilot's seat of the blue and white Cessna Skyhawk. A scraggly beard made him look about ten years older than Theo. Lines on his face from flying too close to the sun and a sagging jawline showed the difference. "Trent paired me up with this old guy, Robertson. He was a grizzled old son of a bitch, but the best crop duster in east Oklahoma. Learned everything from him. How to fly his old Grumman Super Ag Cat, how to degrease engines, repair carburetors, even how to build my own gliders with spare parts when the tractors broke down."

Theo stared out the window at the endless blue expanse below. Ocean waves tumbled into long, thin lines, creating a uniform pattern that stretched across the water for hundreds of miles in each direction.

"When Trent needed someone to fly the guys out over SCR airspace for high-altitude jumps, of course I volunteered. Little did I know that that was the plan for me all along since I was a kid. I never really got to do anything else. Never got to try. Never had a chance."

Theo watched the compass on the dash begin to wobble and spin erratically.

We're heading in the right direction, he thought, but he couldn't see anything down there.

"So, Robertson got ill from all those years of running the crops. The folks called it a toxic lung, but the doctors had a different name for it. Something more complicated. Things sure would have been different if we had the Aeonite machine back then. When he died, I took over maintaining his planes because there was no one else to do it."

When the clone's leg shook, he tried to hide it by shifting his feet back and forth on the foot controls, keeping the appearance of being busy.

"And how's the leg?" asked Theo.

The clone grunted.

"Not terrible yet. I can still fly, can't I?"

"That you can," said Theo, "but you know that there will be slots opening soon at the Elkhart clinic, don't you? We could rebuild you."

The clone grunted again, this time with a sigh.

"I know," he said and chewed on his lip, "I know. I'm just not too thrilled about some machine ripping me open, that's all. I've seen it work miracles. That's a truth I can't deny, but for me, the thought of those scalpels–"

"It's a weighty proposition, I'll give you that," said Theo. He nodded and added, "When you're ready."

The clone grunted in agreement.

Theo looked out the window. Nothing was visible within a hundred miles in any direction. The frost tendrils began to crawl up the edge of the glass. It wrapped around the aircraft's side mirrors like snaking fingers made of crystals. Theo's heart raced at the thought of setting foot on the island again.

What if it's actually true, he thought? What if he's really there?

The cockpit rumbled.

Or what if he's not?

The nose of the aircraft rose and fell, bounding higher as it was thrashed by gusts of freezing air. The pilot held tight to the controls. He pulled the rudder back and bore down with an iron grip on the yoke. Suddenly, a wall of fog swallowed the plane. It wrapped around every curve of metal and glass and blanketed the aircraft in a suffocating white cloud. It was impossible to see out of the windshield.

Theo exhaled, and a white puff escaped his mouth. The temperature in the cockpit plummeted, and ice began to form in between the stitches of the leather seats.

The airplane dipped. Rivets along the door rattled, and the pilot struggled to correct against the oncoming air.

The wall of fog burst open, and warm sunlight flooded the cockpit. An island appeared straight ahead. Curving shores of golden sand and lush trees as soft as if they were painted with a fine sable brush. And almost without knowing it, two words escaped Theo's mouth as effortlessly as breath itself.

"Calico Hill."

Theo watched as the island loomed closer. Endless fields of green and yellow and burnt orange. A patchwork of brilliant colors, like the fur of a calico cat, extended as far as the eye could see. It touched the horizon with no indication of ever stopping.

The pilot was wide-eyed and speechless. He scanned the instrument cluster and glanced at Theo with a nervous look.

"What... exactly is this place?" he asked.

Theo smiled and let the pause in their conversation fill the cabin.

"Oh, my friend, some things are not for us to know."

The plane descended, circling wide along the beach and swooping back around to line up with a thin stretch of flat land in the middle.

The clone brought them in for a smooth landing.

They stepped out of the aircraft and took in the view. A golden field of knee-high grass. Then, across the way, maybe a hundred yards out, it blended into a flat plain of pastel green, bright as summer limes. Each blade, leaf and stem was a flawless specimen.

Almost too perfect to be real.

"So... how do you expect to, uh, find him?"

Theo considered the question for the first time. He shook his head with a half-smile.

"No idea. Maybe he'll find me."

Theo walked toward the center of the island. It felt like he was traveling south, but he couldn't be sure. At the edge of one field, a small boy sat on the land, playing with a patch of dandelions. Theo kept walking and passed more figures sitting by themselves on their individual patches of grass. An old man was on a rocking chair, watching the sun inch by through the impossibly starless sky. Orange and yellow blades of grass were beneath his feet, swaying like silk in the breeze.

Far in the distance, a woman stood with the sun on her back, arms outstretched, flying a kite high in the cerulean sky. She never turned to acknowledge Theo. She held a beaming smile on her face as she watched her kite ride the jetstreams.

The hills bent and curved in the distance. For a moment, a heavy pit formed in Theo's stomach as he took in the sheer volume of land the island covered. It looked as though it never ended. And maybe it didn't.

Soon, the plane was a distant blip behind him. He dipped into a valley and over a small hill. He passed young men, old women, children playing with dump trucks and swingsets and action figures, and more than a face or two that hauntingly resembled his own.

Then, the warm breeze slowed.

The air stopped moving.

The sky seemed to glow a brighter blue, as pure and smooth as paint smeared across a freshly primed canvas.

He took a deep breath. Closed his eyes. Smelled the eucalyptus and mustard bush on a nearby hill.

Then he opened his eyes.

"My Theo."

He heard a familiar voice.

A quiet voice.

"My dear son."

Arthur walked toward him. He wore his favorite brown shop overalls and a baby blue long-sleeve shirt underneath. The fabric looked new, absent of all the black blemishes that peppered the leather from years of MIG welding in the field.

Theo couldn't speak. He'd dreamed of nothing but this moment for months. And now there were no words.

Arthur smiled, "Oh, son, I'm so happy to see you again."

Theo smiled, and his throat swelled. He reached out with a hand, hesitant at first, then touched his father's shoulder. He felt the cotton of his shirt, smooth as a puppy's fur. He collapsed into his father's arms and wept like a child. And for just a moment, the horrors of the world—the Capital, the death, the terror and murder and cruelty—it all melted away. Suddenly, he was transported and remembered being five years old again, back in the safety of the Ranch, with a crackling log on the fire, a warm blanket on his lap, and not a worry on his mind.

Theo wiped away tears and smeared streaks across his face. He shut his eyes, blinked, and was shocked that his father was still there and hadn't washed away like a dream.

"It's okay, son," said Arthur with a smile, "I'm not scared."

"But I did all this for you, and I was too late, and I couldn't–"

"No, Theo, you did this for them. All the babies, the children, and the old men like me in the Midlands who never had a chance. Now they can breathe again, their murmuring hearts can beat again, their cloudy eyes can see the sky again, and they can live on. You did that, Theo. You gave them a chance at a good life."

Theo fought back more tears. He felt so small.

"I don't know how I can face this world now that you're not here."

"Oh, my son," Arthur said with a deep and rumbling laugh, "of course you can. You already did."

His smile was like hot cocoa and a warm blanket amidst a frigid storm.

Theo looked down at the long scar on his arm where the silicon chip was once lodged.

"And you're not alone. You're never alone. I'll be with you always. I'll be with you when you don't think you can go on. I'll walk alongside you, son, when you need me. Just because you can't see me doesn't mean I'm really gone."

Arthur reached out to touch Theo's hand. He cradled Theo's palm with his fingers, and Theo looked down at an old man's weak hands–bony knuckles and thinning skin–holding up his own strong and youthful hands. The hands of a grown man.

"My Theo, we all have a path to walk in this world. This path is mine. And you have your own. Make yours a good one."

Arthur raised a hand and pointed to the center of Theo's chest.

"You carry a flame, son. And it's your job to keep it burning. I had my time to become an old man, and I loved my life. It wasn't perfect, but I loved it. Now, I want you to love yours. All of my years are mine; those memories are mine, and my heart is so full."

Theo felt the heat of tears welling, but he took a deep breath, and the pressure subsided.

"And now it is your turn," said Arthur.

He opened his hand and pressed softly against Theo's chest.

"Protect it, son. Not for me."

A warm breeze flowed through the trees and rode along the blades of grass. The sky was changing, and the sun inched toward the horizon.

"Can I see you again? Here, in this place?"

Arthur looked up for a moment at the clouds floating like white cotton candy overhead.

"I'm not sure, son," he said with a smile, "some things we can't know... and that's alright. All you need to remember is that I'll always love you, son, and everything's going to be okay."

Arthur kissed Theo on the forehead and hugged him tightly. Theo shut his eyes and breathed in the smell of his father's leather overalls one last time.

When he opened his eyes, he watched his father turn and walk away. His footsteps floated along the golden grass until he took a meandering turn and disappeared around a hill in the distance.

20 YEARS LATER

CHAPTER 36

THE VISITOR

There was a knock at the door.

"Yes? Come," said Theo.

Three children entered the room. A girl wearing a cream-colored sundress carried a woven straw basket. She stepped forward. Two boys in collared shirts and pressed slacks stood behind her with curious and nervous grins.

"I'm so sorry to interrupt, Commander Rousseau, but–"

"Not at all, Lily, don't be sorry, you weren't interrupting anything."

Theo clicked his mechanical pencil and placed it on top of a stack of hand-drawn maps strewn across his desk. Thick orange lines on the paper delineated where one plot of land ended and another began. The afternoon sunlight slanted in from the window, warming the air.

"We've had a new harvest from the hydro-phony farms," said Lily.

"Hydroponic!" whispered one of the boys.

"Hydroponic farms!" Lily corrected. She leaned forward and

held out the basket, presenting it to Theo. The children behind her leaned closer to see. She lifted the bleach-white cloth to reveal a heap of strawberries and a clump of vibrant green grapes.

Theo looked closer in amazement.

"May I?" he asked.

"Yes, of course, Commander, please try one!" said Lily.

He selected a medium-sized strawberry and took a bite. It was juicier and sweeter than anything he had ever tasted. Theo's eyes grew wide. He smiled, and Lily smiled back in response.

"Incredible!" he said, "and to think there was a time when we could barely grow potatoes and garlic in that hard red dirt." He looked at the children standing behind Lily, eager grins on their faces.

"Have you tried them?" he asked the children, gesturing with an outstretched hand to the strawberries and grapes. Their faces glowed with bright smiles, and they stepped forward.

"Please, please, have some," said Theo, "here, this looks like a good one! Take that one."

The children plunged their hands into the basket, and each pulled out a piece of fruit and stuffed them aggressively into their mouths. One boy smiled so wide that a dribble of strawberry juice escaped his lips and ran down his neck. He laughed.

Suddenly, there was a hard knock at the door.

Dee stepped in, followed by two young men from the Eastern Midland Scout Patrols. Their torsos bulged with ceramic plate armor vests, flare guns, sheathed knives on their belts, and pump shotguns with incendiary rounds slung across their chests. Their faces were sunburnt. Pale skin encircled their eyes where goggles had been worn.

"Theo," said Dee, "it's the scouts."

Theo nodded.

"Thank you, children," he said with outstretched arms. "I'm so happy to see the farm is doing so well. Incredible harvest, Lily.

Please tell your mother at the lab I loved every bit of it, and she is doing a very good job! Now, if you'll excuse me," he gestured toward the door, and the children shuffled out. Their cheeks bulged with fruit, and they laughed and chattered down the hall.

Dee waited for the children to disappear from view.

"The scouts found an elderly woman traveling along the west side of the Appalachian Mountain line," said Dee, "and she says she knows you. She asked to see you. She has a girl with her."

Theo frowned.

"Well, who is she?" he asked.

"She wouldn't say. She said she would only talk to you, and only you would understand."

Theo exhaled.

"I don't like it," he said.

He paused to consider the unusual request.

"I don't either," said Dee, "not one bit."

Theo stared out the window, a heavy and puzzled look across his brow.

"But we have to find a way to move forward, Theo. We have to start trusting people."

"I don't trust anyone," he said, letting out a deep sigh, "you're the only one I trust. If you think I should see her, then I will. But tell the scouts to stay close. And I want you here in the room."

"You got it, chief," said Dee.

A moment later, Theo heard two sets of footsteps slowly approaching the door. They slowed to a soft shuffle before a figure appeared in the doorway.

Dee stood beside Theo's desk against the far wall.

It was an old woman. Her pants and top looked hand-sewn, with rough earth-toned materials and uneven seams. She had stark white hair, bundled with a tie and extending down her back to her waist. Her eyes flicked cautiously around the room, taking in the decor of Theo's office—a mix of oak wood furniture and industrial accents, bits of scrap metal bent and hammered into submission to become lamps, tables, and chairs.

She turned to Theo.

Her eyes were blue as the ocean and fatigued by years of hardship. It struck Theo that he had seen those eyes before, sometime in the distant past, but couldn't quite place them.

"Good afternoon," he said. He nodded at the woman and greeted her with a stiff, reserved demeanor. His posture straightened. His arms were tense. His fingers remembered how far he would need to reach to draw Trent's 1911 mounted under his desk.

The old woman smiled.

"Mr. Rousseau... I mean Commander Rousseau, my apologies, thank you for meeting me, I–"

She was interrupted when a tall girl entered the room. Her clothes were just as tattered, crafted from the same dirt-toned materials as the older woman. The girl's hair was a rich chestnut brown, faded in spots from months or years in the unprotected sun. Her eyes were white like milk. She looked blankly around the room, turning her head at times, nostrils moving to take in the scents of Theo's office.

"Come here, my dear," said the old woman. The girl sidled up beside her, and the woman rested her hand on the girl's shoulder.

"Commander, I have been searching for you for so long," said the old woman, "It has been decades, I know, but a long time ago I learned of your mission into the Capital. I watched from afar as the SCR destroyed your home and the people you loved. I wanted to do something to help, I had no way to contribute. Until I picked up a transmission near the wall saying there was an old train headed for the Roanoke gate."

Dee's face flushed ghost-white.

Theo's eyes widened.

"It was the first train," she continued, "to run in nearly a

CALICO HILL

hundred years, maybe more. And something told me it was you. I knew it in my bones that it was you. So I overrode the border network and opened the gate."

Theo's mouth opened in shock. He caught his breath with a sharp exhale.

"My name," said the old woman, "is Aria Sloan."

Memories flooded Theo's mind of the woman's face on that screen all those years ago—the shockwave of fire and dirt that flattened the Ranch in a matter of seconds, and her robotic grin—a face void of a soul, floating in the air on a screen mounted on a mechanical arm. He remembered the Kaipher staring at him from across that white, sterile room.

Before he had a chance to fully process his thoughts, his hand flicked to draw the 1911. He leaped from his chair and stood holding the pistol at his side. The old woman flinched at his sudden movement. She raised her hands, palms open, and took a step back.

"Please, you don't understand," she said, "my family line, we were so powerful. The entire Coastal Republic bowed to my father's whim, and his father before that. I was a prisoner in my own home, as was my family, under constant watch of the Kaiphers. The people, they always said they loved us, but their love turned twisted, and they became a different kind of society. They claimed to worship me, but as the years went by I realized what they really wanted was to possess me, to control me, or the idea of me, so that I would never change. None of this would have happened if Father Charles the Eternal hadn't created the Aeonite machine all those centuries ago."

Aria looked away for a moment, a hint of tears welling in her eyes.

"You don't understand what's it's like to grow up and have your entire life path chosen for you," she said. Then she paused, and looked up at Theo, "Or... maybe you do."

"Commander, what you may have seen or thought you saw in the SCR was not me. The SCR government has been run by a dark council of Kaiphers in secret for the past thirty years. They used my face and my voice as a puppet for their dirty work and exploited my name because of my heritage... my relation to Dr. Charles Sloan. They knew the people would worship me, or at fall in line and comply at the image of me. They took over by force and held me imprisoned for months as they scanned me, prodded me, and studied me to build a model of my digital likeness with imperceptible differences. But one day I managed to escape, barely alive."

Aria's voice choked.

"I fled to the Midlands," she said, "but I knew I would never be accepted here, so I went to the mountains, living in hiding ever since. I knew I could never come to Trent. He would never understand. He'd kill me on the spot or, worse, use me as a tool in his war. But I thought there was a chance that you, Theo... you might understand."

Theo's neck and arm tensed.

Sweat beaded on his brow. He felt the cold grip of the ivory handle, the curve of the precision-tuned trigger smooth against his index finger.

"Why the hell should I believe you?" he said, jaw clenched.

"You'd certainly be in your right to doubt me. I know this is a lot of information all at once, but if you'll allow me thirty more seconds of your time, the real reason I am here is not about me at all. The reason I am here is because I brought a visitor."

Aria glanced at the tall girl by her side.

"I helped her get out of the SCR and disappear before the Kaiphers could track her down and kill her. She said she knows you. Isn't that right, Penny?"

Kristof's daughter, he thought.

The girl from the ship!

"Yes, Mr. Rousseau. We've met before, on my father's scraper ship many years ago. I've come with a request, and I am praying you can help me."

Theo's shoulders relaxed, and he set the heavy pistol down on the desk with a soft thump.

"I need your help to rebuild my eyes, and—"

"Yes, of course, Penny, we have Aeonite clinics set up all around the Midlands."

"Because I have a mission I must go on."

"A mission?" asked Theo.

"Yes, Mr. Rousseau, to find and kill the man who murdered my father."

His mind filled with flashing images of that knife as it plunged into Kristof's neck. His blood fell in a curve like a waterfall. Kristof's massive body crashed to the floor of that ship.

"Penny, the Capital has fallen, and the SCR as a land, as a society, is severely weakened. Many parts of the SCR along the border wall have gone dark for years, but that doesn't mean that there couldn't be very dangerous forces still moving about the region. That was a Kaipher that killed your father. They were ruthless agents of the SCR long ago. They murdered for pleasure, and I wouldn't even know where to begin with—"

"All I need are my eyes, sir, please. I will take care of the rest. And no one can convince me otherwise, so please do not attempt to change my mind."

Theo recognized that tone. He used to sound like that at a time in the distant past, many years ago when the world was different. The outward confidence. The trace of recklessness and arrogance. But he knew what lurked beneath the facade. The terror. The doubt. The crippling fear. And also the untarnished belief that anything is possible if you're willing to lay your blood and body on the line. That was a spark that only came with youth. A spark that all too often dimmed with age.

"So, tell me, Penny, what exactly is your plan?" asked Theo.

"In my life, I've done more than you'd believe without my vision. I'll figure this out," she said.

"I can get her in," said Aria, interjecting quickly, "beyond the wall. That much I know."

"Absolutely not," said Theo, "We'll take care of your vision, but there is no way you're marching up to that wall without a plan. I'm sorry; it's too risky."

"You made it back alive, and you saved the Midlands when you were, what, twenty? Twenty-one?" said Penny, "and the odds are you should've died a hundred times before reaching that wall."

"Penny, dear, you cannot speak to the Commander like that!" said Aria.

Theo raised a hand, "it's fine. She's not wrong."

He sighed and was quiet for a moment.

"Penny, my attention is needed here, where we are rebuilding a strong and prosperous Midlands. We need to focus on the future, on what is possible for our people. Living in the past it... it can take you to dark places."

He looked out at the sun tucking itself behind the distant mountains. Then he looked up at Dee.

She nodded.

Theo looked back at Penny.

"I need to know that you fully understand the dangers of what you're proposing, what you would be walking into. And I also need you to know that my place, our place, the Scouts and the Midland Guard, is here, and once you set foot beyond that wall, I cannot help you. If you choose to go, Penny, you must go alone."

"I understand sir, thank you. I have had many years to think, and this is what I have decided."

Theo exhaled a deep, resigned breath.

"You're going to need weapons."

"I know, sir," said Penny.

"And training."

"Yes, sir."

"And a whole lot of luck."

Penny smiled for the first time since stepping into the room.

"I'm going to kill him, sir."

Theo nodded.

"I know you will."

THE END

Acknowledgements

Calico Hill wouldn't exist without the support of the National Novel Writing Month (NaNoWriMo) organization and the awesome NYC crew run by Sara, aka musesofbacchus. This community gave me the momentum to put those very first words down on a blank page during lockdown in 2020.

Thank you to the many talented editors, reviewers, and beta readers who provided invaluable feedback: Jacquelyn Ben-Zekry, Ana Hantt, Josie Baron, Maxine Meyer, Danny Decillis, Julie Taylor, Lauren Haynes, and Lucija.

Gratitude to Dr. Minhaz Uddin and Mousumi Laila for their love and support and for allowing me to write the majority of my early drafts during vacations camped out in their cozy sunroom.

I look back with deep appreciation at where it all started: the spark of curiosity for writing that struck me in Jerry Mansfield's Creative Writing class at Moorpark Community College. I left that class with an unshakable itch for writing that has followed me all these years.

Thank you to my favorite authors, Blake Crouch and Michael Crichton, for sharing your thrilling stories with the world and inspiring people like me to take a chance on writing my own stories.

Big thanks and massive hugs to Peter Acosta, Scott Brand, Crystabel Rangel, Kawa Hatef, Jessica Bonham, Adam Paschal, Mike Pullano, James Martin and Michelle Scheffler who are all creative, hilarious, wonderful human beings who I am so incredibly lucky to call my friends.

Lastly, tremendous love and gratitude to my wife Moury for her unwavering encouragement and support through the four years it took me to turn scribbled notes in a Mead composition notebook into a real published novel. What a gift it is to have you as my partner in this life. Cheers to many more great things to come.

Calico Hill is dedicated to Ralph Alexander, who passed away in 2019. Dad, if Calico Hill existed in real life, I'd be on the first flight out in the morning to meet you for coffee. Until then, rest easy.

About the Author

Chris Alexander grew up in Southern California. He is an alumnus of University of California Santa Cruz and New York University. His work lies at the intersection of art, design and business. In his free time he practices archery, paints and writes fiction. Calico Hill is his debut novel. He lives in New York.

Made in the USA
Middletown, DE
13 August 2024